DISMISSED WITH PREJUDICE

DISMISSED WITH PREJUDICE

a novel

Christopher Meyerhoeffer

TATE PUBLISHING & *Enterprises*

Published by Tate Publishing & Enterprises, LLC
127 E. Trade Center Terrace | Mustang, Oklahoma 73064 USA
1.888.361.9473 | www.tatepublishing.com

Tate Publishing is committed to excellence in the publishing industry. The company reflects the philosophy established by the founders, based on Psalm 68:11,
"The Lord gave the word and great was the company of those who published it."

Book design copyright © 2010 by Tate Publishing, LLC. All rights reserved.
Author Photograph by Doug Maughan
Cover design by Blake Brasor
Interior design by Jeff Fisher

Published in the United States of America

ISBN: 978-1-61663-026-3
1. Fiction, Thrillers
2. Fiction, Legal
10.03.03

DEDICATION

For Tracey, Cole, Alexis, and Nick, my daily inspiration.

ACKNOWLEDGMENTS

I want to thank my wife, Tracey, and my children, Cole, Alexis, and Nick, for their unwavering support during the writing process. Especially my wife, who read the book more times than I can count. The following people read the manuscript in an unfinished state and offered invaluable criticism and encouragement: Jerry Meyerhoeffer, Pauline Meyerhoeffer, Cole Meyerhoeffer, Alexis Meyerhoeffer, Jason Meyerhoeffer, Michele Meyerhoeffer, Tony Mannen, Carol Morgan, Melanie Hunsaker, Emily Huber, and Teresa Christensen. I sincerely thank them all for their contributions and input.

CHAPTER 1

Thursday morning, October 5

The giant of a man had been standing motionless in the dark for the better part of four hours. The complete lack of movement would have been maddening for most people, but he actually enjoyed the mental challenge. Avoiding detection required complete control of his mind and body. Besides, hiding in the shadows was nothing new to him. For as long as he could remember, Edgar had struggled to blend in with his surroundings. Unfortunately, anonymity was a scarce commodity for a man of his size and physical appearance.

Homes had been bustling with activity when he crept into the middle-class neighborhood shortly before midnight, so he had been careful to position himself so the headlights of passing cars would not illuminate his hiding place. The neighborhood was only a couple of years old, so the surrounding trees and shrubbery were small, certainly not large enough to conceal a man of his dimensions. With his hiding places limited, Edgar had been forced to stand with his back pressed flat against the wall of a house. The house was just like every other house in the neighborhood except for one critical distinction. It had an unobstructed view of the woman.

He watched intently from his hiding place as the pretty, blonde woman went about her business inside the home. Edgar had not seen the little girl, but he knew she was inside the house, most likely sleeping, while her mother readied herself for bed. Between midnight and two o'clock, the lights in the two-story house began vanishing one by one. When she turned off the last light and retired for the evening, he felt strangely disappointed he could no longer see her. By the time four o'clock rolled around, the two-story house had been completely dark for more than two hours. A small exterior lamp above the front door was the only remaining sign of life.

When he sensed the time was right, the large man moved quickly and silently from his hiding place and advanced toward the backyard of the residence. It was finally time for him to carry out his mission. He would eventually enter through the front door but not until he surveyed the layout of the ground floor one last time. All things being equal, the front door was not an ideal point of entry. The door was directly beneath the only burning lamp and easily viewed from the street. But in this case, all things weren't equal. He had a key that opened the front door in his pants' pocket. If everything went as planned, he would be in and out before anyone detected his unlawful entry.

Edgar made his way to the rear of the woman's house without making a sound. The neighborhood was deathly quiet except for the constant hum of speeding cars on Overland Boulevard several blocks away, but he paused briefly anyway to listen for anything out of the ordinary. When he was convinced he was alone, Edgar stepped into a small flower bed adjacent to a ground-floor window. If the information provided by his employer was correct, the item would be somewhere in the lawyer's work papers. The small room was dark, but Edgar could clearly make out the outline of a desk and a file cabinet against the rear wall. He would begin his search there. After peering through the window for several seconds, he was almost positive that no one was moving about on the ground floor. The woman and child were most likely upstairs sleeping. Everything seemed to be in order, so he stepped out of the flower bed and moved silently toward the front door.

Edgar had decided in advance to abort his mission if a car or early morning walker happened by while he was entering the house. He wasn't sure why, but part of him hoped for an excuse to flee the neighborhood before he completed the routine job. His reluctance made no sense; he'd done more distasteful things than this simple job and had not given them a second thought. This job had been playing games with Edgar's head from the start. He was almost expecting something to go wrong during the entry, but it didn't. The key fit both locks perfectly, and nothing out of the ordinary derailed his plan. With the door unlocked, he glanced up and down the street. When he was certain no one was watching his movements, he stepped inside the house and silently closed the door behind him. The home was dark, quiet, and peaceful. Edgar stood in the entryway while his eyes adjusted to the change in lighting and listened for sounds of movement upstairs. Nothing living, either human or animal, was stirring inside the house, and everything seemed to be in order.

He liked the house's clean, fresh smell and its calming essence. For a fleeting moment, he wished he had grown up in a house like this one. Edgar quickly pushed the thoughts of his childhood out of his mind and moved cautiously toward the desk. When he reached the work space, Edgar knelt on the floor behind the small desk and slowly opened the top drawer. The room was darker than he expected, so he pulled the leather glove off his right hand and removed a small flashlight from his pocket. He was about to switch on the flashlight when he detected a slight movement out of the corner of his eye. Edgar instantly froze. It was the pretty, blonde woman he had been watching. She stopped abruptly at the bottom of the staircase as if she sensed she was not alone. He remained deathly still behind the desk, afraid to breathe or even blink his eyes.

Edgar wasn't afraid of the young woman or the legal ramifications of being discovered in her home. He was afraid of what he'd be forced to do if the woman detected his presence. The young woman stood motionless and scanned the makeshift office. A surge of relief shot through Edgar's body when the track of her eyes continued past him without stopping. His relief was fleeting. A second later, the woman's gaze paused for a moment, and then she slowly turned her head until her eyes locked on his.

CHAPTER 2

Thursday morning, October 5

The first rays of sunlight had just begun to brighten the eastern sky when Nick Jelaco's beat-up Ford Mustang crossed the Lincoln Bridge just south of Lakeland. The two-lane architectural relic was built shortly after the invention of the automobile, but it still effectively connected the north and south shores of the Susquehanna River. For Nick, crossing the Lincoln Bridge meant he'd be home in a matter of minutes.

The most important case of his young legal career had ended the day before in Las Vegas. A practical man would have spent the night in Las Vegas and started for home first thing in the morning, but common sense had lost out to compulsion, and Nick had hit the road immediately following the reading of the jury's verdict. Two factors had been responsible for Nick's abrupt departure: his sixth wedding anniversary and an uneasy feeling he couldn't shake.

Even at six o'clock in the morning, heavy traffic in Lakeland made the drive across town excruciatingly slow. After what seemed like an eternity, Nick finally guided the red convertible into his driveway at 434 River Crest Drive. The uneasy feeling that had been his constant companion since leaving Las Vegas immediately intensified. He sometimes experienced unsettling premonitions or vibes, but this morning the feelings were more pronounced than any he could remember. As he shifted his car into park, he took a deep breath and then exhaled slowly in a futile attempt to clear his head. He would know soon enough if the apprehension had some basis in fact or if the uneasiness was merely a side effect of sleep deprivation, too much caffeine, and an overactive imagination.

Unable to shake his anxiety, Nick tentatively exited the Mustang and approached the front door of his home. Just short of the front door, he fumbled then dropped his keys on the sidewalk. As Nick bent to pick up the keys, he noticed the burgundy-colored front door was slightly ajar. He tried to convince himself Julie had failed to close the door tightly when she retrieved the morning paper, but he knew better. It was only a couple of minutes past six, and the paperboy never delivered the morning paper before seven o'clock.

As he entered the house, Nick noticed several muddy shoeprints on the four-foot-by-four-foot, white tile square that served as an entryway. Julie was a compulsive housekeeper and scrambled to keep every inch of their small home spotless. Nick knew Julie would have immediately cleaned up the shoeprints if the mud had been tracked in before she retired for the evening. It was also apparent the muddy shoeprints belonged to a very large person. The shoeprints appeared to be at least size seventeen or eighteen. The tread pattern was worn, but he was pretty sure the mud tracks had been left by an athletic shoe of some sort.

Nick stepped over the muddy shoeprints and cautiously entered the cramped living room. The family room and kitchen were straight ahead toward the rear of the 1,800-square-foot house. A flight of stairs that led to the second floor, and all three bedrooms, was directly to his right. He turned right and began moving upward from one stair to the next, but it did little to alleviate the uneasiness he had been feeling since his return to Lakeland. In fact, as he climbed the staircase his apprehension intensified. When Nick reached the narrow hallway at the top of the stairs, he turned left and quickened his pace slightly as he walked down the narrow hallway that led to his daughter's bedroom.

At the end of the hallway, Nick poked his head into Darby's bedroom, not sure what he expected to find. His daughter's toddler bed was covered with an array of stuffed animals, but the neatly made bed was not an unexpected development. Darby often slept with her mother when her dad was out of town, and even when he wasn't, she'd nestle between the two of them on what she called "special occasions."

After making sure Darby wasn't in her bedroom, Nick turned to leave, but out of the corner of his eye, he caught a brief glimpse of something that seemed out of place. He moved far enough into the bedroom to see it was a small bare foot. Stunned and disoriented, Nick inched his way into the room. When he realized it was his beautiful wife lying face up on the carpeted floor, he crashed onto his knees and frantically crawled to his wife's motionless body.

The scene was surreal and strangely peaceful. Julie's long blonde hair framed her face, giving her youthful features an angelic, almost childlike quality in the morning sunlight. Her blue eyes were clouded and staring at nothing in particular. Even in death, she was the most beautiful woman he had ever seen. His wife's clothes were not torn or bloodstained, and there were no obvious signs of injury except for two indistinct bruises on her neck. Gurgling sobs escaped his constricted throat as he realized his wife had been murdered.

Julie was wearing his extra-large University of Idaho T-shirt she had permanently borrowed from him a couple of years ago. She loved to tease that after six years of marriage and one child, comfort was more important while she slept than sex appeal. The long shirt had ridden up her thighs, exposing her slender, muscle-toned legs, but not so far that her panties were visible. For some reason, perhaps self-preservation, his thinking momentarily shifted from grief stricken to analytical. Nick made a mental note that his wife's murder had not been the result of a sexual assault or overpowering hatred, because victims of passion killings typically sustain multiple injuries, most of them superficial.

"Why, why?" Nick cried softly, even though the why of it didn't really matter. His beautiful wife and best friend was dead. Nick brushed a wisp of blonde hair from her delicate cheek and gently kissed her on the lips. The tears that flowed steadily from his eyes now glistened on her soft skin.

"I love you," Nick sobbed then struggled to his feet.

Nick was reeling from his wife's murder, but he reluctantly left her body to search for his missing daughter. He quickly made his way from Darby's bedroom to the bedroom he had shared with Julie since returning to Lakeland. A hectic and crazed search of the master bedroom and the entire second floor confirmed his worst fears. Darby was not in the master bedroom, her bedroom, or any of the other rooms on the second floor. Nick's fragile hope of finding Darby had already begun to fade as he hurriedly made his way down the staircase to continue his frantic search on the ground floor.

Nick's family lived in a fairly small home, yet it seemed enormous as he searched. He ran from room to room screaming Darby's name and exploring any place a child might hide. After a frenzied and unsuccessful search of the downstairs that ended abruptly in their family room, he knew for certain his daughter was nowhere in the house. Several months before, Nick had crammed an old desk and file cabinet against the east wall of the family room. He used the small area to work on cases when he could no longer tolerate the loneliness of his downtown office. The papers and folders on top of his beat-up old desk had been ransacked, and two metal drawers were dangling from the file cabinet. Nick absentmindedly wondered why the intruder had messed with his work papers. But given his other discoveries, it didn't really matter.

Without a clear purpose in mind, Nick ascended the staircase for a second time. His second trip was strangely easier than the first. This time he knew what awaited him on the second floor and, more importantly, what he would not find there. He returned to the master bedroom and stood at the foot of the bed while he tried to formulate a plan of action. Nick didn't have a clue where he could turn for help or what his next move should be. Countless hours of training and combat experience were supposed to prepare him for any contingency, but it had not prepared him for this personal nightmare.

Nick was standing at the foot of their king-sized bed, dazed and confused, when the unbearable reality of the moment hit him like a ton of bricks. The only woman he had ever loved was dead in their daughter's bedroom, and his sweet, vulnerable three-year-old daughter was missing, most likely abducted by the same person who had killed her mother in cold blood. Perhaps it was caused by grief, or a lack of food and sleep, but the bedroom began to telescope. His body felt as if it were shrinking under the enormity of his pain, while his bedroom seemed to be expanding.

Nick pushed through the surreal feeling and slowly made his way toward the telephone on the nightstand beside the bed. He felt as if he were trying to move underwater as he clumsily picked up the telephone and attempted to dial 911. After blindly jabbing at a third digit, he shouted, "This is Nick Jelaco, send help!" into the telephone. Without knowing for sure what numbers he had punched on the telephone or if anyone had heard his plea for help, he dropped the phone to the floor as the room faded to black.

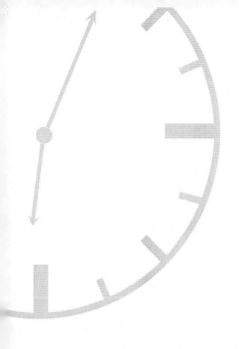

CHAPTER 3

Thursday morning, October 5

Nick blinked several times in an attempt to clear the fog from his throbbing head. It took a moment. When his vision was restored, he discovered a short heavyset man wearing a tight-fitting police uniform standing over him. The officer's cheeks were flushed, and he had a pained expression on his round face.

"I'm Officer Peters, first responder to your 911 call," he offered as an explanation for his presence.

"911 call?" Nick mumbled.

"Are you hurt?" the officer asked.

"No, I don't think so." Nick hesitantly replied.

"Is there anyone else in the home?"

"My wife is in our daughter's bedroom."

"Is there anyone in the house besides your...uh...wife?" Officer Peters stammered, clearly uncomfortable with his own question.

"I don't know," Nick answered without hesitation. "I can't find my daughter."

Officer Peters appeared to be in his mid to late thirties. Nick heard someone moving in the bedroom down the hall, and for an instant he thought it might be his daughter. After a brief moment, he realized it was probably another police officer assessing the crime scene.

Officer Peters noticed his quick glance in the direction of the movement and said, "That's my partner, Officer Jones; he's trying to get a handle on the situation."

As Nick struggled to sit up, Officer Peters extended a hand to help him to his feet.

"Let's go downstairs, Mr. Jelaco. The detectives blow a gasket when they take over a contaminated crime scene."

"Crime scene?" Nick murmured under his breath.

Officer Peters put his hand on Nick's shoulder and guided him down the staircase into the living room. The officer motioned toward the worn leather sofa that Julie had purchased at a garage sale shortly after Nick had graduated from law school, and he took a seat without objection. Officer Peters sat down heavily in a matching recliner positioned directly across from him. The police officer slumped in the chair, massaged his forehead, and exhaled deeply. Officer Peters avoided eye contact, and Nick assumed he was trying to figure out how he should handle the situation. Should he treat the victim's husband like a secondary victim of the violent crime or his prime suspect? Nick wanted the officer to start asking the right questions. If Peters and the rest of the cops eliminated him as a suspect, they could focus their attention on his missing daughter.

Officer Jones came down the stairs a few minutes later and motioned for Officer Peters to join him in the kitchen. Officer Jones was younger than Officer Peters, but he was clearly the officer in charge—the alpha male. Officer Jones was at least six foot four and easily carried two hundred and thirty pounds of muscle on his broad frame. Thick black hair was cropped close to his head, military style. The two police officers spoke briefly in whispered voices, with Officer Jones doing most of the talking, and then they returned to the living room.

Officer Jones spoke first.

"What's your connection to the deceased female in the upstairs bedroom?"

"She's my wife, Julie Jelaco," Nick said, choking back a sob.

"Were you and your wife both residing in this residence at the time of her death?" he asked, making no attempt to hide his suspicion.

Officer Jones lacked the skills of a good interrogator. He was obviously trying to determine if Nick and his wife were having marital difficulties prior to her death, but he was going about it in the wrong manner. Nick hoped the aggressive young cop wasn't the best the Lakeland Police Force had to offer.

"Yes, my wife and I live here with our three-year-old daughter, Darby," Nick answered, before quickly adding, "I know you're trying to figure out who murdered my wife, but my daughter is missing. Her whereabouts should be your first priority."

Officer Jones seemed annoyed by Nick's advice about how to prioritize the investigation and angrily countered, "You don't need to tell me how to do my job, Mr. Jelaco."

Nick nodded, but didn't respond to the officer's tongue-lashing.

When Officer Jones appeared convinced that Nick knew who was in charge, he asked, "When did you last see your daughter?"

"I've been out of town for several days on business, but we spoke on the telephone last night. It was about nine o'clock," Nick added before Officer Jones could ask the time.

"When did you get home from your business trip?"

"It was about six o'clock this morning," Nick answered truthfully.

Officer Jones frowned and made no attempt to conceal his suspicion. "When you returned home, your wife was dead, and your daughter was missing. Is that what you're trying to tell me?"

"Yes, that's correct."

The young police officer briefly discontinued his questioning in order to make a few mental calculations. If the confused look on his face was any indication, math was not his forte. After several seconds, he resumed his impromptu interrogation.

"It took you nine hours to get home? Where were you conducting your business, Mr. Jelaco?"

"I was in Las Vegas litigating a civil case, and the jury came in with a verdict at about seven o'clock last night," Nick answered, his frustration mounting. "I know where this interrogation is headed. I've taught criminal justice and criminology courses at the local university, and you're wasting time with this line of questioning."

Officer Jones puffed up his chest and said, "What do you mean by that, Mr. Jelaco? Are you trying to intimidate me?"

"No, of course not," Nick answered just as forcefully. "The majority of homicides are committed by someone close to the victim, especially if the victim is female. Initially it's standard procedure to consider persons related to the victim as a suspect. Right?"

Nick had been fairly calm up to this point in the interrogation. His calmness may have been the result of shock or denial. Whatever the reason, he had somehow managed to avoid an emotional breakdown. Perhaps, it was because he had been analyzing the horrific events from a detached legal perspective. *Should they have given me Miranda warnings before asking questions? Would their questioning qualify as an on-scene interrogation exempted from Miranda? Why haven't the officers taken more precautions to protect the homicide scene from contamination? I'm a potential witness or suspect. Why haven't I been removed from the scene?*

When Nick ran out of trivial distractions to keep his mind busy, the stark reality of the situation hit him again, and the fragile protective barriers created by Nick's subconscious came crashing down. His wife's lifeless body was upstairs, and his three-year-old daughter was nowhere to be found. The analytical calmness that had typified his demeanor up to that time was suddenly replaced by an unrestrained display of pain and grief.

"Give him a few minutes," Officer Peters pleaded, sympathetic to Nick's fragile mental state. "Can't you see the guy's about to lose it?"

The headstrong officer ignored Peters' plea for compassion, but before he could resume his questioning, a middle-aged man wearing faded blue jeans, a white button-down shirt, and a paisley tie came cautiously through the front door. A black .38 caliber revolver with a wooden grip protruded from the leather holster slung across his shoulder. It was clear from his confident demeanor that his carefully measured movements were necessitated by his desire to preserve trace evidence and not because of a timid or unassertive personality. There was a tattered tweed sport jacket slung across the man's left arm, and he was wearing a pair of cowboy boots that had seen better days. His graying hair was cut short, and his lean, wiry build seemed to exude energy. As soon as he entered the room, it was evident that the power dynamics had changed dramatically. Officer Jones's cocky swagger was immediately replaced by nervous insecurity.

"Good morning, Detective Gates," Officer Jones stammered.

"What's good about it?" Detective Gates grumbled. "Were you two morons absent the day they taught police work at the academy?"

Neither Officer Jones nor Officer Peters responded. Officer Jones stared intently at his freshly polished boots, and Officer Peters mumbled something indecipherable under his breath.

Detective Gates looked in Nick's direction for the first time and stared at him for several unwavering seconds.

"What's his connection to the victim?" Gates asked with a quick nod in Nick's direction.

"His name is Nick Jelaco. He lives here, and the deceased female is his wife," Peters answered nervously.

Detective Gates shook his head in disgust.

"He needs to be removed from the scene immediately. Peters, take Mr. Jelaco down to the station, and make him as comfortable as possible. Take his statement, but no one questions him until I'm present. Is that perfectly clear?"

"Yes, sir," Officer Peters responded.

Nick lacked the self-composure needed to formulate a full sentence, but Officer Peters must have been reading his mind, because Peters looked questioningly at Detective Gates.

"Spit it out, Peters," Gates bellowed when he noticed the red-faced police officer's inquiring gaze.

"Mr. Jelaco's daughter is missing, sir," Officer Peters replied meekly.

"Jeez, Peters," Detective Gates replied. "Get a detailed description of his daughter and a recent photo from Mr. Jelaco. Provide local law enforcement agencies and media outlets with the description and photograph. Also, plug the pertinent information into the Amber Alert system. Let's cover all our bases until we have more information regarding the girl's disappearance."

"Yes, sir, I'll get right on it," Peters responded, clearly relieved he had been granted permission to leave the scene and Gates's watchful eye.

Gates turned his attention to Officer Jones.

"Get a few more patrol officers down here to secure the crime scene. Establish a perimeter around the entire residence, including the yard. Don't let anyone in unless they have my approval."

"Yes, sir, consider it done," Jones replied.

"The point of entry appears to be the front door. No one, and I mean no one, enters through the front door until the crime scene guys are done processing the area."

It was apparent that Detective Gates knew his way around a crime scene. Even though Nick had just met the man, his intuition was telling him Detective Gates was the right man to head up the investigation. Nick thought it was odd that he and a complete stranger could be so quickly connected by a common objective, though he also found it a little disheartening that the surly detective considered him a suspect rather than an ally.

CHAPTER 4

Detective Phillip Gates was not well liked by his coworkers at the Lakeland Police Department. Still he was undeniably the most respected officer on the force. When it came to working a crime scene or interrogating a suspect, Detective Gates was the best the police force had to offer. His supervisors tolerated what they called a lack of "people skills" and his blatant disregard for departmental policy because of his extraordinary, almost uncanny, skills as a detective. Detective Gates had been promoted to detective sixteen years ago, and during that time, the ill-tempered detective had successfully closed more investigations than the rest of the detective division combined. His methods weren't always by the book, but his methods got results, and results kept the chief and Lakeland taxpayers happy.

Gates glanced at his watch and made a mental note of the time. He expected Detective Sato to arrive within the hour, armed with a search warrant and Mr. Jelaco's written consent to search his home. Gates didn't need both the search warrant and Mr. Jelaco's consent for a lawful search of the murder scene, but he had instructed Sato to get both just the same. He knew from experience that legal technicalities could sometimes make or break an investigation, and he wasn't about to take any chances with such a high-profile crime.

Officer Jones and two youthful-looking patrol officers were encircling the entire yard with crime-scene tape as Gates made his way to the northeast corner of the Jelacos' modest home. The patrol officers would keep the crime scene free from curious onlookers and media types while Gates waited for the rest of the homicide investigative team to arrive. Over the next few days, Gates and his team would scour every inch of the crime scene looking for any evidence that would provide even the smallest clue to the killer's identity. It was difficult, time-consuming work, but it had to be done and done meticulously. Right now, Gates had to figure out what made this guy tick; he needed to get inside the head of the cold-blooded killer.

On his initial walk around the house, Gates had noticed several very large shoeprints in a muddy flower bed near a window at the rear of the house. Those same large shoeprints were also present on the front step and just inside the front door on the tile entryway. Detective Gates's mental reenactment of the crime needed to follow in the footsteps of the actual killer. When Gates arrived at the rear window, he tried to clear his head of peripheral thoughts as he stood stoically on the damp grass near the muddy shoeprints.

"Trying to think like a psychopath is one messed up way to earn a living," Gates muttered under his breath. Gates pushed the unproductive clutter from his thoughts as he stood motionless near the small flower bed and stared intently at the large shoeprints in the mud. If he wanted to catch the killer, he needed to understand the man's true motivation for the crime. *Was the perpetrator trying to find a point of entry, or was he trying to view something inside the Jelacos' home? Was Julie Jelaco the victim of a random burglary gone terribly wrong, or did the intruder specifically target Mrs. Jelaco or something else inside the home?* After some deliberation about the angled shoeprints under the window, Gates decided the intruder was most likely trying to view the contents of the Jelacos' family room.

The detective found no evidence that indicated the intruder had attempted to open this particular window or any of the windows on the ground floor. Still, Gates couldn't help but wonder why the killer had entered through the front door. It was the worst possible point of entry due to the undeniable fact that it could be easily viewed from the main road. In addition to the visibility factor, the front door was the most secure of the four entrances located on the ground floor. It was the only door that had both a key lock on the doorknob and a separate dead bolt. Gates made a mental note to inquire about Julie Jelaco's door-locking tendencies. He thought it unlikely that Mrs. Jelaco would leave the door unlocked, especially with her husband out of town. When Gates was convinced that the killer had not entered through a window, he returned to the front door.

Gates knelt on the front porch and examined both locks on the heavy, metal door. He was careful not to compromise the dried shoeprints. Gates was well aware of the limitations of ordinary shoeprint evidence, but he was cautious to preserve it nonetheless. Unique shoeprints could place a suspect at the scene of the crime, and that was the kind of simplistic evidence juries could really sink their teeth into.

It did not appear as if either lock on the front door had been jimmied or forced. In any case, Gates would have the forensic experts check the locks for tool marks and paint transfers. He was certain they wouldn't find anything, but Gates wanted perfection on this investigation. The simplistic lock on the doorknob would take a professional burglar about five seconds to open. The dead bolt was another story. It was a fairly sophisticated lock that would pose a challenge for a seasoned professional. Gates's intuition told him that the guy he was looking for was a thug—hired muscle—certainly not a professional. *So how did the killer get in? Was the door unlocked? Did Julie Jelaco know her killer? Did the killer have a key?* Gates had lots of questions. What he needed were some answers.

Detective Gates entered the house in the same manner as the nameless, faceless man he was pursuing—through the front door. Once inside, the detective systematically made his way from the entryway to the family room at the rear of the home. Gates tried to imagine covering that same distance in the dead of night with Julie and Darby Jelaco upstairs alive and most likely sleeping. *What was the killer feeling? Was his main objective theft or sexual assault? It probably wasn't murder and kidnapping.*

As Gates slowly moved toward the family room and Nick Jelaco's makeshift home office, his gut told him that the key to the investigation lay in the cluttered, ransacked workspace. In a moment of optimism, he hoped the crucial evidence had avoided the intruder's detection. Deep down, he knew better. *What was this guy looking for? Did its value warrant murder? Obviously it did to someone, but whom?* He knew all investigations started with more questions than answers, but this one had enough questions to give Gates a headache.

Nick Jelaco's desk and file cabinet gave Gates his first rush of adrenaline. Two drawers had been pulled from the file cabinet and were dangling on their runners. A good portion of the drawers' contents had been tossed onto the floor. The papers on top of Nick's desk had been rifled through as well. *What does a lawyer keep in his home office? Client files from old cases? Client files from cases he's still working on?* Gates was certain that Mr. Jelaco's chosen profession was somehow connected to the initial break-in, but how? The detective made a mental note to look into Mr. Jelaco's business dealings.

Gates's gut told him the killer's first contact with Mrs. Jelaco had been in this area of the house. He wondered why she had come downstairs to confront the intruder. She could have phoned the police from the safety of her bedroom upstairs, yet there had been no 911 calls reported from the Jelaco residence. Maybe Mrs. Jelaco had ventured downstairs because she believed her husband had returned early from his business trip? Once again, Gates's instincts kicked in, and he realized that Mrs. Jelaco had probably ventured onto the scene unknowingly. After surprising her killer, he had most likely pursued her back upstairs. At this point, Gates did not believe that the killer would have ventured upstairs had his trespass gone undetected.

After one last look, Gates reluctantly left the family room and made his way to the second floor and Mrs. Jelaco's lifeless body. A murder victim's body could provide a great deal of evidence about a crime and its perpetrator. Gates hoped the murder site would tell him something about the killer, his motive, and the cause and time of Mrs. Jelaco's death. As Gates entered Darby Jelaco's bedroom, he was struck by the comforting environment her parents had created for her and how out of place Julie Jelaco's lifeless body seemed in the otherwise cheerful room. Mrs. Jelaco was dead. Gates hoped her daughter would not suffer the same fate.

Gates's concern for the Jelacos' little girl brought back memories of his own daughter. They had not spoken a word for more than three years, and Gates wondered if she ever thought about him. The mistakes he had made and the solitary life he had chosen had doomed their relationship many years ago. Gates quickly pushed the guilt and regret from his mind. Those feelings were buried deep, and only occasionally did he allow them to surface. Today they had snuck up on him. A frustrated Gates massaged his temples in an attempt to alleviate the throbbing in his head and then returned his focus to the task at hand.

Gates was almost certain Julie had been pursued from the family room to her daughter's bedroom by the killer. The chase had ended in a deadly confrontation in the far corner of the little girl's bedroom. Gates tried to imagine the terror Julie must have felt as she stared into the eyes of her killer, cornered with no chance of escape. Gates walked methodically toward the body, trying to visualize the horrifying events as they unfolded. When Gates reached Julie's lifeless body, he noted its condition and the state of her scant clothing. She was wearing an old T-shirt and underwear but no bra. Gates assumed Mrs. Jelaco had removed her bra and donned the T-shirt prior to retiring for the evening. It did not appear as if the struggle was prolonged or overly violent. It appeared as if the killer had exerted just enough force to cause her death and then fled the scene. She had suffered no obvious broken bones, lacerations, or deep contusions. Her youthful face was free of makeup and showed no signs of trauma. Gates was struck by how beautiful the young woman looked in the natural morning light. Her nightshirt was not bloodstained or torn, and Gates was certain the rape kit would be negative.

Gates stood next to the body and scanned the child's bedroom. *Why did she run into a room with no telephone or lock on the door? Was Mrs. Jelaco trying to lead her attacker away from her daughter? If so, why did she venture back upstairs?* The rumpled bedding on the king-sized bed in the master bedroom indicated the bed had been slept in by one adult and one child. *Did the little girl hear her mother's screams and leave the safety of her parent's bed? Is Darby Jelaco alive or dead?* Gates had to operate under the assumption that the little girl was still alive, an assumption he prayed was accurate.

Gates had investigated hundreds of crime scenes over the years, and he believed a police officer could determine a lot about a person's character by the way he or she lived. The Jelaco home was modest by contemporary standards but tastefully decorated. Multiple pictures had been placed around the house, pictures that told the story of a playful, loving family. Detective Gates doubted that the Jelacos were involved in any criminal activities. Gates paused at a fairly recent picture of Mrs. Jelaco and her daughter. *What a waste,* he thought. *Lakeland's south side is overrun with rapists, murderers, and drug dealers, but it's a loving wife and mother who gets murdered in her suburban home.*

CHAPTER 5

Gates completed his initial walkthrough just as Detective Sato, Detective Styles, and Detective Mitchell arrived at the crime scene. Detective Sato was armed with the search warrant and Mr. Jelaco's written consent to search, as he had been instructed. Gates had specifically asked the chief to assign Detective David Sato to his investigative team. Sato was one of the few members of the Lakeland Police Force that Gates could tolerate.

David Sato had made detective after only three years on patrol. Unlike most of the young detectives on the Lakeland Police Force, he had earned his promotion through hard work, not brownnosing. Detective Sato was in his early thirties but looked much younger. Sato was small for a police officer, only five foot eight with a slim build. His shoulder-length, black hair and scraggly goatee came in handy when Sato worked narcotics undercover.

Detective Gates had never worked with either Detective Styles or Detective Mitchell. He assumed both detectives would be reassigned after a couple of weeks due to the persistent manpower shortages plaguing the Lakeland Police Department, but Gates hoped he could get some productive work out of the detectives while they were part of his investigative team. Mitchell and Styles's first assignment would be to interview the Jelacos' neighbors and local businesses. Maybe a neighbor or store clerk had seen someone out of the ordinary. Gates knew it was a long shot, and he certainly wasn't optimistic, but he couldn't afford to take any shortcuts with this investigation.

Stan Smith, a crime scene investigator employed by the Idaho Bureau of Investigation, arrived shortly after nine o'clock. Stan's primary duty was to collect and perform laboratory analysis on the forensic evidence. As a short, balding man in his early forties, Stan didn't fit the male-model stereotype that had become the norm on primetime television.

The final member of the investigative team, medical examiner Katie Holt, arrived a few minutes after Stan Smith. Katie worked for the Monroe County coroner, and she would determine the time and cause of death. Gates hated working with doctors, because they never gave him a straight answer, but he felt differently about Katie. Katie was a licensed physician who wasn't afraid to speak her mind or take a chance on tricky cases. Most people who worked with Dr. Holt thought she was ex-military. She wore her brown hair short, almost in a crew cut, which made her look like she had just completed twelve weeks of basic training.

There were persistent rumors in the law enforcement community about her sexual preferences, but Gates couldn't have cared less about her personal life. It was her business whom she slept with when she was off duty. Guys around the police station often joked that it was a good thing Katie worked with dead people given her unpleasant bedside manner, but Gates disagreed. He had worked with Katie Holt on numerous occasions, and he liked the direct no-nonsense approach.

When the investigative team was all present, Gates called them together for a brief pep talk and gave each member of the team their initial marching orders.

"This is a messy case with multiple dimensions and few clear-cut leads to follow," Gates began. "We have a murdered housewife and mother in an upstairs bedroom, and the victim's three-year-old daughter is missing. The husband claims he was driving back from Las Vegas at the time of the murder, so we'll need to check his alibi."

After his brief introduction, Gates turned his attention to Detective Sato.

"Get a hold of his cell phone records and interview anyone he had contact with in Las Vegas. Also check out flights from Las Vegas to Lakeland on the night of the murder."

"I'll get right on it," Sato confirmed.

"One more thing, take a look at his law firm and find out if Jelaco is working on any cases that might interest us. He's at the station right now making an official statement. Get a copy of it when he's done, and reference it for the specifics of his story, but don't question him."

Gates turned to Detectives Styles and Mitchell.

"I want you to canvas the local area from top to bottom. Interview everyone who lives on River Crest Drive and everyone who lives on the street directly behind the Jelaco residence. When that's done, talk to all employees who worked a shift at the convenience store on the corner of River Crest and Shoreline during the past week. I want to know if there were any suspicious characters or unfamiliar cars hanging around the neighborhood prior to the murder. Take detailed notes—you never know what might be important."

Styles and Mitchell nodded.

Detective Gates was used to giving orders, and he didn't miss a beat.

"Katie, I want a preliminary estimation of the time of death. Also, check the victim for signs of lividity. I want to know if the victim was moved postmortem."

"This is not my first homicide, Phil. I know the drill."

"I know, but this one is important. We can't afford any screwups," Gates tried to explain.

"I never screw up, Phil."

Katie's cockiness brought a fleeting smile to Gates's face, but he moved on without comment.

"Stan, check the front door for signs of forced entry," Gates instructed. "I also want impression casts of the shoeprints in the flower bed outside the family room window and scale photographs of the shoeprints in the front entry. Get me the manufacturer and shoe size as soon as possible."

"How about fingerprints?" Smith asked.

"Don't waste your time with that stuff unless you've got a hunch you want to work. A couple of crime scene techs can photograph the crime scene and dust for latent prints," Gates replied.

Smith nodded and said, "I don't want to examine the locks until they've been dusted for prints."

"The front door isn't going anywhere," Gates sarcastically replied before directing his next comment at Katie. "Let me know when you're done with your preliminary examination of the body. I want Stan to check Mrs. Jelaco's body for trace evidence before it's removed. Does anybody have any questions?"

"Where's the body?" Dr. Holt demanded.

"It's on the second floor in the little girl's bedroom."

There was no small talk between Gates and the medical examiner as she followed him to Julie Jelaco's lifeless body. Gates hated meaningless chitchat and made no effort to start a conversation. When they arrived in Darby's bedroom, Katie made a beeline to the body and removed a small tape recorder and a pair of latex gloves from her jacket pocket.

"She was a pretty girl," Katie remarked as she pulled on the gloves.

"Yeah, she was," Gates agreed.

"I need to jot down a few preliminary notes before Stan checks the body," Katie said. "We need to get her body to the morgue as soon as possible."

"Let me know when you're ready for Stan."

"Were the lights on when the patrol officers arrived at the scene?"

"Yes, but the husband could have turned them on when he returned from his business trip."

"The ambient room temperature is currently seventy-two degrees. Does the furnace operate on a timer?" Katie asked.

"I don't know, but I'll check it out."

"It could be important in pinpointing the exact time of death," Katie said and then quickly qualified her statement, "The temperature variance was probably small enough that it won't matter a great deal, but I'd still like to reference it in my report."

She kneeled and began to speak methodically into a small, black tape recorder.

"The victim is a white female, approximately thirty years of age, weight 110, height five foot four. The victim exhibits no signs of blunt force trauma, lacerations, or surface wounds. Victim has superficial bruises on her neck and broken blood vessels in her eyes. Manual strangulation is a possible cause of death. Check victim for breakage of the hyroid bone and vegal inhabitation. Postmortem lividity patterns indicate that the body has not been moved post death."

"Do you have an estimate on the time of death?" Detective Gates interrupted.

Katie turned off the tape recorder and stood up. "I can't be sure without a more comprehensive examination of the body."

"What's your best guess?"

Katie glanced at her watch.

"I would estimate time of death between three and four o'clock this morning. I'll need to check her liver temperature and stomach contents before I can give you a more precise time, but I'm confident my estimation is pretty close."

Gates did some quick math in his head.

"That time of death would fit with my original theory," he said to no one in particular.

"Let's get Stan up here to do his job. I want her on the table by this afternoon."

Gates left the room and returned a couple of minutes later with a civilian crime scene technician named Kelly Colter and Stan Smith. Kelly held a small video camera in the palm of her right hand. Departmental policy required that the entire forensic examination be recorded in enough detail to satisfy the most paranoid defense attorney. Stan Smith brought up the rear of the three-person procession. The pudgy, balding crime scene investigator carried a black leather medical bag in one of his gloved hands. Without hesitating, Smith took a digital camera from the black medical bag and snapped several photographs of Julie's body from various angles.

The investigator had already returned the camera to his black bag and removed a sterile drop cloth by the time the last camera flash had vanished from the air. Smith carefully spread the sterile drape next to the body and then placed several stamp-sized paper envelopes, glass vials, a box of toothpicks, and a pair of stainless steel tweezers on the drape. Smith was slow but Gates wasn't about to rush the investigator. His experience working with Smith had taught him that the crime scene investigator was plodding and meticulous, but that caution translated into Smith being an unflappable witness at trial.

Smith pulled a pair of black-framed glasses from his breast pocket and slid them onto the bridge of his nose. He slowly and methodically began to scrutinize every inch of the victim's body. When his well-trained eyes detected a foreign hair or fiber, Smith would carefully remove the foreign object with a pair of tweezers and then place the potential evidence in a paper bindle. After securing the bindle, he would place the bindle in a glass vial. To avoid any confusion about the original location of the evidence, Smith marked each bindle with a black pen and made a corresponding notation on a diagram of the victim's body. Before removing larger pieces of trace evidence, Smith would snap several photographs of the evidentiary item in question.

After about thirty minutes, Smith spoke for the first time.

"I recovered a couple of long black hairs, and, judging by the photos I was shown, the hairs don't belong to the daughter. Does the husband have long black hair?" Smith asked.

"Nick Jelaco has black hair, but it's cut pretty short," Gates answered.

"These hairs are between nine and ten inches in length," Smith added for clarification.

"Definitely not the husband's hair," Gates replied. "He's got that clean-cut, G.Q. look going for him."

"I want to scrape her fingernails before we turn the body over," Smith said as he stared intently at the victim's right hand. "It appears as if there's some blood and tissue under a couple of her fingernails."

Gates felt a momentary rush of excitement. *Could it really be this easy?* he wondered. *If the killer's in a DNA data bank, we may get a quick match.* His excitement faded just as quickly. Gates knew very few offenders were required to register a DNA profile, and law enforcement agencies were slow to input DNA information when it was mandated. A DNA match was a long shot at best.

Smith removed a white plastic toothpick and scraped under the index fingernail of the victim's left hand. After the first fingernail had been scraped, Smith placed the toothpick in a paper bindle and then placed it in a glass vial. Smith then marked the vial to indicate which finger the sample had been removed from. Smith repeated the process with each of the victim's fingernails. When he was finally done, Smith placed all ten glass vials in his black medical bag. He then stood and let out a soft groan as he stretched his arms above his head.

"Okay, Phil, it's time to flip her body over." Gates started to move toward Julie Jelaco's body. "Put on a pair of gloves!" Smith blurted out.

Gates donned a pair of latex gloves as instructed and positioned himself near the victim's shoulders. Gates and Smith gently rotated Julie's small, lifeless body After the body had been turned, Smith continued the slow process of removing trace evidence and preserving it for analysis.

After several minutes, Smith stood and let out a sigh.

"Let's get her on a sterile sheet and remove her clothing."

Katie asked, "Is there a clean drop cloth in your medical bag?"

"Yeah, check the big zippered pocket on the right side," Smith replied.

The medical examiner retrieved a sterile drape from Smith's medical bag and flattened the clean, white linen sheet on the floor next to the body. Gates and Smith once again moved into position and carefully lifted Julie's body onto the white sheet.

"There is something beneath her body," Katie pointed out.

Smith removed a ballpoint pen from shirt pocket and carefully picked up a small gold chain and heart-shaped locket.

"It must have come loose in the struggle," Gates surmised.

Smith held the locket in the sunlight and softly read the words engraved on the back of the locket.

"It was probably a gift from her husband," Katie said softly.

The crime scene investigator nodded before he dropped the necklace into an envelope.

Smith reached into his black bag for the last time and removed two clear plastic bags. The crime scene examiner removed Julie's faded T-shirt and placed it in one of the plastic bags. He carefully sealed the bag and marked it. Smith returned to the body one more time and repeated the process with Julie's underwear. He then folded the sheet inward, bindle style, around Julie's nude body to preserve any trace evidence that might become dislodged during the trip to the morgue.

When he was done, Smith stepped aside. "Some days I really hate this frickin' job."

Katie removed a cell phone from a clip on her belt and dialed a phone number from memory.

"The body is ready for removal and transport," she said before hanging up. Within minutes, two young men arrived with a black body bag and small gurney. They placed Julie's body into the black bag before the smaller of the two men pulled the zipper closed around her face. Both men lifted her body onto the gurney and secured the safety belts. Katie Holt, Detective Gates, Kelly Colter, and Stan Smith followed in silence as the two young men wheeled Julie Jelaco from her home for the last time.

CHAPTER 6

"Hello."

"It's me," Edgar's unmistakable voice greeted him.

"You inept moron, I told you never to call me at this number."

The insult infuriated Edgar, but he managed to hold his temper in check. He'd been called demeaning names his entire life, and years of personal insults had taught him how to control his inner rage.

"I had no choice. My news was too important to wait for the scheduled call," he explained in a deceptively contrite tone.

"It better be important, and it better be good," Edgar's employer hissed.

"Things got complicated," Edgar said in his slow, droning voice.

"Complicated?" He growled. "What do you mean by complicated?"

Edgar hesitated for a second before skirting the question. "We need to meet."

"Have you lost what's left of your mind?" his employer barked. "Get to the point, and get there fast."

"The wife—ah…she must have been awake or something because she came downstairs while I was searching the desk."

"Fool! Did she get a look at you?"

"Yeah."

"Your screwup had better not end up on my doorstep."

"Don't worry. The wife won't be pointing a finger at me or anyone else for that matter."

"How can you be sure?"

"I did what had to be done," Edgar answered without emotion. "I suppose it was her time to die."

After a brief silence, Edgar's employer said, "Unfortunate but necessary. Did you get the item?"

"I wasn't sure which one to take, so I took them all."

Edgar's employer laughed softly. "Good work. That'll make it almost impossible to connect me to the break-in."

"There's still the matter of payment," Edgar reminded him.

"Leave the commodity at the drop point, and when I'm satisfied that your stupidity hasn't put me at risk, I'll arrange a time and place for the final payment."

"There was one additional complication," Edgar hesitantly continued.

"Spit it out!"

"The little girl woke up and came into the room while I was taking care of her mother."

"And?"

"I took her," Edgar explained.

"You took her where?"

"She's at my apartment with my girlfriend," Edgar explained.

"Are you completely insane?" the angry man snarled at Edgar. "Every cop in Lakeland will be looking for that kid."

"I had no choice," Edgar replied defensively.

"If you want to get paid, you had better clean up this mess."

"How?"

"Make your girlfriend and the little girl disappear."

"Okay, it's done."

"Do it quickly, and don't call me again," his employer demanded. "I'll call you at the scheduled time and place."

Edgar Ellenwood was enraged by the time he hung up the telephone. He was sick and tired of that pompous egomaniac criticizing his every move. He was even more arrogant and controlling than his narcissistic boss. He wasn't about to make his girlfriend disappear, and Edgar didn't want to kill the little girl. At least not yet. He had other plans for his small houseguest, and they didn't involve her death.

Edgar had heard stories about rich suburban couples who were willing to pay a lot of money for a healthy little white girl. With the right contacts, a guy could make a tidy profit facilitating a black market adoption. Edgar estimated $50,000 to $100,000 if he played his cards right. Times had been tough for him and Shavonne. That much money would get them far away from Lakeland.

Right now, the situation was a little too hot, but he could wait a week or two until things cooled down.

"After all, isn't patience a virtue?" Edgar mumbled to himself. If the cops got too close, he could always kill the little girl. *What a shame that would be,* he thought. *Wasting such a perfect opportunity for a fresh start far away from Lakeland.*

CHAPTER 7

Thursday afternoon, October 5

Officer Peters escorted Nick to his black and white Chevy Impala. The Lakeland City Council had recently approved the purchase of eight new patrol cars, and evidently Officer Peters had been one of the lucky recipients. Nick stood beside the police car, not sure if he was supposed to ride in the backseat like an arrested suspect. Peters climbed into the cramped driver's seat. The overweight police officer then leaned across the front seat and opened the passenger door. Nick felt disoriented and confused as he slumped down low in the front seat. A multitude of strange and random thoughts were bumping around inside his head when Officer Peters' voice jarred him back to the present.

"What's your daughter's date of birth?"

"Excuse me?" Nick replied in confusion.

"What's your daughter's date of birth? I need to call in a missing person report," Officer Peters repeated.

"Darby's birthday is the twenty-third of December. She'll be four."

"Oh, a Christmas baby…," Officer Peters cheerfully started and then stopped midsentence. "Can you give me a physical description?"

"Darby has brown eyes and light brown hair that hangs well past her shoulders."

"Do you know her height and weight?"

"I think she's about three-and-a-half feet tall and weighs around forty pounds, but I'm not sure," Nick answered.

"Can you describe the clothes she was wearing at the time of her disappearance?"

"I don't have any idea," Nick angrily replied. "I would assume she was wearing a pair of pajamas or one of her silky nightgowns."

"I'm sorry, Mr. Jelaco," Peters apologized. "I forgot that you were out of town last night."

The realization that Julie would never pick out another outfit for their daughter or fix her long brown hair caused a tear to roll down Nick's cheek.

"I might be able to figure it out if I look through her pajama drawer but probably not," he answered softly. "Julie paid more attention to that kind of stuff than I do."

Officer Peters tilted his head forward and starting speaking methodically into his left shoulder. Peters had relayed all Darby's pertinent information before Nick realized he was speaking into a radio that was attached to his blue shirt just below the neckline. Nick knew from experience that the radio could also function as a recording device, and he wondered in an offhand way if Officer Peters had been recording their conversation. When Officer Peters was done talking into the radio, he slowly backed his black and white patrol car out of the Jelacos' driveway.

Nick turned to look at 434 River Crest Drive through the rear window of the patrol car as they drove away. He knew it was his home, but it seemed as if he were seeing it for the first time, or maybe the last. He watched the houses in his neighborhood slowly pass by as Officer Peters drove west on River Crest Drive. It seemed strange that his life had changed so drastically yet the lives of his neighbors were virtually unaffected by those same life-altering events. His neighbors would talk about the crime for a week or two, and then it would be mostly forgotten. A few of Nick's neighbors stood in their yards, craning their necks to get a good look at the events taking place down the block. At the end of the street, Officer Peters turned his patrol car left onto Overland Boulevard and headed south toward Lakeland's city center and the police station.

Overland Boulevard was one of the busiest streets in Lakeland, which made travel toward the downtown area slow. Nick had mixed feelings about reaching the police station. The grieving husband part of him was not ready to face the reality of his wife's death, but the frantic father part of him needed to start the seemingly impossible process of finding his daughter. Julie's fate was now beyond his control, which meant Nick had to put his grief aside and focus on things he could change. It was up to him to find his little girl as soon as possible.

They drove in silence for a mile or two before Officer Peters spoke again. "It's common knowledge among us cops that Gates is the best detective on the Lakeland police force. He's not always the most pleasant person to be around, but he'll find your daughter and the guy who murdered …" Peters' voice trailed off, but the painful truth of his unfinished statement hung in the air.

"When will I be able to return to my house?" Nick asked. "I need to be home just in case Darby tries to get in touch with me."

Officer Peters knew it was unlikely the three-year-old would attempt to contact her father via the telephone, but he answered Nick's question just the same.

"I can't give a definite time frame. Processing a complex crime scene usually takes at least two or three days. We'll keep one of Lakeland's finest on sight twenty-four-seven just in case somebody tries to contact you."

"Thanks," Nick quietly replied.

"I'll run you by your house to pick up a few things if I'm still on duty when Gates is done questioning you," Peters offered. "Do you have any family members in the area that you could stay with for a few days?"

"No, not really," Nick answered. "My father died when I was in high school, and my mother and I haven't been close since she remarried."

"This might be a good time to reach out to her," Officer Peters suggested.

"Maybe..."

"Do you need to give anyone a heads-up before the story hits the newspapers and television?" Officer Peters asked.

"I probably should call my father-in-law, but I'm dreading that conversation," Nick replied before quietly adding, "He never believed I was good enough to marry his daughter, and to be honest with you, he was probably right. I should have been home last night."

Officer Peters took his eyes off the road for a second and looked Nick directly in the eyes. "I don't know about any of that personal stuff, Mr. Jelaco. I do know your wife's family should hear the news directly from you and not from some news reporter who sensationalizes other people's tragedies for a living."

"You're probably right," Nick answered without conviction. "I'll call my father-in-law when we get to the station."

Officer Peters and Nick rode the rest of the way to the police station without speaking to one another. Nick could tell that Officer Peters was trying to think of something to say that might help him deal with his personal tragedy. Nick knew only the return of his beautiful, brown-eyed daughter unharmed could lessen the unbearable pain that consumed him.

The Lakeland Police Station was located on Second Avenue East in one of the oldest and most rundown sections of downtown Lakeland. The old building had been constructed adjacent to the Monroe County Jail and sat directly across the street from the Monroe County Courthouse. All three buildings were an eclectic mixture of old-style architecture and modern budget-impacted additions. Officer Peters pulled his patrol car into the alley behind the police station and parked beside a no-parking sign. Nick wondered if Peters was following standard operating procedure or if the sympathetic police officer was trying to avoid the media onslaught that might be gathering at the main entrance.

They entered through an unlocked service entrance in the garage area. Once inside, Officer Peters escorted Nick through a maze of hallways to a dingy, depressing interrogation room that contained a metal table, three metal chairs, and a large mirror on the west wall. The other three walls were bare and grey except for a circular clock and calendar that boldly displayed the date his life had changed. The interrogation room had poor lighting and no windows to the outside, which served to intensify the room's gloominess. Officer Peters placed a yellow pad of paper and two black pens on the metal table.

"You should have some privacy here to make your phone calls and work on your statement. Can I bring you something to eat or drink?" Officer Peters asked.

"Just some water, thanks," Nick replied.

Officer Peters patted Nick on the shoulder and quickly left the interrogation room without further comment. Nick removed his cell phone from his pants' pocket and took a seat on one of the metal chairs. The chair was uncomfortable but not nearly as uncomfortable as the thought of speaking to Julie's father. His father-in-law, William Forsthye, came from a family of wealth and influence. Real-estate development and a bull stock market in the 1980s and 90s had made him a very wealthy man, a man used to getting his way by whatever means necessary.

Nick's thoughts wandered to Julie's father while he waited for him to pick up the call. William Forsthye was sixty years old but appeared younger due to his daily regimen at the gym. His graying hair and tanned face gave him a distinguished look that belied his true personality. William should have been a politician, because he knew how to use his appearance and physique to intimidate or impress, depending on the situation. Nick wasn't intimidated by his father-in-law, but he did try to keep his distance whenever possible. According to gossip in the Forsthye social circle, William was quite the ladies' man, and the institution of marriage didn't impede his extra-marital activities. Nick knew his wife was aware of the rumors, but she had never mentioned them to him. An obvious lack of moral character was just one of many reasons that Nick despised the man.

He had dialed William Forsythe's private business line and prayed Julie's father would not answer the incoming call. Unfortunately, he answered after the third ring. Nick was expecting the worst, but nothing could have prepared him for the blame and hatred William unleashed on him.

CHAPTER 8

Detective Gates strode through the door of the interrogation room at precisely the same moment Nick finished writing his statement. He suspected the detective had been watching him through the one-way window on the west wall of the interrogation room. Nick's limited exposure to police investigations made him believe that he was probably a suspect or at least a person of interest. He truly hoped Detective Gates's investigative skills warranted the praise Officer Peters had heaped upon him. Nick needed the lead detective to get the investigation on the right track as soon as possible, and to help Gates get on the right track, Nick was willing to take risks he would never permit a client to take.

The metal chair Nick was sitting in clanged against the cement floor when he abruptly stood to greet the detective.

"Do you have information about my daughter?" Nick immediately asked.

"Not yet, Mr. Jelaco," Gates answered. "I have a couple of detectives and six patrol officers going door to door in your neighborhood, and the appropriate state and federal law enforcement agencies have already gotten involved. At this point, we don't have a lot to go on."

"She's a little girl," Nick mumbled. "There's got to be something more we can do."

"Child abduction cases are law enforcement's worst nightmare," Gates continued. "Your daughter's picture and description were sent out over the Amber Alert warning system, and media outlets will make sure everyone in the country knows her face and story. The FBI and Idaho State Police are talking to known sex offenders in the area. To be brutally honest with you, these cases are like looking for a needle in a hay stack."

"You make it sound so bleak."

"The odds aren't good," Gates admitted. "By this afternoon we should have a couple of National Guard helicopters in the air and search parties organized on the ground."

"Will any of that stuff matter?" Nick asked dejectedly.

"We definitely need a break, and I was hoping you could point the investigation in the right direction."

"I don't know anything," Nick replied, his frustration mounting.

Detective Gates sized Nick up for a couple seconds before responding. "With proper prodding, you might give me something I can use. I'd like to ask you a few questions and then let our polygraph man follow up while you're hooked to the little black box."

"Let's get a move on," Nick replied with as much optimism as he could muster.

"It's departmental policy to make an audio and video recording of all interviews," Detective Gates casually informed him.

"Do whatever it is you people do, but do it quickly. We both know time is working against my daughter."

Nick had scarcely given permission to record the interview when a young woman with bleached-blonde hair opened the door to the interrogation room. The woman, who appeared to be in her early twenties, hastily entered the room carrying a digital recorder on a stainless steel tripod. The woman made eye contact with Detective Gates, and he nodded toward a spot directly across from the chair where Nick had been sitting. She effortlessly positioned the tripod and recorder as Gates had instructed and handed him a remote control.

"Thanks, Dana."

The young woman winked at the detective as she left the interrogation room and said, "No problem, Detective Gates. Whistle if you need anything else."

As the door closed behind her, Nick wondered who else was watching from the other side of the one-way window. Gates walked over to the digital recorder and bent to look through the viewfinder. He made a couple of minor adjustments to the position of the lens and then returned to the metal table. The detective nodded toward the only chair that was in the direct view of the digital recorder, and Nick took a seat. Gates positioned his chair so the recorder's view of Nick would not be obscured. When everyone was in position, Gates offhandedly pointed the remote control in the direction of the digital recorder. A flashing red light on the camera turned green.

"Are you ready to begin, Mr. Jelaco?" he asked.

"Yes."

Detective Gates glanced at his watch and spoke to no one in particular. "It is approximately 1:20 p.m. on Thursday, the fifth day of October, year 2007. This is Detective Phillip Gates interviewing Nicholas Jelaco. Mr. Jelaco, I would like to advise you of your Miranda rights before proceeding with the interview."

"Fine, Detective, but I know my rights," Nick impatiently informed him.

Gates proceeded with the Miranda warnings in spite of Nick's assertions. " Do you understand your rights, Mr. Jelaco?"

"Yes," Nick snapped. "Like I told you before, I'm a lawyer."

"Are you willing to waive your right to remain silent and your right to an attorney's presence during this interview?"

"Yes."

"Where were you this morning between three a.m. and four a.m.?"

"I don't know exactly," Nick answered truthfully. "I was probably fairly close to Wells, Nevada."

Gates nodded and then immediately shifted gears. "When was the last time you saw your wife alive?"

"About ten o'clock Sunday morning," Nick answered, choking back tears as he recalled the last time he had seen her.

"When was the last time you spoke with your wife?"

"She called me last night around midnight."

"Last night?" Gates repeated. "Where were you when she called?"

Nick racked his memory in an attempt to recall where he had been when he received Julie's phone call. "I was just past Tonopah, Nevada, on Highway 95, or maybe it's Highway 6. I don't know. Anyway, she called me on my cell phone."

"Where did she call you from?" Gates asked without pausing.

"She called from our home. The number came through on the caller ID. It should be stored in the memory if you want to see it," Nick offered, reaching for his cell phone.

"That won't be necessary, Mr. Jelaco. Where's Tonopah?"

"I believe Tonopah is about seventy miles south of Ely on the highway from Las Vegas," Nick answered and then added in frustration, "We're wasting time. All this information is in my statement."

"Bear with me, Mr. Jelaco. I'm trying to establish an accurate timeline," Detective Gates explained. "What were you doing in Las Vegas?"

"I was litigating a personal injury case."

Gates looked at Nick with skepticism. "It seems strange your client hired an out-of-state lawyer."

"I'm licensed to practice law in Nevada."

"Nonetheless, isn't it unusual to retain the services of an out-of-state lawyer?" Gates asked.

"It's not common practice, but my client had just moved to Las Vegas from Lakeland."

"What is your client's name?"

"Bill Peterson was the named plaintiff, but his wife, Dorothy, actually retained my law firm."

"Did you win?" Gates asked, with a hint of a smile on his face.

"Nobody really wins when someone is permanently disabled, but the jury did award the damages we were seeking."

"How much money are we talking about?" Gates asked casually.

"Three point five million."

Gates raised his eyebrows and whistled. "That's a boatload of money. What's your cut?"

"My firm is contractually entitled to forty percent or approximately 1.4 million. I won't share in the judgment personally, because I'm not a partner in the firm," Nick explained.

"That's got to make you mad," Gates pressed. "You do all the hard work, and your boss walks away with all the money."

Nick shook his head. "Not really, I knew how things worked when I signed on with the firm."

"Why did you drive to Las Vegas? There are four direct flights daily to and from the Lakeland airport. I would think a law firm could afford to pay the cost of your airfare," Gates said in a tone of voice that led Nick to believe the detective was not overly fond of lawyers.

"Personal preference. I don't like the hassle of rearranging my flight plan every time my schedule changes and renting a car is even worse."

Gates nodded before continuing with his questions. "When was the last time you spoke to your daughter?"

"Last night around nine o'clock, Darby told me good night and then asked if she could have a puppy," Nick said, his voice choked by emotion again.

"When did you last see your daughter?"

"Sunday morning at approximately ten o'clock," Nick methodically replied. "I told my wife and daughter good-bye right before I left for Las Vegas."

"What was the date?"

"I believe it was October first, but I'm not positive on the exact date," Nick hesitantly replied. "Anyway, it was last Sunday."

"Are you involved in illegal conduct that may have placed your family in harm's way?"

"No, of course not," Nick emphatically replied.

"Why the big hurry to get home?" Gates asked. "You had to be wiped out after your big trial, and Las Vegas is a great place to blow off a little steam."

Nick wasn't about to tell Gates that intuition had been a major factor in his decision to race home. The detective had enough problems without adding Nick's mental stability to the list. "I prefer driving at night, and today is my sixth wedding anniversary," Nick explained softly. "Mostly, I was anxious to see my wife and daughter."

"Did you and your wife argue last night?" Detective Gates asked in a casual tone that seemed to imply Nick's answer didn't matter to him one way or the other.

"No, not even close," Nick angrily replied. "She was excited about the verdict in my case, and she was anxious for me to get home."

"Did you sense anything out of the ordinary or get the impression that something was wrong?"

Nick could remember every minute detail of his last conversation with Julie, and nothing except his sixth sense had led him to believe she was in trouble. "No, she seemed fine, a little tired, but that's all. Julie has—had—a hard time sleeping when I was away on business."

"Why did she have a hard time sleeping?" Gates immediately followed up.

"I don't know. I guess she was used to me sleeping beside her, or maybe being alone in the house with Darby made her uneasy."

Maybe she wasn't asleep or was sleeping lightly and heard the intruder downstairs. If that was the case, I wonder why she went to investigate without first calling the police. Gates thought to himself. "Was your wife having an affair, Mr. Jelaco?"

"Of course not!" Nick almost shouted. "Julie wasn't that kind of person."

"Were you having an affair, Mr. Jelaco?"

"Absolutely not! I had the perfect wife and daughter. There's no way I would have jeopardized the life we shared."

Gates narrowed his eyes and leaned forward in his chair. "Did you kill your wife, Mr. Jelaco?"

Nick returned Detective Gates's stare for several seconds prior to answering his question. "No, I did not kill my wife. She was undoubtedly the best person I have ever known."

"Do you know who killed your wife?"

"I don't have the slightest idea who killed my wife," Nick firmly asserted. "Julie didn't have an enemy in the world."

"Have you ever killed another human being, Mr. Jelaco?"

"Yes," Nick responded without further explanation. He was certain Detective Gates knew all about his military record.

"Explain the circumstances if you wouldn't mind, Mr. Jelaco."

"My Special Forces unit was ambushed by Mohamed Aidid's militia in Mogadishu, Somalia, during what was supposed to be a routine extraction mission in 1993. My commanding officer ordered me to engage the enemy, and I followed orders without hesitation," Nick responded without emotion.

"How many men did you kill, Mr. Jelaco?"

"I don't know, Detective. I wasn't keeping score," Nick sarcastically replied. "Me and the guys from my unit were just trying to stay alive from one minute to the next."

"You were a member of Delta Force, isn't that right, Mr. Jelaco?"

"Yes, I was assigned to Delta Force during the majority of my military service."

"I heard you Delta Force guys are as tough as they get," Gates pushed. "Highly trained killing machines."

"Don't believe everything you hear."

"It surprises me you fainted at your home earlier today," Gates commented, exaggerating his skepticism.

The detective's comment was intended to get a rise out of Nick, but he kept his emotions in check.

"I was trained to do a job, Detective. Unfortunately, the army didn't teach me how to respond if my wife was murdered and my daughter kidnapped."

Gates leaned back in his chair and stared at Nick as if he was trying to see inside his head. "Did you suffer from any psychological problems when your tour in Somalia was up?"

"Yeah, but nothing serious," Nick answered. "I had a hard time sleeping and suffered from reoccurring nightmares for a short time. The military psychologist assured me that my post-combat symptoms were to be expected and actually quite normal under the circumstances."

"Are you currently taking any medication for depression, psychological problems, or post traumatic stress?"

"No, I'm not, Detective Gates," Nick replied with a frustrated shake of his head. "I left the military ten years ago, and my civilian life had been fairly uneventful until this morning."

"Do you know your daughter's current location?"

"If I did, she'd be in my arms right now."

"Have you formulated a theory in regard to the abduction?" Gates asked.

"Maybe she woke up alone and went to look for her mother," Nick said hopefully. The thought of his three-year-old daughter lost, alone, and frightened was terrible but not nearly as horrifying as the other scenarios Nick could not push from his thoughts.

"Has the kidnapper contacted you about a ransom?"

"No, Detective. I'm not a rich man."

"Is it possible your work was somehow connected to the break-in?"

Nick shook his head emphatically from side to side. "The majority of my work is routine civil stuff. Breach of contract disputes and personal injury cases."

"How about criminal cases?" Gates asked.

"I haven't taken on any criminal defense work in months."

"Have any of your clients made threats or tried to intimidate you in any way?"

"Nothing out of the ordinary—a few angry complaints about unconscionable billable hours and excessive contingency fees but nothing that stands out," Nick answered. "It's fairly typical when a client complains about the bill once his case has been resolved."

"Do you have a strained working relationship with any of your coworkers, or, more importantly, do any of your coworkers have a problem with you?" Gates asked with a noticeable edge to his voice.

"What do you mean by 'problem'?"

"Do you get along with your coworkers?"

"I don't have any close friends at work, but I don't have any enemies either."

"What did you keep in the file cabinet that was ransacked?"

"Documents, but nothing overly important—things like tax returns, travel receipts, case files."

Detective Gates leaned forward in his chair and asked, "What kind of case files?"

"Client files from cases I'm working on."

"Is it possible one of your clients was behind the break-in?"

"Absolutely not," Nick answered without hesitation. "As I told you before, my case load is comprised of routine civil litigation."

Something about Nick's case files had obviously piqued the detective's interest. "Can you provide me with a list of the client files you kept at home?"

"I could probably figure it out, but right now everything is kind of a blur," Nick replied.

Gates appeared to be disappointed, but he didn't push the issue. "We can deal with your case files a bit later. Right now, I'd like to bring in the department's polygraph examiner."

"Okay, let's get it over with," Nick said without enthusiasm.

Detective Gates aimed the black remote control at the digital recorder. The green light vanished, and the flashing red light reappeared.

"I'll be right back," Gates said, the metal door to the interrogation room banging shut behind him.

Gates returned about fifteen minutes later accompanied by a huge, middle-aged black man with the baldest head Nick had ever seen. Nick surmised that Gates had spent the past fifteen minutes prepping the polygraph examiner for their upcoming interview.

Gates nodded toward the large black man. "This is Detective Reginald Johnson. He'll be conducting the polygraph exam."

Reginald Johnson was an enormous man, yet he went about his business with surprising agility. He swiftly moved across the interrogation room carrying what appeared to be a laptop computer and an assortment of bizarre-looking attachments. He placed the laptop on the metal table and immediately started plugging cables and wires into the back of it. Once the setup was complete, Detective Johnson powered up the computer and deftly punched a series of letters and numbers on the small keyboard.

"I'm ready to go. Phil," Johnson said as the computer screen came to life, "I don't want you in the room during the examination."

"Sure thing, Reggie," Gates replied and quickly exited the interrogation room.

After Detective Gates's departure, Nick returned to the metal chair he had occupied for the better part of the past two hours.

"Do you know how a polygraph examination works, Mr. Jelaco?"

"I know the basics, but that's about it."

Up to that point, Nick's knowledge on the subject of polygraph examinations had come primarily from watching police shows on television and a fuzzy recollection of the one he had taken prior to joining the Delta Force. He had been expecting a large metal box, scrolling paper, and jumping needles. Obviously technology had progressed faster in the real world than it had on television. Nick felt surprisingly relaxed, given the circumstances surrounding his upcoming lie detector test. The only anxiety he felt came from an overwhelming desire to get it over with. Once the police eliminated him as a viable suspect, they could focus on the real problem, finding his daughter and bringing his wife's killer to justice.

Detective Johnson momentarily halted his preparation and looked directly at Nick. "The polygraph examination is designed to detect deception by monitoring heart rate, respiration, and skin conductivity while the subject responds to a series of specific questions. I am going to ask you several questions regarding your wife's murder and daughter's disappearance. I'll record your body's reaction to my questions throughout the course of our interview. Each question should be answered with a simple yes or no response."

Nick nodded at the detective and said, "I understand."

Detective Johnson looped a coiled rubber tube around Nick's stomach and a second identical tube around his chest. He then wrapped a blood pressure cuff around Nick's left bicep. When that was finished, the detective clipped a V-shaped fingerplate to the tip of Nick's index finger and attached a second fingerplate to his ring finger. Detective Johnson positioned himself behind Nick so both the detective and his computer were outside Nick's range of vision. Nick could no longer see the detective, but he certainly recognized his deep voice.

"Focus your attention on the wall directly in front of you, Mr. Jelaco. It's essential you remain as motionless as possible. Even slight movements can alter the results of a polygraph examination."

Nick nodded and said, "I'm ready to begin."

Detective Johnson expected an affirmative response and no deception to his first question. "Is your name Nick Jelaco?"

"Yes."

"Do you currently reside at 434 River Crest Drive in Lakeland, Idaho?"

"Yes."

Detective Johnson followed with a couple of questions that were unrelated to the investigation. Nick assumed the detective was expecting his responses to indicate deception. "Have you ever stolen anything of value?"

"Not that I can remember."

"Answer yes or no," Detective Johnson instructed in a voice that clearly conveyed his annoyance.

"No."

"Have you ever lied to your employer?"

"No."

Nick could hear the distinct sound of Detective Johnson's fingers rapidly striking a series of keys on the laptop computer. When the data entry stopped, Johnson asked, "Did you return from Las Vegas at approximately six o'clock this morning?"

"Yes."

Now that the preliminaries were complete, the detective

could get down to business. "Do you know who killed you wife?" he asked in a flat tone of voice.

"No."

"Did you kill your wife?"

"No," Nick answered firmly.

"Did you help plan or facilitate your wife's murder?"

"No."

"Have you ever killed another human being?"

"Yes."

"Have you ever killed a citizen or resident of the United States?"

"No."

Detective Johnson's questioning ceased just long enough for his fingers to record something of importance with his fast-paced key strokes.

"Did you last see your daughter on Sunday, October first?" he asked.

"Yes, that's right," Nick answered truthfully.

"Do you know the current whereabouts of your daughter?" Johnson asked and then firmly added, "Please sit still, Mr. Jelaco. I can't get an accurate reading if you are fidgeting."

"No."

"Do you know the current location of your daughter?" Detective Johnson repeated.

"No."

The large detective had a good rhythm going, and Nick sensed they were nearing the end of the lie detector test.

"Do you possess knowledge about the party responsible for your daughter's disappearance?"

"No."

"Are you responsible for your daughter's disappearance?"

"No."

"Did you kill your daughter?"

"No."

"Do you possess any information that would lead you to believe your daughter is no longer alive?"

"No," Nick responded without hesitation.

"Have you ever been involved in the buying or selling of illegal drugs?"

"No."

"Have you been involved in any fraudulent financial transactions?"

"No."

"Thank you, Mr. Jelaco. That concludes our business here today."

Detective Johnson closed the laptop and removed the blood pressure cuff. "Give me a couple of minutes to discuss the polygraph results with Detective Gates."

The massive detective exited without further comment. Nick had no idea how long he had sat there in silence battling his dark thoughts before Gates returned.

"Detective Johnson and I have reviewed the results of your polygraph exam," Gates explained with an edge to his voice. "Do you want to clarify any of your responses before we discuss the end product?"

Nick shook his head wearily from side to side. "No, Detective Gates, I've told you and Detective Johnson everything I know. Now I would like some answers of my own."

"Nick, I honestly believe you know more than you realize," Gates said, using Nick's given name for the first time. "Detective Johnson is convinced you're telling the truth, but maybe we didn't ask the right questions. I've got a gut feeling the key to this entire investigation is locked away in your memory."

"I can assure you my family wasn't targeted."

"This wasn't a random burglary that escalated to murder. The man who broke into your house was searching for a specific item in your file cabinet."

"You're barking up the wrong tree, Detective."

"Take my word for it—a file cabinet is not the first place most burglars look for valuables."

"I want to help!" Nick forcefully countered. "But there was absolutely nothing of value in that file cabinet."

When Detective Gates stood up, Nick knew the interrogation was officially over.

"I hate to inconvenience you any further, Nick, but you won't be able to stay at your house for a few days."

"That's fine with me," Nick quickly agreed as he tried to push images of Julie's lifeless body from his mind's eye.

"I'll drive you by your house so you can pick up your car and a change of clothes when we're done here," Gates offered.

"Thanks."

"If you're feeling up to it, maybe you could take a quick look around your office to determine if anything is missing."

"I'll take a look at my office, but I'm positive there wasn't anything worth stealing in that file cabinet."

CHAPTER 9

Nick and Detective Gates exited the Lakeland Police Station through the public entrance. Nick was surprised by the odd mixture of people seeking police assistance. Some were young, and some were old, though most were somewhere in between. A handful appeared homeless, while a few appeared quite affluent. Most of the people waiting to speak to a police officer were Caucasian, but Lakeland citizens of Hispanic and African-American origin were also seated patiently in the bleak reception area. Nick deduced from the eclectic mixture of people who packed the Lakeland Police Station that no one was immune from victimization. The ache in his heart and the empty feeling in his soul were further proof of that reality.

It was unseasonably warm for an October day in southern Idaho as Nick and Detective Gates jaywalked across Second Avenue East and quickly made their way to Gates's Toyota 4-Runner. The bright, blue sky seemed out of place on what was undoubtedly the darkest day of his life. Detective Gates's silver 4-Runner was at least ten years old and it appeared as if the battered and beaten SUV had not been washed since the day it was driven off the lot.

"The passenger door's unlocked," Gates said as they approached his truck.

Nick found it strange that a veteran police officer would leave his vehicle unlocked in the most crime-ridden area in Monroe County. The puzzled expression on his face prompted Gates to offer an explanation.

"The dirt-bags around here know better than to mess with my car," Gates explained. "They leave me alone; I leave them alone. It's as simple as that."

"I suppose that makes sense," Nick answered, even though he found the detective's explanation somewhat illogical.

The interior of the neglected 4-Runner was a bigger mess than the dented and mud-covered exterior. The passenger seat and floorboards were littered with fast food containers, empty soda cans, Styrofoam coffee cups, and a few empty beer bottles. The backseat was buried under an array of what appeared to be both clean and dirty clothes. Nick surmised that Detective Gates spent a great deal of time in his truck. He pushed the garbage that covered the passenger seat onto the floor and climbed into the food-stained bucket seat.

The middle-aged detective climbed into the driver's seat and removed a key from the visor above the steering wheel. The Toyota's 4-cylinder engine whined a couple of times before it finally turned over.

Unless they are on foot, Lakeland's criminals don't have much to fear from Gates in the form of a high-speed pursuit, Nick thought.

Without buckling his seatbelt, Detective Gates engaged the clutch and shifted the 4-Runner's manual transmission into first gear. The old SUV lurched away from the curb, and Gates skillfully forced his way into the bumper-to-bumper traffic heading east on the one-way street. Nick's thoughts again wandered to a happier time as he and Detective Gates drove for several blocks in silence. Less than twenty-four hours ago he had been on top of the world. He had a beautiful wife and daughter eagerly anticipating his return. His wife had been planning something for their sixth wedding anniversary, and he had just won a multi-million-dollar verdict in the most significant case of his fledgling legal career. Now his entire world was in ruins, and trying cases for monetary judgments seemed less than trivial.

Nick would have given anything to turn back the clock for a second chance. If he had refused to litigate the Peterson case, Julie would be alive, and Darby would be safe at home with her mother. Julie's father had never hidden his contempt for Nick. He felt his daughter had married beneath their social class, and he let everyone know it. In an attempt to prove him wrong, Nick had lost sight of the most important thing in his life—family. The pursuit of wealth, power, and prestige was a poor substitute for lost time that could never be recaptured.

After several minutes of silent driving, Detective Gates interrupted Nick's self-loathing. "The first forty-eight hours are crucial in child abduction cases. Any potential lead could make the difference."

Nick racked his brain for several seconds before responding, "I don't know anyone who could commit such an awful crime. It had to be a random break-in, some junkie looking for something to hawk in order to score a fix."

Gates thought about Nick's theory before he replied, "I don't think so, Mr. Jelaco. The crime scene doesn't fit the M.O. of a random burglary."

"Criminals don't have a Burglary 101 handbook to follow."

"True, but the intruder ransacked your home office. A junkie would have searched for electronic equipment, a shotgun, a handgun, jewelry—something easy to pawn."

"It's not unheard of to keep a handgun or cash in a desk or file cabinet."

Gates wasn't swayed by Nick's argument. "True, but a couple of things don't add up. A burglary conviction would get the guy probation. A repeat offender might get a couple of years in the state pen. On the other hand, convicted murderers in Idaho are sentenced to life in prison without the possibility of parole or the death penalty. This guy went out of his way to keep your wife quiet. It just doesn't add up to a random burglary."

"None of this makes any sense to me," Nick replied, his eyes filling with tears.

"Violent crime seldom does. But I'm confident the guy we're looking for didn't leave empty-handed. If you can figure out what he took, it may shed some light on his motive, and motive usually points an investigation in the right direction."

"I'll do my best," Nick replied without conviction.

Detective Gates made his way slowly down Second Avenue East through Lakeland's city center. Traffic was thick for a Thursday afternoon, and Gates hit every red light on the congested one-way street. There were quicker routes to Nick's house, but it didn't appear as if the detective was in a big hurry. Traffic on the outskirts of Lakeland's downtown had thinned by the time Gates turned left onto Shoreline Drive.

In many ways, Lakeland was two distinct cities with a couple of main thoroughfares connecting Lakeland's south side to its more affluent north side. Shoreline Drive was one of them. The four-lane highway was lined with an array of seedy motels, biker bars, and all-night strip joints.

Gates continued driving north on Shoreline Drive until he passed over the North Fork Bridge and out of the nightclub district. Lakeland's degenerating south side slowly gave way to gated communities, swimming pools, and well-manicured parks. The contrast between the two worlds was shocking. Gates exited Shoreline Drive at the Orchard intersection and guided his dilapidated 4-Runner through an endless maze of two-story houses and neatly trimmed lawns. The sight of children laughing and playing as they made their way home from school did little to lighten Nick's melancholy mood. His life had been damaged beyond repair, but for the rest of Lakeland it was just another day.

After weaving through a maze of newly constructed neighborhoods, Gates turned onto River Crest Drive. The familiar surroundings only deepened the depression that had overcome Nick. Gates parked on the street directly in front of the Jelacos' house and turned off the ignition. Nick's red Mustang was still parked in the driveway exactly where he had left it some ten hours ago, and several law enforcement officers continued to mill about inside the yellow police tape that surrounded his house. It occurred to Nick that his family's home was now a place of death and sorrow.

Gates looked at him with genuine concern. "We can come back later if you're not ready to do this."

"I can handle it," Nick hesitantly replied. "Is Julie still inside?"

Gates shook his head. "Her body was taken to the morgue for an autopsy."

The agonizing thought of his beautiful wife lying nude on a cold metal autopsy table sent a sharp pain searing through his chest.

"When can I see her?" Nick asked, not sure exactly how he wanted Gates to respond.

"Police business usually takes two or three days, but I'll check with the medical examiner."

"I'll need to take care of her funeral arrangements," Nick said more to himself than the detective.

Nick and Detective Gates entered his home through the cluttered two-car garage. Julie's late-model Honda Accord was parked in the only spot that wasn't buried under dusty boxes or some type of sporting equipment. Nick felt a lump in his throat when he recalled his wife's constant pleas for him to clean and organize the ever-expanding mess. It was too late to grant her simple request, and that added to his deepening sadness.

Gates followed Nick to the master bedroom. The king-sized bed was unmade, and the outline of two small bodies was clearly visible in the crumpled bed coverings. Nick quickly turned his gaze from the bed and proceeded straight to the bathroom. As soon as he crossed the threshold, it occurred to him that his toiletries and a suitcase full of clothes were still locked in the trunk of his car. Unpacking had not been high on his list of priorities when he returned from Las Vegas in the chilly predawn hours. Nick also remembered the Xanax that was tucked away in his suitcase. He hoped the prescription medication would stop his mind from spinning long enough to allow him a few hours of sleep. Dr. Roberts had written the prescription to help him deal with the anxiety he had expected during the Peterson trial. The trial had progressed so smoothly that he had drifted off to sleep each night without the need for chemical assistance. However, Nick was certain that tonight sleep would not come easily, if he slept at all.

Nick returned to the bedroom, where he found Detective Gates staring blankly at an Ansel Adams photograph of Yosemite National Park. Julie had purchased the print to commemorate their honeymoon in Northern California. The detective appeared to be lost in his own thoughts and didn't hear him return to the bedroom. Nick didn't know why, but he felt a connection to the gruff detective. It was evident Gates was familiar with pain and loss, and Nick's intuition told him the detective's sorrow was not entirely the result of his chosen profession. Nick was pretty sure the detective knew torment and heartache on a personal level as well.

"I didn't unpack after my trip," Nick said, interrupting Gates's thoughts.

"What?" Gates asked, startled.

"I didn't unpack when I returned from Las Vegas. My overnight kit and suitcase are in the trunk of my car. I packed for an entire week, but the trial ended two days early," Nick explained.

"Do you need anything to get you through the next couple of days?"

Nick shook his head and said in a voice choked with emotion, "Right now, I just want to get out of here. This room brings back memories I'm not ready to deal with quite yet."

"That's understandable," Gates replied. "Are you feeling well enough to take a quick look around your office?"

Nick shrugged his shoulders. "I'll give it a shot, but I honestly don't believe there is a link between the junk I kept in my office and the break-in."

"Humor me, Mr. Jelaco. I've been doing this a long time."

Nick was not obsessive about keeping his home office organized, but he found his small work space in more disarray than usual. It was obvious the area had been ransacked by someone, but Nick didn't have a clue who or why. He had to admit the intruder's inexplicable interest in his office lent some credibility to Gate's implausible theory; still, Nick was skeptical. Several drawers had been pulled out and their contents dumped on the floor. Papers, pens, and tax papers had been strewn about the rear corner of the family room. Investigators had brushed black fingerprint powder over the wooden surfaces of both the desk and file cabinet.

"Did the police make this mess?" Nick asked.

"Cops dusted the place for latent fingerprints, but we left the rest of the stuff pretty much as we found it. Take a look around; I need to know if anything is missing."

"Is it okay if I touch this stuff?" Nick asked.

"That's not a problem. The crime scene guys are done with this part of the house. You might get some fingerprint dust on your hands, but it comes off with a little soap and water."

Nick took a seat in the worn leather chair behind his desk. He had spent hundreds of hours seated at the old desk but none as uncomfortable as this one. He wasn't preparing for trial or reviewing a case; he was trying to figure out why someone had killed his wife and kidnapped his little girl. He felt like a stranger in his own home.

Nick studied the desktop and the contents of the three small drawers on the right side of the desk. His things had been rummaged through, but nothing appeared to be missing. He quickly glanced at the papers that were spread across the floor. Nothing important—just some old tax returns and travel receipts. He moved from the desk to the file cabinet expecting more of the same.

"That's strange," Nick said. "Are you sure the police didn't remove anything from the file cabinet during their search?"

"I'm positive. Why?" Gates asked, clearly energized by Nick's question.

"All my client files are missing. I usually keep them in the top drawer of the file cabinet, but it's been cleaned out, and I didn't see any client files on the floor either."

"Can you list the client files that were in that drawer?" Detective Gates asked as he removed a ballpoint pen and small notepad from his jacket pocket.

"I think so, but I may need my hourly logs to jog my memory."

"Do your best, Nick," Gates encouraged. "I know you're wiped out, but this could be the break this investigation needs."

Nick searched his memory as he stood by the file cabinet. "If I remember correctly, there were six or seven files in the cabinet but nothing overly exciting."

"Let me decide what's exciting," Gates immediately countered.

"One file contained information for a minor breach of contract case. My client, Jonathon Holladay, is a local contractor, and the defendant, Michael Lindsay, hired him to do a major remodel of his office building. Both parties agreed that Lindsay had breached the contract, and we reached an agreement on the actual damages a few weeks ago."

Gates scribbled a few words in his notebook, but it was obvious the Holladay case did not pique the detective's interest. "Okay, what else?" Gates asked when he had finished writing.

"The Colton Straub vs. Donald R. Smith case file was also in the cabinet. My client had a long-term lease on Mr. Smith's farmland, but Mr. Smith received a better offer from a real-estate development company out of California. My client was seeking an injunction to stop development of the land until the duration of his ground lease had expired. The lease was bulletproof, so the defendant seemed agreeable to liquidating my client's future damages."

"I'll check out Donald Smith and the development company, but they're probably legit," Gates said without enthusiasm.

After Gates had jotted down the landowner's name, Nick continued, "David Gibson vs. Randy Ross was a wrongful termination lawsuit. My client, David Gibson, decided to drop the lawsuit prior to the start of discovery. I believe Mr. Gibson realized that his termination was justified."

"Any chance Mr. Gibson could be responsible for the break-in?" Gates asked.

"David Gibson is a frail, sixty-five-year-old computer programmer. The guy's afraid of his own shadow. Mr. Gibson was angry when he got fired, but he actually stumbled into a better job shortly after he dropped the lawsuit. He's definitely not the man you're looking for, Detective."

Gates seemed disappointed by the lack of progress. "What other case files are missing?"

"I was working on two small personal injury cases, Lawrence Lewis vs. Tiffany Wayne and Katie Alderson vs. Clifford Hobbs. Both lawsuits involved minor automobile accidents. The damages in both cases were minimal, and the liability of the defendants was undisputed. The defendants' insurance companies were anxious to settle and more than willing to negotiate. I was the one holding out for a better offer. The numbers haven't been finalized, but we're close to a settlement in both cases."

"Anything else?" Gates asked.

"Nope, that was about it."

The detective was clearly disappointed by the mundane nature of the lawyer's clientele. "Sounds like routine stuff for an attorney. Are you sure nothing else was taken?" Gates prodded.

"I'm not positive," Nick replied and then after a brief pause added, "There may have been a file from a closed criminal case in the cabinet. I never really got started on the client's defense, but I vaguely remember bringing the case file home."

"What kind of criminal case?" Gates asked, obviously more interested now that Nick was talking his language.

"It was a felony drug possession case, State of Idaho vs. Janis Jones. The public defender had a conflict with Ms. Jones, so Judge Mills pawned the case off on a private law firm. I'm not sure how, or why, but my firm ended up defending Ms. Jones.

The case never really amounted to much, because the defendant died from a drug overdose before the state had a chance to prosecute her."

"Is it common practice for your firm to take conflict cases from the public defender's office?"

Nick thought for a second, and the answer he came up with surprised him. "I've been with the firm for six years, and as far as I know, the Jones case is the only conflict we've ever taken."

"Who made the decision to take on Ms. Jones's case?"

"I don't know," Nick replied. "I suppose one of the senior partners was doing Judge Mills a favor."

"Was there anything about Ms. Jones's case that was out of the ordinary besides the fact that she died?" Detective Gates asked with a hint of excitement in his voice.

"I don't want to sound unsympathetic, but Janis Jones was a delusional crackhead. She had been arrested numerous times for drug possession, theft, prostitution—you name it—but she always managed to avoid any serious jail time."

"She probably ratted out a fellow scumbag so the prosecutor cut her a deal," Gates said in disgust.

"Anyway, she wanted to meet with me but refused to come to my office. I reluctantly agreed to meet her at a dive restaurant, Chief's Diner, down on the south side. Ms. Jones showed up thirty minutes late, high as a kite. She was paranoid and kept rambling on and on about a secret that was worth plenty to people in high places. It was almost impossible to decipher her incoherent babble, but I believe she was claiming to have information about an old murder case that involved some high-ranking public officials and police officers."

Nick thought he detected a trace of fear on the detective's face, but the look was gone so quickly, he wondered if he'd imagined the detective's reaction. When Gates spoke, he was in complete control.

"Did she give you any names?"

"No, I'm not really sure about the specifics of her story. She bolted before I could pin her down on the details. About a week later, I got a phone call from Julie Hoffman at the prosecutor's office informing me that Ms. Jones had died of an apparent drug overdose, case closed."

"Did Ms. Jones tell you anything that can be verified, like the defendant's name or the year the case was prosecuted?" Gates asked hopefully.

Nick shook his head slowly. "No, but I got the impression the case had been closed for quite some time. She wanted me to run her story by the prosecutor. If the prosecutor was interested in what she had to say, she was willing to trade the rest of her story for a "get out of jail free" card. Obviously we never got to that point in her representation."

Gates tapped the tip of his pen against his notebook while he considered Nick's recollection of Janis Jones's story. "It sounds like Janis Jones had a good imagination, but there is usually a hint of truth in most fantasies. I'll check her criminal history and known associates just in case. If you remember anything else she told you, let me know."

"I will, but to be honest with you, I think she was just another spaced-out addict trying to play me for a deal," Nick suggested.

"You're probably right, but a dead junkie trying to sell a conspiracy theory is the best lead I've got at the present time," a frustrated Gates replied.

Nick was sure his facial expression conveyed his dissatisfaction as he stared at Detective Gates. "That's more than a little disappointing. If all you've got are the bizarre ramblings of a small-time drug addict, you've got nothing."

"Actually a lot of successful investigations start with a small scrap of information from some degenerate," Gates replied defensively. "Maybe the man who broke into your home didn't want to deal with the scrutiny that would follow Ms. Jones's accusations."

"Janis Jones overdosed months before the break-in, which means her story died with her."

"That's true, unless there was something in her case file you overlooked," Gates responded hopefully. "If we can figure out which case Ms. Jones was referring to, maybe things will start to add up."

"I'm positive there wasn't a single thing in the file that could lend a shred of credibility to Ms. Jones's story," Nick replied. "I took maybe a page of fairly general notes at our meeting. The arrest report, the officer's probable cause statement, and my scribbled notes were the only things in the file. We hadn't even begun the discovery process before she died."

"It might be a dead end, but there's something about Ms. Jones's sudden death that piques my interest. I'll check with my snitches on the south side," Gates said. "Gossips and the rumor mill aren't reserved for Lakeland's social elite. Degenerates and dopers can be great sources of information if you know how to tap into their knowledge. Rest assured someone out there has information regarding Janis Jones and her untimely death."

"I don't understand how a doper's death is going to help me find my daughter."

"Some investigations are similar to a game of connect the dots. You can't see the big picture until all the dots are connected."

"I sure hope you're connecting the right dots."

CHAPTER 10

Nick and Detective Gates shook hands and parted company in the street directly in front of his house. Nick wasn't the type of person who needed constant companionship, and he actually enjoyed being alone on occasion, but when Detective Gates's silver 4-Runner had disappeared from view a feeling of loneliness overcame him like nothing he had ever experienced before. This time, his solitude was not of his choosing, and there was no relief in sight.

Nick sat in the driver's seat of his Mustang staring through the windshield without a clue of what his next move should be. His brother lived in Lakeland, but Luke was not the type of person he could to turn to during an emotional crisis. To escape the cold winters of Idaho, his mother and her new husband had taken up residency in a small mobile home park just south of Tempe, Arizona. Nick knew his mother would return to Lakeland for Julie's funeral, but the comfort her presence had provided him as a child was now a distant and foggy memory.

For all practical purposes, Darby was his only family now. Unfortunately, he had no idea where she was or how to go about finding her. Prior to this morning, Nick had been trying to balance his duties as a husband, father, and lawyer. Now, his once complicated life was painfully one dimensional. Gates had warned him that the wait for information would be maddening, but his daughter was out there somewhere, and he wasn't about to go crazy sitting by the phone in a motel room.

Nick started the Mustang's engine and slowly backed out of the driveway with no clear destination in mind. Finding Darby was his first and only priority, but he didn't have any idea how to conduct a missing person investigation. Finding a three-year-old little girl in a city the size of Lakeland seemed impossible. "How does a person with no investigative skills follow the trail of a cold-blooded killer?" Nick asked himself. Investigative skills or not, he needed a viable plan of attack, and he needed it fast. Unfortunately, sleep deprivation and paralyzing grief were making coherent thought almost impossible.

Darkness descended on Lakeland while Nick drove randomly back and forth through the city's crowded business district looking for any sign of his daughter. He was abundantly aware of the futile nature of his search, but any action was preferable to the seclusion of a motel room. During the maddening drive, mental images of his vibrant, brown-eyed little girl provided some measure of solace. In fact, the memories were so vivid he could almost feel the touch of her soft skin and the smell of freshly shampooed hair as she would settle into his lap for a bedtime story. Nick had phoned the Lakeland police station several times as he drove around the city, and each time a pleasant public relations officer had told him there was nothing new to report. Before ending each call, the woman had promised to contact him immediately if anything happened with the investigation.

Sometime past midnight he lost his battle with fatigue and decided to check into a motel for the night, pulling into the Best Western on Overland Boulevard. The young college girl at the front desk probably thought he was drunk or high on drugs after their brief encounter. His responses to the simplest questions were labored and nonsensical. After several miscommunications, he finally rented a single room with a river view for just one night. Nick chose the more expensive room with a view of the river because Julie would have preferred it to a view of the parking lot. He didn't have the energy or the inclination to worry about his sleeping arrangements beyond the one night.

The small room was clean and exactly the same as a hundred other motel rooms he had stayed in over the course of his marriage, but this time there was no one at home waiting for his return. Nick had just enough willpower to remove the white dress shirt and wrinkled suit pants he had been wearing for the past thirty-six hours and stumble into a hot shower. He was hoping the scalding water would wash away some of the pain and torment that had been his constant companions since his return to Lakeland.

Unfortunately, the twenty-five-minute shower did little to improve his state of mind, so Nick reluctantly resorted to Plan B. He needed a short break from reality and decided the Xanax in his suitcase was his best shot at a few minutes of peace. One little blue pill would usually stop his unwanted thoughts from spinning out of control long enough for sleep to overtake him. Tonight he swallowed two of the blue pills down with a gulp of water straight from the bathroom faucet. Nick then climbed into bed and waited for sleep. After tossing and turning for a couple of hours, he resigned himself to the fact that even drug-aided sleep was not in the cards. He reluctantly crawled out of bed and dressed himself in a pair of khakis and a mock turtleneck.

Nick left his motel room not knowing where he was headed, but the cool October night was preferable to the claustrophobic motel room. He avoided eye contact with the desk clerk as he exited the motel's lobby. Once outside, he paused briefly on the sidewalk and then started walking south on Overland Boulevard. Nick was somewhat of a night owl himself, but he was surprised by the number of people roaming around Lakeland's business district at two a.m. on a Friday morning.

Lost in a drug- and grief-induced haze, he staggered down Overland Boulevard. The lateness of the hour and the backlog of cases piled on his desk at Burton, St. James, & Summers no longer held any power over him. He wandered aimlessly for an hour or so before entering a rundown watering hole called the Wind Jammer. The patrons of the Wind Jammer were a diverse group who scarcely noticed Nick's early morning intrusion into their sanctuary. They were a rough-looking crowd, but there was something about the solemn group that made him less alone in his misery.

The collection of lost souls was unremarkable except for a young woman who sat alone at the end of the bar with a can of Diet Pepsi in front of her. Her youth and striking appearance clashed with the squalor and despair that surrounded her. Without really thinking his decision through, Nick took a seat at the bar and ordered a gin and tonic. He vaguely remembered Dr. Roberts cautioning him about the dangers of mixing alcohol and Xanax, but he didn't give the doctor's warning a second thought when the bartender placed his drink in front of him.

Denial and self-pity were Nick's only companions until the gin started to blur the harsh edges of coherent thought. About halfway through his third gin and tonic, he again noticed the young woman sitting at the end of the bar as she engaged in whispered conversations with the bartender whenever he wasn't busy pouring a drink or retrieving a bottle of beer from the refrigerator behind the bar. Nick assumed the attractive young woman was keeping her boyfriend company while he worked the graveyard shift. The shortness of his time with Julie caused a surge of jealousy to shoot through him. Nick had truly believed he and Julie would be together forever.

By the time Nick finished his fourth gin and tonic, the alcohol was firmly in control of his thought processes. In fact, his thinking was so muddled and convoluted that it was impossible to focus on any single topic for more than a few seconds. Mercifully that included thoughts of murder and kidnapping. Nick's future as a lawyer was one of the random topics ricocheting around his alcohol- and drug-impaired brain. He was now a single parent, which added a new dynamic to long days and billable hours. Darby would definitely need a full-time father more than Burton, St. James, & Summers needed a full-time associate lawyer.

When Nick's wandering mind rejoined his body at the Wind Jammer, he noticed something strange about the woman seated two stools down. She was absentmindedly thumbing through the pages of a tattered textbook. He squinted in the dim light to make out the book's title: *Criminal Procedure for Criminal Justice Professionals.* After noting the legal text and that the young woman seemed out of place in the Wind Jammer, Nick promptly returned his attention to the drink in front of him.

Nick was lost in another wave of random thoughts when the sound of a female voice startled him. "Excuse me, but I think you dropped something."

"Are you talking to me?" Nick slurred.

"Yes, you dropped something on the floor," the woman said, pointing to a spot near his barstool.

Nick stared in the general direction of her pointing finger, but the combination of poor lighting and his own blurred vision left him gawking at nothing in particular. After a few seconds of watching him stare at the floor, the young woman slid off her bar stool and retrieved a twenty-dollar bill from the grimy floor near his feet. She handed Nick the worn bill and returned to her seat.

"Can I buy you a drink or something?" Nick asked, hoping she would refuse his offer.

She held up her Diet Pepsi and politely said, "No thanks, I don't drink much."

An uncomfortable silence followed her drink refusal, prompting Nick to ask her a second question. "I noticed the legal textbook. Are you a law student?"

"I study the law, but I'm not a law student," she answered without elaborating.

"Most people don't read criminal procedure texts for enjoyment," Nick mumbled, thick tongued from the liquor and Xanax.

"I find the law both fascinating and at the same time very frustrating, but no, I'm not a law student—at least, not yet."

Nick wasn't overly talkative around strangers, but evidently the alcohol and Xanax had lessened his inhibitions. "My job might be a little more tolerable if the law fascinated me."

"What's your job?" she asked.

"I'm a lawyer," Nick answered, not sure why he was sharing personal information.

The young woman gave Nick a quizzical look, and asked, "Are you really a lawyer, or is that your idea of a come on?"

The bluntness of her question caught him off guard. "I'm really a lawyer, but take my word for it; what I do for a living is nothing to get overly excited about."

"Really?" she remarked, seemingly surprised. "It sounds exciting to me."

"It's not. The vast majority of my work day is spent sitting behind a desk dealing with mundane disputes that have no business clogging up the legal system."

"Isn't it satisfying to protect the rights of a wrongly accused defendant?" she asked.

"Most criminal defendants are arrested because they're guilty," Nick cynically replied. "Perry Mason's the only lawyer who saves an innocent person from injustice once a week."

The young woman studied his face for several seconds before asking, "What's your name?"

"Nick," he answered, intentionally omitting his last name.

"Hi, Nick. My name's Simone."

"Simone," Nick repeated. "That's an unusual name."

"It's Hebrew. It supposedly means 'to hear or listen.'"

Without really thinking about it, Nick replied, "Your name suits you."

A slight smile turned up the corners of her mouth. "Not according to my brother. He thinks I only hear what I want to hear."

The bartender, who had been washing drink glasses at the other end of the bar, returned just in time to overhear the end of their brief conversation. "My shift's almost over. Do you want another drink before I check out?" he abruptly demanded.

"Sure, I'll have one for the road," Nick slurred.

The bartender poured Nick's drink with a scowl on his face and then removed the night's receipts from the cash register. It was obvious from the bartender's exaggerated movements that Nick's conversation with his girlfriend had made him angry. After he emptied the register, the bartender turned to Simone and said, "It will take me about ten minutes to count my till, and then we can get out of here."

"That's fine," she agreed, seemly unconcerned by her boyfriend's display of jealousy.

After his terse comment, the bartender took the money and disappeared into a small office behind the bar.

"I don't think your boyfriend is overly thrilled you're talking to me," Nick remarked.

"He's not my boyfriend. He's my older brother, and I don't really care what he thinks," Simone replied matter-of-factly.

"Oh," Nick said, surprised he had misread their relationship.

Simone must have picked up on Nick's confused expression because she offered an unsolicited explanation. "His driver's license is suspended, so I drive him home after work when he can't find another ride."

"Why's his license suspended?"

"DUI and driving on a suspended license," Simone replied with a disgusted shake of her head. "One more screwup and the judge will probably give him some serious jail time."

"Most likely," Nick agreed. "Unless his judge is in a good mood or your brother gets himself a top-notch lawyer."

Simone's brother returned to the bar about the same time his replacement showed up. He handed her a jacket and purse.

"Let's get out of here," he commanded curtly.

Simone waved good-bye as her brother practically dragged her out the side door. Nick felt compelled to say something, but he sat there in silence instead.

The brief distraction Simone had provided was gone, so Nick returned his full attention to the drink in front of him. When he finished his fifth gin and tonic, the line between what was real and what was imagined had blurred to the point that Nick decided to call it a night. The new bartender, who was much older and friendlier than Simone's brother, called him a taxi, and Nick dejectedly returned to his nondescript room at the Best Western.

Sleep didn't come easily, but Nick finally drifted off into a restless state of unconsciousness sometime after sunrise. Alternating visions of Julie's naked body on a cold steel autopsy table and Darby searching frantically for her daddy filled his troubled sleep. While Nick lay in bed, the combination of alcohol, Xanax, and exhaustion made it difficult for him to determine whether he was dreaming or hallucinating. Either way, the images that filled his mind were not pleasant.

Just before Nick crawled out of bed to face his first day without his family, Julie appeared to him in a dream. She was the same—young and beautiful—but also strangely different. Julie was not the same vibrant fun-loving woman he had been married to for the past six years; she was more serious and fueled by a steely determination. The melodic voice was hers, but it was more intense and desperate. Like most dreams it was clear and coherent while it unfolded before him but fuzzy and elusive when he tried to recall the details upon waking. In his dream, Julie was imploring him to pull himself together for their daughter's sake. She told him to accept the fact that her fate had been decided. She was gone, but their daughter needed him to be strong. Julie warned him that some of his old friends could not be trusted. She wanted Nick to understand that assistance might come from an unexpected ally and told him to follow his instincts. When Nick tried to touch her beautiful face, a melancholy expression replaced her firm resolve, and she was gone. The fog slowly cleared, and he awoke alone to ponder the meaning of his strange dream.

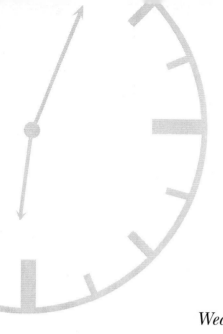

CHAPTER 11

Wednesday afternoon, October 11

The past six days and nights had been a surreal mixture of grieving for his wife and searching for his three-year-old daughter. Before the sun set each day, a great deal of Nick's time and energy was exhausted making arrangements for Julie's funeral while trying to avoid contact with her dysfunctional parents. William Forsythe's control fetish and overt hatred for his son-in-law had sparked more than one confrontation between the two of them. Nick wasn't in the mood for socializing, and, ironically, the ongoing investigation the Lakeland police department was conducting in his home had saved him from an endless stream of well-wishers who were unable to ascertain his whereabouts.

At night, Nick spent his time hanging out in drinking establishments on the south side that serviced a somewhat questionable clientele. The police investigation had stalled at the starting line, and Nick was beginning to believe that information regarding his daughter's kidnapping would not be unearthed by traditional police methods. A brief conversation with Detective Gates had convinced him that associating with Lakeland's criminal element was the quickest path to such information. Nick and Detective Gates had been standing in the street in front of his house when the detective had informed him valuable information flowed freely between Lakeland's deviants. As illogical as it was, Nick was trying to tap into information about Darby's kidnapping by associating with the bottom rung of Lakeland's social ladder.

A nonstop obsession with his daughter's whereabouts had allowed Nick to postpone the acceptance of his wife's death for the past six days. Wednesday, October 11, the day of Julie's funeral, brought his nonstop running to an abrupt end. The day of the funeral there wasn't a cloud in the bright, blue sky, and the temperature felt more like a warm summer day. It was almost as if Mother Nature were mocking the dark cloud that had settled over Nick's life.

The architecture of Saint Peter's Catholic Church was reminiscent of a bygone era with an ornate altar and large stained-glass windows. For some reason, the grandeur and excess of the chapel seemed to accentuate the senselessness of his wife's death. It was still ten minutes before one o'clock, the scheduled start time, but a steady stream of casual acquaintances, friends, family, and people Nick didn't know had almost filled the large chapel. Nick sat next to his mother and Pastor Richard Clark, her second husband, on a hardwood pew in the front row. His mother was wearing the same dark blue dress she had worn at his father's funeral ten years ago.

His mother's presence beside him at another funeral wearing the same blue dress caused a flood of childhood memories to wash over him. In stark contrast to Julie's upbringing, Nick's family had not been wealthy or even comfortable by most standards. When he was growing up, his father, Jonathon "Buck" Jelaco, had always struggled to provide for his family. Buck Jelaco had been an uneducated man who had never held a job that could be considered a career. Instead he had earned a living through an indistinguishable series of odd jobs. Even though they had been poor, Nick had never doubted that both his father and mother loved him. He knew his parents had sacrificed on a daily basis so Nick and his brother would have every chance to succeed. Nick had taken advantage of the opportunities, but his brother, Luke, had not.

Luke believed education was a waste of time and money, and, predictably, he did not finish high school. Luke worked infrequently but always had enough money to indulge in his numerous vices. Nick worried about the source of his brother's income and dreaded the day Luke asked for representation in a criminal matter. A message on Luke's answering machine had been his only contact with his younger brother since Julie's death. If Luke had made it to the funeral, his presence had escaped Nick's detection.

When they were growing up, his mother would have been referred to as a housewife for lack of a better description. Her primary responsibility had been taking care of her husband and two sons, but she had worked countless other jobs as well. Nick clearly remembered her cleaning houses and working at the local diner for a little extra money when times were especially hard. Sharon Jelaco had been a devoted mother who had frequently gone without necessities so her sons would not have to. She was small in physical stature but had a toughness about her that commanded respect. When Nick was a kid, he hadn't fully appreciated her sacrifices, but he knew that he could confide in her like a friend. When Nick looked back with the benefit of time, he realized that Buck Jelaco's death had derailed his mother's life more than it had Nick's or his brother's.

His father had been diagnosed with lung cancer in November of Nick's senior year of high school. He was not alive to see Nick graduate the following June. Buck Jelaco's death seemed to take a piece of his mother's soul and her identity as well. For some reason, not being a wife impacted her ability to be a mother. After Nick graduated from high school and moved away, he and his mother had grown apart. Nick's mother had phoned during his sophomore year at the University of Idaho to inform him that she planned to marry Pastor Clark from the First Christian Church. His mother had explained how Pastor Richard Clark's wife of twenty-five years had passed away a few months before her husband's death. Nick had congratulated his mother and wished her the best. His mother and Pastor Clark were married in a small, private ceremony before a local magistrate in Lakeland. When Sharon Jelaco became Sharon Clark, Nick and his mother had drifted even further apart. Although his mother and Julie had never shared a close relationship, Nick could tell her grief was heartfelt.

Nick pushed the childhood memories from his mind and returned his attention to the funeral proceedings. Julie's parents were seated just to the right of Richard Clark, but both parties were trying to avoid the other. In fact, Nick had scarcely spoken a word to his in-laws since their arrival in Lakeland. William Forsythe had insisted on a formal Catholic funeral, and for once, Nick was in agreement with his overbearing father-in-law. Nick was not familiar with the rituals that accompanied a Catholic funeral but respected Julie's unwavering commitment to her faith. The absence of Julie's body, which was still evidence in the custody of Monroe County, had forced some last-minute alterations to the traditional Catholic funeral hierarchy. The vigil service and rosary had been celebrated the night before without Julie's body present, and no graveside service would be held after the funeral mass due to the fact that the bronze casket at the front of the chapel was empty. Nick's favorite picture of Julie had been placed on top of the casket as a stand-in for her body.

Once the police released her body, there would be a small Rite of Committal ceremony at the Lakeland cemetery. Julie's body would be interred at the conclusion of the ceremony, and the Catholic funeral process would be complete. Nick was dreading the burial service, because deep down he knew he had not even begun to accept Julie's death.

Nick had asked a young Hispanic priest named Father Rodriguez to preside over the services. He did not know Father Rodriguez personally, but Julie had spoken of the priest with genuine fondness and respect. Julie's father had reluctantly acquiesced to Nick's insistence that Father Rodriguez conduct the mass. He had a feeling it would be the last time they agreed on anything.

Father Rodriquez conducted the hour-long funeral mass in a decorative white funeral robe and leather sandals. The young priest could have passed for a Latin version of Jesus with his long, flowing hair and beard. Nick floated through the entire funeral in a dreamlike state, barely comprehending the priest's words. During the funeral, Nick's mother rested her hand on his knee just as she had at his father's funeral some twenty years before. Time had passed, and this time his spouse was dead, but in many ways history had repeated itself. After his father's death, part of Nick's mother had remarried Pastor Clark and moved on with her life, but the other part of her had died when his father passed away. Nick missed the part of his mother that was gone and vowed to be whole for his daughter.

After the funeral mass, cold cuts, cookies, and punch were served in the old church's gymnasium. Nick followed the crowd to the gym but stayed at the reception just long enough to greet a handful of the guests. As soon as an opportunity presented itself, he escaped into the alley. He wanted to remain so he could convey his appreciation to the family and friends in attendance, but their expressions of sorrow were suffocating him. His mother and Richard were already leaning against the Mustang when he arrived at the car. In his haste to escape the reception, Nick had completely forgotten they had ridden with him. His desire to deal with his grief in solitude would have to wait a few more hours.

His mother and the pastor bought him an early dinner at the coffee shop in their hotel. Nick didn't have much of an appetite, but he did his best to choke down a dry club sandwich and a few cold French fries. At first, his mother had tried to ease his pain. After several failed attempts, his mother gave up and ate in silence. Nick wanted to let her presence comfort him, but he just couldn't let her inside the barriers he had built around his emotions.

Following their early dinner, Nick drove his mother and Pastor Clark to the Lakeland airport. His mother gave him a tentative hug, and Pastor Clark shook his hand. Nick promised to let them know if he needed anything and to keep them updated on the police investigation. There was no invitation to wait with them inside the terminal, which came as a big relief to Nick. He should have welcomed their support, but for some reason he felt compelled to face his demons without the support of family.

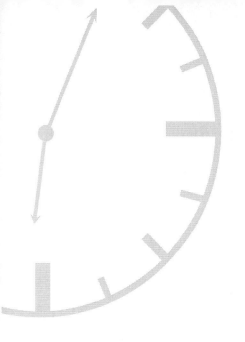

CHAPTER 12

Nick almost sprinted to the short-term parking garage as soon as his mother and Pastor Clark had disappeared inside the terminal. He remembered seeing a convenience store about a mile north of the airport on the road into Lakeland. There were a million things he could be doing, but, true to recent form, the convenience store was his first stop after leaving the airport. Nick knew alcohol wasn't the solution to his problems, but an entire week without any news about Darby was driving him mad. Every waking thought and most of his troubled dreams were filled with images of his daughter. Nick was a man of action, but there was no protocol to follow when your daughter was missing. He had never felt so helpless and inept. He needed to pull himself together, but it wouldn't be today. Julie's funeral and another day without a shred of information about his daughter were too much for him to face in the same day.

Nick drove around the back roads of Monroe County drinking beer and listening to classic rock 'n' roll on the radio intending to formulate a viable strategy for finding his daughter. Instead, he found himself reminiscing about the past. He and Julie used to drive through the farmland of Monroe County on Sunday afternoons when they had first moved to Lakeland.

After Darby was born, she had joined them for the Sunday drives. Julie would dress her in a cute outfit, and then she would sleep peacefully in the backseat while they drove aimlessly around the countryside with no destination or schedule to guide them. It was a chance to spend time together with no interruptions or distractions. Now Nick would have to navigate the rest of his life without Julie seated by his side.

The first six beers dulled the acute pain, but unfortunately the alcohol caused his focus to shift to his failures as a husband. He remembered with profound regret that once he had settled into a routine at Burton, St. James, & Summers, those Sunday afternoon drives with Julie and Darby had ceased entirely. Instead, his time was spent in the office dealing with trivial cases that he had long since forgotten. Financial security had been the driving force, or at least the excuse, behind his decision to work obscene hours. The dream of an early retirement and growing old with Julie had allowed him to justify sacrificing the present for the future. Today he would have given anything to go back in time.

Nick continued to drink beer and drive aimlessly around the tranquil countryside for hours. The headlights of the old Mustang were almost hypnotic as they danced eerily on dead, unharvested cornstalks and barren fields. Every once in a while he passed a car or an isolated farmhouse with lights burning in the windows. Most of the time, he was alone with his thoughts and self-loathing.

Every so often, Nick felt an inexplicable need to hurry home to his family. He had experienced the same feeling a hundred times while working late at the office, but this time there was no one waiting at home for him. In fact, he didn't even have a home to return to anymore. When Nick did return to Lakeland, his daughter wouldn't be up past her bedtime waiting for him to tuck her in. She wouldn't be peering out the living room window with her accepting smile and long brown hair framing her delicate face. Their home was empty, and his vulnerable, trusting little girl was out there with no one to protect her. It was close to midnight when Nick finished the last can of beer and turned his car toward Lakeland.

It was after midnight when Nick slammed his car into a cement parking block in front of the Log Tavern. His forehead bounced off the steering wheel as the car came to an abrupt stop. The name of the bar was supposed to conjure up images of a friendly neighborhood pub, which the Log Tavern certainly was not. It was actually a small, square, one-story building constructed of drab gray brick. Black iron bars covered all the windows, and the front door was constructed of impenetrable wrought iron.

The Log Tavern was not known as one of the rougher bars on the south side; still, it was a place where information flowed freely between the small-time drugs dealers, petty criminals, and strippers who drank there around the clock. Nick was desperate for information regarding Darby's disappearance and hoped one of the degenerates drinking at the Log Tavern would send a little information his way.

The smell of cheap liquor, stale cigarette smoke, and various unidentifiable odors filled his nostrils as he entered the dingy drinking establishment. Nick made his way to the bar and promptly ordered a draft beer and a shot of house whiskey from the bartender. The amount of colorful ink on the bartender's exposed skin made Nick think that he probably served as a human canvas for the local tattoo artist on his days off. *Freedom* was prominently tattooed across the right side of his neck, which was a dead giveaway the bartender was not a stranger to the Idaho penal system.

When the bartender returned with the drinks, he gruffly said, "That'll be four bucks." Nick paid with a five-dollar bill and wondered if the cold reception was the product of poor social skills or if all newcomers to the Log Tavern received a similar welcome. The whiskey shot was downed in one swallow, followed immediately by a sip of the lukewarm beer.

Nick's plan was to ply the bartender for information, but his tattoo-covered arms, overdeveloped biceps, and unpleasant disposition temporarily put that plan on hold. Nick figured the bartender's physique was the result of countless hours spent in the state penitentiary's weight room. He sipped his beer in silence, trying to understand how his life had gone so terribly wrong in a matter of days. A second shot of rotgut whiskey bolstered Nick's courage enough to engage the bartender in conversation.

"Do you ride a Harley?" Nick asked, pointing to the Harley-Davidson logo on his leather vest.

"You talking to me?" the bartender replied with the same warmth he'd shown since Nick's arrival.

"Yeah, I noticed the Harley leathers and wondered if you rode," Nick explained.

The bartender sadly shook his head from side to side. "Not anymore. My ex forced me to sell my bike to pay back child support. The cold-hearted witch threatened to have me thrown in jail if I didn't get caught up."

It was clear from the heartfelt sorrow in his voice that his kids' welfare was secondary to his precious Harley. It pissed Nick off that this self-centered derelict had kids he couldn't care less about while Nick's own daughter had been kidnapped. He wanted to punch the tattoo-covered bartender in the face, but instead Nick did his best to appear miserable over the loss of his Harley.

"That's harsh, man. What did you ride?" Nick said, trying to look as sad as humanly possible.

"My last bike was a Two Thousand Night Train," the bartender said with sincere regret in his voice. "How about you? You ride?"

Nick remembered the model of Harley Davidson an associate in his firm had purchased a few months before and confidently answered, "Yeah, a 2002 Springer Softail."

"Is it outside?" the bartender asked as he glanced longingly toward the front door.

"No. I just moved here from Portland, and my stuff wouldn't fit on the bike. My brother's driving it down next weekend," Nick lied.

"That's a downer."

"My name's Paul," Nick lied again.

"I'm Leroy."

"Hey, Leroy, I was thinking about selling my bike. Let me know if you're interested," Nick said, trying to sound indifferent.

"I'm interested, dude, but no cash," Leroy sadly replied. "My blood-sucking ex is bleeding me dry, and the pay at this lousy job barely covers my rent and child support."

"I'll tell you what, if you like the bike, maybe we can work out a deal that works for both of us," Nick countered. "I don't need the cash right now, and it would be nice to hook up with someone who's connected in Lakeland."

Leroy stared skeptically at Nick and replied, "No offense, dude, but you don't strike me as the deal-making, Harley-riding type."

Before Nick had a chance to respond to Leroy's suspicions, the bartender was summoned to the opposite end of the bar by an odd-looking couple. The man requesting Leroy's services was at least six foot nine inches tall and had to weigh well over three hundred pounds. His scraggly black hair was hanging out of a knit ski cap, and the enormous man was wearing sunglasses in the dim lighting of the Log Tavern. The woman accompanying the giant of a man had stringy bleached-blonde hair she wore past shoulder length. There was nothing remarkable about her appearance except for the fact that she looked like she was suffering from a terminal illness. Her rotting teeth and emaciated body reminded Nick of the countless women and children he saw being starved to death while he was stationed in Somalia. Nick's instincts, though dulled by alcohol, told him the woman's physical ailments were most likely self-inflicted.

Leroy's body language as he approached the couple made it crystal clear that he was not pleased to see them. The hulking giant of a man raised his hands to chest level, palms facing out, as if he were preparing to ward off an attack from the agitated bartender. The man's imposing stature and contrite appearance did little to slow Leroy's aggressive advance. When Leroy reached the couple, he leaned over the bar and repeatedly thumped the big man's chest with the index finger on his right hand. Each thump to the chest graphically reinforced whatever message Leroy was trying to convey with his words. As soon as Leroy finished his admonition of the man, he stepped away from the bar as if he was waiting for an explanation.

From a distance, the huge man looked like a child pleading his case to an angry parent. The man pointed to his alarmingly thin companion and then tried to hand something to the bartender. Leroy's anger was apparent as he slammed the man's hand into the hardwood bar. The large man's docile demeanor changed in an instant. His face flushed with anger as he grabbed the bartender around the neck with one of his giant hands and pulled him close. The massive man whispered something into Leroy's ear and then effortlessly pushed the bartender to the beer-soaked floor. Leroy quickly sprang to his feet as if he wanted to physically engage the man, but something about the large man's appearance stopped the bartender dead in his tracks. The giant man stared at Leroy for several seconds and then put his arm around his female friend and helped her toward the door. Leroy stood motionless behind the bar as he watched the mismatched pair exit the Log Tavern.

Leroy slowly returned to Nick's end. His clash with the strange-looking man had put the leather-clad bartender in an even worse mood. Nick attempted to pick up their conversation where they had left off, but Leroy was no longer in a talkative mood.

"We were talking about a deal for my Harley before we were interrupted," Nick began in an attempt to get their discussion back on track. "I'd be willing to bet a guy like you knows all the right people."

"What do you mean by 'all the right people'?" Leroy angrily replied.

"I need you to put me in touch with people who are willing and able to provide a very unique service," Nick continued.

Leroy narrowed his eyes. "What service?"

"Services of questionable legality," Nick explained.

"I'm not in the mood for any more of your double-talk, so get to the point."

"I'm looking for a young girl—" Nick began before Leroy abruptly cut him off.

"You're not a bad-looking guy. Why do you need someone to find you a woman? Take a look around," Leroy said, nodding toward a table where six or seven strippers were partying. "Most of the girls in here moonlight when they're not dancing."

"I'm not looking for a date."

"Then what are looking for?" Leroy asked.

"I want to adopt a three- or four-year-old little girl, and I'm willing to pay."

"That's sick, man! What kind of pervert are you?"

"You don't understand. My wife can't have kids, and we can't adopt because of my record."

"Either you're the dumbest man on the face of the earth, or you're a cop. Nobody in their right mind would ask a complete stranger for something that bizarre," Leroy snapped. "Finish your beer and get out of my bar, and if you know what's good for you, you won't show your face around here again."

"Sorry, I wasn't trying to piss you off," Nick muttered. "I'm a little drunk, and my old lady's been nagging me about a kid. Just forget I brought it up."

"First that psycho, Edgar, shows up with his strung-out girlfriend, and then you try to set me up. I'm on parole, but I'm not an idiot," Leroy grumbled. "Tell whichever cop you're working for to get off my back."

"I don't work for anybody. I just made a mistake, that's all."

"You made a big mistake," Leroy agreed. "Now get out of here."

Nick left the Log Tavern with his tail between his legs. Four years of training for covert operations, and he had broken every rule in the book. Information was a commodity that was acquired through patience and discretion. Nick's intuition was telling him that someone like Leroy could be a valuable source of information. Then again, he didn't have a lot of time. If the subtle approach didn't work, and work quickly, Nick could always resort to force and intimidation.

CHAPTER 13

Monday morning, October 16

During the daylight hours, Nick could almost convince himself that time really did heal all wounds. He remained in daily contact with the Lakeland police, state police, and the FBI. Although the investigative updates were always the same, he at least felt a connection to his daughter. Nighttime was a completely different story. When the sun set each night, it seemed to take his hope and optimism with it. While the rest of Lakeland gathered with family and friends, he was alone and homeless trying to deal with the agonizing reality of his daughter's situation. Nick's frantic search for Darby, combined with the maddening wait-for-a-break nature of a child abduction investigation, made his thoughts race like a car engine with the accelerator pressed to floor while the transmission was stuck in neutral.

Nick wanted to believe that hanging out in seedy bars on the south side was a necessary evil in his search for Darby, but deep down he knew his alcohol consumption was nothing more than a futile attempt to stop the thoughts spinning around in his head. Detective Gates had given Nick permission to return to his house, but he had checked into a cheaper motel on the south side of Lakeland instead. Being alone in the home he had shared with his wife and daughter was definitely more than he was ready to deal with. Nick's new residence, the El Rancho Motel, cost twenty-five dollars per night or $150 for an entire week. The El Rancho was one step above a flophouse, but that didn't stop him from paying for an entire week in advance. Phone calls to his home number had been forwarded to his cell phone just in case someone phoned with information about Darby.

Self-preservation had been the catalyst for Nick's decision to return to work ahead of schedule. Now that Julie's funeral was behind him, his mind was free to dwell on the plight of his daughter, and the police had no tangible leads to lessen the agony. Nick was still searching for Darby, but he had reluctantly come to the realization that finding his three-year-old daughter would take a lucky break. His daughter was the only thing that mattered, but he needed something to fill his day besides the hourly phone calls to law enforcement agencies involved with the investigation. Burton, St. James, & Summers was the only viable option that didn't involve sitting in a bar. Nick's new plan was to be as productive as possible during work hours and then survive each night alone the best he could.

On Nick's first day back at work, he had purposely snuck into the office about an hour before his typical eight o'clock arrival time. His plan was to be locked safely away in his office by the time the staff and other lawyers descended on the firm. He was not overly anxious to face his coworkers but had decided a return to work was necessary. It was still uncomfortable for him to respond to clumsy offers of sympathy and heartfelt, but completely useless, pledges to help him through his personal tragedy. His wife was dead, and nothing anyone could do was going to change that undeniable reality.

Nick dropped the case file on his desk in frustration after his third attempt to comprehend a set of fairly routine interrogatories. His impromptu decision to bury himself in work had already hit a snag. Nick's mind was so preoccupied with thoughts of his wife and missing daughter that he couldn't complete even the simplest of tasks. He was mulling over the pros and cons of requesting a temporary leave of absence when a light knock on the door interrupted his one-man debate.

Walter Burton poked his silver-haired head through Nick's office door just as Nick said, "Come in."

Walter tried to appear concerned as he entered Nick's office, but the troubled expression on his face was forced and unnatural. Walter was wearing pinstriped suit pants that were pulled up almost to his armpits, and about two inches of floppy sock was showing between the cuff of his pants and the top of his shoes. The sleeves of his white shirt were rolled up, and a red paisley tie hung loosely around his neck. Nick usually found Walter's lack of fashion sense amusing, but today it didn't even bring a smile to his face.

"I didn't expect you back in the office so soon," Walter said in the same patronizing voice he used with juries and clients. "I've been worried about you, son. You're like family to me."

"Thanks, Walter, I really appreciate your support," Nick replied, trying not to sound as insincere as his boss.

Walter gave Nick one of his forced smiles. "Don't mention it, Nick. Your well-being is the firm's top priority."

Nick was trying to figure out Walter's true agenda but merely said, "Your support means a lot to me."

Like most conversations with his boss, this one quickly shifted to make Walter the focal point. "When I was the prosecutor, Lakeland was a safe place to raise a family. Now the criminal element has free reign over the city, and nobody does a thing about it. Do the police have any promising leads?" Walter asked with a frown.

"Not that I'm aware of," Nick reluctantly admitted. "Detective Gates hasn't been overly communicative about the progress of the investigation."

Walter scoffed at the mention of Gates's name. "Detective Gates was a snot-nosed patrolman when I was the Monroe County prosecutor. Personally, I don't care for the man, but he does seem to get the job done. Rumor has it that he's not above bending a few rules."

Nick found it almost comical that Walter was passing judgment on another man for bending a few rules. He ignored Walter's comment and said, "He does seem competent."

"I'm sure he is," Walter said, without the slightest attempt at sincerity. "But my experience tells me this senseless crime was a random act of violence perpetrated by a drug addict who needed fast money to feed his habit. No matter what Gates tries to tell you, random crimes are almost impossible to solve without some dumb luck."

Nick had only been at work for a couple of hours, and Walter's know-it-all attitude was already getting on his nerves. "You're probably right, but Gates seems convinced the intruder was looking for something specific."

Walter was clearly annoyed that Gates's explanation for the break-in was different than his own, and he let Nick know it. "Why in the world does he think that? Is Detective Gates a mind reader now?"

For some reason, Nick found himself advocating Gates's theory regarding the actual motive behind the break-in.

"Gates said the crime scene was too focused to be a random burglary."

"That doesn't make a bit of sense," Walter scoffed.

"When you take a close look at Gates's rationale, there does seem to be certain logic to it," Nick countered. "The intruder went through my desk and file cabinet, and the only things missing from my house were a few client files."

The blood vessels on Walter's temples bulged. Nick was somewhat concerned his boss might have a stroke right there in his office.

"That's ridiculous," Walter said. "The man who murdered your wife was probably an amateur burglar who figured you kept cash in your desk or file cabinet. When your wife woke up, he panicked and killed her. It's not like dopers are the most logical thinkers in the world."

"You might be right, Walter, but Gates has a reputation for successfully closing cases," Nick replied almost entirely to annoy Walter.

Walter's reaction to Detective Gates's explanation for the break-in was puzzling. Walter's dislike for the detective was obvious and perhaps it was clouding his objectivity. Then again, Walter thought he was an expert on just about everything, which probably included police investigations. Still, his insistence that Detective Gates was off base seemed excessive even for Walter. Nick made a mental note to keep pertinent information regarding the investigation close to the vest. His instincts were telling him Walter had an ulterior motive.

The sound of Walter's voice interrupted Nick's deliberation. "Why would anyone want your client files?"

Nick shrugged. "I asked Gates the same question, and he wasn't sure. Just the same, he wanted to know which files were missing."

Walter's face flushed red. "Did you tell him? There might be client privilege issues that we need to consider."

"I did provide Gates with the names of six or seven client files that were taken. It was right after Julie's murder, so I was still pretty shaken up," Nick said defensively. "I'm sure the disclosure didn't violate the attorney/client privilege," he continued, confused by Walter's illogical concern about the files.

Walter glared at Nick with total contempt. "I'll need the names of those clients. I don't want Gates offending them with his abrasive manner."

"I don't think Gates will contact our clients directly."

"I didn't ask for your opinion. I want the names," Walter replied, still red faced. Walter's paranoia about a few missing files was over the top even for him.

"Sure, Walter. I'll get that information to you. One of the clients, Janis Jones, died before her case went to trial. The other clients are still active, but Gates was only interested in the Jones case file."

"Janis Jones? That name doesn't ring a bell," Walter said, a puzzled look on his face.

"It was a felony drug possession case. We took it from the public defender's office due to a conflict of interest," Nick explained. "I was under the impression that you were the one who agreed to take the case."

Walter's momentary calm was a thing of the past. "I wouldn't recommend my firm take on a low-rent drug possession case," he bellowed. "Monroe County only reimburses the firm fifty dollars per hour, and the cases are low profile. The firm actually loses money on those conflict cases. In case you've forgotten, this is a business, not a charitable organization."

Nick shrugged and continued with his explanation. "Well anyway, Janis Jones died of a drug overdose, so there was no trial, no plea bargain, or any anything else of significance."

Walter nodded, seemingly pleased to hear that Janis Jones had passed away. "At least Ms. Jones had the decency to save the taxpayers the cost of a trial," he noted without a trace of sarcasm in his voice.

Discussing the police investigation was clearly irritating his boss, so Nick changed the topic. "Julie's Rite of Committal is this afternoon, so I'll be leaving early."

"Of course, of course—you deal with your family issues first. Don't rush back too quickly, Nick. The grieving process takes time."

"Thanks, Walter."

"Forget my criticism of Detective Gates," Walter added. "As an old prosecutor, it's my nature to second-guess the police. Take all the time you need, son. We'll all pick up the slack until you're back on your feet."

"I appreciate your understanding," Nick replied as Walter turned to leave his office.

Walter abruptly stopped in mid-stride. "I almost forgot to congratulate you on the verdict in the Peterson trial. It would have been hard to screw up such a strong case, but you never know when it comes to a jury trial."

In typical Walter fashion, he had found a way to downplay Nick's part in the judgment. "The jury got it right this time," Nick agreed, ignoring his boss's snub.

Walter wrinkled his nose as if he had just smelled something unpleasant before he continued, "The Petersons are such a disgusting group that I wasn't sure the jury would relate to them. Did the defendant's attorney tell you when we could expect payment?"

Walter had finally gotten around to what really mattered to him. Money. "No, the defense counsel didn't say anything about the payment. In fact, I got the impression the defendant is considering an appeal."

Walter was mumbling to himself as he left Nick's office. The prospect of having to wait for his share of the multi-million dollar judgment had clearly upset him.

As the door slammed shut behind Walter, Nick thought about the man he had worked for his entire legal career. It was difficult to work for Walter, but it was even harder to respect him as a person. Walter was arrogant, mean spirited, and lacked a moral compass. Yet he had a knack for making money. Even though his boss hadn't tried a case in almost five years, his overstated reputation as a trial lawyer and his ability to self-promote kept the big-ticket cases rolling in.

Like many successful attorneys, Walter had started his legal career in the public sector. He had graduated from the University of Washington in 1970, and Charles Beckman, the Monroe County prosecutor, had hired him a few months later. After six years as a marginal deputy prosecutor, Walter ran for Monroe County prosecutor against his boss. His election bid was successful, and Walter became the youngest prosecutor in Monroe County history.

Walter's tenure as an elected official had its share of highs and lows, but one case seemed to define his career as a prosecutor. In the 1980s, Walter prosecuted a young man named Cole Panache for the first-degree murder of an eighteen-year-old Lakeland girl named Brooke Schaffer. Walter got his conviction and the recognition of his political party. Most people assumed Walter's next job would be at the state capital, but for some reason, Walter didn't take advantage of his time in the spotlight. Shortly after the Panache verdict, he surprised everyone by abruptly leaving the public sector and bankrolling a new law firm.

After opening his firm and embarking on a new career as a plaintiff's attorney, Walter surprised the legal community by winning the largest civil judgment ever awarded in the Northwest. The amount of the judgment was shocking, given the fact that most legal experts claimed the case was a surefire loser for Walter's upstart firm. Walter's accomplishments in the legal profession had always amazed Nick. Especially given the fact that he had no innate legal ability and local judges and attorneys despised him.

Nick had watched Walter Burton try a couple of cases, and he wasn't impressed. In fact, he was quite unimpressed. Walter's style was uninspiring and droning, almost painful to watch. He was always over-prepared on tangential issues and belabored points that had little to no relevance to the crux of the case. Boring a judge and jury seemed to be Walter's most obvious attributes as a trial lawyer. Nick could almost feel sorry for the guy, but his greed, power fetish, and overpowering ego made sympathy nearly impossible.

CHAPTER 14

Monday afternoon, October 16

Nick had last visited the Lakeland cemetery in June of 1994. The army had granted him a surprise two-week leave that summer, and he had decided to stop by his father's gravesite, having gained a new appreciation for the fragility of life from his time in Somalia. More than ten years later, he was returning to the cemetery following the worst week of his life. Nick had been dreading the ceremony for days. Nick had begun to accept the reality of his wife's death; he just wasn't emotionally prepared to deal with the finality of her once vibrant body being lowered into the cold earth.

Julie's parents were already waiting at the gravesite when he arrived. Her mother looked even worse than she had at the funeral. Nick assumed that after Julie's death, she had retreated even further into the sanctuary she found at the bottom of a vodka bottle. It was evident from the Forsythes' body language that the death of their daughter had not narrowed the chasm that existed between them.

Nick and Julie had enjoyed a very open relationship, yet she had seldom spoken candidly about her dysfunctional family. As he waited for the service to begin, Nick remembered one occasion when his wife had talked openly about her mother's problems. She hadn't come right out and blamed her mother's troubles on William, but Nick had been able to read between the lines.

Sandra Denning had been an intelligent, beautiful, young woman with a bright future before she married William. When she became Sandra Forsythe, her bright future came to a screeching halt. Sandra and William Forsythe had met at Stanford University during her sophomore year of college. She was a motivated journalism student with talent and ability. He was a charismatic senior studying business and finance. It had not taken William long to realize that he wanted Sandra, and he always got what he wanted.

William and Sandra had been married in a lavish ceremony in Sun Valley, Idaho, less than a year later. With their union, Sandra Denning ceased to exist for all practical purposes. She became just another asset William manipulated and controlled. William's years of philandering and mental abuse had certainly taken a toll on Sandra. Mrs. Forsythe, once vibrant and beautiful, now had the appearance of a bitter old woman who drank too much. Nick was certain that Julie's death would hit Sandra much harder than it hit her self-absorbed husband. Sandra Denning's story was a sad tale, and Nick was pretty sure it wouldn't have a happy ending.

Father Rodriquez, the same young priest who had conducted the funeral mass, presided over the Rite of Committal. Unlike the funeral, only a small group of family and friends was present for the burial service. The graveside service was brief, formal, and conducted according to the rituals of the Catholic Church. Immediately following the Rite of Committal, Julie's body was interred in the Lakeland cemetery for all time and eternity. Nick was overcome with grief as he watched the bronze casket disappear from view.

Reeling from the finality of his wife's internment, he slowly walked away from the gravesite. He had almost made it to his car when he noticed Julie's self-absorbed father rushing toward him, obviously itching to do battle.

"You ruined my life, and now I'm going to ruin yours," Mr. Forsythe hissed at his son-in-law.

Nick wanted to knock some sense into William, but, given the circumstances, he tried to reason with him instead.

He calmly replied, "I know you're hurting and you blame me for Julie's death, but this is not the right time or place."

"You're a failure and a loser," William continued. "I'll never understand what my daughter saw in you."

"I'll cut you a little slack given the circumstances, but it'll be the last time," Nick angrily replied.

"A loser like you threatening me, that's a laugh." William spat. "I have more power and influence than a man like you could possibly fathom."

"Enough is enough—I'm not going to listen to anymore of your drivel," Nick said as he turned his back on William.

"Go ahead, walk away, tough guy."

Nick ignored him and kept on walking.

"Here's something for you to chew on," William called out. "I hired a private detective to find my granddaughter, and when he does, I plan to seek full custody of her."

Nick stopped abruptly and turned to face Julie's father. "Call off your private detective, William. Let the police do their job."

"You weren't fit to be a husband, and you're certainly not fit to raise my granddaughter," William countered in a mocking tone of voice.

Common sense was telling Nick to walk away, but testosterone was telling him to stay and fight it out. Testosterone won. He got face to face with William, and said, "No judge in his right mind would give a raving maniac like you custody of a three-year-old."

William smiled at Nick like a poker player with a straight flush. "So you think some conservative Idaho judge will decide that an unbalanced, ex-soldier, who drinks himself into a stupor every night is a more suitable custodian than a stable, financially secure grandparent?"

William's reference to his excessive drinking hit the mark, but Nick did his best to appear unconcerned.

"There's no chance a judge is going to take Darby away from her father," Nick confidently shot back. "She just lost her mother."

"Don't kid yourself. Your legal system doesn't provide justice for people like you," William boasted. "There's not a verdict in this world money can't buy."

"Then get prepared for battle," Nick threatened without a trace of fear in his voice. "Your scare tactics don't intimidate me."

William appeared to be amused by his son-in-law's unwillingness to back down. "You just don't get it, do you?" he laughed. "Your entire life you've been a pawn for people of wealth and influence—people just like me. In the military you were an expendable asset at the mercy of politicians. Now you're a small-time lawyer who snatches up the crumbs tossed aside by his boss."

Before William could finish his tirade, Nick turned his back on his ex-father-in-law for a second time and walked away. He wasn't stupid enough to take William's threats lightly, yet he knew beyond a shadow of doubt that his father-in-law's arrogance and conceit would ultimately lead to his downfall.

CHAPTER 15

Nick's anger had reached its boiling point by the time the Lakeland Cemetery had disappeared from view in his rearview mirror. William's arrogance and lack of compassion never ceased to amaze him, but this time, his behavior had crossed the line. William was threatening to take his daughter away from him, and Nick wasn't about to let that happen. Julie's father was seldom accurate or objective when it came to evaluating Nick's shortcomings, but this time he was right on target in regard to his excessive drinking. Nick vowed to cut back on his alcohol intake first thing tomorrow morning.

His less than subtle attempts to acquire information about his daughter's abduction had proven futile. Detective Gates had warned him about child abduction investigations, but contrary to his pragmatic nature, Nick had assumed that Darby's case would be the exception to the rule. He needed a new plan of action, but he didn't have a clue where to begin. Perhaps a couple of drinks followed by a good night's sleep would give him a fresh perspective and renewed vigor. Tomorrow all his efforts would be focused on finding his daughter. Tonight he needed to grieve the loss of his wife one last time. Without really thinking about his destination, Nick turned the Mustang onto Moore

Hollow Road and headed straight for the Crazy Horse Saloon. It never occurred to him that the south side was a curious choice if his actual intent was to grieve his wife's death.

The Crazy Horse Saloon was one of the more upscale drinking establishments on the south side, which wasn't saying a great deal. The proprietor, an alleged mobster from the East Coast, had attempted to capture the essence of pre-Castro nightlife in Cuba but had failed miserably. Rumor had it that a lack of capital and entrepreneurial vision had doomed the venture from the get-go.

The Crazy Horse's parking lot was packed for a Monday night. Evidently, the inhabitants of the south side considered every night just another opportunity to party. The parking lot was filled with an odd mixture of barely operational economy cars and $60,000 luxury cars. The obvious disparity in wealth made it easy to distinguish the suppliers of illicit goods and services from the less fortunate consumers of those same goods and services. Nick finally located an empty parking spot at the back of the lot and pulled in beside a late-model Mercedes. He threw his car keys on the floor and exited the Mustang without bothering to lock the doors.

Nick paid the five-dollar cover charge at the front door and pushed his way past a crowd of people milling around the entrance. Once inside, Nick had to fight his way through a sea of men and women. When he finally reached the bar, Nick found all the stools occupied by what he assumed were Crazy Horse regulars. He ordered a double Jack Daniels on the rocks from the harried bartender and stepped away from the bar.

As Nick stood by the bar slowly sipping his Jack Daniels, the profound sadness that had overtaken him was slowly replaced by an irrational anger. He found it maddening that the boisterous patrons of the Crazy Horse were completely unaffected by the events that had knocked his life off course. After a second trip to the bar and no mental relief from the alcohol, Nick began contemplating a change of scenery. He swallowed the last of his drink and turned for the door just as a table opened up near the sound stage. With nothing better to do, Nick changed his mind and headed for the empty table.

The instant he sat down, a bubbly cocktail waitress with Erin inscribed on her nametag bounded up to his table. Nick ordered another double Jack Daniels on the rocks and when the waitress returned a few minutes later, he handed her a ten-dollar bill for the five-dollar drink. The big tip instantly made Erin his new best friend for the remainder of the evening. He had initially intended to drink in moderation, but just like every other night since Julie's death, a couple of drinks turned into six or seven. He was drunk, lonely, and about to call it a night when the house band took its first break of the evening. The momentary reprieve from the ear-splitting music was such a relief, Nick decided to finish his drink before returning to depressing emptiness of his motel room.

Nick wasn't sure how long he had been sitting there, tormented by thoughts of the fate that awaited his daughter and images of Julie's lifeless body when the young woman he had met at the Wind Jammer slid into the chair across from him. Her sudden arrival was completely unexpected but not entirely unwanted. Even though Nick had no interest in the woman, he was tired of being alone with the painful memories and haunting scenarios his mind kept conjuring up.

"Hi, Nick, do you remember me?" she asked, her nervousness apparent. "We met at the Wind Jammer a few nights ago."

"I remember you," Nick replied in a flat tone. "Your name's Simone."

Simone was young, probably midtwenties, and very attractive. She was wearing tight-fitting, faded jeans and a snug V-neck sweater. Her ethnicity was difficult to pinpoint, but he suspected her family roots originated somewhere near the Mediterranean Sea, perhaps North Africa, Italy, or Spain. She had dark skin, long brown hair, and eyes that appeared almost black in the dim light of the bar. But it was not her appearance that caught his attention—it was the sadness in her eyes. Nick knew from personal experience that sadness as profound as hers was probably the after effect of a life-altering event. He wondered if the melancholy aura surrounding the beautiful, young woman had been caused by the death of a loved one.

"I was really sorry to hear the news about your wife and little girl," she said, her eyes suddenly brimming with tears.

Simone's condolences momentarily shocked him into silence, and after an awkward pause, he asked, "How did you know it was my wife and daughter?"

"I've been following the story on the local news, and I finally put two and two together."

Simone's simple explanation didn't add up, so Nick pushed for specifics. "You didn't answer my question," he bluntly informed her. "I want to know how you knew it was my family."

"Like I said before, I put two and two together," Simone repeated.

"Put them together for me," Nick demanded.

Simone shrugged as if it was no big deal. "The Channel 8 News and the local newspaper both reported Julie Jelaco's husband was a local attorney named Nick Jelaco. The night we talked in the Wind Jammer you told me you were a lawyer and your name was Nick. Something about our conservation stuck in my mind, so I searched Nick Jelaco on the Internet. It all added up when I found your picture on your law firm's Web site."

"You searched the Internet after a five-minute conversation?"

"Why not?" Simone casually replied. "By the way, you look much younger in person."

After considering the plausibility of her explanation, Nick asked, "Why all the interest in the sordid details of my life?"

Simone wrinkled her nose and grimaced slightly. "You're going to think I'm crazy, but here goes. After I left the Wind Jammer..." Simone's voice trailed off before she finished her sentence.

"What about that night?" Nick pushed.

Simone quickly glanced at her fidgeting hands. "I got the feeling there was unfinished business between us."

Nick gave Simone one of his "have you lost your mind" looks and said, "What unfinished business? I don't even know you."

"Feelings and impressions are hard to explain, but I'll try," Simone started slowly. "My family had just received some devastating news on the day we met." Simone abruptly stopped to qualify her statement. "What happened to your family was much worse."

Nick nodded but didn't speak.

"Anyway, my brother has been wasting away in prison since 1985, sentenced to life for a murder he didn't commit," Simone continued. "A few hours before our brief encounter, the legal hacks who sit on Idaho's Supreme Court denied Cole's most recent and probably last appeal. I didn't know it at the time, but you work for Walter Burton, the man who prosecuted my brother, Cole. Another lawyer in your law firm, Jackson St. James, assisted with his prosecution."

Erin suddenly reappeared while Nick was processing Simone's bombshell. Against his better judgment, he ordered another double Jack Daniels on the rocks. Simone asked the waitress for a glass of water. Erin gave Simone a disappointed look and then scampered off to fetch his double Jack.

"I'm somewhat familiar with the basics of your brother's conviction, but I don't know the specifics of the prosecution's case," Nick admitted. "With that said, I don't understand how there could be unfinished business between the two of us. Your brother was arrested, convicted, and sentenced ten years before I graduated from law school. I didn't even meet Walter Burton or Jackson St. James until six years ago."

Nick was actually more familiar with her brother's case than he was willing to let on. While preparing for his pre-employment interview with Burton, St. James, & Summers, he had researched a few of Walter's more noteworthy cases. The Cole Panache murder conviction was one of those cases. Nick knew that Cole Panache had been convicted of first-degree murder in 1985. The victim was a local teenager named Brooke Schaffer. He also had a vague recollection that both of Cole's parents had died in the late 1980s.

Newspaper reports at the time of the murder portrayed the Panaches as a lower middle-class family. Cole Panache was portrayed as an average student but an above-average athlete. During his research, Nick came across a few pictures of Simone's brother. He was a good-looking kid with a muscular build, dark skin, and unruly black hair. According to newspaper reports, Cole had been in some minor scrapes with the law but nothing atypical of normal teenage behavior.

Nick also remembered thinking that Walter could have used the Panache conviction to advance his political career, but for some reason, he had not. Shortly after the successful and controversial prosecution of Cole Panache, Walter Burton had unexpectedly left public law and embarked on a very successful career in private practice. Walter's move was surprising given the fact that the local media considered him a viable candidate for governor. Idaho is a state that elects politicians who are tough on crime, and a successful murder prosecution was political gold.

The sound of Simone's voice brought him back to the Crazy Horse Saloon, and the reason for his drunken detour into the Panache family history. Evidently Simone had grown tired of waiting for him to mentally shift through the details of her story and wanted to continue their discussion.

"I don't believe in coincidences, Nick," Simone said with an odd sense of urgency in her voice. "Life has taught me everything happens for a reason, good or bad. Why did you end up in the Wind Jammer the night your wife was murdered?"

"I honestly don't know," Nick admitted.

"Had you ever set foot inside the Wind Jammer before that night?"

"No."

"The bar was practically empty," Simone pointed out. "Why did you sit down next to me and start a conversation?"

Nick felt sorry for the desperate young woman sitting across from him, but her problems weren't his concern.

"I know you're searching for answers," Nick replied sympathetically. "Sometimes bad things happen, and you just have to accept your fate and move on."

"We can change the future," Simone argued.

"My wife is dead, and nothing will change that reality," Nick answered with an edge to his voice. "If we had met under different circumstances, I would make time for your brother's case. Right now, finding my daughter is the only thing that matters to me."

"I wasn't asking you to represent my brother," Simone replied, clearly frustrated. "I merely wanted to ask a few questions about the men you work for—Walter Burton and Jackson St. James."

"And what will that accomplish?" Nick demanded.

"Perhaps nothing, but something tells me we can help each other."

Nick wanted to tell Simone she was delusional if she believed her brother's conviction was somehow connected to his daughter's abduction, but instead he said, "Look, Simone, you seem like a good kid, but I'm drowning in my own problems."

"Most drowning men would welcome a helping hand."

"I really don't have the time or the inclination to get sidetracked," Nick answered dismissively.

"Will you think about my proposition after you sober up?" she urged. "I'm only asking for a couple of hours."

When Simone was done talking, she handed him a scrap of paper with her name and a phone number neatly printed on it. Nick took the paper and stuffed it into his shirt pocket.

"Sure, I'll think about it, but my answer won't change," Nick replied without enthusiasm. "I can't afford peripheral distractions right now."

Simone walked away without further comment, but Nick continued to think about their conversation. Even though he thought she was nuts, she had mentioned one thing that made sense. His unfocused attempts to find his daughter had been all wrong. He was a lawyer trained to evaluate factual evidence and then draw logical conclusions from that evidence. He wasn't a cop who shook down bartenders and intimidated snitches. The

Jack Daniels was making it difficult for him to think logically. Still, Nick knew he had to start from the beginning. He needed to look at the facts, all the facts. Then he would go wherever those facts led him. Tomorrow morning he would take a good hard look at the case files that had been taken from his house.

Nick picked up his Jack Daniels, intent on downing it in one gulp but instead returned the half-full glass to the table. His new plan called for a clear mind, not more self-destructive behavior. Nick tossed a ten-dollar bill on the table and headed for the parking lot and fresh air. The front door was within view when a rough-looking guy with a ponytail grabbed him by the shoulder. Nick wasn't good at estimating ages, but he figured the man was approaching thirty. The man was accompanied by three friends of similar age and sloppy appearance. Something was obviously bothering their ringleader, and he wanted to discuss it with Nick.

"I haven't seen you around the Crazy Horse before," he shouted over the blare of the band.

"If you're bucking for a job as a hostess, you're a little late," Nick replied with a straight face. "I was about to call it a night."

The man glanced at his friends and said, "You're pretty cocky for a guy who's about to get his tail kicked."

"Why don't you and your band of losers run along before someone gets hurt," Nick shot back, half hoping the man would give him a reason to knock some sense into him.

The man with the ponytail narrowed his eyes in an attempt to look tough. "Someone's going to get hurt, but it ain't me."

"Get to the point, your tough-guy act is starting to wear thin," Nick demanded.

"A dude your age should know better than to mess with another man's woman," Ponytail angrily replied. The guy's misplaced jealousy brought a smirk to Nick's face. "I wasn't messing with anyone's girlfriend."

"Don't lie to me, faggot. I saw you hitting on Simone," he screamed in Nick's face.

Nick was trying to decide if he should slap the idiot silly or try to explain the situation when the man made his decision easy by taking a wild swing at his head. Even in his drunken state, Nick could tell the buffoon wouldn't pose a significant problem. He raised his left forearm and easily deflected his attacker's roundhouse punch, while he simultaneously thrust the butt of his right hand into the bridge of the man's nose. The force of the blow caused Ponytail's nose to flatten, and he collapsed in a heap.

Nick determined Ponytail's heavyset friend would be the next contestant to take a shot at him. The man paused briefly to assess the extent of his friend's injuries, and judging by his reaction, what he saw infuriated him. Their fearless leader was wriggling around on the floor as blood flowed from between his fingers. Ponytail's chubby friend let out a bellow and rushed at Nick like a blitzing linebacker. Nick quickly spun to his right and delivered a side kick to the outside of his knee. The snap of his attacker's knee was followed immediately by his wailing. The heavyset man crashed to the floor, and Nick knew from the pop that the man's knee was dislocated.

Nick quickly turned to his left in an attempt to locate the third man in Ponytail's welcoming party. When Nick picked up his movements, he was somewhat alarmed to find the man was brandishing an eight-inch knife. The man obviously wasn't an experienced fighter: fear and indecision had delayed his attack long enough for Nick to regain a defensive posture. By the time he had summoned enough courage to make his move, Nick was ready for it. The man jabbed at Nick with the knife, but his thrust was tentative and unskilled. The blade came up a few inches short, which allowed Nick to grab the wrist of the man's knife hand. As he struggled to free his hand, Nick jammed the palm of his hand into the underside of his attacker's elbow. The man's elbow hyperextended with a resounding crack, and the knife fell harmlessly to the ground.

Adrenaline raced through Nick's body as he scanned the onlookers for another willing participant. It felt good, really good, to unleash his pent-up rage and frustration. After determining there were no more takers, he stepped over Ponytail's writhing body and rushed toward the front door. He needed to get out of the Crazy Horse before someone called the police. As he pushed his way through the murmuring crowd, Nick felt a thump on the side of his head and the faint sound of shattering glass. He was conscious just long enough to realize he was in trouble—big trouble.

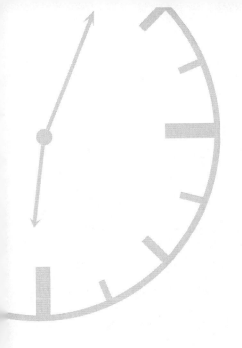

CHAPTER 16

Tuesday morning, October 17

Detective Gates stormed into the drab conference room at precisely ten minutes past the hour, a full ten minutes after the meeting's eight o'clock start time. He quickly surveyed the solemn group and determined the entire investigative team was assembled. Tardiness usually infuriated the detective, but he offered no explanation for his own late arrival.

"Let's get down to business," Gates said, after pouring himself a cup of coffee. "The Jelaco crime is almost two weeks old, and we still don't have squat. Detective Sato, what can you tell us about Mr. Jelaco's activities around the time of the murder?"

Detective Sato removed a small notebook from the back pocket of his faded jeans. "His story checks out to the letter," he began with an air of confidence. "Jelaco was driving home from Las Vegas at the time of the murder. Records provided by Mountain Cellular confirm that his mobile phone received a call from the Jelacos' home phone number at 12:08 a.m., which was approximately three hours before Mrs. Jelaco was murdered. The routing of the call indicates it was bounced off a tower just north of Tonopah, Nevada. It's a six-hour drive to Lakeland from Tonopah driving eighty mph. There is no way he was in Lakeland at the time of the murder."

Gates didn't appear overly impressed by Sato's deductive reasoning. "What if someone else was using Jelaco's cell phone on the night of the murder?"

"The same thought crossed my mind, but he charged a tank of gas at a Texaco gas station in Ely, Nevada at about 1:15 a.m."

"Did anyone at the gas station get a good look at Jelaco on the evening in question?" Detective Gates asked in a tone that implied he had no interest in Sato's answer.

Sato nodded and began flipping the papers of his notebook. "I faxed a picture of Mr. Jelaco to the White Pine County Sheriff, Dennis Weaver. Weaver had one of his deputies run a photo lineup past the night clerk on duty that night. The clerk was a kid named Trent Hogan. He picked Mr. Jelaco's photo out of the lineup without any problem. The kid even remembered that Mr. Jelaco bought a large coffee and commented he had a long drive ahead of him."

"Any chance Mr. Hogan was mistaken?" Gates inquired.

"It's not likely, Boss. Sheriff Weaver claims the station's surveillance tape shows Mr. Jelaco pumping gas."

"Ask Weaver for the videotape," Gates instructed.

"It's in the mail."

"Okay, I'm convinced. Jelaco was driving home from Las Vegas at the time of his wife's murder," Gates agreed. "What about the Jelacos' personal finances? Anything suspicious there?"

Sato frowned and slowly shook his head from side to side. "Absolutely nothing out of the ordinary. Mr. Jelaco's annual salary is approximately $75,000. The only debt he carries is a $980 a month house payment and a $325 car payment, both of which he pays on time each month. The balance in the Jelacos' joint checking account is around $3,400.00 and they have approximately $17,000 in savings. There have been no large deposits or withdrawals since the accounts were opened in July 1999."

"Did the grieving husband purchase any large insurance policies near the time of his wife's murder?"

Sato quickly flipped through the pages of his notebook. "The Jelacos owned two life insurance policies, one on the wife for $100,000 and one on Nick Jelaco for the same amount. Both policies were purchased five years ago."

Detective Gates leaned forward in his chair and dropped his pen on the table. "It's basically the routine type of background I expected. I never figured he was our guy, but we had to jump through all the hoops just the same. We all know how much the chief hates an incomplete file. Sato, is there anything you want to add before we move on?"

Sato hesitated for a moment before he added, "I'm not sure it's relevant to the investigation, but I thought you should know Nick Jelaco was a soldier. In fact, he saw some fairly heavy combat in Somalia. President Clinton even gave him a medal for heroic conduct."

"I'm well aware of Nick Jelaco's military service," Gates said. "He was assigned to a Special Forces unit called Delta Force during his stint in the military. Delta Force is supposedly the best of the best."

"I never would have guessed he was Special Forces," Sato said with a disbelieving shake of his head. "There is something about Jelaco's recent behavior that's been bothering me."

"Spit it out, Sato. We've all got work to do," Gates grumbled at the young detective.

"Mr. Jelaco has been conducting his own amateur investigation."

Gates furrowed his brow and stared intently at Sato. "Amateur investigation? What does that mean?"

"I pumped a couple of my informants, and they told me some yuppie type, not a cop, has been snooping around the south side asking questions about the Jelaco murder and kidnapping. I did a little follow-up, and it turns out Mr. Jelaco has been hanging out in some pretty rough nightclubs, sticking his nose in places it doesn't belong."

"Are you sure it's Nick Jelaco who's asking the questions?" Gates demanded.

"Positive," Sato confirmed. "I shadowed him a couple of times. He's becoming a regular in some of the south side's more notorious hangouts."

Gates leaned back in his chair and exhaled in frustration. "That's just great! The friggin' idiot will probably get himself killed; or worse, he'll dry up our information pipeline."

"It gets worse. He's drinking himself into a stupor most nights. It's a minor miracle traffic division hasn't popped him for a DUI."

"Keep an eye on Mr. Jelaco, and let me know if I need to bring him in for a heart to heart," Gates angrily told Sato. "Anything else?"

Sato closed his notebook. "Not right now. I'm following up on some whispers about a botched burglary for hire, but the information's pretty thin at this point."

"Thanks, Detective Sato," Gates said and then turned his attention to the Monroe County medical examiner. "Katie, update the group on the autopsy results and the official cause of Mrs. Jelaco's death."

"Sure, Phil," Katie said as she passed out a copy of her preliminary report. "Mrs. Jelaco died from vegal inhabitation brought on by excessive stimulation of the vagus nerve."

Gates raised his eyebrows, and dryly asked, "What's that mean for those of us who didn't spend twenty years in medical school?" Katie smiled and said, "Sorry, Phil, you know how I like big words. Mrs. Jelaco was manually strangled to death by her attacker. Bruise patterns on her neck indicate the killer used his hands as the murder weapon. I believe her killer was very strong."

"What facts led you to that conclusion?"

"Compression of Mrs. Jelaco's neck caused a breakage of the hyroid bone. It's kind of complicated, but the compression and breakage of the hyroid bone stimulated the neck's vagus nerve, which caused Mrs. Jelaco's heart to stop beating."

"So, in layman's terms, Mrs. Jelaco was strangled to death by a very powerful man?"

"Yes and no," Katie hedged. "She was strangled to death, but she didn't die from a lack of oxygen. Strangulation caused her heart to stop, so heart failure was the actual cause of her death. It's not that easy to kill a person with your bare hands," Katie added. "Her attacker was probably bigger and stronger than an average man."

Gates knew that Katie didn't like to speculate, but she had opened the door. "What makes you think the killer was bigger and stronger than average?"

"Julie Jelaco was a small woman but in excellent physical condition. She was definitely strong enough to put up a good fight against a man of average size and strength. Most strangulation victims have multiple injuries as a result of their assailant's initial attempts to subdue them prior to the actual strangulation. Mrs. Jelaco had no additional bruises, lacerations, or broken bones. The examination indicated her killer was strong enough to effortlessly control her."

"Was Mrs. Jelaco impaired by alcohol or drugs?" Gates asked.

"No, her toxicology report came back clean. There was no trace of alcohol or drugs, illegal or prescription in her system. In fact, she was so well adjusted she didn't even take antidepressants," a cynical Katie added.

"Was she sexually assaulted?" Gates asked.

"No, Phil, our guy wasn't into sex, torture, or mutilation. The attack on Mrs. Jelaco was limited to the strangulation."

"Do you have an approximate time of death?" Gates asked.

"Considering postmortem lividity and body temperature, I would estimate between 3:30 and 4:00 a.m. on the fifth of October It was a real break her husband discovered her body so close to the time of the murder."

"Yeah, a real break," Gates sarcastically agreed. "Thanks, Katie."

Gates scribbled a few notes on the pad of paper in front of him and said, "Okay, Stan, you're up. What can you tell us about the forensic evidence at the crime scene?"

"The crime scene was relatively clean if it was an unplanned homicide," Smith started.

"What do you mean by relatively clean?" Gates demanded.

"The killer didn't use a weapon, and he didn't sexually assault the victim, which translates to a lack of forensic evidence at the scene," Smith answered defensively.

"I'm more interested in the evidence that was present at the crime scene," Gates said with more than a trace of annoyance in his tone.

"The killer definitely entered through the front door, which seems odd unless he had a key or Mrs. Jelaco left the front door unlocked. Otherwise, it seems illogical that he would choose the only illuminated entrance with a dead bolt."

"So the killer didn't force the lock?" Gates asked for clarification.

"That's right, Phil. There were no tool marks or paint transfers on any of the ground-floor doors or windows," Smith answered confidently.

Gates thought about the crime scene investigator's answer for a couple of seconds. "Did the same key pattern open all the doors?"

Smith shook his head. "The key that opens the front door won't open the garage door or the back door."

Gates began speaking to no one in particular. "Mr. Jelaco is certain that his wife would have locked and then double-checked the doors before retiring for the evening. Evidently she was the nervous type and a little bit compulsive when her husband was out of town on business."

"If that's the case, the guy we're looking for probably had a key," Smith noted.

Gates turned his attention to Detective Sato. "Are all the Jelacos' keys accounted for?" Gates asked.

"Unless there's a copy Mr. Jelaco doesn't know about," Sato answered without hesitation. "The Jelacos had three keys that fit the lock on the front door. One key was in the wife's purse at the time of her death. Mr. Jelaco has one on his key ring, and he keeps a spare at his office."

"Something doesn't add up," Gates replied dryly. "If Smith is right, there has to be a fourth key Mr. Jelaco doesn't know about."

"It's unlikely, but I'll check it out," Sato replied skeptically.

Detective Gates nodded at Stan Smith, indicating his side bar with Sato was over. The crime scene investigator immediately continued his summary of the forensic evidence.

"We found two latent fingerprints and a partial palm print we haven't been able to match to the husband, the victim, or anyone else who had a reason to be in the house. One fingerprint was removed from the light switch in the master bedroom, and the other fingerprint was lifted from the doorknob inside the front door. The palm print was removed from the handrail on the staircase."

"Where on the handrail?" Gates asked.

"Near the bottom, about three stairs up," Smith replied. "The FBI has agreed to enter the prints into AFIS, but it may take a few weeks."

"A few weeks—are you kidding me?" Gates shouted. "Turn up the heat or call in a favor, but get the FBI to run those prints. Tell those pencil-pushers a three-year-old girl has been missing for eleven days, which means we don't have 'a few weeks.' Somebody who works for the FBI should be able to understand the concept of prioritizing a workload."

"I'll do what I can, Phil, but I don't have a lot of pull with the federal government," Smith nervously replied.

"I realize the FBI has their own agenda, but we need to pull out all the stops," Gates urged.

Smith nodded before continuing with his summary of the evidence. "We recovered a couple of long black hairs that don't match the hair samples of the family members. One of the hairs was removed from Mrs. Jelaco's body. The characteristics of the hair samples are fairly unique, so a microscopic comparison is a realistic possibility if we get a viable suspect."

Gates looked up from his notepad and asked, "Unique in what way?"

"The hairs are unusually thick and course, quite similar to an African American's hair, except the hairs are straight. If you forced me to hypothesize, I would say Inuit, Native American, or one of the other Mongoloid races."

"Inuit or Native American—that should narrow the field of potential suspects," Gates remarked dryly. "Did you uncover anything else of interest?"

"You already know about the shoeprints in the flowerbed and the mud tracks on the tile entryway," Smith said.

Gates nodded but didn't appear overly enthusiastic about the shoe-print evidence.

"The killer's a big boy, size eighteen shoes. The tread was worn, which is good for comparison purposes. The tread pattern matches a style of Air Jordan's manufactured by Nike in the late 1990s. Nike sold millions of those shoes, but a size eighteen is pretty unusual. Bring me the right pair of size eighteen Nikes, and I'll tell you if they left the tracks in the Jelacos' flowerbed."

"Based on the forensic evidence, our suspect should stick out like a sore thumb. There can't be that many large Native Americans running around Lakeland in size eighteen Nikes," Gates replied sarcastically.

"Smith's description doesn't ring any bells," Sato said with a slight smile. "I'll put some pressure on my snitches and see if anyone can give Smith's Big Foot a name."

Smith ignored Sato's subtle jab and continued his summary, "My team found half a dozen wool fibers we couldn't match to any fabric source in the house. Two of the fibers were removed from Mrs. Jelaco's T-shirt. The fibers were most likely transferred from the killer's jacket when he came in contact with the victim."

"Did the fibers possess any unusual characteristics?" Sato asked.

Smith narrowed his eyes, nodded slowly, and said, "Funny you should ask. We couldn't match the dye to anything in our database, and the weave of the wool fiber is fairly primitive. The dye was either homemade or an uncommon off-brand, and the wool was homespun. If you find the right jacket, I should be able to match the fibers to it, no problem," Smith answered with confidence.

"Remember the good ol' days when police work instead of lab work solved cases?" Gates asked, without expecting an answer from the youthful group seated around the conference table. "Is the hair sample suitable for mitochondrial DNA typing?"

"Possibly, but we don't need to type the hair," Smith coyly replied. "Mrs. Jelaco may have been overpowered by her attacker, but she did get in one good shot before he killed her. We found foreign blood and tissue beneath three fingernails on her right hand. Evidently, she gouged him pretty good."

Smith now had Gates's full attention. "Has the lab typed the blood and tissue samples for a DNA comparison?"

"That's not the way it works, Phil. The samples have been preserved, but the typing process won't take place until we have a viable suspect."

"Why not?" Gates demanded. "There a chance our guy's DNA profile is in the CODIS database."

"I don't need to tell you the state crime lab is backed up," Smith answered with a pained expression on his face. "I contacted the FBI lab at Quantico, but they're several months behind as well."

"Convince the lab to move this case to the top of the list," Gates angrily countered.

"Every case is a priority, and besides, it's a long shot at best. Only a fraction of convicted offenders actually have their DNA profile in the database, because Idaho law only requires a sample for felons convicted of a sex crime. Given the fact our suspect had no sexual interest in Mrs. Jelaco, it's highly unlikely we'd get a match."

Gates shocked everyone in the room by kicking the leg of the table with the sole of his boot.

"That's great, Stan!" he shouted at the crime scene investigator. "Our entire case hinges on laboratory analysis, and the labs are too busy to process the evidence. Put some pressure on the director of the state lab. Tell him Darby Jelaco's blood will be on his hands if he drags his feet. If there's a chance our guy's in the system, we can't overlook it."

Smith had worked with Gates before and knew from experience not to take the detective's outburst personally. "I'll do my best, Phil, but the state lab services the entire state, and everybody's case is a priority."

"Just get it done," Gates said in a softer voice. "I don't care if you have to call the governor himself. We need results, not excuses.

"Detectives Styles and Mitchell, did your canvassing of the Jelacos' neighborhood turn up anything of interest?"

"Nothing earth shaking, but we're trying to chase down a couple of leads," Detective Mitchell answered.

Gates stared at the young detective for a moment, and when no explanation was forthcoming, he said, "Perhaps you could elaborate, if it wouldn't be too much trouble."

Mitchell looked to his partner for help, but Styles was shuffling through his notes trying to avoid eye contact.

When Mitchell realized he was alone on the hot seat, he said, "The night clerk at the Chevron Station on Overland, a college student named Brandi Lohman, remembers a strange lady buying cigarettes and beer three nights in a row around the time of the murder. The lady stuck in her mind because a man waited in an old Lincoln Town Car while the woman was inside the store."

"Lots of guys are lazy," Gates offered as a possible explanation.

"The clerk thought it was odd the man parked his car to the side of the store even though the parking lot was empty. Ms. Lohman got the impression he didn't want her to get a good look at him."

"What color was the car?"

"It was either white or beige. She wasn't sure."

"That's a busy convenience store," Gates noted. "Why did this couple make such an impression?"

"According to Ms. Lohman, she was afraid they might rob the store. The station primarily serves the local neighborhoods; strangers are somewhat of a rarity."

"Did Ms. Lohman get a look at the tags?"

"She didn't get the license number, but she noticed the plates were from Idaho. When I pressed her for specifics, she told me she thought the man was in his midforties and Hispanic."

"What about the lady?"

"Ms. Lohman couldn't identify her from Monroe County booking photos, but she gave us a fairly good description."

"How good?"

Mitchell glanced at his notes for the first time. "She was a white female, between forty and fifty, with shoulder-length bleached-blonde hair. She figured the woman's height at about five feet six inches and her weight at around 105 pounds. I got the feeling from Ms. Lohman the woman looked a little rough around the edges."

"Rough around the edges?"

"Ms. Lohman said it appeared as if the woman had some hard-earned miles on her. When I prodded her to explain, she couldn't point to anything specific except for the fact that the woman looked like a young person in an old person's body."

"I know the look Ms. Lohman is referring to quite well," Gates agreed. "The description fits half the crackheads living on the south side."

"Detective Styles and I staked out Mrs. Jelaco's funeral service and photographed anyone who seemed out of place. Most of the unidentified people have been eliminated as potential suspects, but we are still trying to positively identify a couple. We definitely didn't observe anyone that fits Investigator Smith's description of the suspect. Based on the evidence we have at this point, it's unlikely the killer attended the funeral."

"Don't waste your time with the photos. Unless he's a relative, the killer only shows up at the victim's funeral on TV shows. In the real world, it takes cops longer than sixty minutes to solve a homicide case," Gates commented sarcastically.

Now it was Detective Gates's turn to keep his team optimistic while they worked an investigation that was going nowhere.

"My theory regarding Darby Jelaco's abduction defies conventional wisdom," he began. "I believe she's still alive and her mother's killer is trying to decide what to do with her. If he planned to kill her quickly, he would have done it at the scene. Furthermore, I don't believe this was a random burglary gone awry. The evidence doesn't support such a conclusion. I believe Mrs. Jelaco's killer was seeking a specific item, an item that was virtually worthless to everyone except the killer or a person who hired him. The only things missing from the Jelacos' house are the little girl and a few of Mr. Jelaco's case files."

"Do you think Mrs. Jelaco's killer intended to kidnap the little girl all along?" Sato asked for clarification.

"Absolutely not," Gates immediately answered. "I think our intruder was looking for a specific case file when Mrs. Jelaco interrupted him. The abduction of the little girl was probably an afterthought born of necessity."

"Why would the perpetrator want some lawyer's case files?" a puzzled Stan Smith asked.

"That's the million-dollar question," Gates remarked. "I can't be sure, but I assume the content of the file, or files, implicates the party responsible for Julie Jelaco's murder in some way."

"What do we know about the missing files?" Sato asked.

"Mr. Jelaco represented a junkie named Janis Jones a few months ago. Ms. Jones claimed she possessed information about a high-profile homicide. Before Jelaco could get the pertinent details, Ms. Jones died of an overdose. Her case file was one of the files removed from the Jelaco residence," Gates informed the group. "I did some digging, and it appears the cause of death was determined without the benefit of an autopsy."

"I'm vaguely familiar with the Janis Jones case," Dr. Holt responded, somewhat defensively. "Maybe the coroner's file will refresh my memory."

"Relax, Katie. I'm not pointing an accusatory finger at anybody. I know it's impossible to autopsy every Jane Doe who overdoses in Monroe County, especially when there aren't any suspicious circumstances surrounding the death."

"No offense taken, Phil. I was just thinking out loud," Katie replied in a more relaxed tone of voice.

"Anyway, I'd like to exhume Ms. Jones's body so Dr. Holt can do a complete autopsy, including toxicology," Gates explained.

"Do you remember the date of her death, Phil?" Katie asked.

Detective Gates opened the manila folder he had placed on the table in front of him. "The patrol officer who took the call filed a cursory report; I'll summarize the high points. Ms. Jones's body was discovered in room twenty-one of the High Desert Motel on July 7 of this year by Mark Olson, the manager. Mr. Olson was certain she had been dead for less than twenty-four hours when he discovered her body. Apparently Ms. Jones was a couple weeks' behind on the rent, and she was willing to perform services of a sexual nature in order to square her delinquent account. According to Mr. Olson, she had made a "payment" the day before her death. The officer found a small amount of methamphetamine in the room but nothing significant."

"It's good to know the barter system is still alive and well in Lakeland," Katie replied sarcastically. "An autopsy won't be a problem, but we'll need a court order to exhume the body. I'll talk to Judge Montgomery this afternoon about the order. If there is anything unusual about her death, I'll find it."

"Thanks, Katie. If Ms. Jones's death was not your run-of-the-mill overdose, I'll need to take a closer look at her story about a police cover-up."

"Why don't we ask Mr. Jelaco about the contents of her case file?" Detective Mitchell asked.

"Jeez, Mitchell, I never thought about that," Gates curtly replied, before adding, "Nick Jelaco only met with Ms. Jones one time, and according to Mr. Jelaco, she was paranoid and reluctant to share information without a plea bargain in place. He assumed she was a crackpot, so he didn't press her for details. She turned up dead before a second meeting could be arranged."

"In other words, there's probably nothing in the file that implicates anyone," Detective Mitchell added.

"There was something in Jelaco's files that will lead us to the killer. Otherwise, why would the perpetrator risk a burglary and then cover it up with murder? I know it's a shot in the dark, but we're running out of options. Let's meet Wednesday morning for a status report. Any questions?" Gates asked as he looked around the table.

Each member of the team gave their team leader a solemn shake of the head.

CHAPTER 17

Tuesday morning, October 17

The faint lyrics of a popular rock-n-roll song comingled with an unsettling dream to awaken Nick from a disturbed sleep. The singer's deep voice belted out lyrics about creating his own prison, while Nick simultaneously dreamed that a jury of his peers had found him guilty of his wife's murder. As he awoke, Nick hoped his dream was the result of the song's subliminal message and not an eerie premonition of things to come.

His head was resting on a perfume-scented pillow, and his feet were dangling over the armrest of a couch. Nick had absolutely no idea where he had spent the night, but he was certain he was not lying on the threadbare couch in his motel room at the El Rancho. He had a hazy recollection of pounding double Jack Daniels at the Crazy Horse Saloon and remembered a nonsensical conversation with Simone Panache about her brother's case. After that, the details of the evening were a blank slate. Nick tried to open his eyes, but a throbbing pain at the base of his skull convinced him to temporarily postpone his return to the world of the living.

"How are you feeling?" a cheerful female voice asked. "I thought you were going to sleep the whole day away."

Pain or no pain, Nick's eyes flew open when he heard the strange female voice. He was more than a little surprised to find Simone Panache standing at the foot of the couch in a pair of tight-fitting exercise shorts and a sleeveless shirt. "What have I done?" he groaned into the pillow.

"Relax, Nick. You spent the night on my couch, and that's the extent of it."

"I spent the night here," Nick repeated.

"You weren't exactly the life of the party last night," Simone replied playfully. Her smile was quickly replaced by a frown. "It's kind of insulting you think I'd take advantage of an unconscious man."

Nick wasn't in the mood to play games. "How did I wind up in your apartment? I don't remember leaving the Crazy Horse."

"That's because you were out cold when the bouncers dragged you out the front door."

"I passed out?" Nick asked in disgust. "I'm never taking another drink as long as I live."

"Technically, you didn't pass out, but cutting back on your alcohol consumption is still a good idea," Simone agreed. "I had to use all my female charm to keep you out of jail."

"Keep me out of jail," Nick moaned. "What happened last night?"

"You were the main attraction in an ugly bar room brawl," Simone explained. "You did some pretty serious damage before one of the bouncers cold-cocked you with a beer bottle."

Nick rubbed his head and mumbled, "That explains the knot on the side of my head."

"My brother, Dominic, helped me bring you here. He thinks I'm crazy to get mixed up with you," Simone said matter-of-factly.

"Letting me sleep off a drunk on your couch is not getting mixed up with me," Nick replied over the throbbing in his head. "I appreciate your help, but that's the end of the story."

"I stuck my neck out to help you last night," Simone reminded him. "That should be worth thirty minutes of your precious time."

"I don't remember asking for your help."

"You didn't ask for help, but your behavior didn't leave me many other options."

"I'm a big boy," Nick replied defensively. "I can take care of myself."

Simone raised her eyebrows and said, "Rumor has it the owner of the Crazy Horse is an East Coast mobster with a nasty disposition. He was trying to decide if he should call the cops or let a couple of his goons do a tap dance on your head when I came to your rescue."

"Why would an East Coast mobster listen to you?"

"I convinced him it would be bad for business if the cops started poking around in his affairs."

"How did you manage to do that?"

"I told him you were a high-powered lawyer with connections at City Hall and the prosecutor's office," Simone answered with a coy smile.

Nick slowly swung his feet off the couch, and after a brief pause, he raised himself into a sitting position. His head had nearly exploded when he first lifted it off the pillow, but after several seconds of sitting upright, the pain subsided enough for him to respond to Simone.

"It sounds like you're quite the storyteller," Nick remarked. "Those punks who jumped me last night—I take it they were friends of yours?"

"Not exactly," Simone replied hesitantly.

Nick gently rubbed the bump on the side of his head and asked. "What do you mean by 'not exactly'? If I remember correctly, the one who took a swing at me claimed he was your boyfriend."

Simone wrinkled her nose in disgust. "That was Jake Paulson. In case you've forgotten, he's the one whose nose you splattered all over his face."

"If memory serves, he was charming and quite handsome," Nick deadpanned.

"We dated for about two weeks when I was a senior in high school. I guess he's having a hard time letting go of the past."

"You should take his obsession as a compliment."

Simone ignored his sarcasm and said, "Jake and his friends are into some pretty bad stuff. They'll come looking for you, Nick, so watch your back."

"I appreciate the warning, but I can take care of myself."

"Yeah, I noticed. Where did you learn to fight like that?"

"I was in the army for a few years."

"My brother Dominic was in the army, but he's no match for Jake and his buddies," Simone countered.

Simone wasn't easily discouraged, so Nick gave her a bit of the truth. "I was assigned to a special unit during my stint in the military, and our training focused on basic self-defense skills."

"If the fighting skills you exhibited last night are an indication, the army taught you a few offensive skills as well. Jake and his two buddies had to be taken to the hospital."

Nick didn't want to know the particulars, but he asked Simone to enlighten him just the same. He winced as Simone gave him the gory details of his encounter with Jake Paulson and his friends. After she finished, he felt compelled to explain the source of his pugilistic abilities.

"What you saw was a form of martial arts called kajukenbo."

Simone looked at him quizzically and slowly repeated, "Ka ju ken bo? I've never heard of it."

"Not many people have. It's a martial arts hybrid that merges the disciplines of karate, judo, jujitsu, kenpo, and kung fu. The style of kajukenbo I studied is heavily influenced by kenpo, which is an aggressive form of martial arts, and means 'way of the fist.' After I left the military, I continued to study kajukenbo as a way to stay in shape."

"You're full of surprises, Mr. Jelaco. I figured you for one of those pampered lawyers who wouldn't know a hard day's work if it hit you in the side of the head."

"I may be a lot of things, but pampered certainly isn't one of them."

"Do you want a cup of coffee? I just made a fresh pot."

"That sounds good," Nick admitted. "I'm having a hard time motivating myself this morning."

"That's not surprising," Simone replied with a quick smile. "You drank the Crazy Horse out of whiskey, put three guys in the hospital and then topped the evening off by using your head as a backstop for a beer bottle. You need to take it easy on the booze if we're going to be partners."

Simone left to fetch the coffee, which gave him a chance to take a look at her living quarters for the first time. Her apartment was small and sparsely furnished, but it had a comfortable feel to it. The living room, the room where he had spent the night, was so small it was difficult to determine where it ended and the kitchen began. There was an open door on the wall to his left, which probably led to Simone's bedroom and the bathroom. In many ways, it reminded him of the first apartment he had shared with Julie while they finished college. There were two pictures prominently displayed on a bookshelf next to the television. One picture was of a young girl and two older boys. Nick assumed it was a photo of Simone and her brothers. The picture had obviously been taken before Cole's murder conviction had changed the course of their lives. Cole had his arm wrapped around Simone's shoulders, and her delight was apparent. The other picture was the same young girl and an older woman. The physical similarities between the two women were striking. His heart ached at the thought of Simone's loss, and he made a silent promise that he and Darby would share many father and daughter moments in the years to come. Simone returned to the living room and handed him a coffee mug that had *Justice is Reserved for the Rich* inscribed across the side.

"Thanks, Simone," Nick said as he accepted the hot coffee from her.

"You're welcome."

"Before this goes too far, we need to talk about the partnership you mentioned. Partners are supposed to have the same objectives. You know—common goals and priorities. Your first priority is proving your brother's innocence and getting him released from prison. My only priority is finding my daughter, and if circumstances permit, killing the psychopath who murdered my wife."

Simone did not immediately respond, but after a brief silence she said, "I called the emergency room before Dominic and I brought you here. I was worried about that lump on your head and thought you might need medical attention. The duty nurse told me how to monitor your breathing and sleep patterns throughout the night. Watching you sleep gave me plenty of time to think about things."

The thought of a complete stranger watching him sleep off a drunk was embarrassing. "I'm sorry you had to babysit me, Simone. It doesn't excuse my conduct, but yesterday was a really bad day."

"I wasn't looking for an apology or your gratitude. I just wanted you to know I had plenty of time to think about your situation last night."

"I'm not trying to be rude, but my situation has absolutely nothing to do with you."

Simone stared at him with an unwavering resolve. "I really believe fate brought us together. I've been studying every facet of my brother's case for the last three years. I know every piece of evidence inside and out: police reports, depositions, trial transcripts—the whole works. There has to be a reason our paths crossed. Take a look at his case. If something doesn't pique your interest, I'll never bother you again," Simone promised.

Nick was about to politely excuse himself when he remembered the strange dream he had the night Julie was murdered. In his dream, Julie had begged him to follow his instincts and warned him that assistance could come from an unexpected source. He wanted to trust his instincts, but since his wife's murder, his instincts had been clouded by alcohol and prescription drugs. He didn't know anything about Simone Panache, and he certainly didn't believe fate had brought them together. He did know his search for Darby was stuck on square one and hearing Simone out wouldn't make things worse.

"All right, Ms. Panache, I suppose I owe you that much. I'll listen to what you have to say," Nick reluctantly agreed. "Just for the record, you have an uphill battle ahead of you."

Simone disappeared into her bedroom without saying another word. Nick wondered if she was afraid he might change his mind if she gave him half a chance. She returned carrying a large cardboard box with a bright red apple logo and the words *Washington Apples* stenciled across the side.

"I've got three boxes full of documentation, but most of the really good stuff is in this box," Simone said as she dropped the box on the floor in front of him. Simone wiped some dust off her black exercise shirt and sat down cross-legged on the floor beside the apple box. "There's so much to cover, I don't know where to start," she said excitedly.

Nick had hoped Simone's enthusiasm would rub off on him, but it hadn't. "Let's take things chronologically so I can create a mental timeline. Start with Cole's relationship with the victim, and then we'll move on to the police reports. I'm curious about the probable cause for Cole's arrest and the factual evidence that supported his conviction."

"Cole and Brooke dated on and off for a couple of years, but they weren't going out at the time of her murder," Simone began.

"Were they both high school students?" Nick interrupted.

Simone nodded. "They were both seniors at Lakeland High."

"When did they start dating?"

"The summer after their sophomore year," Simone replied. "According to Cole, Brooke was beautiful but very insecure. She played mind games with him the whole time they were going out."

"What kind of mind games?"

"Brooke used to openly flirt with other guys just to mess with Cole's head. Cole admits he was the jealous type and got into more than one scuffle because of her."

"Was Cole ever physically abusive with Brooke?" Nick asked.

"No ... not really," Simone slowly answered.

"It was a simple yes or no question, Simone."

"Cole told me Brooke had a mean streak. She even came

after him a few times—you know, scratching and slapping at him in anger. He defended himself, but he was never the aggressor." Simone must have picked up on Nick's skepticism, because she immediately followed up her explanation by saying, "I know that sounds like a justification, but Cole insists it's the truth."

"Was there anything unusual about their relationship that might be relevant to the prosecution's case or your brother's defense?"

Simone hesitated while she searched for the right words. After a noticeable pause, she said, "This might sound weird, or paranoid, but here goes. Cole told me that Brooke used sex to manipulate older men, men who could help her in some way."

"You lost me," Nick replied, confused by the accusation. "What exactly are you saying?"

"Cole believes Brooke used her physical appearance and sex to get what she wanted from powerful men—school teachers, cops, employers, you name it. Cole said he dumped her for good about a month before she was murdered because she was so screwed up emotionally."

"If Cole's perception of Brooke was accurate, she was a young woman with a lot of problems. Anyway, it sounds like their relationship had more than its share of problems."

"No doubt about it. Cole readily admits he was far from perfect."

"Do you have the initial police report filed by the responding officers?" Nick asked.

Simone dug into the cardboard box and pulled out a thick manila folder. "This file contains all the police reports," Simone said as she placed the folder on her lap. "The first police report was filed by a patrol officer named Clyde Parks. Coincidently, Officer Parks discovered most of the incriminating evidence and located the only eyewitness, Jefferson Hughes. Cole is certain Clyde Parks was a crooked cop."

"Was? What happened to Officer Parks?"

"Lung cancer killed him a few years back."

"Did Cole and Officer Parks have a history?"

"Cole had a few run-ins with Officer Parks, but no more than any other boy at Lakeland High."

"What kind of run-ins?"

"Officer Parks made it his business to know what the teenage boys were up to," Simone answered. "Cole was ticketed for drinking beer a couple times, and Officer Parks pulled him out of a couple of fights but nothing serious."

"Why would Officer Parks frame your brother?" Nick asked. "I find it hard to believe a career cop would take that kind of risk without a compelling reason."

"Cole's had a lot of time to think about it. He believes Officer Parks was working for the actual killer," Simone explained. "I'm sure Cole's rocky relationship with Brooke made him an easy target."

"Most female murder victims are killed by someone they know quite well," Nick agreed.

Simone nodded her head. "Walter Burton stated over and over again during the trial that Cole's motive for the murder was plain, old-fashioned jealousy. The people of Lakeland are a fairly simple bunch; the old spurned lover motive was a big hit with the jury."

"Do you have a copy of the police report?"

"Of course," Simone replied as she opened the folder and handed him a worn photocopy of the original police report dated February of 1985.

Since Officer Parks was the first officer on the scene, it was his responsibility to describe his actions and what he found at Brooke Schaffer's apartment on the night of the murder. Nick took the police report and started to read Officer Parks's narrative. He didn't get far. The first line of the police report stopped him dead in his tracks. The twenty-year-old report began, *Officer Phil Gates and I were dispatched to apartment B7 of the Vine Street Apartments at approximately 11:40 pm.* It had to be the same Phil Gates who was investigating Julie's murder and Darby's kidnapping. Could Detective Gates be the connection Simone was sure existed, and if so, what was the connection? After composing himself, he continued to read the police report.

Dispatch informed me and Officer Gates an anonymous caller had reported a major disturbance at the Vine Street location. The caller claimed a man and a woman had been engaged in a heated argument inside apartment B7. The fighting and shouting abruptly stopped after a loud scream by the female. A couple of seconds later the front door slammed, and everything was silent inside the apartment.

"I have a couple of questions about the police report," Nick declared. "First, did Brooke Schaffer live alone, and second, did the police ever locate the anonymous caller?"

Simone's enthusiasm reminded him of an overeager student who possessed the correct answer.

"Brooke celebrated her eighteenth birthday in November and immediately moved out of her parents' house. The way Cole remembers things, Brooke wasn't willing to live by her father's rules, so she moved into an apartment by herself. In regard to your second question, the anonymous caller was never identified."

"The caller wasn't a tenant in her building?"

Simone slowly shook her head from side to side. "The police and Cole's investigator both interviewed all of Brooke's neighbors. Each one claimed they didn't hear anything unusual on the night of the murder."

"Who made the phone call?" Nick wondered aloud. In spite of his reluctance to get involved, his instincts as an attorney were starting to kick in. "It's unlikely a passerby would have heard something when Brooke's neighbors did not."

"Cole doesn't believe Brooke was killed in her apartment, and the physical evidence tends to support his theory," Simone insisted.

"If he's right, whoever made that anonymous phone call was lying to police dispatch," Nick said with a little more interest.

"Cole believes the actual killer made the call to help the police establish the time and place of Brooke's murder."

"Back up a little bit. What do you mean, 'the physical evidence supports Cole's theory of the case'?" Nick asked.

"Both medical examiners agreed Brooke's death was caused by blunt force trauma to the head; in fact, that was the only fact they agreed on."

"How did their opinions differ?" Nick prodded.

"The state's medical examiner was an incompetent quack named Dr. Wilkes. He testified Brooke's traumatic brain injury was caused by a moving object striking her on the left side of the head. He thought the murder weapon was a club of some sort—like a baseball bat or tire iron. He hypothesized the force of the blow was strong enough to fracture Brooke's skull and cause instantaneous death. The instantaneous death claim was important because he used it to explain why there was practically no blood at the murder scene."

"Was the medical examiner who testified for the defense a paid expert?" Nick asked.

"I'm not sure," Simone admitted. "Why does it matter?"

"When a defense witness is paid to testify it makes them easier to impeach on cross-examination."

"Cole's lawyer hired Dr. Howard, but the State of Idaho paid his fee," Simone explained.

"Then technically, he was a paid expert for the defense."

"The prosecution's medical examiner was on the Monroe County payroll," Simone countered.

"In theory, he wasn't getting paid specifically for his testimony."

"So the prosecution's medical examiner was more credible because of the way he was paid?"

"It's a glitch in the system," Nick admitted.

"Our justice system has a lot of glitches for supposedly being the best in the world," Simone remarked sarcastically.

"It's far from perfect," Nick agreed. "Do you remember the crux of Dr. Howard's testimony?"

"The problem wasn't the content of the doctor's testimony. It was his address."

"I don't follow."

"Dr. Howard was a board certified medical examiner from California. Mr. Burton emphasized his place of residence non-stop. He made it seem like no respectable medical examiner from

Idaho was willing to stake his reputation on such a preposterous theory. Anyway, the jury seemed to discount Dr. Howard's testimony because he was a hired gun from California."

"How did Dr. Howard explain the cause of Brooke's death?" Nick asked.

"He agreed Brooke's head injury was caused by blunt force trauma, but he disagreed about the source of the trauma. Dr. Howard was certain Brooke's injury wasn't caused by a moving object striking her head."

"What facts led him to that conclusion?"

"He conducted experiments on various animal skulls and found an accelerating object, like a baseball bat, caused more damage than the injuries found on Brooke's skull. Based on her injury, Dr. Howard concluded her head struck a fixed object like the corner of a coffee table or fireplace hearth. In other words, he believed Brooke fell and hit her head on something hard."

"How does Dr. Howard's testimony help Cole?" Nick asked.

"He didn't believe Brooke's skull fracture was serious enough to cause instantaneous death. It was his opinion Brooke was alive for at least thirty minutes after the initial trauma to her brain. The force of the blow left a fairly nasty gash in her scalp, which means there should have been blood all over the place, because head wounds bleed so much."

"How much blood was found at the crime scene?"

"The carpeted floor beneath her head was virtually blood free," Simone replied. "There was a little bit of blood on Brooke's scarf, but not enough to satisfy Dr. Howard. Which, according to him, indicated Brooke was killed somewhere else."

"Expert testimony is typically based on the opinions of the testifying witness—heavy emphasis on the 'opinion' aspect of the testimony," Nick explained. "Expert testimony is not always an infallible science, and the jury is forced to pick a side. Did Dr. Howard have any other evidence to support his opinion?"

"As a matter of fact, he did," Simone answered. "I almost forgot to mention one of the most important pieces of evidence that was not found at the crime scene. And in my nonexpert opinion, Dr. Howard pointed out a major flaw in the prosecution's case."

"What's that?" Nick asked.

"Dr. Howard testified that when an accelerating object strikes a person's head with enough force to kill, the force of the blow usually causes blood to spatter on the surrounding area. There was not one speck of blood anywhere near Brooke's body. Not on the walls, the coffee table, the carpet, or anywhere else in her apartment."

"You seem to know your brother's case inside and out," Nick commented.

Simone nodded her head. "I've read every document that's tangentially connected to Cole's case at least three or four times. Cole also sends me two or three letters every month. Most of his letters discuss his life before the conviction, the police investigation, and his trial. Yeah, I know his case inside and out," Simone replied sadly, her black eyes brimming with tears.

"We kind of got sidetracked; let's get back to the police reports," Nick suggested softly.

Nick picked up the photocopy of Officer Clyde Parks's report and resumed reading.

Officer Gates knocked on the door of apartment B7 several times. We waited for approximately thirty seconds, and when no one responded from inside the apartment, Officer Gates and I announced our presence and entered through the unlocked front door. As soon as we entered the victim's residence, we observed the deceased female lying face up in the main living area of the apartment. Officer Gates did a protective sweep of the residence to make sure the assailant was no longer in the apartment. I confirmed the victim was dead and called dispatch for assistance. I determined from my training and experience the victim had been dead for less than one hour. The victim had one large wound on the right side of her head. The hair on the right side of her head was matted with blood, but no additional injuries were immediately apparent. Officer Gates and I secured the crime scene and did a quick search of the apartment for the murder weapon. No murder weapon was found in or around the victim's residence.

Nick wasn't overly familiar with the nuances of criminal defense work, yet the police report seemed contrived to him.

"I find it interesting Officer Parks estimated the time of death in his police report," he remarked. "The time of death is usually determined by the medical examiner, and it seems beyond the scope of Officer Parks's area of expertise."

"Yeah, I totally agree," Simone replied excitedly. "It's almost like he put his opinion in the police report so the estimated time of death would coincide with the disturbance reported by the anonymous caller."

As much as he hated to admit it, Nick found himself agreeing with Simone. "I get the same feeling," he admitted with less enthusiasm than Simone.

"I have a question that's a little off topic, but it's been bugging me for a while," said Simone.

"What's your question, Simone?"

"Was it illegal for the police to search Brooke's apartment without a search warrant? Not that it matters. They didn't find any incriminating evidence anyway. The cops had already planted most of the incriminating evidence in Cole's car."

"It was a legal search," Nick assured her. "The police didn't need a search warrant for her apartment because Brooke lived alone. When she died, no other person had a constitutionally protected interest in her living quarters. The Fourth Amendment only prohibits searches that violate a living person's expectation of privacy."

"So the police would have needed a search warrant if Cole and Brooke had lived together?" Simone asked with a puzzled look on her face.

"Yeah, that's kind of right," Nick agreed, not wanting to get into a drawn-out discussion about exigent circumstances and emergency searches. "Criminal procedure law can be complicated when discussed in the abstract; just ask most newly hired public defenders. Right now, it's the time of death determination made by Parks that is really bugging me. It seems way too convenient for the cynical lawyer in me."

"I agree with you, but unfortunately Dr. Wilkes's testimony supported Officer Parks's conclusions. The good doctor testified under oath that Brooke was murdered a few minutes before the anonymous caller reported the disturbance. If you believe Dr. Wilkes, Brooke was murdered approximately thirty minutes before the police discovered her body."

"Why was the time of Brooke's death so critical to Cole's defense?" Nick asked.

"Cole had an airtight alibi earlier in the evening," Simone explained.

Nick had a lot of questions about the evidence and hoped that Simone could help connect the dots for him. "What else did the medical experts disagree about?"

"Cole's expert vehemently disagreed with the state's expert in regard to her time of death. He testified the evidence indicated Brooke had been dead for several hours by the time her body was discovered."

"Which would have definitely helped Cole," Nick commented.

"Dr. Wilkes claimed Brooke's body had not been moved postmortem," Simone said with a disgusted shake of her head. "And Dr. Howard testified Brooke's body had undoubtedly been moved after her death."

"Why did Dr. Howard think Brooke's body had been moved?"

"Dr. Howard's conclusions were based on the crime scene photos, the autopsy photos, and the coroner's report. He compared the crime scene photos, which supposedly showed the position of Brooke's body immediately following her death, with the photographs from Brooke's autopsy and the coroner's report. When he analyzed the postmortem lividity patterns evident in the autopsy photos, the blood patterns were inconsistent with the positioning of the body in crime scene photos. Of course the jury ignored this evidence, just as they did the rest of Dr. Howard's testimony."

Nick held up his hands to stop Simone's overly technical explanation. "Whoa, back up, Simone. I'm a lawyer, not a doctor. I've never represented a defendant charged with murder, so these forensic concepts are completely foreign to me."

"Sorry, Nick. I've read the medical reports and trial transcripts so many times they actually make sense to me. "

"No problem. But what is postmortem lividity for us laymen?"

"Lividity is the reddish color on the surface of a body where the blood settles following a person's death."

"So blood moves to the lowest part of a dead person's body?" Nick asked for clarification.

"Exactly," Simone confirmed. "According to Dr. Howard, lividity patterns are irreversible. If a body is moved to another location and repositioned, the pattern of the lividity will reveal it. That's what Dr. Howard claimed happened in this case."

"Be more specific, Simone. What exactly did Dr. Howard claim in regard to the movement of Brooke's body?" Nick asked.

"That Brooke's body had been positioned facedown for a substantial period of time after her death. If you remember the police report, Officer Parks stated the body was face up when he first entered the apartment. Dr. Howard claimed the prosecution's theory of the case was full of holes. Namely that the time of death was incorrect and the body had been moved postmortem."

"In Dr. Howard's opinion, how long had Brooke been dead when the officers discovered her body?"

"That's kind of a hard question to answer," Simone admitted. "Dr. Howard admitted on cross-examination that determining a precise time of death was extremely difficult."

"Why?"

"Dr. Howard did not perform the autopsy or examine Brooke's body. His opinion was based on the report filed by the state's medical examiner, which was lacking in many respects. To make matters worse, Idaho only had one medical examiner in 1985, and he was located in Boise. It took almost two days to transport Brooke's body to Boise for the official autopsy."

"What time did Dr. Howard think Brooke was killed?" Nick asked again.

"Based on the information available, Dr. Howard thought she was murdered earlier in the evening at about six p.m. His opinion was based primarily on body temperature readings taken by the Lakeland coroner and the contents of Brooke's stomach. Dr. Wilkes evaluated the same information and estimated her time of death between ten and eleven p.m.—approximately thirty minutes before Officer Parks found her body. Once again, the jury believed the testimony of Dr. Wilkes."

"Did Cole have a solid alibi if Dr. Howard was correct about the time of death?" Nick asked.

Simone emphatically nodded her head, and replied, "Cole was at work until eight thirty on the night of the murder. He unloaded delivery trucks for Mincy's grocery store, and he never worked alone. If Brooke was murdered before eight thirty, there's no way Cole could have been the killer. His coworkers and his time card provided proof he was at work."

"Okay, Simone, let's see if I've got this straight," Nick said slowly. "Dr. Howard claimed Brooke's death was caused by trauma to the brain, probably the result of a fall, and her body was moved postmortem."

"That's right," Simone agreed. "He also thought Brooke died several hours before her body was discovered by Officer Parks."

"Dr. Howard definitely presented some compelling arguments and poked some holes in the prosecution's case."

"Nick, do you want some more coffee or something to eat before we continue?"

"I'll take some coffee, but food doesn't sound all that appetizing right now," Nick answered with an involuntary grimace.

"Still hung over, huh?" Simone asked with a smirk.

"I'm not hung over," Nick answered defensively. "It's this lump on my head that's making me queasy."

Simone rolled her eyes, picked up his coffee mug, and said, "Sure, whatever you say."

She returned shortly with another steaming cup of coffee and asked, "What do you want to look at next?"

"My main concern is the eyewitness who put Cole at the murder scene and the physical evidence the cops found in his car. All the expert testimony about blunt force trauma and post-mortem lividity is great, but it was the eyewitness and physical evidence that put Cole in prison."

Simone stared at Nick with a steely resolve. "The eyewitness lied, and Cole has no idea how the scarf and necklace ended up in his car."

"Okay, let's assume Cole is telling the truth—"

"He is," Simone interrupted.

"Then the witness lied, and the physical evidence was planted in his car," Nick calmly replied. "Why would the witness lie, and who planted the evidence? The answers to those two questions should lead you directly to the real killer."

"I can't answer those questions yet, but I do know Cole is innocent."

Cole Panache's conviction had piqued his interest, but Nick needed to focus on his own problems. "It's an intriguing case, Simone, but I can't help your brother right now," Nick firmly replied. "I can't afford to let peripheral issues distract me."

"I agree," Simone immediately chimed in. "Your daughter should be your only priority, but I honestly believe we can help each other."

Nick felt sorry for Simone Panache and wished her the best. She was a young woman whose life had been turned upside down by her parents' deaths and brother's conviction, but he wasn't the solution to her problems.

"After I find Darby, I'll take a look at your brother's case," he promised.

The disappointment on Simone's face was evident, but she seemed to understand. She nodded and said, "It wasn't fair of me to dump my problems on you. Cole's case is making me crazy. Dominic told me to let it go before it kills me like it killed our parents."

"Don't give up," Nick urged. "If you believe in Cole's innocence, stay the course. You've got some compelling arguments here."

Simone smiled weakly in response to Nick's encouragement. "I've been preoccupied with this case since I was a little girl.

Then that crazy phone call turned my preoccupation into an obsession."

"What phone call?" Nick asked.

"It turned out to be nothing," Simone replied quietly. "Some lady called about six months ago claiming to have information about the people who framed Cole. Unfortunately she was a nut and never called back."

Nick stopped edging his way toward the door. "What woman?" he asked. "Did she happen to mention her name?"

"She actually called twice," Simone said. "The first time she was scared to death and hung up after a few seconds. The second time she was more talkative, probably because she was stoned out of her mind."

"Think, Simone, this might be important," Nick pressed. "What did she say?"

"She told me she had reliable, firsthand information about Cole's murder conviction," Simone recalled. "She was really messed up, so it was hard to follow her story."

"Try to remember," Nick pleaded.

Simone closed her eyes and tried to remember the specifics of the long-past conversation. "She wanted money in exchange for information about Cole's conviction. She was babbling about someone framing Cole and something about the eyewitness."

Nick could feel his heart pounding. "Did she give you her name?"

"Like I said before, she was hard to understand."

"Her name!" Nick demanded. "What was her name?"

"Something like Jane Jones or Janis Johns," Simone tentatively answered. "I don't know, Nick, it was a long time ago."

Simone's words stunned him into a momentary silence while he processed the possibilities. *Was it possible the strange caller was Janis Jones? The same Janis Jones who died suddenly while he was representing her and whose case file was taken from his house the night Julie was murdered?*

"How about Janis Jones? Is it possible the woman's name was Janis Jones?"

"Yeah, I guess so," Simone replied with a quizzical look on her face. "Why—do you know a Janis Jones?"

"I had a client named Janis Jones. She tried to sell me a similar story, but she was less specific about the details with me."

The excitement in Simone's voice was palpable, "Could it be the same person?"

"The odds are pretty good."

"We need to talk to her as soon as possible," Simone blurted out. "She could be the break we've been looking for."

"Communicating with Ms. Jones could be problematic."

"Why's that?"

"She died from a drug overdose while she was my client."

The excitement seemed to drain out of Simone's entire body. "In other words, Janis Jones is just another dead end."

"Maybe not. Ms. Jones's case file was stolen from my home the night my wife was murdered. The detective investigating the case thinks the intruder may have been looking for her case file."

"How do we verify a dead person's story?"

"Tell me about the eyewitness who put Cole at the murder scene," Nick said as he returned to Simone's couch. "If there's a shred of truth in Janis Jones's story, the eyewitness was lying, and she found out about it somehow."

"The prosecution's star witness was a career criminal named Jefferson Hughes—lots of petty crimes, but nothing that had gotten him any serious prison time," Simone said without referring to any of the documents in her apple box.

"Any violent crimes?"

"Not that I'm aware of. Most of his arrests were for burglaries and drug offenses."

"Did he have any ties to Brooke Schaffer?"

Simone picked up her coffee cup and took a small sip before answering. "There was no evidence Jefferson Hughes and Brooke had ever crossed paths."

"Okay, so he's probably not the killer," Nick commented. "But I'll give you money he knows who is. What exactly did Mr. Hughes say on the witness stand?"

"Should I summarize his testimony, or do you want to look at the trial transcript?"

"Give me a condensed version of his testimony. You probably know it word for word anyway," he joked. "I'll read the trial transcript when I get back to my motel room."

Simone adjusted her position on the carpeted floor and stretched her arms above her head before beginning her synopsis of Jefferson Hughes's testimony.

"Jefferson Hughes came forward three days after Brooke's murder. He supposedly didn't realize the significance of his observations until he read about the murder in the *Lakeland Times*. Mr. Hughes didn't seem like the type of guy who would read anything, let alone a newspaper. Anyway, Jefferson was a snitch for the Lakeland police department, specifically Officer Parks, so he called his old buddy when he realized he had valuable information."

"What did Jefferson Hughes claim he saw that night?"

Simone closed her eyes and exhaled deeply. After a couple of seconds, she opened her eyes and started to speak softly. "He testified he was in the hallway outside Brooke's apartment on the night she was murdered. He wasn't positive about the precise time, but he estimated it was between ten thirty and midnight. Jefferson claimed he heard shouting, some loud banging, and then a female scream. He also claimed he was still in the hallway when Cole burst through her door in a state of panic a few seconds later."

"How did Hughes categorize your brother's appearance as he left the apartment?"

Simone shook her head in disgust. "In my opinion, he described it exactly like the police and prosecutor had coached him. Mr. Hughes made it sound like Cole was fleeing the murder scene after engaging in a deadly tussle with Brooke. He said something like Cole's hair was messed up and his face appeared flushed from physical exertion. He also said Cole was carrying something in his right hand and appeared to be in a hurry. Officer Parks put Cole in a lineup shortly after his arrest, and Hughes identified him."

"Jefferson Hughes was a dream witness for the prosecution."

"It gets worse. Jefferson claimed he followed Cole out of Brooke's apartment building and got a really good look at the getaway car. He accurately described the make, model, and color of Cole's car, and then to top it off, Mr. Hughes even wrote down the license plate number as the car sped off. Pretty convenient for the prosecution, don't you think?"

"Jefferson Hughes may be the best witness in the history of the criminal justice system. Does he still live in Lakeland?"

His simple question seemed to catch Simone off guard, but she quickly regained her composure. "Jefferson Hughes moved to Blaine County immediately following the trial."

Nick assumed there was more to the Jefferson Hughes story than Simone was telling him, but he let it slide for the time being. "I take it Cole was the sole focus of the police's investigation after Jefferson came forward."

"The police were swimming in probable cause after Mr. Hughes's performance. The judge issued an arrest warrant for Cole and a search warrant for his car and my parents' home."

"Did the police find anything in your parent's house?"

Simone shook her head emphatically. "An entire team of Lakeland police officers searched my parents' house on two different occasions. They found some old love letters from Brooke that weren't a problem for the defense and some old hate letters that were. The prosecution claimed the letters were circumstantial evidence of motive and a volatile relationship."

"Old love letters aren't enough for a conviction."

"Like I told you before, the incriminating evidence was found in Cole's car," Simone replied wearily.

"What precisely did the cops find in his car?" Nick asked.

"Officer Parks found a bloody scarf that belonged to Brooke under the driver's seat. DNA testing wasn't available at the time, but the blood on the scarf matched Brooke's blood type. I believe her blood type was fairly rare—something like O negative. In addition to the bloody scarf, good ol' Officer Parks found a charm necklace in the glove compartment. Brooke's best friend,

Sarah Walker, testified Brooke was wearing the necklace on the day she was murdered."

Nick grimaced. "The prosecution wasn't lacking for evidence. Still, Jefferson Hughes's testimony was the most problematic for the defense. Was he a resident of the Vine Street Apartments?"

Simone rolled her eyes in disbelief. "That's the real icing on the proverbial cake. Jefferson Hughes originally claimed he was visiting a friend at Brooke's apartment building, but when the defense pressed him for details, Jefferson admitted he was at the apartment complex to commit a burglary. On redirect, the prosecution used Jefferson's willingness to incriminate himself as proof of his honesty. It was almost laughable how quickly the jurors abandoned their common sense."

"Sometimes juries believe what they want to believe." Nick said.

"Jurors should be given IQ tests before they are allowed to serve on a jury," Simone said sarcastically.

"IQ tests would certainly limit the size of a jury pool," Nick replied with a laugh. "Let me play devil's advocate for a moment. If Brooke was murdered somewhere else, who moved her body to her apartment?"

"That's the crucial question, and it's probably the key to finding the actual killer," Simone answered. "Cole believes Officer Parks was involved somehow. He discovered Brooke's body, Jefferson Hughes was his snitch, and he discovered the evidence in Cole's car. It stands to reason he was mixed up in moving Brooke's body."

"Why would Officer Parks murder Brooke or participate in a cover-up? What's his motive?"

"Cole doesn't think Officer Parks murdered Brooke, but he does believe Officer Parks covered up the murderer's trail and perjured himself at trial."

"If Officer Parks was an accessory after the fact, who was he protecting?"

"There is one important fact I forgot to mention. One of Brooke's neighbors, a real busybody named Renee Moore, reported seeing a police car parked in the alley directly behind

Brooke's apartment on the evening of the murder. The neighbor didn't notice the car number, but she estimated the car was parked there about an hour before her body was discovered."

"Could police dispatch identify the vehicle?"

Simone slowly shook her head. "No police officers admitted to being in the area, and patrol cars weren't equipped with GPS in 1985. Because there was no evidence to support Ms. Moore's statement, the judge would not allow her to testify for the defense. Cole's attorney did get a transcript of police dispatch's communication on the night Brooke was murdered."

"Was there anything of note on the tape?"

"Not really, but something worth mentioning wasn't on the tape," Simone replied.

"Oh yeah?"

"Officer Parks and his partner did not respond to dispatch calls for almost an hour. In 1985, Lakeland police officers did not carry handheld radios. If a police officer was away from his squad car, dispatch could not contact him by radio. The officers' radio silence coincided with the time frame when Ms. Moore claimed she saw a police car behind Brooke's apartment. When pressed for an explanation, both officers insisted they were involved in a foot pursuit of a suspected burglar."

Nick respected Simone's faith in her brother's innocence, but he hoped it wasn't blind faith. "The defense was fighting an uphill battle from the beginning," he explained. "The prosecutor had great evidence: an eyewitness who put Cole at the scene and the incriminating physical evidence found in his car. To be honest with you, I've never litigated a case with such compelling evidence. Maybe that's why I think there's some validity to your notion of a police frame."

"I'm not a lawyer, but the prosecution's case seemed too good to be true," Simone agreed.

"I wonder why the prosecution chose not to seek the death penalty." Nick mused aloud.

Simone shrugged. "According to Cole, that decision was made by Walter Burton. Walter's deputy prosecutor, Jackson St.

James, was pushing hard for the death penalty, but Mr. Burton refused to entertain the idea."

"That's interesting," Nick replied slowly. "A capital murder charge would have forced your brother to think real hard about a plea bargain. It's common practice for a prosecutor to seek the death penalty in first degree murder cases and then offer to drop the death penalty as part of a plea bargain."

"It was all so frustrating," Simone said, tears welling up in her eyes. "My mother gave Cole a rock-solid alibi when she testified, and no one believed her. I thought the prosecution was supposed to prove its case beyond a reasonable doubt. My mother's story was consistent from the start. She claimed Cole was home at the time of the murder, and her story never changed. Mr. Burton tried repeatedly to confuse and manipulate her during his cross-examination, but she was unshakeable. My mother was a very religious woman. There's no way she would commit perjury or lie under oath even to save her son. During closing arguments, Walter Burton told the jury that any loving mother put in her position would lie to protect her child. When it was all said and done, the jury believed Jefferson Hughes's testimony over my mother's."

"That's the problem with alibis provided by family members, especially the defendant's mother. It's easy to convince the jury the witness is lying to protect her child," Nick explained. "Could anyone corroborate your mother's testimony?"

"My father was out of town at the time of the murder; he was a long-haul truck driver."

"Did you or your brother Dominic testify?"

"Cole's attorney decided we were too young to be taken seriously by the jury, and my mother agreed with his decision. He thought the jury would discount our testimony because Cole was our big brother," Simone sadly replied. "I remember the night he was arrested like it was yesterday."

Nick's mind flashed to images of Julie's body, and he said, "I'm sure you do."

"Cole was a great big brother. When the cops handcuffed him and shoved him into the backseat of the police car, it was devastating for all of us."

"How old were you when Cole was arrested?"

"I was six, and Dominic was nine."

After some quick addition, Nick determined Simone's current age to be twenty-six or twenty-seven. Whatever her age, she was far too young to have buried both her parents and lived through the murder conviction of her oldest brother. Nick was still skeptical of a link between Cole's suspicious conviction and the break-in at his house, but Janis Jones's connection to both cases and Simone's dogged persistence had convinced him to follow the evidence trail for a day or two at least.

Nick let out a heavy sigh and ran his fingers through his short black hair. "Okay, Simone, you win," he reluctantly agreed. "We'll work together for the time being. But let me make one thing perfectly clear; I'm calling the shots."

"I wouldn't have it any other way," Simone said with a playful smile.

"Okay, here's the plan. First thing tomorrow morning we head north to Sun Valley for a heart to heart with Mr. Jefferson Hughes."

Simone nodded her approval, but something in her eyes led Nick to believe the prospect of a confrontation with Jefferson Hughes was unsettling to her.

"Before we make this partnership official, it's important we're on the same page," Nick continued. "My search for Darby is all that matters to me. If Mr. Hughes doesn't give me something tangible, ours might be the shortest partnership in history."

"That's good enough for me," Simone immediately accepted. "I'm positive we'll get something from Jefferson Hughes."

"I hope you're right," Nick said with less enthusiasm. "Do you have the trial transcript and the medical examiner's report? I'd like to take a look at them before tomorrow morning."

Simone pulled the apple box toward her and rummaged through it. "The trial transcript is super long, eight bundles of five hundred pages each. The third and fourth bundles contain most of the really important witnesses like the medical examiner, Jefferson Hughes, and Officer Parks."

"Just give me bundles three and four for now. I definitely won't get through the entire trial transcript before tomorrow morning," Nick said as Simone handed him a thousand Xeroxed pages and a red file folder containing the medical examiner's report. "I'll pick you up tomorrow morning at eight o'clock sharp."

"What's your phone number?" Simone asked and then added, "Just in case I need to contact you."

Nick hesitated before giving Simone his cell number. When he realized his reluctance was silly, he gave her the number.

She jotted it down on an old envelope and said, "I'll be ready at eight o'clock sharp."

CHAPTER 18

Tuesday night, October 17

Nick slowly guided the old Mustang through the unusually quiet streets of Lakeland's south side. His head was aching, and his stomach was still doing flip-flops even though a full day had come and gone since he had been carried unconscious from the Crazy Horse Saloon. Nick was a little surprised to find the darkness of another night had descended on Lakeland.

The thought of another night alone in the El Rancho Motel was depressing, but Nick needed some time to process Simone's accusations of perjured testimony and planted evidence, and his dingy motel room would provide the solitude he needed. Unfortunately, the egg-sized lump on the side of his head was making coherent thought difficult. Even with a headache and a hangover, the circumstances surrounding Cole's murder conviction were bugging him. If there was any validity to Simone's theory, Lakeland police officers, and perhaps other city officials, had manufactured evidence and suborned perjury. Two weeks ago Nick would have considered the notion of a police frame complete nonsense. Today, he believed anything was possible.

There weren't any empty parking spaces near his motel room, so Nick parked beside the manager's office and walked the short distance to room twenty-three. The cool October air felt good on his throbbing head after being cooped up inside all day. As he slid his room key into the lock and turned the door handle, Nick got the distinct impression someone was waiting inside his motel room. For whatever reason, the unexpected presence of a visitor didn't concern him, so Nick pushed his way past the partially open door without hesitating.

The smell of fresh cigarette smoke filled his nostrils the instant he entered the room. The small motel room was completely black except for the orange glow of a lit cigarette on the far side of the room.

"I stopped by to give you an update on the investigation and a little friendly advice," the familiar voice of Detective Gates informed him from the darkness.

"This is a no-smoking room, Detective. I'd hate to get thrown out of such a nice place because you can't follow a simple rule."

"You've got bigger problems than getting kicked out of this dump," Gates curtly replied.

"Yeah! Like finding my daughter," Nick agreed in a tone meant to convey his frustration with Gates's investigation.

Gates took another drag off his cigarette and mumbled, "I quit six years ago, and two weeks into this investigation, I'm smoking like a coal furnace."

"My daughter's been missing for thirteen days, so you'll have to forgive me if I don't care one whit about your long-term health concerns," Nick snapped back.

"I warned you about the paralyzing nature of child abduction cases," Gates replied defensively. "There's no playbook to follow when a complete stranger runs off with a kid."

"We're not talking about statistics or probabilities," Nick reminded him. "The missing kid is my three-year-old daughter."

"Law enforcement agencies across the Northwest are throwing everything they've got at this investigation," Gates insisted.

Nick flipped on the light switch and nonchalantly dropped the medical examiner's report and trial transcripts on a small circular table situated just inside the door. Detective Gates squinted and shaded his eyes while his vision slowly adjusted to the light. Nick was shocked by the detective's appearance when he pulled his hand away from his face. Already thin, Gates had lost several pounds since the last time Nick had seen him. His face was gaunt, unshaven, and a sickly shade of gray. Nick recognized the large black circles beneath the detective's eyes as proof that he had not been sleeping much.

Gates nodded toward the trial transcript and asked in a mocking tone, "Did your new friend give you some reading material? I'm surprised you have the time or energy to take on a new client given your family situation."

Ignoring the detective's snide comment was easy. Ignoring the .38 caliber Smith & Wesson on the coffee table in front of Gates was a different story. Nick wondered if Gates was trying to send a subtle message.

"You mentioned something about an update on the investigation," Nick reminded him.

"The crime scene investigator came up with some forensic evidence that's being evaluated by the state crime lab," Gates gruffly replied.

Nick was trying not to read too much into the detective's surly demeanor, but he had a sneaking suspicion the pace of the investigation wasn't the only reason for Gates's foul mood.

"What kind of forensic evidence?" he asked.

Detective Gates leaned back on the couch and assumed a more relaxed posture. "A couple of latent fingerprints were lifted from the crime scene."

"Did you get a match?"

"Not yet," Gates admitted.

"Why not?" Nick pushed. "Fingerprint identification systems are computerized."

Gates shrugged. "It's possible the killer's fingerprints aren't in the system or the prints might belong to your paper boy."

Nick scoffed at Gates's explanation and asked, "Did the crime scene investigator find anything that might actually help the investigation?"

"He discovered foreign blood and tissue under three finger-nails of your wife's right hand. Evidently, she took a chunk out of her killer's face."

The detective's descriptive answer caused a torrent of ugly mental images to fill Nick's mind. The thought of his wife fighting frantically to save her life solidified his wish to see the animal responsible for her death suffer.

He quickly pushed the unpleasant images from his thoughts and asked, "Can the blood and tissue sample be used for a DNA comparison?"

The detective casually picked up his revolver from the coffee table and returned it to his shoulder holster. "I tried to take a little cat nap, and that thing kept poking me in the ribs."

"What about a DNA comparison?" Nick demanded.

"Once we find him, DNA analysis will put the man who murdered your wife on death row, but the sample will sit in a refrigerator until then."

Nick couldn't understand the detective's pessimism regarding the killer's DNA, so he pushed for an explanation. "A few months ago I scanned an article about DNA profiles in a legal journal. If I remember correctly, the article mentioned that all states are currently recording the DNA profiles of convicted felons. Chances are, murder and kidnapping aren't this guy's first felonies, which means his DNA profile could be on file."

"Not exactly," Gates began slowly. "Most states, Idaho included, only require convicted sex offenders to submit DNA samples for recording. Stan Smith, the state's crime scene investigator, doesn't think our guy's DNA will be in the system because he didn't sexually assault your wife."

"It's worth a shot even if the odds are one in a million," Nick angrily replied.

"You won't get an argument from me," Gates agreed. "I'm pushing hard to get the sample processed as soon as possible."

"And when might that be?"

"Crime labs are so backed up, it could take months," Gates said with a grimace.

"Are you kidding me?" Nick shouted at Gates. "Law enforcement has a powerful tool like DNA profiling at its disposal, and it's underutilized."

Gates held up his hands in mock surrender and said, "Don't kill the messenger. You're a lawyer—you know it's unconstitutional for us law enforcement types to violate a criminal's reasonable expectation of privacy."

"Why does our legal system pander to the social deviants?"

"Maybe you should move to England. I hear they're not so hung up on privacy and civil rights over there," Gates sarcastically added.

"When is the law-abiding majority going to regain control of the justice system?" Nick asked in disgust.

"Never," Gates answered matter-of-factly. "Most law-abiding citizens would rather live in constant fear than relinquish any of their precious civil liberties."

"As stupid as that sounds, I know you're right," Nick admitted as he lowered his head in an attempt to hide his tear-filled eyes from the detective. "Did Julie suffer?"

Nick detected a trace of emotion in the hardened detective's voice when he answered, "No, Nick, she died quickly. The medical examiner was certain her death was instantaneous. Evidently the killer was an exceptionally large man and very strong."

"Did he strangle her?" Nick asked.

"The official cause of death is kind of complicated unless you're familiar with medical jargon," Gates answered. "The simplest explanation is heart failure caused by manual strangulation."

"Julie's dead, so it really doesn't matter to me one way or the other," Nick replied. "I just pray her death was painless."

Gates's eyes softened as he responded, "I'll send you a copy of the medical examiner's report."

Nick thought about the detective's offer before politely declining. "Thanks, Detective, but I don't think I'm ready to deal with that reality quite yet."

"Let me know if you change your mind."

Nick nodded. "You mentioned the killer was a big man." Nick could tell Detective Gates was thinking about how much he should disclose about the investigation.

After a brief pause, he said, "That conclusion was based on the forensic evidence found at the scene. The intruder left size eighteen shoeprints in a flowerbed and on the white tile in the entryway. Based upon the depth of the impressions in the flowerbed, the killer probably weighed in excess of three hundred pounds."

"Julie barely weighed a hundred pounds," Nick mumbled to himself.

"That's between you and me," Gates added. "We haven't gone public with that information yet."

Nick nodded again before asking, "Any news about my daughter?"

Nick had phoned Detective Gates at least fifty times in the past two weeks, and each time he had asked for news about his daughter. After every phone call, Gates would promise himself that there would be something positive to report the next time Nick called, but the next call always ended like the calls before it.

"Nothing new," Gates repeated for the fifty-first time. "In my thirty years of police work, I've never seen the streets this quiet."

"I suppose no news is better than bad news," Nick remarked with as much optimism as he could muster.

"Child abductions that aren't resolved within the first forty-eight hours typically don't end well," Gates cautioned.

Nick locked eyes with the detective and asked, "Do you believe my daughter is still alive?"

Gates met Nick's stare and said, "My instincts are telling me your daughter is still alive. We both know my opinion goes against traditional wisdom when it comes to child abductions, but then again, I don't think the guy we're looking for is the ordinary run-of-the-mill child molester."

Detective Gates wasn't the kind of guy who tried to placate his audience, so Nick was somewhat encouraged by the detective's point of view. He nodded and said, "I know Darby is still alive."

"This guy's an odd one," Detective Gates added. "I sure can't figure out what makes him tick."

Nick's initial skepticism about the relevancy of his missing client files had softened after his lengthy conversation with Simone. In fact, he now wanted to know if Gates had uncovered anything of note in regard to the Janis Jones file, but he wasn't willing to disclose the strange phone calls Simone had received about her brother's case.

Nick casually asked, "Have you learned anything new about the client files that were taken from my home?"

Detective Gates narrowed his eyes and stared at Nick for a good ten seconds.

When he finally spoke, Gates said, "I think you know more about the missing case files than you're willing to let on."

"I've racked my brain, but I keep coming up empty."

"I can't do my job if you're not completely honest with me."

"I have no idea who took my client files or why the files were taken," Nick insisted. "That day at my house, you had a particular interest in Janis Jones's case file."

Gates smiled and said, "Her unfortunate death, coupled with the theft of her case file, does pique my interest. Then again, druggies die every day, so it's probably nothing."

"I've thought about her accusations of police misconduct and no high-profile murder trials come to mind," Nick said without emotion. "Which old murder case do you think she was talking about?"

Anger flashed in Gates's eyes, but his voice remained level and composed, "It's hard to say given the sketchy nature of Ms. Jones's story. Are you sure you don't remember the specifics of her conspiracy theory?"

"I'm positive," Nick said, trying to appear frustrated by his inability to remember any details. Detective Gates smiled ever so slightly, and Nick wondered if he had caught on.

"The Monroe County medical examiner has petitioned Judge Montgomery for a court order authorizing the exhumation of Ms. Jones's body," Gates said matter-of-factly.

"Was there something wrong with the first autopsy?" Nick asked.

Detective Gates shook his head. "The circumstances surrounding her death weren't suspicious, so no autopsy was performed."

"That seems odd," Nick remarked, obviously surprised. "A woman is found dead in a motel room, and the medical examiner signs off on her death without an autopsy."

"It's actually fairly common," Gates corrected him. "Dr. Holt assumed that Ms. Jones's long history of drug abuse was the cause of her death, and there was nothing at the scene to indicate otherwise. If Montgomery grants the exhumation order, which he should, Dr. Holt will be able to determine if foul play was a factor in her death."

"How does that help my daughter?" Nick asked, even though he already knew the answer.

"If Janis Jones was murdered, we know someone wanted to shut her up real bad."

"Then the question becomes, who killed her in order to shut her up?" Nick added, acutely aware it was probably the same person who murdered his wife.

"That's true," Gates said with a shrug. "Once I know why she was murdered, I'll figure out who actually killed her."

"Will you figure it out in time to help my daughter?"

"I'll do everything within my power," Gates promised.

"Let me know when Janis Jones's autopsy is completed," Nick said. "I'd certainly like to know what we're up against."

"No problem, but I'd appreciate a little quid pro quo," Gates countered. "If you come across information pertinent to this investigation, I expect you to share it with me."

"That goes without saying," Nick replied in an offended tone, even though he was actually thinking, *If Clyde Parks was dirty, then so are you, and if you're dirty, you'll figure out soon enough the murder case Janis Jones was talking about.*

"I have one final question regarding Janis Jones," Gates continued. "Did you ever discuss her case with the other lawyers in your office? More specifically, did you mention the fact that she claimed she possessed information about a fixed murder case?"

Nick thought for a moment before answering the detective's question. "I'm not positive, but I probably discussed Ms. Jones's representation and her story with all three partners. We used to meet every Monday morning to discuss our workload for the upcoming week."

"So Walter Burton was made aware of Ms. Jones's storytelling abilities?" Detective Gates remarked without expecting an answer. "I find that very interesting."

Detective Gates stood up, indicating his unannounced visit was over. "You also mentioned something about some friendly advice," Nick reminded him.

The detective's relaxed demeanor immediately became more aggressive. "Why are you staying in a dump like this?" he barked. "You're a decorated war hero and a successful lawyer. The people you're associating with are the dregs of society."

The ferocity of Gates's unexpected attack caught Nick off guard, but he managed to hold his ground. "It's none of your business, but I'm not ready to return to the scene of my wife's murder."

"Why the south side?" Gates demanded.

"Money's a little tight right now, and the cheapest rooms are all on the south side," Nick lied.

Gates's face flushed red with anger. "That's a load of crap, and we both know it. You fancy yourself some kind of amateur sleuth, and you're poking around in places you don't belong."

Gates's combative demeanor had Nick's blood boiling. "I don't have any idea what you're talking about," he shouted at the detective.

"Lakeland is my city," Gates bellowed. "I know you're out there conducting some kind of half-baked investigation."

"You weren't getting anywhere, so I took matters into my own hands," Nick shot back.

"I can't do my job if you're muddying up the water."

"I'm sorry if I've bruised your ego, Gates. I just want my daughter back."

Gates's demeanor softened somewhat, and he said in a calmer tone, "Fair enough, Nick. But getting mixed up with Simone Panache is a big mistake. That family of hers is nothing but trouble. Her oldest brother is a convicted murderer, and the other brother, Dominic, is in and out of the county jail more often than the deputies who work there."

Nick felt compelled to offer Gates an explanation of sorts even though he wasn't willing to open up completely. "I'm not mixed up with Simone Panache or anyone else for that matter," he insisted. "She helped me out of a tight spot last night, nothing more."

Detective Gates lowered his eyes and glared at Nick like a disbelieving parent. "It appears as if she's more than a casual acquaintance to me. You spent the night in her apartment."

Nick didn't have a logical explanation for his seemingly inappropriate conduct, so he tried to deflect the detective's accusation with a vague response. "It's a long story," he said with a dismissive shrug. "But you know that appearances can be misleading."

"Don't let Simone Panache take advantage of your situation," Gates cautioned. "She definitely knows how to use her physical attributes and female cunning to get what she wants."

"Gates, get to the point," Nick demanded.

"She's into some bad things, Nick. I've heard drugs, prostitution—nothing good, that's for sure."

Nick had only known Simone for a couple of days; still, the detective's warnings seemed off the mark. He started to tell Gates that he trusted Simone but instead said, "Thanks for the heads-up. You don't need to worry about me, Detective. All my time and energy is reserved for my daughter."

"That's good, Nick, real good. Your first and only priority should be your daughter's safety. Don't go sticking your nose into other people's business. That's how people wind up dead."

After a thirty-minute scalding hot shower, Nick dragged his exhausted body to bed. The past twenty-four hours had been a wild ride, but, in a strange way, hitting bottom had been good for his overall outlook on life. He now realized that hiding behind alcohol wouldn't change Julie's fate, and it certainly wasn't helping his daughter. Detective Gates had been right about one thing: he could not change the past. He could only accept it and move forward. He had decided to attempt sleep without the aid of alcohol or drugs. Much to his surprise, sleep came quickly. It wasn't the fitful, restless sleep that had plagued him since his life had been turned upside down. Instead, it was the deepest and most peaceful sleep he had experienced since his daughter's disappearance. Nick awoke for the first time at around five o'clock. After a quick trip to the bathroom, he returned to the warmth of his bed. His intent had been to lie in bed while he mapped out a plan for the upcoming day, but instead he drifted off.

In the dream, Nick was running blindly through a dense forest. The wind whipping through the trees seemed to be calling out to him in a melodic singsong voice. With each step, the strange voice grew clearer, and it soon became evident that the indistinct sounds were the cries of his little girl. Nick strained to pick up his pace, but there was no path through the dense forest. Branches, leaves, and pine needles slapped his face and arms as he moved toward the sound of his daughter's pleas for help.

Nick's pace had slowed to a maddening crawl, and he was considering a change of direction when he suddenly broke free of the trees. Just like that, he was alone in a circular meadow that was guarded on all sides by one-hundred-foot pine trees. A large ravine cut through the middle of the grass-covered clearing, and the ravine seemed to be pulling him toward it. Near the edge of chasm, it became apparent that Darby's desperate cries for help were drifting out of the gorge. Nick carefully inched his way to the edge of the ravine and gazed into the black nothingness below. Then he saw her, clinging desperately to a jagged rock wall while she struggled to maintain her balance on a small sandy ledge. Chunks of the ledge were breaking loose and falling into the blackness beneath her. The sheer horror of the moment nearly paralyzed him. He knew that within minutes, the ledge would cease to exist and his daughter would plummet into the darkness below. Nick dropped to his stomach and extended a hand into the gorge, but Darby's tiny hand was just beyond his grasp.

Nick scrambled to his knees and was frantically scouring the grassy floor of the meadow for anything long enough to reach his daughter when a familiar voice froze him. It was Julie's voice. Julie motioned to him and then floated to the edge of the precipice while Nick clumsily followed.

As he approached, she extended one of her delicate white hands and softly whispered, "Take my hand."

Nick grasped her hand, which was familiar, soft, and warm but stronger than he remembered. He was certain that Julie's strength could hold him while he pulled their daughter from the chasm.

"Soon we'll be a family again," Nick said in a hopeful tone.

Julie's blue eyes filled with tears as she replied in a scarcely audible voice, "I can stay until you save our daughter." When Nick tried to assure her that they would be together forever, she gently touched her finger to his lips and said, "Fate has taken us down different paths."

Julie tightened her grip on Nick's hand as he reached into the gorge. His outstretched hand inched lower and lower until he felt his daughter's tiny hand. The instant their hands touched, Julie's reassuring voice said, "I can hold you for a minute, Nick, but your strength must save our daughter."

Julie held the weight of his body as he clutched Darby's hand and slowly pulled her from the ravine. When Darby was safe in his arms, he rolled onto the damp green grass of the clearing and pulled her tiny body tight against his chest. When he turned to embrace his wife, she was gone. Nick sprang to his feet and quickly scanned the clearing. He caught a fleeting glimpse of his wife's silhouette just before she disappeared into the dense cover of the forest. He was about to pursue her into the woods when Simone Panache emerged from the same spot where Julie had just vanished. Simone's face was shrouded in profound sadness—the same sadness that caught his attention the night they met.

"She's gone," Simone said matter-of-factly. "She needs you to let go."

"I can't let go," Nick replied as he tried to push past Simone.

"Julie loves you, Nick, but she can't come back again."

"Why not?"

"She made a deal."

"What kind of deal?" Nick demanded.

"She traded her life for Darby's."

Before he could follow her into the trees, Nick awoke in a pool of his own sweat calling out his wife's name. He knew it was just a dream, but he clutched his pillow and sobbed like a baby just the same.

CHAPTER 19

Wednesday morning, October 18

Simone was sitting on the concrete steps outside her apartment when Nick arrived for the trip north. She tentatively waved and began walking slowly toward the sidewalk as he brought the Mustang to a stop beside the curb. The excited energy she had exuded the day before had been replaced by a look of uneasiness. Simone's nervous expression and lethargic movements made him wonder if her night had been as strange and troubling as his.

"Rough night?" Nick asked as she climbed into the passenger seat.

"I've had better," she answered with a forced smile.

"Me too," Nick said without elaborating.

"I'm scared to death," she admitted. "I've hated Jefferson Hughes most of my life, and in a couple of hours, we'll be face to face with him."

"Hopefully he'll be willing to talk to us, but if he perjured himself at Cole's trial, he might tell us to take a hike."

"What if Jefferson won't talk to us?" Simone asked with a panicked look on her face.

"Then I'll beat the truth out of the old man," Nick answered with a straight face.

The panicked look on Simone's face changed to a look of sheer terror, but all she said was, "Nick..."

"I'm kidding," Nick assured her. "If Mr. Hughes isn't the talkative type, we'll get in the car and drive back to Lakeland." Simone looked at Nick as if she was waiting for more, so he added, "We can't force him to talk."

"Leaving empty handed is not an option," Simone insisted.

"Let's cross that bridge when we come to it."

Nick and Simone drove without speaking for several minutes before he broke the silence. "I need to make a quick stop before we head north."

"That's fine. I've been waiting for this moment since I was a little girl, and now I'm in no big hurry to get there," Simone nervously admitted. "In fact, part of me is dreading it."

"Don't worry about the things you can't control," Nick suggested. "Experience has taught me that the apprehension before a dreaded event is usually far worse than what actually occurs."

Simone smiled and said, "I'll try, but I'm a natural worrier."

They drove through the streets of Lakeland talking about the weather, urban decay, and various other topics they had no control over. Noticeably absent from their chitchat was any discussion involving Jefferson Hughes, wrongful convictions, murder, or kidnapping.

Memories of Julie caused a lump to form in his throat when Nick turned the Mustang onto River Crest Drive. Actually every street and building in Lakeland filled his head with memories of Julie, but River Crest Drive was the worst. He had no idea if the memories would ever go away or, more importantly, if he wanted them to. He pulled into the driveway of 434 River Crest Drive for only the second time since his dreamlike return with Detective Gates. His only other visit had been a hasty ten-minute stop to retrieve a change of clean clothes.

"Is this your house?" Simone asked in a quiet almost reverent voice.

Nick heard Simone's question, but it didn't immediately register. His attention was focused on the bright pink curtains that hung in two of the second-story windows. Julie had sewn the bright window coverings for Darby's bedroom about a month before she was killed.

When Simone's question finally registered, Nick said, "Yeah, this used to be my house."

"Are you sure this is a good idea?" Simone asked.

"It's just a house," Nick replied a bit too quickly.

"It's not any old house," Simone reminded him.

"I have to face the truth sooner or later," Nick snapped. "Avoiding the place where my wife was murdered won't bring her back."

It was obvious from the concerned look on Simone's face and the tone of her voice, she didn't agree with his decision to return to the scene of his wife's murder, but she merely said, "I suppose you know what you're doing."

"You can come inside, or you can wait in the car," Nick said. "But there's something I need inside."

"Which would you prefer?" she asked tentatively.

"It doesn't matter to me one way or the other."

Simone unfastened her seatbelt and opened the passenger door. "Let's get moving. We're not going to find your daughter sitting in the driveway."

Yellow police tape still surrounded the entire yard, and several strips were draped across the front door. Nick assumed his neighbors were not thrilled by the constant reminder of the violence that had occurred in their neighborhood. He didn't care what his old neighbors thought; still, he made a mental note to clean up the mess when he returned from Sun Valley.

Simone was nervously pacing back and forth on the sidewalk when he caught up to her. An uncomfortable silence hung in the air as they walked to the front door together.

"Do you have your house key?"

"You sound like my mother," Nick said as he pulled the key from his pants' pocket.

"Sorry, I'm really nervous," Simone offered as explanation. "I talk too much when I get nervous."

The muddy footprints of Julie's killer greeted them when they entered the house. Time and foot traffic had faded the tracks somewhat, but the faint outline of the large shoeprints was still visible. The house was cold, quiet, and gloomy. Nick was certain the warm cozy feeling the home had exuded before the tragedy was gone forever.

"If you're thirsty, there should be some water or soda in the refrigerator."

Simone glanced nervously around the living room. "I'm fine," Simone answered quietly, before adding, "I probably should have waited in the car."

"This will only take a minute," Nick said before bounding up the staircase.

The police officers investigating Julie's murder and Darby's abduction had never asked if he kept a handgun in the house. It seemed like a fairly substantial oversight but understandable given the fact that Julie's murder had not involved a weapon. Had the police asked, he would have disclosed the weapon-safe hidden beneath the carpet in the walk-in closet. Given his recent concerns about the honesty of certain police officers, he was relieved his small weapons stash had gone undetected.

Julie wasn't a big fan of guns, yet she had reluctantly permitted him to keep two handguns in the house. In an effort to ease her fears, he had asked the contractor to install an eighteen-by-eighteen-inch gun safe in the floor of his closet. The carpet that covered the small vault was tucked under the molding, but it was not stapled to the floorboards. Nick dropped to his knees and gently tugged on the carpet in the back corner. The combination was easy for him to remember. It was the date of their wedding anniversary; and now, it was also the date his wife was murdered.

The vault contained two handguns, a .40 caliber Glock semi-automatic and a .45-caliber Smith and Wesson. Nick removed the Glock and its fully loaded magazine from the safe and quickly inspected the weapon. Satisfied everything was in order, he jammed the eleven-round magazine into the handgun's grip but did not chamber a round. Before leaving the closet, he locked the safe and returned the padding and carpet to their original positions.

Simone was in the living room thoughtfully gazing at family pictures when he returned to the ground floor.

"Your wife was a beautiful woman, and your daughter is an absolute doll," Simone said, without taking her eyes off the pictures.

"Yeah, I was the luckiest man in the world until about two weeks ago."

Simone's olive-colored complexion paled a shade or two when she noticed the Glock protruding from his right hand. "What's that?" she asked with a nervous nod in the direction of the handgun.

"It's nothing that concerns you," Nick replied forcefully.

The panicked look on Simone's face intensified. "Nick, it's a gun. Don't you think a gun is a bit excessive?"

"My wife was murdered, my daughter is missing, and if your theory is correct, your brother was framed for murder by police officers. So to answer your question, no, I don't think a handgun is excessive given the circumstances," Nick said with a little too much aggression.

His combative demeanor momentarily shocked Simone into silence. He wanted to apologize but instead said, "If you're not comfortable with the way I'm handling things, I'll take you back to your apartment right now."

"I trust you, Nick," she replied meekly. "It's just kind of shocking to see you carrying that gun."

Nick wasn't sure why he had been angry with Simone all morning. Perhaps he subconsciously blamed her for his unsettling dream. Whatever the reason, the defeated look on Simone's face caused his tone to soften. "I'm sorry. There's no reason to go looking for trouble; I'll lock the gun in the trunk," Nick offered in a conciliatory tone.

Nick wrapped the handgun in an old towel and stowed it in the trunk of the Mustang. With the gun out of sight, they climbed into the passenger compartment of the vehicle. Simone appeared upset by the possibility of trouble, so Nick downplayed his decision to bring a handgun.

"I'm sure we won't need a weapon, but being in the military taught me to be prepared for any contingency."

It was evident from Simone's reaction that the prospect of a gun battle wasn't something she had even remotely considered. "Can we leave it in the car when we get to Jefferson's place?" she asked hopefully.

"Relax, Simone, I don't plan on rushing Jefferson's place with guns a blazing."

Simone smiled slightly and said, "That's real comforting, Nick."

"Do you know how to get to Jefferson Hughes's place?" Nick asked after she had fastened her seatbelt.

Simone nodded. "I got the address from the Blaine County Courthouse when I first started researching Cole's case. Jefferson lives on a secluded piece of property about five miles north of Ketchum."

"Have you been there before?"

Simone looked out the side window and didn't immediately respond to his question.

"Have you been to Jefferson's place?" Nick asked again.

Simone turned to look directly at him before answering. "I was there once, a couple of years ago."

"Why?"

"I was really confused," Simone said softly. "My parents were dead, Cole was in prison, Dominic was in the County Jail, and for some reason I blamed Jefferson Hughes for all my family's problems."

Nick shifted the Mustang into park and took his foot off the brake. "What did you do?" he demanded.

"You'll think I'm completely insane, but here's the ugly truth," Simone almost whispered. "I got Jefferson Hughes's address from the Blaine County Courthouse. I drove by his place a couple of times, but I never worked up the courage to actually confront him. After several months of planning and then chickening out, I finally did it."

"Did what?"

"Dominic and I were sharing an apartment at the time, but he was in jail for drunk driving. He kept a handgun in a shoebox beneath his bed, and in a very confused moment, I took Dominic's gun and drove to Sun Valley."

Nick couldn't believe what he was hearing. "How far did you go, Simone?"

Simone pulled some wadded up Kleenex from her coat pocket and wiped her eyes. "Way too far. I was actually face to face with Jefferson Hughes on the front porch of his cabin."

"What do you mean by 'face to face'?"

Simone exhaled deeply, brushed a loose strand of hair from her eyes, and then continued her confession. "I parked my car on a gravel road about a quarter of a mile from his cabin. My harebrained plan was to pose as a helpless woman in need of assistance in order to get close to him. I walked down the dirt road that led to his place, knocked on his front door, fully intending to shoot him dead if the opportunity presented itself. The man who opened the door wasn't the demon I expected him to be. Mr. Hughes was a small, sickly man, old enough to be my grandfather."

"You obviously didn't shoot him," Nick interrupted.

"Nope, I sure didn't," Simone replied with a sheepish grimace. "I lied to him about my car breaking down and then asked if I could use his telephone. Mr. Hughes apologized profusely, because his telephone had been disconnected. He told me times were hard and he couldn't afford to pay the bill. He politely directed me to his neighbor's house and apologized again. I thanked him, turned around, and then ran away from his cabin crying like a baby."

"At least your visit to Jefferson Hughes's cabin accomplished one thing," Nick said trying to suppress a smile.

Simone seemed confused by his reaction. "Oh yeah, what's that?"

Nick shifted the car into drive and pulled away from the curb. "Now we don't need to stop at a gas station for directions."

North of Shoshone, the farmland gave way to an odd mixture of desert, sagebrush-covered hills, and odd-shaped lava flows. The harshness of the landscape made Nick wonder if the early settlers had ever second-guessed their decision to move west when they discovered the strange and seemingly uninhabitable land. Nick really tried to lose himself in the scenery as they drove in silence, but his thoughts always returned to Detective Gates's remarks about Simone's personal life. After thirty miles of questioning the accuracy of Gates's information, he decided to ask Simone about the detective's less-than-flattering comments.

"A cop was waiting in my room when I got back to the El Rancho last night," he casually mentioned.

"He was waiting inside your room?"

"Yep, he just let himself in."

"That seems odd. Did he have information about your daughter?"

Nick tried to think of the least offensive way to phrase what he was about to say. "Not exactly..." he answered slowly. "He did update me on the investigation, but he also warned me to stay away from you."

Simone was visibly upset by the direction their conversation had taken. "What did he say about me?"

"He informed me that you and your brothers were nothing but trouble," Nick answered in a nonaccusatory tone. "He made some other unflattering accusations as well."

"What kind of accusations?" Simone demanded.

Nick silently chastised himself for opening his big mouth, before answering, "He said you support yourself by selling things."

"Your cop friend obviously didn't tell you I was selling Girl Scout cookies door to door," Simone snapped.

Nick shook his head.

"Do I have to guess?" Simone asked with a noticeable edge to her voice.

"Gates said you were mixed up in drug trafficking and perhaps even prostitution," he replied weakly.

The concern on Simone's face was replaced by a look of disappointment. "My personal life has been the subject of whispered rumors and hurtful lies for as long as I can remember."

"You certainly don't owe me an explanation," Nick assured her.

"I don't have an explanation, except to say that people assume the worst because Cole's in prison and Dominic's a screwup."

"For whatever it's worth, Gates's accusations didn't ring true."

Simone smiled and said, "I'm guilty of spinning my wheels, but I'm definitely not a criminal."

"Spinning your wheels?" Nick asked.

"I pictured myself in a different place at twenty-six," Simone explained. "But it's hard to move forward when you're stuck in the past."

"You're not over the hill." Nick laughed. "You've still got a few good years ahead of you."

"Who knows? I might go back to college," Simone answered with a shrug. "Believe it or not, I was a pretty good student in high school."

"What would you study?"

"I've considered social work as a stepping stone to law school."

"Oh no …" Nick groaned. "Not another woman who wants to save the world."

"I know the world is beyond saving, but people who care can make a difference," Simone said with conviction.

"I would have agreed with you ten years ago."

"So now that you're old and cynical, you've basically given up on mankind?" Simone joked.

"Yeah, something like that," Nick agreed.

"Who knows, maybe your faith in mankind will be restored when you least expect it."

"I'm not holding my breath," Nick said in a more serious voice.

The Wood River Valley is a narrow strip of land bordered to the east and west by the Sawtooth Mountains. The limited availability of usable land in the valley had driven the cost of real estate to unbelievable heights. Actors, entertainers, and corporate bigwigs were buying million-dollar homes and then leveling the structure for the property beneath them. This practice had led to the term "scrapers" being coined in the area, which referred to the practice of purchasing a home with the intent of scraping it off the land. Once the house was scraped from the land, it wasn't uncommon for a twenty million-dollar mansion to spring up in its place.

The influx of wealth into the area had not been without a price. The astronomically high cost of living had forced some long-term residents to sell their properties and move out of the valley. In addition, the survival of many locally owned businesses was constantly in doubt. Their very existence was contingent upon snowfall and a good ski year. The business prospects for the upcoming tourism season looked good. It was only the middle of October, and the mountains on either side of the valley were already covered in snow.

As they continued north on Highway 75, the more-rounded and sparsely wooded slopes of the Sawtooth Mountains turned into the high jagged, pine covered peaks that made Sun Valley a world-famous ski resort. Conversation had been on hold while Nick and Simone admired the majestic scenery, but after an extended silence, Nick spoke.

"Tell me about your brother, Dominic. You said he's been in jail a couple of times?"

"Dominic's a smart guy, but he's mad at the world."

"What do you mean by 'mad at the world'?" Nick asked.

Simone thought about her response for a moment before answering. "Dominic believes the entire world is conspiring to keep him down. Every time things don't go his way, he has some lame excuse for his failure."

"Give me an example," Nick coaxed.

"This is just one of many," Simone said. "Dominic applied for a job at a truck stop last week, and a black man ended up getting the job. Dominic blamed affirmative action for the snub. It never occurred to him that he didn't get the job because he's messed up so many times."

"So Dominic needs to get his act together?"

Simone raised her eyebrows and said, "That's an understatement. Dominic has made one mistake after another since he dropped out of high school in the tenth grade. He drinks too much, and partying is always his first priority. When an ex-employer doesn't give him a good recommendation, he blames it on reverse discrimination. According to Dominic, he didn't get the job at the truck stop because his skin wasn't dark enough. If the company would have hired a woman or a Baptist, he would have claimed sexual or religious discrimination. Never mind the fact that he's been fired from his last five jobs for showing up to work drunk or not showing up at all."

Nick found Simone's maturity and realistic outlook on life surprising. "I know exactly what you mean. In fact, Dominic sounds just like my younger brother, Luke."

Simone clinched her fists and scrunched up her face. "Then you know how frustrating it can be when someone you love is a total screwup," she said. "Dominic has a ton of ability, but he'll end up a broken-down drunk unless he figures it out."

"It's the same with my brother," Nick agreed. "I used to pressure him to make something out of his life, but now I just stay out of his way. Hopefully both of our brothers will get it together before it's too late."

"I'm not holding my breath," Simone joked.

"Me either."

About a mile north of the Ketchum city limits, Nick said, "I'm going need directions to Jefferson's cabin."

Simone flinched at the mention of Jefferson's name and quietly replied, "Keep heading north for another four or five miles.

When you see a brown sign that says Foxtail Creek Road, take a left."

"How far once we turn off the main road?"

"It's another three or four miles to his place down the gravel road."

"Ol' Jefferson lives out in the sticks, huh?" Nick remarked. "Evidently he's not the type of guy who likes visitors dropping in unannounced."

The gravel road quickly turned into a tree-lined dirt road that obviously wasn't maintained by the Blaine County Highway District. Deep tire ruts made progress difficult, especially in the low-riding sports car.

After bumping and skidding for ten minutes, Simone said, "His cabin is on the other side of that dried up creek bed."

Nick pulled the mud-covered Mustang off the dirt road and parked beside the creek.

"Remind me to borrow an SUV if we come up here again," he said in an attempt to lighten the mood, but Simone didn't hear a word he said. She was staring blankly into the trees on the far side of the creek.

"Maybe coming here was a mistake," she mumbled. "We don't even know if Jefferson lives in the same place."

"There's only one way to find out," Nick confidently replied as he opened the driver's door. Simone was still staring blankly at the trees and hadn't budged an inch. "It's fine with me if you want to wait here," he added softly.

Simone unbuckled her seatbelt and picked up her purse. "This wild goose chase was my idea," she reminded him. "I'm certainly not going to bail out on you now."

Simone was so unhinged by the prospect of confronting Jefferson Hughes that she had forgotten all about the .40 caliber Glock in the trunk. Nick briefly considered retrieving the handgun, but his better judgment convinced him that a weapon wouldn't be needed. After Simone joined him beside the creek bed, they silently began the hike to Jefferson Hughes's remote cabin. They had been tripping and stumbling through the underbrush for a couple hundred yards when Simone grabbed Nick's arm and whispered, "There it is."

CHAPTER 20

Wednesday morning, October 18

A small, fragile-appearing man stepped on the front porch as Nick and Simone approached the cabin.

"That's him," she said in a barely audible voice. Nick had constructed a mental picture of Jefferson Hughes, and the old man on the porch did not match the image in his head. Jefferson was a small man dressed in baggy denim overalls and a long-sleeved plaid shirt. His long gray hair was braided in a single braid that hung nearly to his waist. The old man was an unimposing figure, except for the double barrel shotgun he clutched firmly in both hands.

"What can I do for you folks?" he called from the porch.

Nick placed his hand on Simone's forearm, indicating that he wanted to do the talking. "We'd like to ask you a couple of questions, if you don't mind," Nick casually replied.

"What kind of questions?" Jefferson shot back. "I don't know nothing about the stock market or anything else for that matter."

Nick decided the direct approach was the best course of action. "We'd like to talk to you about Cole Panache's murder trial."

Jefferson relaxed his death grip on the shotgun. "Oh that,"

he calmly replied. "I figured someone would show up sooner or later asking questions about that trial." Jefferson invited them into his cabin with a wave of his hand and said, "Come on inside. My place ain't much, but it's warm inside."

"Thanks, Mr. Hughes. We won't take much of your time," Nick promised.

"Take all the time you need. I sure don't have any pressing social engagements this morning," Jefferson said with a chuckle.

When they were beside Jefferson on the porch, he said, "Sorry about the shotgun. I've been a little on edge."

"No problem," Nick replied. "We're the ones who barged onto your property without an invitation."

Jefferson extended a hand. "I'm at a disadvantage. You seem to know me, but I don't know you."

"I'm Nick Jelaco, and this is my friend Simone," he said, intentionally leaving out Simone's last name.

"Come on inside, and let's hear what the two of you got to say," Jefferson said without a trace of apprehension in his voice. Nick and Simone followed the old man into his squalid living quarters. "I know it ain't much, but it's been my home for the past twenty years."

Simone took a quick look around the cabin, "It's a nice place, real peaceful."

Jefferson let out a soft chuckle, "You're a sweet kid but a lousy liar. I know this place is a dump."

Jefferson pointed at a small circular table beside the refrigerator. "We can talk right there," he offered. Nick and Simone took a seat at the table while Jefferson retrieved a filthy mug from the kitchen counter. Before he joined them, he asked, "Would either of you care for something to drink before we get down to business? I might have a soda or some grape juice in the refrigerator."

"No thank you," Nick and Simone answered in unison.

"Sorry about the limited menu," Jefferson apologized. "I don't get to town much these days. It's a seven mile walk one way unless someone offers to drive me, and to be honest with you, it's been a while since I had company."

"We're fine," Nick assured him.

Jefferson took a seat at the table and promptly said, "You mentioned that you had some questions."

Simone stared at Nick with panic-stricken eyes. Nick gave her a reassuring look before turning his attention to Jefferson Hughes.

"That's right. We'd like to ask you about your testimony at Cole Panache's murder trial."

"Ask away," Jefferson replied, seemingly unconcerned about the prospect of discussing his testimony.

Nick didn't want to get thrown out of Jefferson's cabin after his first question, so he started with a softball: "Are you positive it was Cole Panache you saw leaving the murder scene?"

Jefferson took a big swallow from the grimy mug he'd been holding. If the pinched look on his face was any indication, whatever he was drinking had some kick to it.

Placing the mug on the table, Jefferson casually replied, "I'm positive all right—positive I didn't see no one leaving the murder scene. Truth be told, I wasn't nowhere near those apartments on the night of the murder or any other night."

Nick could have been knocked over with a feather. "What?" he stammered.

Jefferson was obviously enjoying the moment. "I wasn't even in Lakeland that night," he continued. "I was down in Twin Falls burglarizing a sporting goods store."

Simone let out a small gasp.

"Why did you testify that you saw Cole leaving the victim's apartment on the night of the murder?" Nick asked, still stunned by the old man's admission.

"Now that's one hard question to answer," Jefferson acknowledged. "I've been asking myself the very same question for the past twenty years. Never did come up with a good answer, except maybe greed or stupidity."

"Greed?" Nick repeated. "I don't understand."

"Clyde Parks kicked in my door one night and made me an offer I couldn't refuse," Jefferson replied, clearly amused by his *Godfather* reference.

"What kind of offer?"

"Ol' Clyde offered to pay me $50,000 in exchange for my testimony," Jefferson explained matter-of-factly.

"You committed perjury for $50,000?"

The old man gave Nick a look that seemed to say, "Try to keep up boy. It's not that complicated."

"That's exactly what I'm saying," Jefferson replied a bit more forcefully. "Clyde told me what to say and how to say it. He even made me rehearse my story before he would give me a little front money."

"That's absolutely incredible..." Nick said in amazement.

"Can we take a little break?" Jefferson asked. "I'm not feeling my best."

"I think we could all use a break," Nick agreed as he glanced at Simone. If her wide eyes and open mouth were any indication, she was even more shocked than he was.

Jefferson pulled a hand-rolled cigarette from the breast pocket of his bib overalls and stuck it between his lips. After leaning back in his chair, he removed a disposable lighter from same pocket and lit the cigarette. The tip of the cigarette glowed red as the old man inhaled deeply. Nick had been to enough fraternity parties to recognize the distinct smell of marijuana.

After expelling a cloud of smoke, Jefferson asked, "Would you mind throwing a log on the fire? I can't afford to fill the propane tank, so I don't run the furnace much." Nick did as the old man had asked and returned to his seat.

Jefferson nodded his thanks to Nick and took another drag of his joint. "I don't even get high off this crap anymore," Jefferson sadly explained. "But pot does help me tolerate the pain, and it keeps me from puking most days. I grow a handful of plants down by the creek strictly for medicinal purposes. The creek's not on my property, so the cops can't prove the plants belong to me unless they catch me during harvest."

"Are you sick, Mr. Hughes?" Simone politely inquired.

"Honey, I've been sick for as long as I can remember," Jefferson answered as he snuffed out the marijuana cigarette and returned it to his pocket.

"Have you seen a doctor?"

"I've seen a doctor, and he's seen me," Jefferson responded in flat tone. "I got what the medical types call an aggressive cancer all through my body."

"Modern medicine has progressed to the point where most cancers can be treated," Simone suggested.

"That dumb doctor down in Ketchum gave me two choices, and neither of 'em was worth a darn in my opinion." When Simone didn't comment, Jefferson continued, "That worthless quack told me the cancer will kill me in less than a year if I don't take no treatment. My other option is to undergo chemotherapy and radiation treatment, which would make me sicker than the cancer—and most likely I'd still die within a year or two," Jefferson added with a bemused shake of his head. "I told that lame excuse for a doctor to stick his chemotherapy where the sun don't shine."

"I'm sorry," Simone said.

"I done so many bad things, I don't deserve no sympathy from a nice girl like you," Jefferson assured her. Then the old man took another swig from his mug and said, "Okay, I'm ready for more questions."

Jefferson seemed more upbeat after his short smoke break, so Nick decided to introduce Simone properly. "Mr. Hughes, this is Simone Panache. You testified in her brother's murder trial."

"I know who she is," Jefferson shot back. "I may be old and sick, but I'm not a fool."

Simone was visibly shaken by Jefferson's acknowledgement. "How did you know, Mr. Hughes?" she asked meekly.

"I thought you looked kinda familiar when you stopped by my place a while back. It took me a day or two to figure it out, but it finally came to me. You got a definite resemblance to your older brother."

"I do?" Simone mumbled.

"You're both real good-looking kids. Especially you ..." Jefferson said with a wry smile.

"So you knew I was Cole's sister when you invited us into your home?"

"Sure," Jefferson said with a shrug. "I figured if you was out to get me, I probably had it coming and then some."

"We don't want to hurt you, Mr. Hughes. We just want to hear the truth," Simone said softly.

"Call me Jefferson," the old man said in an obviously flirtatious manner.

"Okay, Jefferson."

"Today is your lucky day, little lady, because the truth is the one thing I can give you."

"What really happened that night?" Simone pleaded.

Jefferson focused his gaze on the mug in front of him and began speaking in a low, almost monotone, voice. "It all started when Clyde and his cocky little partner convinced me that your brother had murdered his girlfriend in a jealous rage. Those two cops claimed he was guilty, but they needed my testimony to make the charges stick." Jefferson looked up from his mug and spoke directly to Simone. "I ain't gonna lie to you, honey; I was pretty easy to convince. I wanted the money Clyde was offering in the worst way."

"So it was Clyde Parks who solicited your testimony?" Nick asked.

"That's right. He told me what to say, and I repeated it for the jury just like he told me," Jefferson admitted with a sad shake of his head. "I knew he was playin' me, but I went ahead and ruined your brother's life for the money."

"Why did Officer Parks seek you out?"

"Clyde knew I'd sell my soul to the devil for a couple of bucks. I was hooked on hard drugs back then, and he used my weakness against me. Turns out I didn't need no rehab to get clean, just a change of scenery. I've pretty much stayed off the hard stuff since I moved up here," Jefferson boasted.

"Do you know why a veteran police officer would risk life in prison for this particular case?" Nick asked. "Is it possible he murdered Brooke Schaffer?"

The look on Jefferson's face made it abundantly clear that the old man thought Nick's question had missed the mark. "Absolutely not! Clyde Parks wasn't the brains behind the cover-up,"

Jefferson snapped. "That idiot never had an original thought in his life."

"How can you be sure?" Nick pressed.

"Clyde couldn't throw together $50,000 if he'd just won the lottery. He was definitely the front man for someone else."

"If that's the case, who put up the cash?"

"I don't know, but it was that strutting rooster of a cop, Gates, who delivered the bribe," Jefferson shot back, his contempt obvious.

The reference to Detective Gates sent a chill down Nick's spine. "You've got to have some idea who Clyde Parks was working for?"

Jefferson sadly shook his head from side to side. "I honestly don't know who killed that young woman. I sold what was left of my self-respect and then bought my own prison cell with the blood money," Jefferson said. "I can tell you straight up, I'm still alive because I don't know who killed that young woman."

Nick believed Jefferson's story. Still he decided to push the old man just a little. He shook his head skeptically and said, "You know more than you're letting on."

Jefferson stared directly at Nick, and his eyes didn't waiver one iota during his answer. "Rest assured, I'd give you the maniac's name in a heartbeat."

"Convince me," Nick pushed.

"You seem like a good guy. Still, you've got the look of a man who is out for blood," Jefferson correctly surmised. "I want that animal to pay for murdering my kin, and I believe you'd get the job done."

"You were related to Brooke Schaffer?" Nick asked, confused.

Jefferson rolled his eyes. "I didn't even know Brooke Schaffer, but I'm certain the same guy killed my sister's little girl."

Jefferson's latest revelation made no sense, and Nick wondered if the marijuana had jumbled the old man's thoughts. "Your niece was murdered, Mr. Hughes?"

Jefferson took another swig from his grimy mug before answering. "I don't have no direct proof," he admitted. "I only have what lawyers call circumstantial evidence."

"I don't understand. Who died?" Nick asked.

Jefferson picked up his dirty mug, but he didn't take a drink this time. "I kept my mouth shut about that murder for twenty years. I broke my silence six months ago, and now my niece is dead."

Nick ran his fingers through his black hair and said, "Maybe you should start from the beginning."

Jefferson was clearly frustrated by Nick's inability to understand. "My sister's little girl came to visit me a while back, and the two of us started drinking. After we got drunk, she told me she was looking at some serious prison time for a felony drug possession charge. I wanted to be a big man, so I told her about the police framing Cole Panache."

"How could Cole's conviction help your niece?"

"It was a dumb idea, but I thought she might be able to use the information to cut a deal with the Monroe County prosecutor," Jefferson answered with an embarrassed shake of his head. "Anyway, a couple months later, she turns up dead. I'll tell you right now, it wasn't no accidental overdose, because she never used a needle in her whole life. She was scared to death of needles ever since she was a little girl."

Nick felt sick to his stomach, but he asked the question just the same. "What was your niece's name?"

"Janis," Jefferson sadly replied. "Janis Ann Jones."

"Janis Jones was your niece?" Nick asked, his shock apparent.

Jefferson nodded his head. "She was good people. Janis and her mother was my only blood relations that hadn't written me off." Jefferson wiped his eyes with his sleeve. "I killed her by opening my big mouth."

Nick was stunned. Just like that, they had a motive for the break-in at his home as well as information that could get Simone's brother out of prison. Now Nick needed to figure out how he could use the information to find his daughter.

"Why come clean after so many years?" he asked.

"I'm going to die, son," Jefferson answered matter-of-factly. "No way I get into heaven unless I set the record straight with God. Besides, someone has to pay for ruining so many lives."

Even though he'd done some terrible things, there was something about the old man that Nick found likable. In a strange way, Jefferson was a victim just like the rest of them.

"Mr. Hughes, I knew your niece. In fact, I was assigned to represent Janis in her drug possession case."

"You was Janis's lawyer?" Jefferson asked, hopeful that Nick had an explanation for her death.

"I represented Janis for a short time. She gave me bits and pieces of your story, but she was killed before our second meeting," Nick admitted.

Jefferson looked even more crestfallen after hearing that his niece had in fact repeated his story. "I never should have involved Janis in this awful mess. I was trying to help, but I handed her a death sentence instead."

"This sordid tale doesn't end with your niece's death, Mr. Hughes," Nick said softly. "Someone broke into my house and stole Janis's case file."

"Why would someone—"

Nick cut Jefferson off midsentence. "The intruder murdered my wife and kidnapped my three-year-old daughter."

Jefferson hadn't looked healthy before, but after hearing about his family, Nick was afraid the old man might die on the spot. He slumped in his chair and gasped for air.

"It never ends," he moaned. "Good people keep paying for the mistake I made all those years ago."

"Will you help us find Nick's daughter?" Simone pleaded.

"I already told you everything I know," Jefferson assured her. "Clyde's the only one who knew the whole truth, and that SOB died a while back."

"At least two other people know what really happened," Nick speculated. "Clyde's partner and the person who actually murdered Brooke Schaffer."

"I suppose that's true," Jefferson agreed. "But you still don't know who put up the cash, and Phil Gates ain't the talkative type."

"You let me worry about Gates," Nick countered. "Can I ask one more favor?"

"Name it, son."

"I'd like to get you on videotape."

Jefferson narrowed his eyes and asked, "What good will that do?"

"I'm not sure," Nick admitted. "Still, I'd like a permanent record of the story you just told us. I thought we'd come back in a day or two with a video recorder."

Jefferson nodded his head in agreement. "No need to call first," he joked. "My schedule is wide open."

Simone offered to pick up supplies before their next visit, and Jefferson reluctantly provided her with a short shopping list. They said their good-byes on the front porch of the old man's cabin before Nick and Simone made the return trek through the woods. They hardly spoke to one another until they were driving south on Highway 75.

After several miles of silence, Simone asked, "What do we do now?"

"I've been asking myself that same question," Nick remarked. "Not in my wildest dreams did I think Jefferson would spill his guts."

"I think I'm in shock," Simone added.

"We definitely know more than we did this morning, but I'm not sure how Jefferson's confession helps Darby."

"That's easy," Simone said. "Now we know your daughter was kidnapped by the people who framed Cole."

Nick thought about Simone's assumption for a moment. Jefferson's self-indictment had answered some of his questions, but it had created just as many new ones. *If Cole didn't murder Brooke Schaffer, who did? Was it the same person who paid Jefferson Hughes to lie under oath? Was it the same person who murdered his wife and kidnapped his daughter? If so, how did he go about finding the man? What was Detective Gates's connection to the murder and subsequent cover-up?* The original euphoria Nick had experienced after leaving Jefferson's cabin was already beginning to fade. He was a little closer to finding his daughter, but not much.

"There are more layers to this mess than I can unravel," Nick finally replied in frustration.

"Maybe talking about it will help," Simone suggested.

"For starters, Jefferson implicated the detective investigating Julie's murder. He was Clyde Parks's partner, and he delivered the $50,000 payoff. To make matters worse, my boss prosecuted your brother. It's unlikely Walter Burton was oblivious to the methods employed by the police officers who investigated the case," Nick said dejectedly.

"It does seem as if the past and present are on a collision course," Simone agreed.

"Oh, I almost forgot," Nick continued, "The police officer who warned me about you and told me to mind my own business?"

"Yeah?"

"He was the same police officer who delivered the bribe money to Jefferson Hughes."

After mulling over Nick's disheartening comments for a mile or two, Simone said, "How do you prepare for a trial, Nick?"

"It's a process. I evaluate the facts of the case and then develop a plan of attack."

"That's how you need to approach this situation."

"Since you're the expert, what's our next step?" Nick asked.

Simone playfully patted Nick on the thigh and said, "I don't have the slightest idea." It was an innocent gesture, yet Nick's demeanor hardened the instant she touched him. "I'm sorry, Nick," she immediately apologized.

"You didn't do anything wrong," Nick replied unconvincingly.

"Spending time with me can't be easy," Simone continued. "I know you're trying to deal with the death of your wife."

Nick's eyes filled with tears. "It's hard to explain, but I feel like I'm betraying Julie's memory just by getting out of bed in the morning."

"You have nothing to feel guilty about," Simone said softly. "You're a good guy—don't blame yourself for things that are beyond your control."

After an uncomfortable silence, Nick said, "The so-called experts say grieving is a process. I don't have any idea how long the process usually takes—but it may be forever in my case."

"Finding your daughter will help," Simone quickly countered. "It won't change the past, but it's the best we can do."

"You're right about that," Nick agreed. "We need to figure out who murdered Janis Jones and who forked over $50,000 for Jefferson Hughes's perjured testimony."

Simone raised her eyebrows as she said, "I have a sneaking suspicion it's the same person."

CHAPTER 21

Thursday night, October 19

Thursday night at the Log Tavern was typically the slowest night of the week, but this one had been downright stagnant. Leroy usually preferred nonstop action when he bartended, because it made his eight-hour shift fly by, but tonight the leisurely pace suited him just fine. He was taking advantage of the peace and quiet to map out a plan for his immediate future. A string of cops had paraded through the Log Tavern asking questions about a murder and kidnapping in the suburbs. Leroy wasn't paranoid. Still, he got the feeling that he was in the path of an approaching storm. As soon as he saved up a little travel money, Leroy was planning to put some distance between Lakeland and himself.

He had just conjured up a soothing image of himself on a white sandy beach when the creak of the front door interrupted his train of thought. His good mood vanished the instant Edgar Ellenwood came shuffling through the front door.

"And a good night is ruined just like that," Leroy mumbled under his breath.

Edgar came lumbering up to the bar like a grizzly bear shaking off the effects of a long hibernation. "Shavonne's sick again," he said, skipping the pleasantries. "She needs some stuff to make her feel better."

"I'm working, Edgar. I don't have time to deal with your crap tonight," Leroy replied dismissively.

Edgar leaned his massive body over the bar until his scarred and pockmarked face was only a few inches from Leroy's.

"Can you score me some heroin?" he asked, ignoring the bartender's brush-off. "Even some morphine would fix her up."

"I'm permanently retired from that line of work," Leroy lied. "The heat's been sniffing around here for the past week or so. I'm not about to go back to prison because of some penny ante dope deal."

Edgar spoke in a slow drawl, "Quit giving me the run-around—I know you can get your hands on some heroin or something almost as good. Shavonne needs some medicine to get her through the next few days."

"Look Edgar, I'm sure there's a small-time dope dealer around here looking to unload some meth, but it sure ain't me," Leroy snapped.

"Shavonne's not a crackhead," Edgar said with more intensity. "She's really sick."

"I'm not jerking you around," Leroy insisted. "Dealers can't afford to inventory heroin, because everybody wants meth these days. It's cheaper, the high lasts forever, and it's easy to find on the street. "

"Shavonne doesn't need meth. She needs heroin," Edgar growled. "She's not one of those brain-dead zombies who buy that poison."

"Yeah, heroin is practically health food," Leroy said with a roll of his eyes.

"She needs the heroin to get rid of her pain."

"Yeah, whatever you say," Leroy scoffed. "Shavonne's a real Mother Teresa."

The drug dealer's insult caused Edgar to stiffen. Leroy sensed that the large man was nearing his boiling point.

"I may be able to track down some oxy, but that stuff's not cheap," Leroy offered in a conciliatory tone.

"How much?"

"We're talking at least twenty bucks a tab, minimum," Leroy countered. "Someone with Shavonne's, uh … history, will probably need ten hits to get her through a couple of days."

A trace of a smile appeared on Edgar's stoic face. "I have a valuable asset that could be worth a bundle to the right buyer," he whispered. "Once I find a buyer, I'll have more than enough cash to buy whatever you're selling."

"Then we can talk after you liquidate your asset."

"I was thinking you could find a buyer," Edgar suggested.

Leroy hated doing business with Edgar under the best of circumstances, and he wasn't about to enter into a consignment deal with the head case.

"Look Edgar, I'm not a pawn broker or credit union," Leroy said impatiently. "You hand me a wad of cash, and I provide you with a product—that's the way it works. If you don't have any money, you're wasting my time."

Edgar gave Leroy a piercing stare that sent chills up the bartender's spine. "I've got several irons in the fire; I just don't have the cash right now."

The deranged look on the large man's face caused Leroy to backtrack. "Okay, Edgar, you win," he relented. "I'll front you some dope, but only for a day or two. My suppliers aren't the type of guys who do business on credit."

"A couple of days is all I need," Edgar promised.

"So what's this valuable asset you're so anxious to move?"

Edgar grabbed Leroy by the forearm. The muscular bartender wanted to yank his arm from the giant's vice-like grip, but instead, he stood there frozen by fear.

"What I'm about to tell you is worth killing for," Edgar murmured in a low voice.

Leroy was certain he didn't want to hear the rest, but he also knew it was too late to turn back. "Get to the point, Edgar," he demanded with as much bravado as he could muster. "I've got customers waiting."

"I've got a little girl I'd be willing to sell for the right price," Edgar said. "She's a perfect little white girl."

Leroy didn't know what he was expecting, but this lunacy was off the charts. "I don't understand ..." he stammered. "How did someone like you get your hands on a little girl?"

"Her mother ... passed away, and Shavonne's too weak to take care of her, so we decided to sell her," Edgar explained as if he was trying to pawn a bicycle or a car stereo.

Leroy stared at Edgar in disbelief. "What about the father?" he asked. "Does he know you're trying to hawk his kid?"

"Her father's probably looking for her right now," Edgar casually replied. "And that's why we can't afford to screw around."

"You're talking about kidnapping and human trafficking. If you get caught, you'll spend the rest of your life in prison."

"Then I won't get caught," Edgar answered indifferently.

Leroy shook his head in disbelief. "I've sold every chemical known to mankind, but a kidnapped kid is way out of my league."

"You're a resourceful guy," Edgar countered.

"Even if I was stupid enough to get involved in your mess, I wouldn't know where to start."

"We can split the money right down the middle," Edgar offered.

Leroy was about to throw out another excuse when it dawned on him what child Edgar was talking about.

"It took me a while, but the pieces just clicked into place," he said.

Edgar narrowed his eyes and asked in a low voice, "What do you think you know?"

"The story's been all over the news for the past two weeks, and cops have been in here asking all kinds of weird questions. You murdered that housewife out in the suburbs and then walked off with her little girl," Leroy blurted out.

"Knowledge can be deadly in the wrong hands."

"You're certifiably nuts," Leroy barked. "Get out of my bar. If you show your ugly face in the Log Tavern again, I'll call the cops myself."

The instant the words left his mouth, Leroy knew he'd made a potentially fatal mistake. The glare on Edgar's face made it crystal clear that Leroy would end up like the housewife if the big man got him alone. One thing was certain; the time frame for Leroy's impending departure had just been put on the fast track.

As he lumbered toward the door, Edgar realized he'd screwed up big time. He never should have trusted a man like Leroy with his secret. His desire to make a tidy profit off the little girl had proven to be more difficult than he had anticipated. Now it appeared as if killing the little girl and cutting his losses was the most prudent course of action. Shavonne wouldn't be happy about it, but she would agree with his logic in the end. How to deal with Leroy was a much easier decision for Edgar. He would kill the bartender when the time was right without giving it a second thought.

CHAPTER 22

Friday morning, October 20

A late-night phone call from Jackson St. James had forced a last-minute alteration to Nick's original plan for Friday morning. He had asked Jackson to postpone the hastily schedule meeting until the first of the week, but Jackson had insisted that they get together first thing in the morning. Jackson had refused to disclose the reason for the meeting, yet there was something about his secrecy that made Nick believe it was serious. Simone had tried to downplay her disappointment when he broke the news to her, but her deflated tone of voice conveyed her true feelings. After an awkward conversation, the two of them made a tentative plan to return to the Wood River Valley and Jefferson Hughes first thing Saturday morning.

Nick arrived at the law offices right on time for his appointment. It caught him off guard when the receptionist, Erma Sliger, asked him to wait in the lobby like a regular, fee-paying client. Erma assured him that the partners wouldn't keep him waiting long as he took a seat in the reception area. Nick absentmindedly thumbed through a magazine while he waited for the partners' impending summons. He had just tossed the magazine onto the coffee table when Erma's intercom beeped. Erma didn't put the call on speaker; instead, she picked up the receiver and spoke in a hushed voice. After a brief conversation, she hung up the telephone and tentatively looked in his direction.

"Nick, the partners are waiting for you in the small conference room."

Nick stood and said, "I know the way."

"We've missed you around here," Erma said with a pinched look on her face. Then she quickly added, "Don't be a stranger."

"I won't be," Nick promised.

Nick thought about Erma's parting comment as he made his way down the deserted hallway. Her remark made sense given his current situation. After all, he'd been out of the office for the past couple of weeks. Still, her demeanor seemed to indicate that the firm dynamics had changed. His heart was racing, but he appeared calm on the surface when he slipped through the closed door without knocking. He was still clueless as to why the partners had demanded his presence, but his instincts were telling him to keep his guard up. He nodded casually at his bosses and then selected a chair at the opposite end of the mahogany table. His thoughts momentarily flashed to a memory of his pre-employment interview, and for some reason, Nick remembered the three partners had occupied the exact same chairs.

"First things first," Walter began in a syrupy sweet tone of voice. "How are you holding up?"

Nick wondered how anybody could take a word Walter spoke at face value. "It's been tough," he answered truthfully. "Some days are better than others."

"Do Lakeland's finest have any viable leads yet?" Jackson St. James asked in a manner that clearly conveyed his contempt for the local police department.

Nick was fairly sure the partners' true agenda didn't involve his mental state or the status of the police investigation, but he dutifully answered their preliminary questions. "Detective Gates is working a couple of leads but nothing overly promising in my opinion."

Jackson's body stiffened, and he leaned forward in his chair. "What kind of leads?" he asked.

If Jackson was looking for specifics, he was barking up the wrong tree. Nick wasn't about to share information with Jackson or anyone else. For the time being, Jefferson Hughes's jaw-dropping confession was he and Simone's little secret.

"I spoke to Detective Gates a couple of days ago, but he didn't get into specifics," Nick replied nonchalantly.

"He didn't get into specifics because his investigation stalled at the starting gate," Walter scoffed.

"I don't know about that. Detective Gates seems more than competent to me," Nick shot back in an attempt to annoy his boss.

Walter's face instantly flushed bright red, and for a moment, Nick thought his boss wanted to debate the detective's investigative skills. Instead, Walter merely said in a patronizing tone, "That's all fine and good, Nick. I suppose everybody's entitled to their opinion. Why don't we get down to the business at hand?"

"That sounds like an excellent idea," Nick quickly agreed.

Walter tried to give Nick his best this-hurts-me-more-than-it-does-you look, but instead, he came off looking insincere and constipated. "I'm the senior partner of this law firm, which means unpleasant decisions come with my job description," Walter said with a sad shake of his head.

The instant Walter finished his sentence, Nick knew the partners had decided to terminate him. He was about to save Walter the trouble of firing him, but after thinking about it, he decided to watch his boss fumble his way through the process.

"What kind of unpleasant decisions?" Nick asked with a puzzled look on his face.

"All kinds of unpleasant decisions—and this one is the most unpleasant of all," Walter replied with a forced grimace.

Nick just sat there with a puzzled expression on his face while he waited for Walter to get to the point. After a fairly lengthy and uncomfortable pause, Walter began speaking again.

"Termination decisions are undoubtedly the toughest of all, especially when the employee has been a loyal and valued part of the team."

"What have I done to warrant termination?" Nick asked, honestly perplexed by the partners' decision to let him go.

"Your continued association with our law firm creates a couple of insurmountable problems—" Walter replied.

"Such as?" Nick cut in.

"You work's suffered as of late," Walter continued. "This law firm is not a charity, Nick. We're in this business to turn a profit."

"Given what occurred two weeks ago, billing hours hasn't been my first priority," Nick snapped.

"There's also the media's coverage of your wife's murder and the negative impact it could have on the firm."

"In other words, my wife's murder screwed up the firm's business plan," Nick angrily replied.

Walter shrugged and said, "Some clients are bound to think you were involved in something criminal or, at the very least, unsavory. When Jackson first brought up the issue of your continued employment, I had my doubts about letting you go. After careful consideration of our limited options, I realized Jackson was right."

Nick was ashamed to have been associated with these men for the past five years. It wasn't so much their greed, narrow-mindedness, and hypocrisy that bothered him. It was the fact that they were about to fire him before he had a chance to quit.

"I'm sorry that my wife's murder and my daughter's kidnapping impacted my job performance," Nick replied sarcastically.

"This isn't personal," Walter said no longer faking sincerity. "We know you've been living through a nightmare, but this is a business. We can't afford to pay someone who's not pulling his weight." Walter slid an envelope across the table to Nick. "We've all agreed two months of severance pay is more than fair."

"Is your decision final?" Nick asked, only because he wanted an opportunity to tell them to shove their lousy job.

Walter quickly glanced at Sean Summers before answering. "I'm afraid so, Nick. The decision to let you go was unanimous."

Nick fought an urge to tell the trio what he really thought

of them. Instead, he took the high road and merely said, "I just wasted an hour that I couldn't afford to waste."

"I hope there are no hard feelings," Jackson St. James chimed in. "You'd understand our decision if you were responsible for paying the bills."

Nick needed to get out of there before he did something he would regret. Nick stood and said, "I'll stop by next week to clean out my office."

"That won't be necessary," Jackson quickly countered. "I cleaned out your office after we made the decision to terminate your employment."

"Were you afraid I'd steal one of the firm's staplers?"

"I thought it would be helpful if I separated your personal belongings from the firm's property," Jackson replied defensively.

"You're a swell guy," Nick replied through clinched teeth. "Where did you put my stuff?"

"I'll get it when we're done here," Jackson offered.

"As far as I'm concerned, we're done," Nick said and abruptly left the conference room.

Nick waited in the reception area while Jackson St. James gathered his personal belongings. Poor Erma Sliger avoided making eye contact with him by trying to look busy. There was something about his spur-of-the-moment termination that caused his instincts to question Walter's true motivation. Firing him made absolutely no sense from a business perspective, or any other perspective for that matter. Nick would still be the firm's most productive associate lawyer even if he didn't bill a single hour for the rest of the year. As for the negative publicity associated with his wife's murder, Walter's convoluted logic didn't hold water. The media had actually portrayed him as a sympathetic victim and war hero. Regardless of their true motives, his termination actually came as a relief. The only thing that mattered to him was finding his daughter, and being employed, especially by Walter Burton, made that task more difficult.

Jackson entered the reception area a few minutes later carrying a small cardboard box. Nick found it depressing that the small box contained the remnants of his legal career at Burton, St. James, & Summers.

Jackson handed him the box and said, "I think that's everything, Nick."

"If not, I know where to find you," Nick replied indifferently.

"Don't forget, Nick, you signed a noncompete and confidentiality agreement when we hired you."

"Since legal work has never been your forte, I'll spell it out for you," Nick said. "The noncompete only applies to voluntary resignations, and you guys fired me."

The insult obviously angered Jackson, but all he said was, "Give me your office key." Nick removed the key from his pants' pocket and dropped it on the floor without saying another word.

Nick had one foot out the door when Erma Sliger suddenly raced from behind her desk and shouted, "Wait! Nick." When Erma caught up to him, she handed him a piece of paper with nothing but a phone number written on it. "This has been such an awful day that I almost forgot to give you a message."

"What's this?" Nick asked.

"Some guy called here this morning."

"What guy?"

"He refused to leave his name or a detailed message," Erma said with a shrug. "He gave me that phone number and told me he needed to talk to you about your daughter."

Nick grabbed the old woman by the shoulders. "What did he say about my daughter?" he frantically demanded.

Erma's eyes pooled with tears. "I don't know," she meekly replied. "He hung up after he gave me that phone number. I wasn't even sure if I should give you the message."

"Why not?"

"What if he's a crackpot who read about your daughter in the newspaper?" she asked and then murmured, "I didn't think you could survive more heartache."

Erma had always been one of Nick's favorites. She had been with Walter from the beginning, yet she had somehow managed to stay out of the political posturing and gossip typical of most law firms.

"Thanks, Erma, but you don't need to worry about me," Nick said before he turned and left Burton, St. James, & Summers for good.

CHAPTER 23

Friday morning, October 20

Nick sprinted to his car and tossed the cardboard box into the trunk. There was a hastily scrawled note from Sean Summers on the passenger seat. It read simply:

Walter lied! The vote to terminate was two to one.

"Thanks, Sean," Nick muttered.

Nick's hands were shaking as he clumsily punched the seven-digit number into his cell phone. A gruff voice answered after the third ring.

"Yeah," was all the man said.

"I was told you have information about my daughter," Nick said in a rush.

There was a long pause on the other end of the line, before the man said, "That all depends."

"Depends on what?" Nick pleaded.

"It depends on how much you're willing to pay."

"I'm not rich, but you can have everything I own," Nick replied without hesitation.

"I appreciate the generous offer, but I'm not greedy," the

man growled. "I just need enough cash to put some distance between me and Lakeland."

"Just tell me how much," Nick replied, desperate for any scrap of information that might lead him to Darby.

"Ten thousand dollars should do the trick."

"I can get the money," Nick quickly agreed. "Now convince me you're on the up and up."

"Life's full of risks," the caller taunted. "So you'll need to trust me if you want to see your daughter again."

"Give me something," Nick begged.

The man sighed as if Nick's pleas were boring him. "I know who took your daughter, and I know she is still alive."

Nick tried to remain calm and somewhat objective about the reliability of the caller's information, but his desperation caused him to throw caution to the wind.

"When can we meet?"

"Give me your phone number, and I'll contact you after I tie up a few loose ends," the man answered before quickly adding, "I may need to leave Lakeland in a hurry, so get the money ready."

Nick gave the anonymous caller his cell phone number and started to inquire about a tentative timeframe for their upcoming exchange. He was about halfway through his question before he realized that the mystery man was no longer on the line.

CHAPTER 24

Saturday morning, October 21

The heart-wrenching sound of the child's whimpering had quieted down a few minutes past midnight. Shavonne had made several trips to the dingy apartment's only bedroom during the course of the evening, but each time her efforts to comfort the child had been unsuccessful. When the child finally drifted off to sleep, Shavonne let out a grateful sigh. After summoning what little courage she possessed, Shavonne approached Edgar.

"Perhaps it was a mistake to take the little girl," she cautiously suggested. "Young children need a devoted parent, and I'm too sick to care for a small child."

"It happened so quickly—I didn't have time to seek the spirits' guidance," Edgar responded defensively. "Perhaps she belongs on the other side with her mother."

Shavonne was frightened by Edgar's obsession with the other side, yet she managed to maintain her charade of acceptance. "For heaven's sake, Edgar, I wasn't suggesting that it was a mistake to spare the child's life," she replied with a dismissive wave. "I want you to return the child to her father."

"That's impossible."

"Her father's been put through the ringer, and so has that baby girl."

Edgar violently shook his head from side to side. "It's too risky," he said with finality. "The child can connect me to her mother's death."

Shavonne tried to reason with the giant man even though she knew it was hopeless. "Edgar, she's three, maybe four years old at the most."

"The child has powers, and she's seen inside my head."

Shavonne ignored his cryptic ramblings and pressed on, "We can drop her outside the emergency room on our way out of Lakeland."

"You told me that you wanted a child of your own," Edgar replied in frustration.

"When I was much younger, I wanted a child. It was selfish, but I figured caring for a baby would force me to get clean."

"That little girl needs a mommy."

"My dreams of motherhood died a long time ago," Shavonne replied. "It's too late for me to make something positive out of my life."

Edgar got a hopeful, almost pleading look on his sallow face. "Maybe it's not too late."

Shavonne had silently promised herself that she would do everything within her power to save the child even if it meant betraying Edgar. Her life had been marked by weakness and failure, but she couldn't live with the child's blood on her hands.

"Edgar, let's do the right thing and give her back to her father," she pleaded.

"It's not for me to decide if the girl lives or dies," Edgar replied in anger. "The spirits will determine the child's fate. Once the spirits speak, I'm merely the instrument that carries out their wishes."

Edgar's erratic behavior had forced Shavonne to do some soul searching since the little girl's arrival. Edgar had taken care of Shavonne for several years, but he was getting more bizarre and unpredictable with each passing day. Lately he had been obsessed with death and, as he called it, the "spirit world." Shavonne had done many things that she was ashamed of because of her addiction. One of them was relying on Edgar for money, but she continued to rely on him because money paid for the drugs her body craved.

Even though Edgar was a social outcast marching to the voices in his head, he had an uncanny ability to get his hands on cash. Over the course of their relationship, Shavonne had intentionally remained ignorant about the source of Edgar's income. Her denial helped preserve what was left of her sanity. She had always known that Edgar engaged in nasty, unpleasant, and even criminal activities, but had never dreamed he was capable of murdering a child, or an innocent mother for that matter. Although Shavonne didn't believe Edgar would harm her, she had always been too terrified of him to test her belief.

Shavonne's time with Edgar had been a drug-blurred haze. She couldn't even remember how she'd first hooked up with the large, strange man. She did know they had been together for what seemed like an eternity and during their time together, they had drifted from one city to another without a place to call home. Even though they were wanderers, the nomadic couple returned to Lakeland every couple of years. Edgar owned a small cabin on the reservoir that had belonged to his uncle. He had even started to fix it up before this mess with the little girl's mother had diverted his attention to more pressing matters.

Shavonne found it unsettling that after all their years together Edgar was still an enigma to her. He was huge in physical stature yet childlike in many ways. He could be the kindest, most gentle person one minute, and a coldhearted sociopath the next. Shavonne, who was five years older than Edgar, had always been more of a mother figure than a girlfriend to the enormous man. Their relationship had never been sexual. Edgar believed sex was a dirty, unholy act that would distance him from the spirit world.

When Shavonne was honest with herself, she had to admit that her relationship with Edgar had always been an odd one, born of necessity. She needed someone to provide for her, while

Edgar longed for the companionship of another human being. Shavonne had learned at an early age that need and love were the only two emotions that kept people together. Her entire adult life had been spent pursuing alcohol and drugs, and the never-ending hunger made it impossible to truly love another person. Edgar did not drink alcohol or use drugs, making their union even more unlikely. On rare occasions when peyote was made available to him, Edgar would smoke the flower in order to seek the spiritual guidance of his Sioux forefathers.

Even though Shavonne did not love Edgar, she felt sympathy for him. His enormous size and unpleasant physical appearance attracted a lot of unwanted attention. He pretended not to care about the insults. Still, she knew the open-mouthed stares and whispered jokes hurt the big man more than he was willing to let on. Shavonne wanted the best for Edgar, but she had slowly come to realize that their destinies would play out on different paths. In one of her rare moments of strength, she had decided to end their dysfunctional relationship and strike out on her own. In her opinion, the dissolution of their codependent relationship was long overdue. Shavonne said a silent prayer for herself and the child before she drifted off into a troubled sleep. She hoped God listened to people who had strayed from his path.

CHAPTER 25

Saturday morning, October 21

Shavonne had passed out on the couch, and the little girl had been asleep in the back bedroom for a while. Edgar had hoped a few moments of solitude would clear his head, but alone in the dark, he was more confused than ever. He sensed that a storm was brewing. Edgar had become quite adept at living his life in the shadows of society, but suddenly he felt vulnerable. What had begun as a simple burglary had spiraled out of control. If more killing was necessary to put things right, he would do what had to be done. Besides, Edgar did not understand Shavonne's aversion to his suggestion of killing the little girl. Death was inevitable and sometimes even welcome. The only unknowns regarding death were when and how. If his childhood was an indication, the little girl would be better off on the other side.

Edgar was no stranger to death. In fact, Edgar considered himself to be a friend of death. In essence, he was a conduit between the earthly world and the spiritual realm. The spirits had given him that special power the day he had watched his mother and father die. Edgar had never questioned his duty to the spirits until he sent Julie Jelaco on her journey to the other side. Since that night, he had been haunted by the heart-wrenching look in her eyes and the anguished sound of her voice before she passed over. He had always understood that his actions were the will of the spirits, but lately he was plagued with doubt. He wondered if he had misread the spirits' wishes. The pretty young woman did not seem ready to die. If the spirits were displeased with him, he needed to make things right.

Edgar struggled to focus on the present, but no matter how hard he tried, his troubled thoughts wanted to return to his youth on the Pine Ridge Indian Reservation. He was a full-blooded Sioux Indian, born and raised as a member of the Oglala Tribe of South Dakota. Edgar had always been proud of his Indian heritage and tried to follow tribal customs, when the white man's world permitted it. He spoke Lakota and respected the traditions of his people, but living in the white man's world was difficult. Edgar had considered returning to the reservation many times during the past twenty-eight years, but he had not set foot in South Dakota since his hasty departure at sixteen.

Most of Edgar's childhood memories were unclear. He found it difficult to distinguish actual recollections from the wishful fantasies of a lonely child. Unfortunately, one memory, the memory he most wanted to forget, was so vivid it could have happened yesterday. Edgar had been only five the day he was sitting on the dusty kitchen floor of his home on the reservation. He had been playing with a hand-carved wooden horse while his mother washed the supper dishes at the kitchen sink. She had had her back to him, and her long, shiny, black hair hung past her waist. It had been a good day, an uneventful day. Edgar's father had left the house shortly after breakfast and had not returned. Edgar liked being alone with his mother. Even though it made him feel guilty, he had secretly wished his father would stay away forever. When he was at home, Edgar's father was usually drunk and always abusive. On the days his father was drunk, he could be exceptionally cruel, and Edgar's mother had typically borne the brunt of his cruelty.

In his mind's eye, Edgar's mother had almost finished washing the dishes when the bright headlights of his father's pickup truck shone through the small window above the sink. Edgar still remembered the fear that had gripped him while he waited for his father to come stumbling through the door. Edgar and his mother had not waited long when Floyd Ellenwood came crashing through the back door of their ramshackle home. He had been very drunk, and in a particularly foul mood. Edgar's father had slung the whiskey bottle he was carrying against the far wall and demanded his supper. Most days, Edgar's mother did exactly as Floyd instructed, but that night was different. She had told Floyd to prepare his own supper.

Floyd Ellenwood had cursed at his wife, spit in her face, and then stormed out of the kitchen. Edgar hadn't believed their luck; his father was so drunk that he was going straight to bed without making his mother suffer. But their good fortune and his mother's life had come to an abrupt and bloody end when Floyd Ellenwood staggered back into the kitchen clutching his old .45 caliber revolver. He had waved the pistol wildly and screamed Lakota and English obscenities at his wife. Edgar's mother had stood her ground and stared defiantly at her drunken husband. Edgar believed that his mother had finally become sick and tired of living each day in fear. Unfortunately, Floyd had been a man accustomed to getting what he wanted, and his wife's defiance enraged him. He had aimed the pistol at her, let out a bloodcurdling shriek, and then shot her twice in the chest.

A shocked Floyd Ellenwood had stood there for several seconds staring openmouthed at the bloodstained floor around his wife's motionless body. Edgar remembered that his ears were still ringing from the pistol blast when his father scooped him up and carried him into the living room. Edgar's sobbing father had plopped down heavily onto the couch with Edgar in his arms.

He had pulled Edgar close to him and whispered, "*Wastelakapi cinks*" in his ear. Young Edgar was still sitting on his father's lap when Floyd Ellenwood pressed the muzzle of the pistol against the side of his head and pulled the trigger. After Floyd's suicide, Edgar had stayed with his dead father a few minutes before he slid off his lap and returned to the kitchen. He had retrieved his wooden horse and then lay down beside his mother's body on the dirty kitchen floor. He was still lying beside his mother when a neighbor discovered the horrific scene the following morning.

His father's last words, *Wastelakapi cinks,* meant *beloved son* in Lakota. As a child, Edgar had wanted to believe his father's final words, yet he wondered why his father had abused him and his mother if he truly loved them. When he was a little older, Edgar's confused feelings toward his father had turned into outright hatred. He had come to the realization that his father was a liar and even his dying words had been untruths. Edgar was certain the spirits would make his father pay in the afterlife.

The months following his parents' deaths had been both lonely and confusing for young Edgar. He remembered white men and women asking him questions about his parents and forcing him to take a variety of tests. He didn't have any relatives on the reservation, so Edgar was passed from one household to another while tribal elders decided what to do with him. Six months after the shooting, Edgar was placed in permanent foster care. His foster mother was a sixty-year-old widow named Maggie Yellow Hawk. It had not taken Edgar long to develop a hatred for his new foster mother. Maggie Yellow Hawk did not physically abuse Edgar, but she had been indifferent to his suffering. She had regularly stood by while the other Indian children beat and ridiculed him. Even though he had been bigger and smarter than the other kids, Edgar wouldn't stand up for himself.

As Edgar had approached his teenage years, he would frequently disappear into the badlands for days at a time. It was not unusual for the young orphan to wander in the desolate country with nothing but water to keep him going. Because of the area's rugged terrain and its lack of water, the Sioux called the ever-changing landscape *Mako Sica,* which means *badlands.* Edgar had been drawn to the badlands because the severe and desolate land made him feel as though he were alone in his own private world. Edgar's favorite place in the badlands was Stronghold Table located at the northwest corner of the Pine Ridge Indian Reservation. The United States Government had proclaimed Stronghold Table a national monument in 1939, but it was seldom visited by tourists because of its limited access by road. The holy land was bleak, yet it held special meaning for the Oglala Sioux. Stronghold Table was the site of a sacred Sioux burial ground, and it was also the location of the last Ghost Dance of the nineteenth century that was cut short by the massacre at Wounded Knee. But to Edgar, Stronghold Table had been the only place where he could find peace of mind.

It was a fifty-mile hike through barren, rugged terrain to reach Stronghold Table. Yet Edgar had made the difficult trek several times a year. He would have made the pilgrimage more often but for the severe weather. During his journeys to the Stronghold, Edgar would fast and pray for enlightened visions of the future. When he was fifteen years old, Edgar had been fasting and praying at Stronghold Table for twelve hours when the Great Spirit had appeared before him in the form of his deceased mother and ordered him to kill Maggie Yellow Hawk. The Great Spirit told Edgar that Maggie's death would free him from his daily torment.

Over the years, the Great Spirit and other lesser spirits had called upon Edgar in a variety of forms. Sometimes they didn't physically appear, but Edgar would hear their voices inside his head. When the Great Spirit ordered the teenager to kill Maggie Yellow Hawk, it was the first time the spirits had given him a holy task to perform. Edgar had been eager to please the spirits and dutifully planned the killing of his foster mother. He had patiently waited for the right time and finally decided to put his deadly plan into action on March 21, 1978. More than two decades had passed, yet Edgar remembered even the minute details of that particular day in March. It was unseasonably cool for early springtime in South Dakota, and the wind had been whipping gale force across the prairie for three straight days. Edgar believed the wind was actually the spirits gathering to witness the fateful event.

Just before midnight, the wind had abruptly stopped, and the reservation was cloaked in an eerie calm. The young Indian boy had sensed that the spirits were present and it was time for him to carry out his sacred mission. After clearing his head of all doubt, Edgar had crept down the hallway and silently entered Maggie Yellow Hawk's bedroom. He had stood by her bed and watched the old woman's rhythmic breathing for several minutes, fully aware that she was taking her last breaths. When it was time for her to die, he had awakened the old Indian woman, because he wanted to savor the fear in her eyes as she passed over. Before she could cry out for help, Edgar had pulled the pillow from beneath her head and pressed it firmly over her mouth and nose. The frail old woman had struggled mightily for a minute or two, and then with a final shudder, she lay still. He had gently placed the pillow beneath her head, smoothed her long grey hair, and returned to his own bedroom. The next morning, one of the younger children had discovered the old woman's dead body. Because Maggie Yellow Hawk was an older woman and in poor health, everyone had assumed that she had died of natural causes, and there was no formal inquiry into the cause of her death. To this day, Edgar truly believed that he had done his foster mother a favor by freeing her spirit from the confines of her sickly body.

Summer on the reservation came and went without further incident. Edgar had been indifferent to his new foster family because he knew the living arrangements were temporary. He had attended his tenth grade classes every once in a while but spent the majority of his time wandering through the badlands. After several months of relative tranquility, Edgar had experienced a second life-altering vision. It was a gray, rainy afternoon in October, and like most days, Edgar had skipped his classes in order to seek spiritual enlightenment in the badlands. After several hours of hiking up and down muddy hillsides and climbing over rugged rock formations, a cold, wet, and tired Edgar had crawled under the shelter of a rock overhang. While he had waited for the rain to let up, his mind drifted into a dreamlike state. In his dream, Edgar and his mother were standing on the sandy shore of an enormous body of water. The two of them were holding hands as the waves crashed against their bare legs. Edgar had never been to the coast—or traveled off the reservation—still he knew the endless expanse of water was the Pacific Ocean. Free of Edgar's abusive father, they were happy, laughing, and completely at peace.

Just before the dream ended, Edgar's mother looked at him and said in her soothing voice, "He won't be able to find us here." Edgar's mother then released his hand and walked into the pounding surf. Edgar stood on the shore and watched as his mother disappeared into the water.

Edgar had awakened beneath the rock overhang alone and confused. He had called out to his mother and then frantically scrambled from the shelter of the small cave. After desperately searching the area surrounding the rain-soaked rock outcropping, he had realized that she was gone. Alone again, Edgar had dropped to the damp ground while he pondered the strange dream. He cried and prayed for hours. Four days later, with everything he possessed slung over his shoulder in a burlap sack, Edgar set out on foot for the Pacific Ocean. Twenty-eight years had passed since that day in the badlands, yet Edgar had still not set foot on the shores of the Pacific Ocean.

When the focus of Edgar's thoughts finally returned to the present, he was alone in the dark solitude of his shabby apartment. He was unsure how long he had been lost in his past, but the first hints of sunlight had already begun to brighten the morning sky. Edgar had not reminisced about his mother or his postponed journey to the Pacific Ocean in years. Perhaps it was finally time for Edgar to complete his journey to the ocean or return to the reservation.

Right now, Edgar needed to return to the path that destiny had chosen for him. Since that unsettling night in the little girl's bedroom, he had been besieged by feelings of self-doubt and uncertainty. Mrs. Jelaco wasn't the first person he'd sent to the spirit world. Still, there was something different about her passing. Not once had she pleaded with Edgar to spare her own life. Her only concern had been for her young daughter's safety. Edgar remembered how profoundly his mother's death had affected him as a child, and he questioned whether killing the young mother had been the right decision. Perhaps killing the little girl would restore harmony to Edgar's universe. If not, at least the child would be reunited with her mother. Edgar was convinced that he needed to pray for spiritual guidance before he acted again; he certainly couldn't afford to make another mistake.

CHAPTER 26

Sunday night, October 22

Nick had never been a patient man, and waiting two days for his cell phone to ring had been nothing short of excruciating. Finally on Sunday afternoon, the mysterious caller made contact for the second time. He skipped the pleasantries.

"Do you have my money?"

Nick did have the $10,000 in crisp, new bills. He had withdrawn the cash from his savings account immediately following the first conversation. The envelope that contained the stack of fresh $100 bills had been close by ever since.

"Yeah, I've got the money," Nick calmly replied.

"The payment better be in cash," the caller added. "I don't take checks or credit cards."

"Yeah, it's in cash," Nick said in a flat tone.

"So far, so good," the caller growled.

"How do we make the exchange?" Nick asked.

"It has to take place tonight, and it has to be someplace off the beaten path."

"Name the place."

"Are you familiar with Hartman Park?"

Nick wasn't thrilled about the choice, but he also realized that balking might scare the man off. "Yeah, I've been there a few times," Nick answered without enthusiasm. "What time do you want to meet?"

There was an extended silence on the other end of the line and Nick wondered if the caller was conferring with a third party.

When he came back on the line, he said, "Eleven o'clock near the bathrooms."

"I'll be there at eleven o'clock sharp," Nick immediately agreed.

"One more thing, Mr. Jelaco."

"Yeah, what's that?"

"Don't try to pull a fast one on me," he warned. "If you're not alone, I'll take a walk, and so will any chance of you getting your daughter back alive."

"I'll be alone," Nick assured him. "You just keep your end of the bargain."

"Don't worry about my end. The information I possess will knock your socks off," the caller said before abruptly ending the call.

Nick shoved his cell phone into his coat pocket and quickly checked his watch. "Great," he muttered to himself. "I've got six hours to kill before the exchange."

Leroy arrived at Hartman Park a full hour before the scheduled exchange time. He had been walking on eggshells since the blowup with Edgar, and he wasn't about to stumble this close to the finish line. Leroy scouted the area around the bathrooms until he found a grove of pine trees with a perfect view of the agreed-upon meeting place. He took up a position in the dense pine trees and began the anxious wait for eleven o'clock and his $10,000 to arrive. Leroy was nervous, but he was feeling good about his plan. He had gone over the specifics several times and truly believed it was foolproof. Once Jelaco showed up, Leroy would monitor the area for a couple of minutes to make sure he was alone. When he was satisfied the lawyer had followed his instructions to the letter, Leroy would make the exchange and then get out of Lakeland.

Forty-five minutes of skulking in the pine trees had convinced Leroy that foot traffic through the neighborhood park was virtually nonexistent. Aside from two rough-looking teenagers who had stopped to smoke a cigarette, he had been without company since he took up his position. Leroy was getting more anxious with each passing minute. *That lawyer better be on time,* Leroy thought. Leroy considered himself to be a tough guy, but every dropping pinecone or rustle of the leaves caused his heart to jump into his throat.

"I should have scheduled this friggin' exchange in a strip mall," he whispered under his breath. The words were scarcely out of his mouth when he heard the snap of a dead branch directly behind him. He realized that his imagination was working overtime. Still, Leroy was almost positive that someone else was in the trees with him. The best scenario he could imagine was a teenager looking to satisfy a nicotine craving or a late-night fitness nut out for a walk. Leroy couldn't bring himself to think about the worst-case scenario.

Leroy was about to attribute his latest heart palpitations to unsubstantiated paranoia when a hulking presence emerged from the darkness.

"Just because I'm paranoid, it doesn't mean people aren't out to get me," Leroy mumbled. Leroy couldn't see the approaching man's face but the size of his massive body left little doubt as to his identity. "Hey Edgar," Leroy greeted him as nonchalantly as possible. "What brings you out at this time of night?"

The large man continued to advance until he was uncomfortably close to Leroy. "I'm checking up on you," he calmly answered. "I was afraid you might be up to no good."

Leroy was doing his best to appear composed and unconcerned, but he wasn't successful on either count. "I'm trying to conduct a little business. If you don't get lost, you'll blow a big deal for me."

Edgar grabbed Leroy by the shoulder and effortlessly held him in place. "I was surprised to find another bartender covering your shift when I stopped by the Log Tavern this afternoon."

"It's no big deal," Leroy assured him. "I'm moonlighting because minimum wage doesn't pay the bills."

"Your absence from work troubled me so much that I waited outside your apartment and then followed you here," Edgar explained in his flat emotionless voice.

"I'm flattered—you're my first stalker."

Edgar tightened his grip on Leroy's shoulder. "You were supposed to track down some heroin for Shavonne."

"Rain or shine, I deliver just like the post office," Leroy said as he pulled a plastic bag from his coat pocket.

Edgar stuffed the heroin in his pants' pocket and asked, "How much do I owe you?"

Leroy glanced quickly around the grove of trees. "It's on the house, big guy," he nervously replied. "Now shove off before my client shows up."

Leroy couldn't see the big man's eyes, yet he could feel their penetrating stare. "Who are you waiting for?" Edgar growled through clenched teeth.

"Some low-budget drug dealer from out of town," Leroy lied.

Edgar tightened his vise-like grip on Leroy's shoulder. "I believe you're about to betray the confidence I placed in you."

Leroy tried to squirm free of Edgar's powerful grip. "Don't worry about me," Leroy almost whimpered. "I know how to keep a secret."

Edgar chuckled softly and said, "I'm big, but I'm not stupid. I know you're waiting for the child's father."

"You don't know nothin' about nothin'," Leroy stammered unconvincingly.

"It doesn't take a genius to figure out who would most covet the information you're trying to peddle," Edgar said matter-of-factly.

"You've got it wrong," Leroy said in a voice thick with fear. "I swear to God—I'm not selling you out."

Edgar smiled at the pleading bartender. "It doesn't matter one way or the other," he said indifferently. "I'm going to kill you because you deserve to die."

Once Edgar made his true intentions known, Leroy realized that reasoning with the large man was hopeless. He began to struggle violently. Leroy was strong, but it didn't take long for him to figure out that he was no match for Edgar's almost superhuman strength.

Edgar wrapped his massive right arm around the bartender's neck, pulled him tight to his chest, and whispered, "I trust your house is in order, because you're about to meet your maker." Leroy fought frantically as Edgar methodically increased the pressure as he simultaneously twisted his neck. Edgar was surprised by the bartender's will to live, but the will of the spirits was stronger. A few seconds later, Leroy's neck snapped, and his body went limp. Edgar exhaled deeply before he dropped Leroy's lifeless body to the ground. It felt good to have taken care of that little piece of business. Now it was time to collect his payment for the Jelaco job, so he could put Lakeland in his rearview mirror. Edgar was about to step from the cover of the trees when he sensed that he was not alone. He quickly scanned the area and noticed a man slowly crossing the open area of the park. Edgar took a step backward into the shadows and silently watched as the man advanced toward the bathrooms. When the man stopped beneath the security light, Edgar recognized him as the little girl's father. Edgar turned and vanished into the neighboring subdivision without a sound.

CHAPTER 27

Sunday night, October 22

Nick headed straight for Hartman Park after his brief conversation with the mystery caller. His military training had taught him to conduct a little preliminary reconnaissance before venturing into enemy territory. He discovered that Hartman Park was just like every other neighborhood park that savvy real-estate developers were cramming into newer subdivisions. The generic park consisted of a play area, a fenced tennis court, a walking trail, and an open grassy area. The north and east boundaries of the park were fenced and bordered the backyards of the adjacent subdivision. The developers had planted pine trees along the fence line in an attempt to provide a little privacy for the neighboring homeowners. Nick assumed the anonymous caller had chosen this neighborhood park because of its somewhat secluded location. Nick's complete survey of Hartman Park had taken a grand total of forty minutes, which left him five hours to kill until the scheduled exchange time. Nick briefly considered showing up early so he could monitor the area but quickly decided that deviating from the caller's instructions was too risky.

Nick parked on Pinecone Loop near the northwest corner of the park at precisely eleven o'clock. He retrieved the .40 caliber Glock from beneath the driver's seat and tucked it into the waistband of his pants before exiting the Mustang. On the street, he paused near the driver's door to give anyone watching an opportunity to identify him. The exposed feeling made Nick uncomfortable, but he wanted his new business associate to be relaxed when they met face-to-face. After a three count, he stepped onto the damp grass and began his slow march toward the bathrooms. His plan was to walk the length of the open grassy area of the park from north to south. Nick didn't want to spook the guy, and that path would expose him to anyone watching for approximately thirty seconds. It would also give him an unobstructed view of the bathrooms and anyone approaching from the south.

Nick didn't expect trouble because he figured the guy was an amateur. Still, his heart was racing as he walked toward the designated meeting area. About twenty yards short of the bathrooms, he picked up a slight movement in the pine trees to his left. Nick didn't turn his head or break stride, because he assumed it was the mystery caller monitoring his arrival from a safe place. When he reached the bathrooms, Nick stopped and waited patiently in the lighted area near the restroom's entrance. His objective was not stealth or secrecy. He wanted to appear calm and nonthreatening to the person watching from the trees.

He stood beneath the security light for five or six minutes even though his instincts were screaming that something was very wrong. His military training had taught him to cut his losses and retreat when a mission went off track, but this wasn't any ordinary mission. He needed information, and he was willing to risk his life to acquire it. Drawn by the movement he had detected earlier, Nick began walking toward the grove of pine trees east of the bathrooms. He kept his right hand near his weapon as he crossed the open area between the bathrooms and the pine trees. He felt vulnerable and exposed, but he tried to appear relaxed as he made his way toward the grove.

The instant he reached the trees, Nick pulled the Glock from the waistband of his pants and quickly assumed a defensive posture. He kept his back tight against the pine trees as he zigzagged his way through the grove. Nick was beginning to think the mystery caller had bolted after a change of heart when he glimpsed a man's body lying face up on the damp grass. Nick had seen death before, but he felt sick to his stomach when he realized the guy staring wide-eyed into the starless sky wouldn't be talking to him or anyone else. He removed a penlight and squatted beside the body.

He shook his head in disbelief and muttered, "You've got to be kidding," when he recognized the tattoo-covered bartender from the Log Tavern.

Nick shoved the Glock into the waistband of his pants and removed his cell phone from his jacket pocket. After contemplating his limited options, Nick dialed Detective Gates's number from memory. He didn't trust the detective, but the old adage "keep your friends close and your enemies closer" seemed appropriate under the circumstances.

Detective Gates was obviously still awake and in a foul mood when he picked up after one ring and angrily bellowed, "Gates" as his only greeting.

"Hey, Detective, this is Nick Jelaco."

"You called the wrong guy if you're looking for a designated driver," Gates growled.

"Actually, I called to report a homicide."

After a brief silence, Gates said, "What are you talking about?"

"I went out for a late night stroll and stumbled across a dead guy in a neighborhood park."

"Have you been drinking, Jelaco?"

"I'm as sober as a judge."

"Do you know how to get to Hartman Park?"

"Don't ask stupid questions," Gates shot back. "I'm a cop who's lived in Lakeland his entire life."

"My car is parked on Pinecone Loop near the northwest corner of the park," Nick said. "I'll wait for you there."

CHAPTER 28

Monday morning, October 23

Nick had been waiting for thirty agonizing minutes when the headlights of Detective Gates's 4-Runner finally appeared in the rear window. The detective killed his headlights before the SUV had skidded to a complete stop behind the Mustang. Nick was anxious to put the Hartman Park episode behind him, but the time alone had given him a chance to organize his thoughts. He was fairly sure the Harley riding, ex-con bartender from the Log Tavern had not been the victim of a random mugging in the middle of suburbia. Leroy was obviously the anonymous caller, and his present condition seemed to indicate that someone wanted to keep him from talking. Nick didn't want to jump to conclusions. Still, he had to assume it was the same person who had murdered his wife and kidnapped his little girl. No matter how he sized it up, the dead bartender had been a huge disappointment, because it put him back to square one in his search for Darby.

Nick stashed the .40 caliber Glock beneath the driver's seat and joined Detective Gates on the sidewalk.

"Good evening, Detective," Nick greeted him with exaggerated cheer. "I hope I didn't pull you away from something important."

"Yeah, I was about to sit down to dinner with the governor," Gates replied sarcastically. "What's this about a body?"

Nick motioned in the direction of the bartender's body. "The dead guy's in a grove of pine trees on the east side of the park." Without offering additional details, Nick set out across the open grassy area of the park with Detective Gates tagging along behind him.

When they reached the pine trees, Nick said, "The body's over there."

Detective Gates switched on the flashlight he was carrying and gruffly barked, "Don't go anywhere, Jelaco. I've got a bunch of questions, and you better have some answers."

When Gates reappeared a few minutes later, his anger was evident. "Your friend back there has a broken neck," he growled.

"It sounds like you've ruled out suicide," Nick remarked with a straight face.

"One more wise-crack, Jelaco, and I'll slap the cuffs on you," Gates angrily shot back. Nick was trying to decide how much information he wanted to share with the detective when Gates added through clenched teeth, "Start talking, or we're headed downtown."

It was obvious from Gates's aggressive demeanor that he was fed up with Nick's evasiveness. Nick didn't trust the detective, but he decided a little candor might get Gates off his back for a day or two.

"Here's the sum total of what I know," Nick said, feigning sincerity. "Some guy left a message at my law firm. When I called him back, he told me that he possessed reliable information about my daughter's kidnapper."

"What guy?"

"It was an anonymous call," Nick replied truthfully. "We agreed to meet at eleven o'clock near the bathrooms. The caller was a few minutes late, so I went exploring. When I found that dead guy in the trees, I called you. It's as simple as that."

"You were planning to meet this phantom caller without backup?" Gates asked with a suspicious raise of his eyebrows.

Nick shrugged his shoulders. "He threatened to walk with the kidnapper's name if I wasn't alone."

"Did you recognize the caller's voice?"

"No, but I'll give you money it was that dead guy in the trees."

Detective Gates shook his head and glared at Nick. "Are you stupid or just arrogant? That could be you lying in the trees with a broken neck."

Nick knew the detective was probably right, but Gates's tongue-lashing angered him just the same. "I'm desperate for information," Nick snapped. "It's been over two weeks, and the police haven't accomplished a thing."

"Your condescending attitude is starting to piss me off," Gates shot back. "You play hide the ball from Detective Gates, and then you criticize my investigation."

"Don't lecture me about *your* investigation. My little girl has been missing for eighteen days, and that guy offered the first tangible piece of information so far," Nick said.

Detective Gates took a deep breath and then smoothed his crew cut with the palm of his hand. "All right, all right, let's start from the top," he said in a calmer tone. "What did the anonymous caller say?"

"A male caller left a brief message with the receptionist at my law firm. He claimed that he had information regarding my daughter's whereabouts," Nick started to explain.

"You went back to work?" Gates asked.

"It was a cameo appearance at best. The partners had scheduled a meeting so they could fire me," Nick replied indifferently.

Detective Gates grimaced and sarcastically remarked, "Ouch, that's harsh even for a bunch of bloodsucking lawyers."

"Yeah, I found the timing a little suspect as well," Nick agreed. "Anyway, when I called the guy back, he told me that he had firsthand knowledge about the man who abducted Darby."

"Firsthand, because he was the kidnapper?" Gates asked.

"It wasn't a ransom demand," Nick said. "He offered to sell me the kidnapper's name for $10,000."

"Let me get this straight," Gates said in an incredulous tone. "You agreed to meet a complete stranger in the middle of the night carrying $10,000 in cash?"

"Evaluating it with the benefit of hindsight, it wasn't the smartest decision I've ever made," Nick sheepishly agreed. "Anyway, the guy finally called me this afternoon with a time and meeting place."

"He chose the location?"

"That's right. When he didn't show at eleven o'clock, I went looking for him."

"Why the trees?" Gates asked. "It's the perfect place for an ambush."

"I picked up a slight movement in the grove when I first arrived at the park," Nick explained. "I thought the caller might be the shy type."

"Your mystery caller was a scumbag named Leroy Demers. Murder and kidnapping are outside his known areas of expertise," Gates remarked.

"He was the means to an end. I never figured Demers was the treasure at the end of the rainbow," Nick replied wryly.

"You got that right," Gates agreed. "Leroy didn't have much imagination when it came to criminal conduct. He was more your petty burglary, dope dealer type of criminal."

The timing wasn't right to mention his previous encounter with Demers, so instead Nick asked about Leroy's criminal associates. "How would a small-timer like Leroy Demers acquire information about my daughter?"

"Leroy tended bar at a raunchy dive on the south side called the Log Tavern. It's possible he stumbled across a legitimate lead, but then again, he may have been working a $10,000 con," Gates hypothesized. "You never know with a piece of crap like Demers."

"Don't ask me why, but I believe Demers was telling the truth."

"Is your conclusion the product of fact or wishful thinking?"

"Here's a fact for you. Someone snapped ol' Leroy's neck."

Gates furrowed his brow while he thought about Nick's interpretation. "Demers hung out with some bad guys," he finally responded. "There's a good chance his murder and your daughter's abduction are unrelated."

"An anonymous caller schedules a late-night meeting in a remote neighborhood park, and Demers is murdered in the same park at the same time," Nick reminded the detective. "There's definitely a connection."

"It could be a weird coincidence."

"I don't like coincidences," Nick said with a skeptical shake of his head.

"Relax Jelaco, I'll follow up on Demers."

"Keep me posted."

"Are you still at the El Rancho?"

Nick was certain the detective kept abreast of his living arrangements, but he answered his question anyway. "Yeah, it's continental breakfast is the best in town."

Detective Gates rolled his eyes. "Go straight to your motel, and don't talk to anyone. I'll stop by for an official statement after I hand Demers off to the coroner."

CHAPTER 29

Monday morning, October 23

Nick considered stopping at a twenty-four-hour liquor store on his way to the El Rancho, but after some deliberation, he returned to his bleak motel room empty handed. When he took a hard look at where things stood, it seemed as if all roads led back to Leroy Demers. Demers allegedly knew the identity of his daughter's kidnapper, and now the bartender was lying in a park with a broken neck. Someone had gone to great lengths to silence Demers, and Nick's instincts were telling him it was the man who had taken his daughter.

Nick had just finished dissecting each word of his conversation with Demers when Detective Gates banged on his door. Nick glanced at his watch and noted that less than an hour had passed since he had left the detective with Demers's body. Gates's quick arrival made him think that the detective was itching to talk about the murder at Hartman Park.

Before Nick could react to the knock, the detective shouted, "It's Gates. Let me in."

Nick dragged his weary body off the sofa and slowly made his way to the door. The instant the door swung open, Gates pushed past him and stood defiantly in the center of the room.

The wiry little detective was itching for a fight, and Nick was frustrated enough to give him one.

Nick slammed the door and asked, "Do you know who murdered Leroy Demers?"

Gates glared at him. "To be honest with you, Nick, you're my prime suspect."

Nick returned to his seat on the couch while Gates continued to stand in the middle of his motel room. "That's ridiculous, Detective, and you know it," Nick answered without the least bit of concern.

"Is it ridiculous?" Gates angrily shot back. "You're a highly trained soldier who's killed before."

"Strong-arm tactics might work on your strung-out snitches, but I'm not in the mood for your mind games," Nick shot back.

"You're in no position to play tough guy with me," Gates angrily replied. "I'm sure you learned how to snap a man's neck during your Delta Force training."

"You can't be serious," Nick replied dismissively. "Why would I kill Demers?"

"How should I know?" Gates bellowed. "Maybe he was playing you for a sucker, and it pissed you off."

"Demers was already dead when I found him," Nick replied more forcefully. "Think about it, Gates. I needed him alive. Alive he could provide information about my daughter. Dead he is useless."

The detective's face was bright red, and veins were bulging on his forehead.

"You're hiding something, and I want to know what it is," Gates shouted.

"Get some sleep," Nick snapped. "You're sounding a bit paranoid."

"I requested your military records, but the Department of Defense informed me in no uncertain terms that your file is classified. I believe the Pentagon's exact words were 'beyond the jurisdiction of my investigation,'" Gates said in a mocking tone.

"The DOD's stonewalling of your investigation has nothing to do with the nature of my military service," Nick assured him. "The Delta Force operates in secret. In fact, the other soldiers stationed at Fort Bragg don't even know who is assigned to Delta Force. They wear civilian clothes or uniforms with no name or rank displayed to keep identities a secret."

"Great, more top secret rhetoric," Gates roared.

"Calm down," Nick shouted in reply. "Ask me your questions—I'll answer them."

Gates's demeanor softened, and he sat down on the foot of the bed. "Why is your military record classified? What kind of top secret stuff did you do?"

"My unit was on the periphery of some sensitive situations, politically speaking, but none of it is relevant to your investigation," Nick answered truthfully.

"Let me decide what's relevant and what's not," Gates shot back. "I know how to read people, and I get the distinct impression that you're hiding something."

Gates was right. Nick was keeping information from him, but it had absolutely nothing to do with his four-year stint in the military. Gates's involvement with Jefferson Hughes and the Panache investigation made it difficult for him to trust the detective.

"What do you want to know?"

"Start from the beginning, Jelaco. Why did a smart guy like you join the army?" Gates asked suspiciously. "At the very least, the air force and flight school seems more up your alley."

"That's a hard question to answer," Nick said with a shrug. "Why did you become a cop?" He could tell by Gates's facial expression that his rhetorical question annoyed the detective, so he continued without waiting for a response. "I can't remember my exact motivation for joining the army. I was confused about my future after I graduated from college. Most of my friends were going on to graduate school or getting jobs. Those options didn't feel right to me. I wanted something different, a new challenge. I suppose the army provided both."

Detective Gates nodded as if he understood the restlessness that had prompted Nick to choose that particular career path.

When the detective remained silent, he continued, "My commanding officer at Fort Huachuca recommended me for the Special Forces. Evidently he saw something in me that I didn't see in myself. Anyway, I completed the Special Forces' Qualification Course at the top of my class and was assigned to Fort Bragg and the Delta Force."

"You obviously saw some pretty heavy combat," Gates interrupted.

"My first assignment was stateside. I facilitated training missions and taught tactical weapons at Fort Bragg. That changed when I was reassigned in August of 1993."

"Is that when the army sent you to Mogadishu?"

"That's right. It was supposed to be a simple three-week mission. Obviously things got complicated."

"Yeah, things went real bad for our guys," Gates agreed.

"The army officially classified 'Operation Gothic Serpent' as a success, but we paid a very high price. Our mission was to capture two of Aidid's top militia leaders, which we did. In and out within thirty minutes, that was the original plan. Unfortunately, even the best-laid plans of mice and men—"

"Often go awry," Gates finished.

"That's an understatement," Nick said with a partial smile. "We captured Aidid's men without incident, but then it all came apart on the ground."

"I watched it on the news," Gates remarked softly.

"Take my word for it. The movies and documentaries don't do it justice," Nick responded. "By the time we were extracted the next day, eighteen of my comrades had died in the battle."

"You were part of the firefight on the ground?"

"I was knee deep in it, and it's not a fond memory," Nick replied quietly.

Gates rubbed his crew cut. "I'm just trying to figure out if there's a connection between your military service and the break-in at your house," he explained. "Aren't Delta Force soldiers trained primarily as a counter-terrorism unit?"

"That was one facet of my job description."

"Maybe a fanatical terrorist is out for revenge."

"No way," Nick replied without hesitation. "You've got a good imagination, but there's no connection between my past and what happened to my family."

"All that cloak and dagger stuff at the Pentagon makes me suspicious. Maybe you pissed off the wrong terrorist," Gates suggested.

"I was in Afghanistan masquerading as a civilian for a couple of weeks in November of 1994 and again in March of 1995. Both missions were for routine training purposes, completely under the radar, and real low profile. If the Taliban has active resources in the Unites States, they wouldn't waste an operative on someone like me," Nick assured the detective.

Detective Gates slowly rose from the foot of the double bed and stood directly in front of Nick. "We're pursuing the same objectives," Gates reminded him, "finding your daughter and putting the man who murdered your wife on death row. My job is that much more difficult if you don't trust me."

Nick nodded at Gates but couldn't bring himself to say he trusted the detective. "You have my word—I won't do anything to jeopardize or impede your investigation."

Gates took a small envelope out of his pants' pocket and handed it to Nick. "This didn't have any evidentiary value, but I figured it might have sentimental value."

Nick looked inside the envelope and nodded. "I gave this necklace to Julie on our first wedding anniversary," he answered, his voice choked with emotion. "It wasn't much compared to her father's lavish gifts, but she cherished this simple locket."

"If you think of anything that could point me in the right direction, you let me know," Gates said.

"You can count on it," Nick replied as Gates exited the room and slammed the door behind him.

CHAPTER 30

Tuesday morning, October 24

Nick and Simone were both cold and a little on edge as they waited in a dentist's parking lot that had a good view of Nick's old law firm. Neither of them needed dental work, which was a good thing, because the dental office had been closed for several hours. Instead, they were killing time until the cleaning crew finished up at the law office. Nick didn't have a clue what he hoped to accomplish by breaking into his old law firm, but his instincts were telling him it was the right move. Walter's role in Cole's conviction and the convoluted rationale they offered for his abrupt termination didn't feel right to him. It seemed like Walter didn't want him around the office, and he wanted to know why.

Nick's plan was to enter the office building through a basement window as soon as the cleaning crew vacated the premises. The window was located in a dark alley, and it had a broken latch that made it the perfect point of entry. With any luck, the understaffed Lakeland police force would be patrolling another part of the city for the next hour or two. The past twenty-four hours had been a wild ride for Nick. He had discovered a murder victim in a quiet neighborhood park the night before and tonight he was about to break into an office building. He shuddered to think what tomorrow might bring. If Simone had looked him square in the eyes and said, "Nick, you've lost your mind," he would have agreed with her.

When he told Simone about his half-baked scheme, his new partner in crime had insisted on joining him. Nick had argued with her for a few minutes before he reluctantly agreed to let her tag along. Now that they were alone in the cold dark car, Nick was actually grateful for her company. Small talk was non-existent while they waited, but the cleaning crew finally turned off the last light. Nick watched as the old, married couple who had cleaned Walter's building for the past fifteen years loaded up their cleaning supplies and slowly drove away from the parking lot.

When the old van disappeared around the corner, Nick asked, "Are you still up for this?"

"I guess so," Simone whispered. "What's the penalty for burglary?"

"Technically, it's not burglary unless we enter with the intent to steal something or to commit a felony once we're inside," Nick explained, tongue in cheek. "What we're doing is more along the line of breaking and entering or criminal trespass."

Nick could tell by the look on Simone's face that his brief summary of the crimes they were about to commit had not lessened her apprehension.

"That's a relief," she said sarcastically. "I was afraid breaking into a building in the middle of the night might be frowned upon by the authorities."

"Don't worry—it's only a crime if we get caught," Nick said as he opened the car door.

Simone sighed and said, "Then we better not get caught."

Simone was definitely dressed for the occasion. She was wearing a black sweater, black pants, black boots, and a black stocking cap. Nick was wearing the same gray sweater, Nike windbreaker, and blue jeans he had been wearing all day. He may have been ill dressed in comparison to Simone, but at least he had remembered to bring a small penlight and pocketknife.

As they walked down the sidewalk, Nick said, "The best

point of entry is a basement window that can be accessed from the alley."

"Are you positive you don't have an extra key? It's hard to look dignified when you're squirming through a basement window."

"I'm positive," Nick replied. "Walter and his buddies almost strip-searched me after I was fired."

Simone responded with a nervous smile. "Then it looks like we'll be climbing through the window."

The two of them walked the length of the alley in complete silence. When they reached the window with the broken latch, Nick stopped and whispered, "That's the window. I'll go first and then lower you into the basement."

"Whatever you say," Simone agreed weakly. "You're the expert when it comes to breaking and entering."

"I completely understand if you've had a change of heart," Nick said. "Why don't you wait for me in the car?"

The apprehension on Simone's face was replaced with a determined look as she said, "Let's get moving. We're not going to find any evidence freezing our tails off in this alley."

Nick carefully lowered himself into the window well and tested the broken latch. The rusty hinges groaned as he pushed the window inward, but it opened. When he had opened it as far as it would go, Nick carefully lowered himself into the basement. With his feet and legs dangling inside the building, he carefully rotated himself until his stomach was resting on the window-sill. After a brief pause, he started to lower the upper half of his body into the basement. Everything was going according to plan until his shoulders got stuck in the window. Nick thought about pulling himself back out but quickly decided that direction was hopeless. Instead, he started swinging his legs from side to side like a pendulum. With each swing his shoulders slipped an inch or two further into the basement. After several seconds of swinging back and forth, he slipped through the window crashing rear-end first into a pile of dusty boxes.

When Nick finally came to rest, he was flat on his back with a face full of dust. After wiping the dust from his eyes, he looked up and saw Simone peering at him through the open window. "Are you okay?"

"Physically, I'm fine, but my ego is a little bruised," Nick admitted as he lifted himself off the cement floor and brushed off his clothing.

"Don't worry. I won't say a word until both my feet are firmly planted on the ground," she joked.

"Slide your legs through the window and then turn onto your stomach," Nick told her. "I'll take hold of your waist and lower you to the floor."

Simone sat down on the windowsill and extended her legs into the basement. Once her legs were inside, she rolled onto her stomach, while Nick tentatively placed his hands on her hips. He then gently held her by the waist as she lowered herself through the window. Just before her feet touched the cement floor, his hands slipped from her waist and brushed against her breasts. It was an accidental and meaningless touch, but for some reason, it made Nick feel like an awkward teenager.

Simone appeared a little bit self-conscious when she turned to face him, but in a teasing tone said, "I'm surprised you didn't drop me."

Nick knew she was trying to minimize his embarrassment by pretending the touch had gone unnoticed, and he appreciated it.

"The thought definitely crossed my mind after you got such a kick out of my ungraceful entry."

After Simone had brushed the dust from her sweater, she asked, "What are we looking for?"

"I'm not sure, but I'll know it when I see it."

"You'll know it when you see it," Simone repeated.

"Hear me out," Nick implored. "The explanation given for my abrupt termination just doesn't add up. I got the distinct impression my bosses didn't want me hanging around the office."

"In other words, this is a wild goose chase," Simone joked.

"I suppose that's one way to look at it," Nick agreed. "Now let's get a move on before someone comes poking around here."

Nick removed the penlight from his jacket pocket and switched it on. The small light provided just enough illumination to show a clear path through the maze of dusty old legal boxes but not enough to attract unwanted attention from outside.

"Let's start in Walter's office; he keeps his confidential files in a cabinet beside his desk."

They had only taken a few steps toward the staircase when Nick stopped and sheepishly said, "If the door leading to the main floor is locked, I'll need to pick it."

"You know how to pick a lock?" Simone asked, clearly surprised.

Nick responded with an uncomfortable grin and said, "Not really, but I know how to kick a door in."

Simone followed him quietly up the cement staircase, and much to his relief, the door leading to the main floor offices was unlocked. It was a strange feeling to be a trespasser in the law firm that had employed him for the past six years.

"Walter's office is in the east hallway, last door on the left," Nick whispered to Simone.

Nick kept the penlight pointed at the carpeted floor as he and Simone made their way down the hallway toward his ex-employer's office. Walter's personal file cabinet was positioned on the north wall within arm's reach of his desk. Nick kept the penlight close to the ground and hooded it with his hand as they approached the open curtains behind Walter's desk. He definitely didn't want to attract the attention of a curious pass-erby or a bored police officer patrolling the area. Simone followed him to Walter's file cabinet and waited for instructions.

"There's only one drawer that isn't labeled and it's locked," he whispered after a quick check of the file cabinet.

"We can't take the whole file cabinet," Simone nervously replied

"Don't worry. I can pick the lock."

"Five minutes ago you didn't know how to pick a lock."

"File cabinets are easier."

Simone rolled her eyes but didn't vocalize her skepticism. The lock was harder to pick than he had expected; still, he managed to pop it open on his fourth try. The file drawer contained twenty-five to thirty files that weren't identified by a client name. Instead, each file had a series of numbers handwritten on the file tab. The numerical code appeared to be a four-digit identification code followed by the year the file was created. The earliest date displayed on any file was 1987, and the most recent date was 2003. Nick handed Simone a file from 1987 and kept a file dated 2003 for himself.

"What exactly are we looking for?" Simone asked.

"I know I sound like a broken record, but I'm not really sure," Nick answered. "Just let me know if something looks fishy."

Simone thumbed through the contents of her file with a confused look on her face. "The stuff in this file looks like a bunch of background checks. Do you think Walter gathers information on potential employees?"

Simone was partially right; the files did contain personal information, but it wasn't gathered for the purpose of evaluating potential employees. The reports graphically detailed the personal transgressions of jurors seated on a civil trial Walter had litigated in 1987. The highly personal summaries had obviously been prepared by a private detective and contained potentially compromising information about each juror. Nick was trying to figure out how their discovery impacted his search for Darby when the bright headlights of a car passing through the alley filled the east window. He quickly dimmed the penlight and motioned for Simone to duck behind Walter's desk. After a couple of seconds, he peeked over the top of Walter's desk and saw a Lakeland police car creeping through the alley directly behind the law office. They continued to crouch behind Walter's desk until the police car turned onto a side street and disappeared from view. When the alley was dark again, Nick turned to Simone and barked, "It's time to go."

"Let's finish what we started," Simone stated with newfound determination.

"It's too risky," he snapped.

"I'm not leaving this place empty handed."

"I have an idea, but if it turns into another dead end, we're out of here."

Nick turned on the penlight and directed its beam into the file cabinet. He was somewhat familiar with the highlights of Walter's legal career, and the Strickland case litigated in 1988 had always intrigued him. Most legal experts had predicted the case would bankrupt Walter's upstart law firm; instead, it had been the civil case that propelled Walter's new law firm to unexpected heights. Nick hastily removed the only file from the drawer that was labeled 1988, and, just as he'd suspected, the 1988 file contained twelve reports with enough detail to satisfy even the pickiest CIA agent. Each summary provided graphic descriptions of a juror's personal weaknesses and shortcomings. As Nick scanned the reports, he saws accounts of drug use, marital infidelity, spousal battery, sexual harassment, and questionable political ideology. He was thinking about photocopying the contents of the file when one of the juror reports jumped out at him. It was the dossier of a local attorney who had been practicing law in Lakeland for the past twenty years.

"Jason Davidson was a juror on the Strickland case?" Nick mumbled to himself.

"Why is that important?" Simone asked.

"It makes no sense from a litigation perspective," Nick said as he thumbed through the report.

"I'm not a trial lawyer," Simone reminded him.

"Jason Davidson is a civil defense attorney," Nick explained. "Any competent plaintiff's lawyer would have challenged him for cause."

"I still don't understand."

"I'll explain it when we get to the car."

Nick shoved the juror reports into the file and hastily returned the file to the cabinet.

"There's a back door that opens into the alley," Nick said as he closed the file cabinet. "It's the only door without a dead bolt, which means I can lock it from the inside and then pull it shut once we're outside."

"That sounds good to me," Simone agreed. "I wasn't thrilled about the prospect of climbing out that basement window."

Once they were safely back in the Mustang, Simone said, "Remember, you promised a lesson on the intricacies of jury selection."

"One of the jurors in the Strickland case was an attorney who specializes in commercial litigation, and he usually defends banks and insurance companies."

"What difference does that make?"

"Walter represented the plaintiff, Adam Strickland. If the scuttlebutt was accurate, the plaintiff had a weak case from a legal perspective, and Mr. Davidson was a business lawyer."

"Which means?" Simone prodded.

"Jason Davidson was the worst possible juror from the plaintiff's perspective," Nick continued. "Walter should have done everything within his power to keep him off that jury."

"Did Walter have the authority to kick him off the jury?" Simone asked.

"He could have challenged Mr. Davidson for cause, and if that failed, he could have used a preemptory challenge to remove him from the panel," Nick said. "It sounds complicated, but it's really quite simple."

Simone thought for a couple of seconds and then said, "What if Walter is just a really bad lawyer?"

If Nick hadn't seen the dossier on Jason Davidson or if Walter had lost the Strickland case, he could have accepted Simone's seemingly plausible explanation. When he considered the facts of the case, Walter's limited ability and the staggering judgment, things didn't add up.

"That snake used the information to manipulate the jurors," Nick mumbled to himself.

Simone realized that she was jumping to potentially illogical conclusions, but she took Nick's conjecture to the next step. "If you're right and Walter Burton is corrupt enough to bribe and threaten jurors, he could be responsible for fabricating the evidence in my brother's case."

"It's possible."

"What's next?"

"I'll have a little chat with Mr. Davidson," Nick said.

"What if he won't talk?"

"I'll cross that bridge when I come to it."

CHAPTER 31

Tuesday afternoon, October 24

Nick parked up the street from Jason Davidson's Main Street law office while he waited for the downtown professionals to rush out of their offices for a quick lunch. Nick hoped Jason Davidson took a lunch break and, if he did, that he would still recognize him. His only contact with Mr. Davidson had occurred several years before when they had met briefly to discuss a breach of contract case. The case had settled prior to trial, which meant most of their contact had occurred over the telephone or via currier. Finally, fifteen minutes past the hour, Jason Davidson Esquire came strolling through the front door of his office complex. His appearance had not changed much since the last time Nick had seen him. Jason's hair was a little longer, and he had put on a few pounds, but otherwise, the short, heavyset man with bushy black hair looked the same.

On the sidewalk, Jason stopped briefly to put on a pair of sunglasses and hike up his sagging trousers. After adjusting his clothing, he turned right and began walking up Main Street directly toward Nick's parked car. Nick picked up yesterday's newspaper and pretended to read as the lawyer passed by the Mustang. When Jason was twenty to thirty feet up the sidewalk, Nick nonchalantly exited his car and followed at a safe distance. He was still trying to work out the specifics of his plan when Jason suddenly veered into Wong's Wok and Grill. Nick waited outside for a minute and then followed him into the Chinese restaurant. After Nick's eyes adjusted to the dim lighting, he spied Jason sitting alone in a corner booth. As he glanced around the restaurant, it occurred to him that the soft lighting and private booths would provide the perfect setting to confront Mr. Davidson.

A petite, Asian hostess politely offered to seat him, but Nick told her he was joining a friend and confidently headed for the corner booth. Jason was scanning a menu when Nick stopped beside his table.

"It's good to see you, Jason," Nick said with as much self-confidence as he could muster. When the chubby lawyer looked up, Nick continued, "We were on opposite sides of a contract dispute a few years ago."

"Sure, Nick, I remember," Jason nervously replied and then added, "I was really sorry to hear the news about your wife and daughter." Conspicuously absent was an invitation to join him.

Nick felt more than a little uncomfortable, but he forged ahead just the same. "Do you mind if I join you for a minute?"

"Sure, no problem," Jason hesitantly responded.

Nick slid into the seat directly across from Jason and said, "I'm here about a personal matter."

Jason's confused expression turned into a look of outright distress. "I'm on a tight schedule, Nick."

"This is going to sound a little bizarre, so please hear me out," Nick offered as a precursor.

Jason glanced at his watch and impatiently said, "Okay...get to the point."

"I'm sure you're aware that my daughter was kidnapped."

Jason nodded. "It's been all over the news."

Nick carefully thought about his choice of words before he continued. "I don't have any concrete proof, but I believe one of Walter's old cases is behind my daughter's kidnapping."

The blood seemed to drain from Jason's face, and it appeared as if he might get sick to his stomach. But before he could respond, a different Asian waitress stopped at the table to take their orders. Evidently Nick's unexpected intrusion had ruined Jason's appetite, because he passed on lunch and ordered a Diet Coke. Nick also ordered a Diet Coke, and the waitress abruptly left to retrieve the drinks.

Nick's theory had seemed logical while he waited alone in the Mustang, but sitting across from Jason Davidson, he suddenly felt like a complete idiot.

"Jason, I'm desperate for any information that might help me find my daughter," he began candidly and then he stretched the truth somewhat. "I have irrefutable proof that Walter bribed witnesses when he was the Monroe County prosecutor."

Jason's already pale face whitened another shade or two. "That sounds like an ethics issue that should be addressed by the Bar Association," he replied weakly.

"I also believe Walter bribed jurors in some of his civil cases," Nick continued.

Jason flinched noticeably and stood to leave. "I'm sorry about your loss, Nick, but I really need to get back to the office."

"If you're too busy, I'll take my suspicions to the police," Nick threatened.

"You're delusional," Jason countered weakly. "Maybe you should look into counseling or something."

"Did Walter bribe you in the Strickland case?" Nick asked point blank. "There's no way you should have been on that jury."

Jason covered his face with the palm of his hand and sat back down just as the waitress delivered their sodas.

"Will there be anything else?" the waitress asked without enthusiasm.

"No, we're fine," Jason replied without making eye contact. The waitress dropped the ticket on the table and left.

"I need your help, Jason," Nick pleaded. "My daughter's life is at stake."

"Believe me, Nick! I would help you if I could," Jason said with heartfelt sympathy.

"Then help me Jason," Nick pleaded.

"How can I?" Jason asked. "I don't have a clue what you're

talking about." Jason stood up again and said, "Now if you'll excuse me, I do need to get back to the office."

Nick grabbed Jason's arm before he could leave. "You're a good guy, Jason. Do the right thing," he urged.

Jason weakly attempted to pull his arm from Nick's grasp. "Nick, you're way off base," he stammered. "There's absolutely no way I would be involved in anything unethical or illegal."

Nick released Jason's arm and said, "I don't care about the friggin' Strickland case. This is about my three-year-old daughter."

"I can't help you," Jason said again.

Nick stared at Jason with piercing eyes. "Can you live with your guilty conscience if my daughter dies?"

Jason sat back down and ran one of his sweaty hands through his curly black hair. They sat there in silence for several seconds until Jason finally spoke, "Walter didn't bribe me."

Nick's heart sank. He had really believed that Jason was about to purge a guilty conscience. "It's my daughter, and you're all I've got," Nick pleaded again.

Jason looked at his Diet Coke and then pushed it away in disgust. "If you repeat one word of this, I'll claim you're crazy and deny it with my last dying breath."

"You have my word," Nick promised.

Jason looked up from his drink and began to speak slowly in a hushed voice. "Walter didn't bribe me. I never would have traded my dignity and integrity for money."

"How did he convince you to fix the verdict?" Nick asked.

Jason's eyes filled with tears and he quickly wiped them away with the back of his hand. "The monster threatened to kill my wife." Nick had been expecting something awful, but Jason's statement momentarily stunned him into silence. When Jason realized Nick wasn't going to prod him for the specifics, he continued. "Walter didn't actually threaten me, but the madman had to be working for him."

Nick shook his head in confusion and disbelief. "I'm sorry, Jason, but you've lost me."

Jason nodded and started from the beginning. "When I was

called for jury duty, I told my wife that there was absolutely no way I'd be selected for a jury trial—you know, being a civil lawyer who specializes in defense work. Once I realized it was the Strickland case, I was convinced I would be the first juror dismissed."

"That's exactly what I'd think," Nick agreed.

"Jeez, Nick, half of my clients are banks and insurance companies," Jason added. "I filled out my juror questionnaire fully thinking that I'd be excused during voir dire."

"Walter didn't challenge you?" Nick asked, surprised.

Jason shook his head. "The judge asked me a few routine questions, and then the bank's lawyer asked me a few questions. The bank's lawyer, some old-timer named Arthur Pike, told the judge the defense considered me an acceptable juror."

"No big surprise there."

"Yeah, I figured the defense would try to keep me," Jason remarked. "Anyway, Walter stood up, all pompous and full of himself. Right out of the box he asked if I would render a verdict consistent with the evidence presented. I answered yes, and Walter said, 'The plaintiff has no objections to this juror.'"

"Were you shocked?" Nick asked.

"I about fell out of my chair," Jason said with a rueful smile. "At that moment, I honestly thought Walter was the dumbest lawyer on the face of the earth."

"What happened next?" Nick coaxed.

Jason took a sip of his Diet Coke before he continued telling his story. "Both parties made their opening statements, and then Judge Smoot recessed court until Monday morning at nine o'clock. I was still in shock, so I went back to the office to tie up a few loose ends. I certainly wasn't expecting to be out of the office for a week or two when I showed up for jury duty. Anyway, I scribbled a bunch of notes for my secretary and then headed home for the weekend. It was Friday night at about ten o'clock, and my car was parked in the lot behind my office," Jason explained. "It was kind of spooky; you know how downtown Lakeland is deserted after six o'clock. When I got to my car, there was this giant of a man leaning against it. I was definitely nervous but figured he was some homeless guy looking for a handout."

When Jason described the guy as "a giant of a man," Nick immediately thought about the enormous shoeprints in the entryway of his house. "How big was he?" Nick asked.

"Six foot nine, six foot ten, easy—at least 350 pounds. He was the biggest man I'd ever seen in person."

Nick's thoughts flashed to his wife and the terror Julie must have felt if it had been the same man. His mind then conjured up an ugly image of his tiny three-year-old daughter being held captive by the gigantic man. "It sounds like he made a lasting impression," Nick said.

Jason nodded his agreement and mumbled, "You have no idea, and his physical appearance was even more unsettling than his size."

"How so?" Nick asked, not sure if he really wanted an answer.

"The guy had long, scraggly black hair, and his face was covered with hideous scars."

Nick wanted to create a complete picture of the man he planned to kill, so he pushed Jason for more detail. "Was he a white man?"

"He wasn't white or African-American," Jason answered without hesitation. "He looked almost Indian or South American."

Nick nodded but didn't interrupt again.

"At first he tried to bum a ride, but I politely declined," Jason continued. "Unfortunately, he wasn't the type of guy who took no for an answer."

"So you agreed to give him a lift?"

"Not exactly," Jason answered with a nervous chuckle. "He thumped me upside the head and knocked me out cold. When I came to, I was locked in the trunk of my own car beside my golf clubs. I don't know how long he drove with me in the trunk, but it seemed like hours."

Nick couldn't believe what he was hearing. "He knocked you out and locked you in the trunk of your own car?" he repeated in disbelief.

Jason picked up his soda, but his hand was shaking so hard that he set it down without taking a drink. "I've never told anybody the whole story, not even my wife," he said in a barely audible voice.

"You have my word, Jason. Your story goes no further than me," Nick promised.

"When the car finally stopped, I was sure he was going to kill me, but he didn't. Instead he pulled me out of the trunk by my hair and dragged me into some old, smelly shack. I'm pretty sure the shack was close to the reservoir, but I don't know the exact location."

"What's your best guess?" Nick asked.

Jason closed his eyes as if he was trying to recall a hazy memory and said, "I was confused and disoriented, but I think it was on the north shore."

Nick felt sympathy for the chubby, little lawyer sitting across from him. Reliving his ordeal was obviously dredging up memories that he had buried deep in an attempt to preserve his sanity. If Darby's life hadn't been at stake, he never would have forced him to recount the disturbing events.

"What happened in the shack, Jason?"

Jason stared off into space and distantly said, "It was so strange, sometimes I can almost convince myself it was all just a bad dream. After he dragged me into the shack, he ordered me to strip down to my underwear."

Jason wasn't looking well, and Nick was feeling guilty about pushing him to talk. "Do you need a minute?" he asked.

Jason shrugged his shoulders. "I'm okay," he replied unconvincingly. He continued in a rush, "At first, I thought the guy was going to sexually assault me. I wanted to scream for help, but I knew it was useless. All the windows of the dingy old cabin were boarded up, and a small kerosene lantern provided the only heat and light. Once I had removed my suit and shirt, he tossed me into a small room and locked the door from the outside. He kept the kerosene lantern, so it was dark and cold as hell inside that room. Once he left me alone, I briefly entertained thoughts of escape, but it soon became apparent that my freedom would be on his terms. The room's only window was boarded up tighter than a drum and the giant was standing guard outside the room's only door. I did manage to stumble across a trap door in the wooden floor, but it was secured with a padlock."

"What did you do?"

"Not much," Jason sheepishly admitted, clearly embarrassed by his lack of ingenuity. "I just paced back and forth in my underwear. I probably wore a rut in the wooden floor trying to stay warm. The whole time I was pacing, I could hear him chanting or singing in some bizarre language."

Jason quit talking and covered his face with both hands. He sat there with his head buried in the palms of his hands for quite some time. When he removed his hands, his eyes were red and swollen.

"I was in a bad spot, Nick. The waiting was a nightmare, but not nearly as terrifying as the thought of his impending return. I was huddled in a corner when he came barreling through the door, and let me say, he had worked himself into a frenzy. He grabbed me around the throat and yanked me to my feet. He choked me until I was about to lose consciousness, but he didn't want me to pass out. Just before I blacked out, he loosened his grip on my neck and slammed me against the wall. I was gasping for breath, trying to pull myself together, when he slapped me so hard that it knocked me to the floor. He left the room while I was sprawled out on the floor, but he wasn't done with me, not by a long shot. He repeated the brutal ritual a half dozen times over the course of the night. He would chant and sing in that strange language and then storm back into the room to inflict more torture."

"He kept it up all night?" Nick asked, trying to imagine the psychological damage Jason had suffered.

"Yeah, I was actually praying for a quick and painless death when the first rays of sunlight shined through the cracks in the boarded-up windows." Jason shuddered involuntarily. "He was calm when he came to see me in the morning, but his composed demeanor was worse than the crazy ranting and raving. I've never seen a shark's eyes, but I've read accounts," Jason tried to explain. "That's what his eyes were like—black and lifeless with no emotion. I knew beyond a shadow of a doubt that he could kill me and never give it a second thought."

"Is that when he threatened to kill your wife?" Nick asked.

Jason nodded his head, wiped his eyes, and said, "Uh huh. After he broke me down mentally, he got to the crux of the matter. He told me what he expected from me and the consequences of failure."

"Consequences of failure?" Nick repeated.

"To this day, I have nightmares about his sales pitch," Jason said matter-of-factly. "That last time, he didn't throw me around like a rag doll. He methodically walked toward me, and I slowly backed myself into the corner. When my back was flat against the wall, he pressed his massive body up against mine, and he moved his face in real close. He was so close I could feel his hot, sour breath on my face. The tone of his voice was emotionless, but his words conveyed pure madness. He told me that he was the instrument of powerful men and death was his calling card."

"What does that mean?" Nick asked with a furrowed brow.

Jason shrugged. "He wasn't making a lot of sense. Still, it came through loud and clear that he was the front man for someone else and the services he brought to the table were death and intimidation."

"Did he happen to tell you which men?" Nick cut in.

Jason frowned and shook his head. "He never mentioned any names, but he definitely told me what they wanted."

"A plaintiff's verdict in the Strickland case?"

"That's right, and at least $6 million in damages," Jason added. "Even though I was scared out of my wits, I still told him he'd lost his mind. There was no way I could deliver such an outlandish verdict."

"What did he do then?"

"He laughed in my face and said that it didn't matter to him one way or the other."

"I take it there were repercussions for failure," Nick suggested.

"Oh yeah, there were serious repercussions," Jason agreed. "He told me if I didn't deliver a plaintiff's verdict, he would kill my wife."

"You're certain it was a death threat?"

"He made it abundantly clear that it wouldn't be a quick, painless death," Jason elaborated. "He said my wife would suffer immeasurably for my failure. I truly believe that he wanted me to fail."

Jason paused long enough to finish his Diet Coke. "When the psychopath was convinced I was taking him seriously, which I certainly was, he threw my clothes at me and told me to get dressed. After I was dressed, he covered my eyes with duct tape and locked me in the trunk of my car again. He drove into the desert near the old internment camp, yanked me out of the trunk, and ripped the duct tape off my eyes. His parting words reiterated the fact that my wife's life depended on the outcome of the Strickland case."

"I can relate to your feelings of helplessness," Nick remarked as his thoughts flashed to his daughter.

"I bet you can," Jason said with sadness in his voice. "After his final threat, I just stood there as he sped away in my car. I started walking toward the highway, and thankfully, a young couple with two small children picked me up. I guess a short, fat man in a business suit didn't appear all that threatening. I can't remember the ride into town, but I'm sure they had second thoughts after they picked me up," Jason said with an uncomfortable smile. "Anyway, the couple was headed downtown, so I asked them to drop me off at my office. Much to my surprise, my car was waiting for me in the parking lot. The psycho had even parked it in the exact same spot. For a fleeting second, I thought I had imagined the whole ordeal."

"Thanks, Jason. I know that wasn't easy," Nick said with heartfelt gratitude.

"Would you excuse me for a second, Nick? I need to use the restroom," Jason said and then abruptly left the table without further comment.

Nick was grateful for a little time to process Jason's bizarre story. He needed to figure out how the lawyer's kidnapping and torture was connected to the other pieces of the puzzle. He knew Walter was an integral player in Cole Panache's case, but he couldn't be certain of his exact involvement. It was also apparent that Walter's role in Cole's prosecution indirectly connected him to Jefferson Hughes and Janis Jones. In regard to Darby's abductor, the murder in Hartman Park seemed to be the most crucial piece of evidence. Nick was convinced that Julie's murderer was the same man who had snapped Leroy's neck. Leroy had claimed to know the identity of his daughter's kidnapper, and now he was dead. Nick didn't have direct proof. Still, his intuition was telling him that the man he sought had also been Jason's tormenter. If he could put a name with the description Jason had provided, it might shed some light on Walter's ties to the killer, and then he just might have enough evidence to unravel the web of lies. The real question was whether or not he would have enough time.

When Jason returned a couple of minutes later, he was as pale as a ghost. Nick wondered if reliving his story had made him physically ill. He felt guilty about putting the timid lawyer through the ringer, but he had to hear the final chapter of the story.

After Jason was seated, Nick said, "So in the end, you delivered a plaintiff's verdict?"

"Yeah, I handed Walter his verdict on a silver platter," Jason sadly replied. "It wouldn't have been hard to sway the jury if Walter had presented a flawless case, but that incompetent boob made my job almost impossible."

"But you pulled it off," Nick interjected.

"It's amazing how persuasive you can be when a loved one's life depends on your success. I argued the case of my life sequestered away in that jury room. I convinced my fellow jurors the rules of evidence prohibited the judge from allowing prejudicial evidence of the bank's prior bad conduct to be heard in court. I lied that I was personally aware of multiple instances where the bank had acted not only improperly but criminally. Maybe

Walter was counting on my expertise as a defense lawyer when he chose me for that jury, because he raked in millions. In fact, I was so good the jury came in with a $12 million verdict. He's not much of a lawyer, but the man knows how to manipulate the legal system. In the end, Adam Strickland and Walter Burton got rich, and I've lived the last eighteen years of my life in shame."

Jason Davidson and Jefferson Hughes seemingly had nothing in common, but each in their own way had been victimized by corruption in the legal system. Jason had traded his self-respect and professional integrity for his wife's life. Jefferson had spent the last twenty years living in fear and isolation with nothing to show for his trouble but a dead niece.

"Aside from one person who deserves the truth, you have my word that I'll take your story to the grave," Nick promised.

"Do you trust him?"

"Her ... and yes, I do."

Jason nodded and looked at him with such genuine sadness that Nick knew the chubby lawyer was no longer thinking about himself. "If that lunatic has your daughter, you need to find her yesterday."

Nick dropped a ten-dollar bill on the table and said, "I know, Jason, I know."

CHAPTER 32

Tuesday afternoon, October 24

Monroe County medical examiner, Katie Holt, tossed a file onto Detective Gates's desk and said, "Sorry, Phil, I screwed up big-time on this one."

Detective Gates glanced at the file. The name Janis Jones had been hastily scribbled across the front cover of the tan folder. "I'm not worried about who screwed up, Katie. Just tell me you have some good news."

"Judge Montgomery was not overly thrilled by my request to dig up Ms. Jones's body, but he finally signed the exhumation order after a lengthy lecture on doing my job right the first time," Katie said with a roll of her eyes.

"Remind me to put the judge on my Christmas list," Gates said sarcastically.

Unable to contain her excitement any longer, Katie blurted out, "It seems as if I'll need to amend the original death certificate from accidental overdose to death by homicide."

"You sound pretty sure of yourself, Katie," Gates goaded. "I thought there were no certainties when it came to forensic science."

Katie raised her arms in frustration and said, "Jeez, Phil. I try to give you something concrete, and you throw it back in my face."

"This case is beginning to take a toll on my sunny disposition," Gates gruffly retorted. "Take a seat and tell me about the autopsy."

"I'm too amped up to sit," Katie replied and then immediately plopped down in the chair next to Gates's desk. "Janis Jones was killed with a lethal dose of potassium," she confidently stated.

Gates thought about the medical examiner's conclusion for several seconds before he asked, "Potassium is a fairly common substance. How can you be certain she didn't ingest it accidentally?"

A smile flashed across Katie's face as if she had been expecting Gates's question. "It's almost impossible to die from accidental potassium poisoning. When a person ingests large amounts of potassium orally, poisoning is usually prevented by the person's vomiting reflex. Aside from puking it up, the body's natural cleansing function removes toxic levels of potassium from the bloodstream. Potassium is a natural substance that is easily absorbed by the various cells of the body, and once absorbed, the kidneys quickly transfer the potassium ions from the bloodstream into the urine."

"Then how did Ms. Jones die from potassium poisoning?"

"It wasn't ingested orally," Katie repeated, clearly toying with the uptight detective.

"That's the only fact we've established so far," Gates impatiently countered.

"Someone injected the lethal dose of potassium into Ms. Jones's bloodstream."

"Any chance Janis Jones injected the potassium herself?" Gates asked.

"There's a chance, but the odds are pretty slim, Phil."

"Wasn't she a junkie?" Gates asked. "She probably thought she was injecting an illicit substance."

"I only found the one injection site on her right thigh," Katie replied. "There was no evidence whatsoever that Ms. Jones was a needle user."

Gates had a puzzled look on his face. "Ms. Jones was a junkie, but she only had one injection site on her entire body?"

"Judging by the excessive scarring in her throat and lungs, Ms. Jones apparently preferred the inhalation method," Katie explained. "The autopsy also revealed extensive damage to her heart, liver, and kidneys from prolonged substance abuse."

"Her death was several months ago," Gates reminded the medical examiner. "Is it possible the passage of time impacted the autopsy results?"

"Time was definitely a concern, but we got lucky in this case," Dr. Holt explained. "The potassium levels we found in her organs and body tissue were off the charts. More than one hundred times the amount of potassium that is found in the human body naturally."

"Just to make sure we're on the same page, are you telling me that someone injected Ms. Jones with potassium?"

"That's exactly what I'm telling you," Katie answered with atypical directness. "Large doses of potassium can cause cardiac arrest and respiratory failure. In Ms. Jones's case, prolonged drug use had weakened her regulatory system to the point where even a much lower dose of potassium would have proved fatal."

"Did you find any illicit drugs in her system?"

"We found trace amounts of methamphetamine and alcohol but nothing to write home about," Katie replied.

Gates leaned forward and tapped the end of his pen on the Jones file. "Were there any signs of foul play?"

"Besides the lethal dose of potassium?" Katie flippantly asked.

"Yes, besides the potassium," Gates replied, annoyed.

Gates could tell that Katie was somewhat embarrassed by the answer she was about to give the detective. "She had three cracked ribs and a fairly substantial contusion on the right side of her neck."

"So somebody roughed her up a little bit before he killed her," Gates muttered under his breath.

"What's that, Phil?"

"I was talking to myself," Gates mumbled again. "Nice work, Katie. Now we can assume the knowledge Ms. Jones claimed to possess was the underlying motive for the Jelaco break-in."

"Sorry about the initial screwup, Phil," Katie apologized again.

"Nobody's perfect," Gates answered flatly.

"You know where to find me if you have any questions," Katie said as she abruptly stood and left Gates's office.

It was becoming more apparent that somebody wanted to permanently shut Janis Jones's mouth, and Gates had a pretty good idea who it was. He didn't like where the Jelaco case was headed. Still, he'd follow the evidence trail just the same. If the investigation led to his front door, he'd cross that bridge when he got there.

CHAPTER 33

Tuesday night, October 24

Nick had phoned Simone following his informative lunch to invite her to an early dinner. Simone had hesitantly accepted his invitation, and Nick wondered if she felt awkward being seen in public with a recent widower. Even if she was comfortable with their alliance, Nick was still battling the appropriateness of having a female friend. In fact, he had chosen a generic franchise as their meeting place, because he feared a charming locally owned restaurant might seem too personal.

Once she arrived, it was his intent to swear her to secrecy before he disclosed the details of Jason Davidson's ordeal. There was also the matter of their return trip to the Wood River Valley. The events of the past three days had convinced him that a second get-together with Jefferson Hughes should be their first priority. Even though he had no direct proof that Darby was still alive, his instincts were telling him that she was out there waiting for her daddy. He was also confident that his daughter's captor had killed Leroy Demers and terrorized Jason Davidson. That realization had heightened—if that was even possible—the terror that had consumed him since his daughter's disappearance.

As Nick ran through the details of his wife's murder, the bartender's death, and Jason's torture, he became more convinced that the killer was actually a henchman for someone else and that someone was probably Walter Burton. Time was his enemy, yet Nick had to fight a compelling desire to confront Walter. If he tipped his hand too quickly, it could provide his ex-employer with an opportunity to cover his tracks. Nick didn't believe that Walter's misdeeds had ended with jury tampering in the Strickland case. If Jefferson Hughes was telling the truth, Detective Gates had delivered the payoff, but the circumstantial evidence seemed to indicate that Walter Burton was behind the old man's perjured testimony and Cole Panache's questionable conviction. Unfortunately, Nick didn't have any hard facts to connect Walter to Jefferson Hughes.

There were countless unknowns, but the elusive giant of a man and Walter Burton were the two known variables that ran throughout his loose-knit suspicions. Nick was guardedly optimistic their next trip to the Wood River Valley would shed some light on the faceless, nameless killer and his connection to Walter Burton. Jason Davidson's description of his tormentor had been detailed and unique, which meant with a little luck, Jefferson Hughes might be able to provide them with a name.

Nick was still deep in thought when Simone slid into the booth across from him.

"Sorry I'm late," she apologized. "Crossing town during rush hour is a nightmare."

Simone was wearing gray pants, black boots, and a black sweater. For some reason, it occurred to Nick that she always wore dark colors, and he wondered if her avoidance of bright clothing was an attempt to downplay her physical appearance.

"No problem," Nick responded flatly, annoyed that he had noticed her attire and attractiveness. "It gave me some time to think."

"Did you solve the case without me?" Simone joked with a relaxed smile.

"To be honest with you, I'm having one heck of a time piecing this thing together."

"You sounded pretty upbeat on the phone," Simone remarked. "I take it your hunch about the Strickland case was right on target."

"At first I was afraid Jason would tell me to take a hike or that I had lost my mind," Nick admitted. "Instead, he told me things that were more shocking and bizarre than anything I could have imagined."

"Shocking and bizarre," Simone repeated. "That's sounds alarmingly familiar after our meeting with Jefferson Hughes and the dead body in Hartman Park."

"The deeper I dig, the stranger this case gets," Nick said with a frustrated shake of his head.

Nick was about to give Simone a condensed version of his exchange with Jason Davidson when a young waitress, who introduced herself as Skye, approached the booth. He fought an urge to order an extra large mug of beer and ordered a small sirloin steak, a baked potato, and an ice water instead. Simone, who had hardly glanced at the menu, ordered the same thing.

When they were alone again, Simone said, "Before you tell me about your meeting with Mr. Davidson, would you give me a little background on the Strickland case? If I remember correctly, the file was labeled 1988, which means I was in first grade when the case was litigated."

Simone was obviously teasing Nick about his age, and for the first time, he realized that he actually enjoyed her company.

"I wasn't a senior citizen back in 1988," Nick replied feigning defensiveness. "I researched the Strickland case before my job interview with Walter Burton."

Simone held up her hands in mock surrender and said, "I didn't realize you were so sensitive about your age."

Nick gave Simone a watch-yourself stare, but instead of continuing the banter, he began his summary of the Strickland case. "Shortly after Walter left the prosecutor's office, he won a huge judgment in a tort case. Most 'legal experts' considered the case a surefire loser for his client, and most local attorneys thought Walter had lost his mind when he accepted the case on a contingency fee basis. In fact, there was widespread speculation the case would bankrupt his upstart law firm. Imagine everyone's shock when Walter ended up getting the last laugh. Defying all logic, the jury awarded Walter's client a twelve-million-dollar judgment. At the time, it was the largest judgment ever awarded by a jury in the western United States."

"Who did Walter sue?" Simone asked.

"Lakeland National Bank."

"It's possible to sue a bank?" Simone asked.

"You can sue Mickey Mouse if you pay the filing fee," Nick replied, only half joking. "Mr. Strickland's business failed, and according to the American way someone else was to blame for his shortcomings. Unwilling to accept responsibility for his businesses failure, Strickland sued Lakeland National Bank for breach of contract, fraudulent misrepresentation, and various other torts. The general consensus in the business community seemed to be that Mr. Strickland was a poor businessman and Lakeland National Bank had carried him longer than they should have. All that aside, the jury disagreed with community sentiment and common sense, and after seven days of deliberations they awarded Mr. Strickland the jaw-dropping twelve-million-dollar judgment. After the Strickland case, Walter Burton was a rich man, and his legal career really took off."

"Jason Davidson was responsible for the jury's decision?"

"He most certainly was, but that's not the most interesting aspect of the story," Nick explained. "Why he was willing to risk his career is the fascinating part."

"Did he do it for money like Jefferson Hughes?" Simone asked in disgust.

"Nope, he didn't see a dime of the judgment."

Simone gave Nick her best get-to-the-point look. "Okay, you've got my attention. Why did he fix the verdict for Walter's client?"

"Because an abnormally large madman kidnapped and tortured him," Nick said matter-of-factly. "And to top things off, he threatened to kill Jason's wife if the plaintiff didn't get a substantial judgment."

Simone grimaced. "What kind of people are we dealing with?"

"Greedy, power-hungry people who will stop at nothing to get what they want," Nick answered truthfully. "The further we delve into this case, the more dangerous it's going to get for both of us."

"Do you really believe we're in danger?"

Nick shrugged and said, "It's a distinct possibility. Maybe I should go the rest of the way alone."

"No way!" Simone emphatically replied. "This partnership was my idea, and I'm seeing it through."

"Are you sure?" Nick asked. "I can't guarantee your safety at this point."

"I've never been more sure of anything in my entire life."

Nick shook his head and smiled. "You need to hear the rest of Jason's story before you make your final decision. The people behind the curtain will do whatever it takes to protect their dirty secrets."

Simone crossed her arms over her chest and stared defiantly at Nick. "Have it your way, but nothing you say is going to change my mind," she said with finality.

Simone sat across from Nick in shocked silence as he recounted the horrifying events that had ultimately led to a plaintiff's judgment in the Strickland case. He didn't sugarcoat any of the ugly details. He told her about Jason Davidson's kidnapping, death threats, humiliation, torture, and subsequent abandonment in the desert. When he was done, Simone said, "Jason's story reminds me of a plot from a bad horror movie."

"Yeah, except it really happened," Nick reminded her.

"What's the old saying—fact is stranger than fiction," Simone remarked.

"There's something else you should know."

"What's that?" Simone asked and then quickly added, "Or should I even ask?"

"I'm almost certain the man who kidnapped and tortured Jason Davidson is the man who killed my wife and the man in Hartman Park."

"Which means he's the man who took your daughter," Simone whispered in a barely audible voice. "You need to contact the police."

"I can't," Nick answered forcefully. "I promised Jason I would never repeat his story."

Even though his promise to Jason was important to him, it wasn't the only reason he was avoiding the police. Nick didn't want to involve law enforcement because his trust level, as far as the police were concerned, was fairly low given Detective Gates's participation in the Panache payoff.

"What do we do now?"

Nick thought about it for a couple of seconds before he said, "Tomorrow morning we pay Jefferson Hughes another visit. He hung out with a rough crowd twenty years ago in Lakeland. It's possible Jason's kidnapper ran in the same circles."

"It's a date…I mean a plan," Simone stammered, clearly embarrassed.

Nick ignored her choice of words and said, "I'll pick you up at nine."

"I'll be ready," Simone replied just as Skye returned with their dinners.

Nick and Simone picked at their meals in relative silence, as they thought about the path ahead. They both sensed the end of their journey was near, yet neither of them had a clue where the road would lead.

CHAPTER 34

Wednesday morning, October 25

Detective Gates had been sitting at his desk since well before sunrise. Frequent trips to the coffeepot had been his only respite from a series of potential leads that led exactly nowhere. He had tried to get a little sleep the night before, but after tossing and turning for a couple of hours, he gave up and returned to the police station. Gates did not sleep well under the best of circumstances, and the past couple of weeks had been positively unnerving for the detective.

Gates typically had no problem remaining distant and emotionally detached from the cases he investigated, but the Jelaco investigation was starting to take its toll on the high-strung detective, and unfortunately, he could see no end in sight. He hadn't slept a night through since the case had been dropped in his lap, and his cigarette consumption had steadily increased since he had resumed smoking. To make matters worse, Gates's typically infallible instincts were sending him mixed signals. For the past couple of days, Gates couldn't shake an unnerving feeling that he was connected—perhaps even responsible—for the Jelaco break-in. After he closed the case, he was definitely going to take some of the vacation time he had piled up over the past twenty years.

He was about to head to the coffee pot for the tenth time when an uncharacteristically excited Detective Sato tossed a worn case file on the detective's desk.

"We've got a match," he breathlessly informed Gates.

"A match on what?" Gates asked as he removed his reading glasses and looked up at the young detective.

"We got a hit on a fingerprint lifted from the Jelaco murder," Sato explained in a rush.

Detective Gates slapped the top of his desk and shouted with atypical enthusiasm, "Are you kidding me? I'd almost given up on the fingerprints."

"He was in the FBI's database," Sato continued.

"You're sure he's our guy?" Gates asked skeptically.

"Positive," Sato confidently answered. "There's no logical reason his prints should have been anywhere near the Jelacos' house."

Gates shook his head in disbelief as he picked up the tattered file. "His jacket's pretty thick; I take it he's a member of Monroe County's frequent flyer club."

Sato slid into a chair next to Detective Gates's desk. "Quite the opposite," Sato countered. "The file is thick because he was arrested when he was a juvenile."

Gates moved the file up and down as if he was estimating its weight and asked, "All this paperwork for a juvenile arrest?"

"Most of the reports are health and welfare, social work type stuff. Mr. Ellenwood is a Native-American from a tribe in South Dakota. I'm sure his ethnic heritage complicated matters for the juvenile justice system."

Gates opened the file and mumbled, "Edgar Lightfoot Ellenwood."

"Did you happen to notice the date?"

"Yeah, he was arrested thirty years ago," Gates replied. "More importantly, what's Mr. Ellenwood been up to lately?"

"Nothing that has made a blip on law enforcement's radar," Sato admitted.

"I'm not much of a reader," Gates said.

"Ellenwood spent the majority of his childhood in foster

care on the Pine Ridge Reservation in South Dakota. Most of the documentation deals with foster care issues, counseling stuff, and the State's rehabilitation efforts."

"Foster care," Gates repeated. "Did he have a history of violence in South Dakota?"

Sato shook his head and said, "No, but he was exposed to violence at a young age. When he was a small child, his father murdered his mother and then committed suicide. Evidently young Edgar had a front row seat for both deaths."

"How 'front row'?"

"He was sitting on his father's lap when his old man blew his brains out with a Colt .45 revolver."

"That's got to leave some emotional scars," Gates said with a grimace.

Sato nodded before continuing with his summary. "Mr. Ellenwood was given an IQ test after he was placed in foster care. His test scores indicated that he had a genius level IQ, but Edgar consistently performed poorly in school until he dropped out in the tenth grade."

"What was he arrested for?" Gates asked. "Let me guess—something really serious like drunk driving or petty theft."

Sato paused briefly. "Edgar Ellenwood was arrested in Monroe County for criminal homicide in December of 1978."

"No kidding," Gates remarked, clearly surprised.

"It took me a couple of hours to find his file in the basement of the old courthouse, but it's all in there in graphic detail," Sato assured his boss.

Ellenwood's violent past had obviously piqued the lead detective's interest. "What were the circumstances surrounding the homicide?"

Sato picked up where he had left off without referencing the case file. "Edgar Ellenwood was a very large teenager, and from the sound of things, not an overly good-looking one. His face was severely scarred by a severe case of acne or small pox. Anyway, Edgar was on his way to the Oregon Coast when he decided to stop in Lakeland to track down a long-lost uncle—some guy named Buddy Red Bird. Apparently, Edgar was panhandling at the Lakeland Mall when some high-school students started giving him a hard time. According to the reports, a kid named Randall Crane was the ringleader. He called Edgar derogatory Indian names and teased him about his physical appearance."

"I take it that Edgar didn't turn a deaf ear to the insults."

Sato slowly nodded his head in response to Gates's question. "The eyewitnesses stated that Mr. Ellenwood grabbed Randall around the throat and snapped the young man's neck like a dry twig. The medical examiner figured Randall Crane was dead before he hit the floor."

"Did Edgar offer a differing view of the unfortunate events?" Gates asked.

"Edgar admitted that he lost his temper, but claimed that he wasn't trying to kill the boy. The eyewitnesses, mostly Crane's friends, believed the killing was intentional."

Detective Gates leaned back in his chair and rubbed his unshaven chin. "It takes a great deal of physical strength to break a person's neck with your bare hands."

"I was thinking the same thing," Sato agreed. "Mrs. Jelaco wouldn't present much of a problem for a man with that much strength."

"Has anyone spoken to the uncle?"

"I tried," Sato replied. "Buddy Red Bird died in 1980, and it appears as if he was a complete loner."

"Why doesn't that surprise me?" Gates mumbled. "When was Mr. Ellenwood released from prison?"

"He didn't actually spend time in prison."

"Why not?"

"He was arrested for homicide, but the Monroe County prosecutor didn't seek a waiver to the adult court system," Sato replied.

"How old was Edgar Ellenwood?"

"Sixteen years and six months," Sato answered. "Old enough to meet the state's presumption of culpability."

"A culpable sixteen-year-old commits second-degree mur-der, or at the very least voluntary manslaughter, and the prosecutor leaves the case in juvenile court," Gates said, looking pensive.

Sato nodded. "Mr. Ellenwood spent approximately eighteen months in a juvenile detention facility, and that was the sum total of his time behind bars."

"And some people think the criminal justice system is soft on crime," Gates countered sarcastically.

"An army of shrinks and social workers all agreed that he suffered from post-traumatic stress and some kind of borderline personality disorder. One shrink from the state hospital actually thought Mr. Ellenwood exhibited symptoms consistent with paranoid schizophrenia. When he was released from the jurisdiction of the juvenile court, Mr. Ellenwood virtually disappeared, which probably means his mental problems have gone untreated for the past twenty-five years."

Gates took off his glasses and began to massage his temples with his right hand. "Who was the prosecutor assigned to the case?'

"Walter Burton," Sato answered. "Given the circumstances, it seems odd that he chose not to prosecute Mr. Ellenwood. The arrest was good, and Edgar made a full confession after being apprised of his Miranda rights. There were no mitigating circumstances to speak of except for Edgar's age. From what I could glean from the file, it appeared to be an open-and-shut second-degree murder case."

"So Mr. Ellenwood commits a murder in 1978, serves a little time in juvenile detention, and then disappears for nearly thirty years," Gates said almost to himself.

"And when he finally resurfaces, it's in the Jelacos' home and the site of another homicide," Sato added.

"Does that seem a little odd to you?"

"It seems more than a little odd. Where's he been for the last thirty years, and what was he doing in the Jelacos' house? A random burglary that escalated to murder doesn't seem like a plausible explanation for his presence at the crime scene."

"I know where Edgar Ellenwood was on Sunday night at about eleven o'clock," Detective Gates said with certainty.

"Oh yeah, where's that?"

"At Hartman Park, murdering a small-time dealer named Leroy Demers."

"I glanced at the Demers homicide report a couple of days ago," Sato commented. "What makes you think Ellenwood was the killer?"

"Demers called Nick Jelaco and scheduled an eleven o'clock meeting for Sunday night. According to Jelaco, Demers claimed he had information about the person behind his daughter's kidnapping. When he showed up for the meeting, Demers was lying in a grove of trees with a broken neck."

"You think it was Edgar Ellenwood?"

"I'm almost positive it was Ellenwood," Gates growled before adding, "He killed Mrs. Jelaco, kidnapped Darby Jelaco, and murdered Leroy Demers. I just don't know why he did it, or who he is working for, but he's our guy."

Detective Gates decided not to mention, at least not yet, what concerned him the most: Walter Burton's connection to both Ellenwood and Nick Jelaco. Walter was the prosecutor who had dropped the murder charges against Ellenwood, and he had been Jelaco's boss for the past six years. And now after all these years, Edgar Ellenwood had reemerged as the primary suspect in Julie Jelaco's murder. Detective Gates didn't like coincidences, especially when they involved someone as slimy as Walter Burton.

"Detective Sato, get an arrest warrant for Mr. Edgar Lightfoot Ellenwood," Gates instructed.

"Probable cause shouldn't be an issue given the fingerprint evidence and his prior arrest for homicide," Sato said, thinking out loud.

"Give patrol and the guys over at county an updated description of Mr. Ellenwood. Make sure everybody knows his arrest is top priority."

"Consider it done," Sato said, standing to leave.

"One more thing, Sato."

"What's that?"

"If we don't turn up something on Ellenwood within the next forty-eight hours, I want you to dig into his life on the reservation. There's a chance someone from South Dakota has remained in contact with him."

"Sure thing, Boss," Sato said on his way out the door.

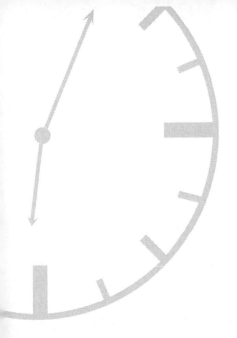

CHAPTER 35

Wednesday morning, October 25

A series of interruptions had forced Nick and Simone to postpone their return trip to the Wood River Valley. Finally, after nearly a week of delays, they were loaded in the Mustang and driving north for a second time. They were armed with the same .40 caliber Glock, a video camera, a bag full of groceries, and a little guarded optimism in anticipation of their second visit with Jefferson Hughes. Nick was hopeful that any shooting would be done with the video camera, but at this point, he wasn't about to take any chances. He had briefly considered leaving Simone in Lakeland but had decided her absence might make the flirtatious old man less willing to talk.

They had barely passed the Lakeland city limits when Simone asked, "Would you mind stopping at a convenience store? I'm not a big coffee drinker, but for some reason, I'm really dragging this morning."

Nick was also dragging, but he knew the cause of his sluggishness. Restful sleep had been a rare commodity since his return from Las Vegas twenty days ago.

"I could use something to get me going as well," Nick replied. "There's a Stop & Go about a mile up the road."

Nick paid for their two large coffees over Simone's insistence that it was her turn to buy.

When they had settled into the Mustang for a second time, Simone said, "Tell me about law school and what it's like to be a lawyer."

"Why don't we discuss a more interesting topic, like global warming," Nick suggested with more than a hint of cynicism in his tone.

"I'm serious," Simone urged. "Law school sounds really interesting."

Nick groaned. "Well I suppose we do have an hour to kill."

"Try to contain your enthusiasm," Simone sarcastically replied.

Nick laughed softly. "For me personally, the rigors of law school were more enjoyable than the day-to-day grind of practicing law."

"Is working for a law firm really hard?"

"Being a lawyer isn't difficult from an intellectual standpoint. Instead, it's kind of boring and repetitive," Nick explained.

Simone raised her eyebrows in surprise and repeated, "Boring..."

"Your brother's case is definitely the exception to the rule," Nick continued. "But I found the theoretical and philosophical nature of law school more challenging than a steady diet of DUIs and fender benders."

Simone shrugged and said, "Law school is for smart people, or rich people, not people like me."

"Don't sell yourself short, Simone. You're definitely smart enough for law school," Nick countered.

Simone smiled weakly and offered an unsolicited explanation for her lack of self-confidence. "I've heard my entire life that I'm not smart enough or good enough. After a while you start to believe the bad things people say about you."

"I've only known you for a week, and it's obvious those people are full of crap."

"Thanks, Nick," Simone softly replied.

"You should talk to someone who's less cynical than me if

you want a less jaded opinion about law school, billable hours, and whining clients," Nick suggested. "I'm not the most objective person in the world when it comes to lawyers and the legal profession."

"Your disclaimer has been duly noted," Simone deadpanned.

After several seconds of silence, Nick said, "I wasn't your typical law student, which may have skewed my opinion of the educational process."

"You seem pretty normal to me," Simone joked.

"In my humble opinion, most professors and law students fail to balance their liberal ideologies with the practicality necessary to function outside of academia," Nick began slowly. "A purely academic viewpoint lacks objectivity when it's created without factoring in the chaos of the real world."

Simone smiled and said, "A lawyer, a soldier, and a philosopher—you're full of surprises."

"My military background was another issue altogether," Nick scoffed.

"Do I detect a hint of self pity in your tone?" Simone asked.

"Let's just say my status as an ex-soldier didn't curry any favor among my professors or the other students."

"That seems kind of narrow-minded for people who are supposed to be educated and tolerant."

Nick shrugged. "Law school is a strange place when it comes to tolerance. The professors and students ramble on about personal freedoms and civil liberties, but anyone with a viewpoint that differs from the ultra-liberal majority is informally censored. I was often the brunt of jokes and ridicule because of my prior military service."

"Did their hypocrisy infuriate you?" Simone pushed. "It makes me mad just thinking about it."

"Not really, but I did find it somewhat ironic," Nick explained.

"Ironic?"

"The professors were paid to teach the students about the Bill of Rights and the US Constitution, but they forgot about the historical development of our country."

"What do you mean?"

"When we discussed the constitution, my professors seemed to think the words written on that piece of paper were enough to ensure their individual rights and various freedoms," Nick said with a sad shake of his head. "The daily sacrifices made by countless others to guarantee their way of life were somehow lost in their rhetoric. Some of my less-enlightened professors actually portrayed the police and the military as the bad guys while the terrorists and ruthless dictators were considered innocent victims."

"Maybe college professors need to spend a year living under the oppression of a fascist dictator before they are permitted to influence impressionable young minds," Simone suggested.

Nick laughed. "I wasn't all that young or impressionable."

"You know what I mean."

"Even though I found some of their personal ideologies and teaching philosophies to be a little naïve and nearsighted, the whole experience made me respect their right to have different opinions."

"It sounds more like ignorance and hypocrisy to me," Simone replied.

"You could be right, Simone, but freedom is a two-way street," Nick countered. "If a person demands protections like freedom of speech or religion, that person must be willing to allow those with differing viewpoints the enjoyment of those same rights."

"I understand what you're saying, but it sounds like your professors need a refresher course on American history," Simone shot back.

"Maybe you should go to law school and get the system back on track," Nick teased.

"Maybe I will."

"Don't get the wrong idea," Nick cautioned. "Several of my professors became good friends. We didn't always agree, but some of my most memorable and illuminating discussions were with professors whose philosophies were the polar opposites of my own."

"Do you like being a lawyer?" she asked.

"Another loaded question," Nick laughed again. "Sometimes I do, and sometimes I don't."

Simone rolled her eyes and said, "Spoken like a true lawyer."

"I wasn't trying to be evasive," Nick assured her. "Certain aspects of my job are rewarding and others make me question the legal system."

"I guess watching my innocent brother languish away in prison has made me want to be a lawyer."

"It does feel good to help someone who doesn't have the ability or resources to help himself," Nick agreed.

"What's the worst part?"

"Sacrificing what's right for what's profitable. I realize law firms are in business to make money, but the profession should do some good along the way."

"An altruistic lawyer with a conscious—maybe you're in the wrong profession," Simone teased.

"One of my more idealistic professors used to deviate from the curriculum to tell his students how the pursuit of money had corrupted the legal system."

"Lawyers aren't alone in that regard; the pursuit of money drives most professions."

"You're probably right," Nick agreed. "I know doctors, psychiatrists, and architects who complain they were forced to abandon their professional vision in an attempt to maximize corporate profit."

"Pro bono work at a woman's shelter or volunteering medical expertise in Africa doesn't pay for a million-dollar house in the hills."

"I suppose not," Nick said softly.

T hey drove for several miles without speaking. Some prolonged silences were awkward, but this one was surprisingly comfortable.

A few miles south of Bellevue, Nick said, "Tell me about yourself—it seems like our conversations always revolve around my life."

Simone's dark complexion couldn't hide the sudden flush in her cheeks. "There's really not much to talk about. My life has been pretty boring," she answered, clearly uncomfortable as the focal point of the conversation.

Nick raised one eyebrow. "I doubt that. I've only known you for a week, and it's been nonstop action."

"The pace of my life has definitely picked up since I met you," Simone said smiling. "Trust me—it hasn't always been that way. Since my parents died, I've spent far too much time waiting for things to get better."

"What kinds of things?" Nick asked.

"When I was a little girl, I was obsessed with my eighteenth birthday," Simone said, seemingly embarrassed by her immaturity. "For some reason, I thought freedom from the foster care system would make me happy again."

"Did it?" Nick asked.

A look of melancholy spread across Simone's face. "Joining the adult world wasn't the liberating experience I thought it would be. In fact, I felt more confused and alone once I struck out on my own."

"It's seems like you've figured it out now."

Simone shrugged and said, "I'm a work in progress, but I'm learning to take control of my destiny."

"How does a person control his destiny?" Nick snapped, suddenly angered by the notion that he could have somehow changed the fate of his wife and daughter.

"You don't. I meant to say future," Simone replied weakly. "A person's destiny is predetermined, but their future isn't etched in stone."

"And you've managed to alter your future?"

"I think so," Simone answered with more self-assurance. "I don't blame my problems on foster care or my family's bad luck. I try to remain centered on the present and focus on the things I can control."

"And you're okay with the path your life has taken?" Nick asked.

"For the most part."

Nick nodded and in a softer tone said, "With a little luck, Cole could be out of prison soon."

Simone gave him a sad smile. "For the first time in a very long time, I actually believe it's a possibility."

"It may take your brother a while to adjust to life on the outside," Nick cautioned her.

"Don't worry. I know Cole's release from prison won't be the fairytale ending I imagined as a kid," Simone said matter-of-factly. "We can't turn back the clock to that night twenty years ago, so we'll move forward and do the best we can if he's released."

Simone was a young woman who had persevered through many hardships and managed to develop the pragmatic perspective of a survivor along the way.

Nick wanted to tell Simone he respected the person she had become, but instead he said, "The road to Jefferson's place is just ahead."

Simone flinched at the mention of Jefferson Hughes's name and asked, "Is Jefferson's confession that he lied on the witness stand all we need to get Cole out of prison?"

Nick knew that it was not unusual for a prosecution witness to change his testimony after a conviction, which meant judges were not easily persuaded by testimony recanted after the fact. They would probably need some additional evidence to corroborate Jefferson's story, but he didn't want Simone worrying about the legal obstacles that lay ahead.

"Cole's conviction is about as solid as a house of cards," Nick replied casually. "Once Jefferson's statement is made public, that house will crumble under the weight of the public's scrutiny."

Simone nodded. If the nervous look on her face was an indication, she was even more anxious about their second trip to the Wood River Valley. Jefferson Hughes was no longer an unknown quantity, but strangely enough, Nick felt more apprehensive as well. Even though he wasn't superstitious, Nick intentionally parked the car in the same spot it had occupied during their first visit with the old man. After shifting the Mustang into park, he removed the .40 caliber semiautomatic from beneath the driver's seat and checked its magazine. Simone frowned when she saw the handgun, but she didn't ask him to leave it in the car this time.

CHAPTER 36

Wednesday morning, October 25

Nick and Simone had just started down the bumpy path to Jefferson's cabin when Nick suddenly halted in midstride.

"Is something wrong?"

"Relax," Nick said with a reassuring smile. "I left the video camera and Jefferson's groceries in the backseat of the car."

A look of relief appeared on Simone's face. "I'll get them," she offered and jogged back to the car without waiting for a response. Once she had returned, Nick took the groceries, and they started down the seldom-used dirt path for the second time. Nick was hopeful the familiar walk would calm his nerves, but instead his uneasiness intensified as they approached Jefferson's weather-beaten cabin. Simone was uncharacteristically silent and stone-faced during the short hike, which made Nick believe the same unsettling feelings had her on edge. When they were within thirty yards of the small cabin, Simone whispered, "Do you think Jefferson's inside?"

"If not, he hasn't been gone long," Nick answered without taking his eyes off the cabin.

"How can you be sure?" Simone whispered again.

Nick motioned toward a thin column of smoke drifting from the cabin's chimney.

Simone nodded and was about to ask another question when they both stopped dead in their tracks. The cause of their sudden alarm was the realization that the front door of Jefferson's cabin had been left slightly ajar.

Nick placed the groceries on the ground, removed the Glock from his jacket pocket, and then gently nudged Simone behind a large fir tree. "Wait here. I'm going to check things out," he said in a hushed voice.

Before Simone could object, Nick began to cautiously advance toward the log cabin. He didn't know what to expect, but adrenaline was coursing through his entire body by the time he reached the porch. Without hesitating he bolted up the front steps, crossed the porch, and flattened himself against the log wall all in one motion. Just to the right of the open door, he paused and listened for movement inside the cabin. The interior of the cabin was deathly silent, so Nick gently nudged the open door with the toe of his boot. When there was no reaction from inside the cabin, he took a deep breath, crouched low, and quickly stepped through the open door.

Once inside, Nick assumed a defensive posture and surveyed Jefferson's dingy living quarters through the sights of his semiautomatic. It didn't take him long to establish the whereabouts of the old man. Jefferson Hughes was lying on the dirty hardwood floor beside the kitchen table where he had so openly discussed his perjured testimony. The old man was flat on his back, staring wide eyed at the ceiling with two pancake-sized bloodstains clearly visible on the front of his gray flannel shirt. Nick lowered his handgun as he walked toward Jefferson's body. He was certain that whoever had killed the old man was gone by now. When he reached the body, it was apparent that he didn't need to check for a pulse to determine if Jefferson was dead. Someone didn't want the star witness talking, and the two bullet holes in his chest had permanently guaranteed his silence.

Nick let out a guttural and indecipherable scream when he realized that another potential lead had turned into a dead end.

The echo was still bouncing off the cabin's walls when Simone barged through the front door to discover Nick standing over Jefferson's lifeless body. Her eyes immediately locked on the old man, and she covered her mouth with a trembling hand, but she didn't speak. Nick was afraid that she was in shock, but after standing there for several seconds with a stunned look on her face, she meekly asked, "Is he dead?"

"He's not taking a nap," Nick answered flatly.

"Who killed him?" she asked and then immediately said, "Sorry, I ask dumb questions when I'm nervous."

Nick wasn't clairvoyant, yet he could determine a couple of things from the murder scene. "I don't know who killed Mr. Hughes, but it wasn't the same man who murdered Leroy Demers," he answered confidently.

Simone looked quizzically at Nick and asked, "How can you be sure?"

"Leroy was a young, body-builder type, and his killer snapped his neck with his bare hands. Jefferson was a scrawny, sickly old man who barely had enough strength to get out of bed in the morning. There's no way the guy who murdered Leroy would have used a handgun to kill Jefferson. We are definitely dealing with two different killers."

"I suppose that makes sense," Simone hesitantly agreed.

"I'll take my hypothesis one step further," Nick continued. "I bet Jefferson was shot with a .38 caliber revolver."

Simone grimaced and asked, "Can you tell that by those holes in his chest?"

"He was shot with a small-caliber handgun, but that's not all. There are no shell casings near his body," Nick pointed out. "Unless the killer gathered up the spent cartridges before he fled, he shot Jefferson with a revolver. The wounds are too big for a .25 caliber, which means the murder weapon was probably a .38."

Nick decided to skip over the fact that Detective Gates, the cop who had delivered the payoff to Jefferson Hughes, carried a .38 caliber revolver.

Simone glanced nervously around the small cabin. "Do you think the killer is out there watching us?"

"The killer's long gone by now," Nick assured her. "With Jefferson dead, it would be stupid to stick around."

"Has he been dead a long time?" Simone asked without taking her eyes off Jefferson's body.

"I'm not a forensics expert, but it appears as if the old man was killed a couple of hours ago," Nick estimated. "Jefferson's fully dressed, and there's brewed coffee on the counter, so common sense would say he was probably murdered shortly after sunrise."

"Let's get out of here," Simone almost whispered. "This place is giving me the creeps."

"Yeah, it's definitely time for a change of scenery," Nick said and started moving toward the door.

"Should we call the police?" Simone asked as she glanced back at Jefferson's body.

Nick stopped and said, "Probably, but I can't afford the risk."

"We can't leave Jefferson like this," Simone protested.

"Take my word for it—he won't care one way or the other."

"I'm serious."

"If we call the police, we're apt to spend the rest of the day trying to answer questions we can't answer," Nick shot back. "The police might even throw us in jail while they try to sort things out."

"Walking away doesn't feel right."

"Darby's running out of time—I can sense it more with each passing hour."

Simone sighed and said, "You're calling the shots. Where do we go from here?"

"We need to find someplace off the beaten path where I can figure out our next move."

"Off the beaten path sounds good to me," Simone agreed. "Someone is obviously worried that we're getting a little too close to the truth."

Nick was thinking the same thing, and he was no longer willing to put Simone's life at risk. He knew she would put up a fight, but Nick had decided to go the rest of the way alone.

"I know the perfect place for us to hide out for an hour or two," Nick said. "Let's get moving before someone else comes snooping around here."

CHAPTER 37

Wednesday afternoon, October 25

Nick and Simone kept glancing at the tree line as they jogged back to the Mustang. Nick was confident the killer was long gone, and he had assured Simone there was no immediate threat, yet the prospect of danger hung in the air. Back at the car, they tossed the video camera and groceries in the backseat, but Nick kept the .40 caliber semiautomatic close by.

They were on the highway driving toward Sun Valley when Simone asked, "Where are we going?"

"Julie's father has a place just north of Sun Valley. We can lay low there until I decide what to do next."

Simone opened her eyes wide in surprise, and said, "Don't tell me you're planning to show up at your father-in-law's house with another woman?"

The shocked look on Simone's face actually made Nick smile. "It's one of his vacation homes," he explained. "My former in-laws only spend two or three weekends a year in Sun Valley."

"How can you be sure the house is empty right now?"

"Golf season is over, and ski season doesn't open until Thanksgiving weekend."

"Do you have a key?"

"Nope," Nick said with a casual shake of his head. "But William keeps a spare key hidden in the garage, and I know the security code for the garage door."

"I hope you know what you're doing," Simone said without attempting to conceal her misgivings.

"I seldom do," Nick replied, only half joking.

T wo miles north of Sun Valley, Nick turned left onto Green Horn Road and navigated his beat-up old Mustang past an eclectic assortment of ten-million-dollar estates. Simone stared openmouthed at the sprawling estates as they drove through the subdivision.

"Are those houses or hotels?" she asked.

"Houses."

"It's hard to believe some people live in such luxury when so many others are living in poverty," Simone remarked.

William's vacation home sat on a wooded five-acre lot at the eastern end of the upscale subdivision. Most of the homeowners who lived on Green Horn Road were famous actors, accomplished musicians, or CEOs of Fortune 500 companies. Making money was William's only real talent, and he liked to demonstrate his proficiency by flaunting his material possessions. At the end of the street, Nick pulled into the driveway of the Forsythe estate and told Simone to wait in the car. He was fairly sure the house was unoccupied. Still, he wanted to take a quick look around the grounds before he entered through the garage.

The Forsythe's vacation home was a fifteen-thousand-square-foot monstrosity that resembled an Austrian chalet, but the Rocky Mountain influence was unmistakable. The massive structure had been constructed from large wooden beams and river rock, and no less than a dozen balconies provided unobstructed views of the surrounding mountains. After a brief inspection of the house and surrounding property, Nick was convinced that the mansion was unoccupied, so he returned to the driveway and punched William's five-digit code into the electronic keypad. The blinking red light turned green, and one of the double garage doors slowly rolled skyward. When the hand-carved door rolled to a stop, he rejoined Simone in the Mustang and pulled the car into the immaculate garage. After parking the car and closing the garage door, Nick retrieved the spare key from its hiding place above the ornate oak door and motioned for Simone. She gave him a nervous smile and hesitantly joined him on the step.

"Breaking and entering should be routine to me by now, but this feels really weird," Simone whispered.

"Don't worry. No one will bother us here," Nick assured her. "Homeowners in this neighborhood mind their own business."

Once they were inside, Simone was visibly shocked by the extravagant manner in which Nick's former in-laws could afford to live.

She surveyed the enormous gourmet kitchen with an amazed look on her face and said, "This place is even nicer than the houses they put in those lifestyle magazines."

"No one ever accused William of being a minimalist," Nick sarcastically agreed.

"It's all so extravagant—I don't want to touch anything."

"William's taste undoubtedly favors the ostentatious over the practical, but there's a well-stocked pantry if you're hungry."

Simone wrinkled her face as if she had tasted something sour and said, "Thanks, but discovering a dead body kind of ruined my appetite."

"How about something to drink?" Nick suggested.

"Something warm sounds good."

"There should be some coffee or tea in there," Nick said with a nod in the general direction of two frosted glass doors with the word *Pantry* etched on both panes of glass.

"Why don't you see what you can find while I start a fire?"

"Won't the smoke from the chimney attract attention?" Simone asked.

Nick shook his head dismissively. "This neighborhood is practically abandoned before the first week of ski season."

"The owners don't live here year around?"

"Believe it or not, these are second or third homes for most of the people who live in this neighborhood."

"It only takes one nosy neighbor to call the police," Simone countered.

"Don't worry about it," Nick replied with an edge to his voice. "We'll be long gone before anyone gets the least bit suspicious."

William Forsythe didn't do anything in moderation. Nick shook his head as he made his way past a collection of seldom appreciated paintings and sculptures that had cost Julie's father millions. His destination was a grandiose entertaining room William called the Great Hall. He paused briefly near the well-stocked bar before he plopped down on a plush leather sofa in front of a stone fireplace that was bigger than the bedroom in Nick's first apartment.

The lavish surroundings of William's mansion made it difficult to fully appreciate the harsh reality that waited outside. Still, Nick was grounded enough to know that he needed to pull out all the stops in his search for Darby. The way Nick saw it there were three paths that led to his daughter. First, there was the disfigured giant who had terrorized Jason Davidson twenty years ago. Nick sensed that the road to the large man and the road to his daughter were one and the same, but the man's name and whereabouts were unknown. He could find the man with a little time, but time was a scarce commodity. His second option was Detective Gates, the man who had delivered the payoff to the late Jefferson Hughes. Gates's hands weren't clean, but Nick wasn't convinced the detective possessed information that could save his daughter. If the streetwise detective did have answers, breaking him down wouldn't be an easy task. And then there was Walter Burton. Nick didn't have any direct evidence that his former employer was involved, yet his instincts were nudging him in that direction.

Nick was still trying to figure out which path to pursue when Simone entered the room carrying two steaming mugs. She handed Nick a mug that smelled of cinnamon and sat down on the matching leather sofa across from him.

"I'm afraid to ask what impact Jefferson's death will have on our investigation," she said softly.

"I won't lie to you. His death is problematic," Nick admitted. "With the old man dead, there's no reason for Gates to talk."

"We still have Jefferson's confession." Simone answered hopefully.

"We have the unsubstantiated ramblings of a dead man."

"Jefferson breaks a twenty-year silence, and his niece winds up dead. He spills his guts to us, and now he's dead," Simone shot back. "That's got to be worth something."

Nick shrugged and said, "Even if you believe every word of the old man's story, we're still missing a crucial piece of the puzzle."

"What's that?"

"Who masterminded Jefferson's perjured testimony," Nick explained. "We know Gates delivered the payoff, but we don't know whose money he delivered or why the moneyman wanted Jefferson to lie."

"What's your best guess?" Simone asked. "Who's the bad man behind the curtain?"

"If Jason Davidson was telling the truth, Walter Burton threatened murder in order to win the Strickland case. It's somewhat of a leap, but I think Walter put up the $50,000 that Gates delivered to Jefferson Hughes."

Simone nodded her agreement and said, "If you ask me, it's not much of a leap."

"I need someone to implicate Walter, but Jefferson's dead, and the big man is a ghost..."

"What about Detective Gates?" Simone interrupted.

Nick pursed his lips and slowly shook his head. "I don't know. He's tough as nails and smart."

"What about Walter? He doesn't seem tough or smart."

Squeezing the truth out of Walter had crossed Nick's mind

on more than one occasion. He was convinced Walter controlled the giant of a man who had terrorized Jason Davidson, and that meant he was behind the break-in at Nick's house as well. No matter which angle he viewed the situation from, Walter was always the common denominator.

"You might be on to something," Nick said with a mischievous grin. "Cracking Walter does seem more feasible than breaking a hard case like Gates."

"Are you actually considering a face-to-face confrontation with Walter Burton?"

"I'm not just considering it. I'm planning on it. When he shows up for work tomorrow morning, I'll be waiting in his office."

Simone wrinkled her brow and asked, "What happens after Walter finds you waiting in his office?"

"That depends on Walter's level of cooperation," Nick answered without hesitation. "I'll do whatever it takes to save my daughter."

"I don't like the sound of that."

"Don't worry. I can read Walter like a book," Nick assured her. "If he's lying, I'll know it."

"That wasn't my concern. Desperate people act without regard for the consequences."

"Walter might be the only person who can lead me to my daughter. I need answers, and I'll do whatever it takes to get them."

"Does that include violence?"

"Let's hope it doesn't come to that, but yes, violence is definitely an option," Nick answered with unwavering resolve.

Simone stood up and slowly walked to a pair of French doors with an unobstructed view of the Western mountains. She stared intently at the snow-covered mountains for a couple of minutes before she said, "I trust your instincts, Nick. But keep in mind, Darby's going to need her father when this ordeal is finally behind us."

"Don't worry about me. I've been in tight spots before," Nick replied dismissively.

"This is about your daughter, not you and Walter."

"Let's try to get a few hours of sleep before we head back to Lakeland," Nick snapped. "Walter usually gets to the office between six and seven o'clock, and I plan to be waiting for him when he gets there.

CHAPTER 38

Wednesday night, October 25

Shavonne did not remember the precise moment she had decided to strike out on her own. She did know she had been planning to leave Edgar for quite some time. A paralyzing fear of being alone and a concern for the little girl's safety were the only things that had delayed her departure up to this point. Even though she was frightened of the unknown, Edgar's increasingly bizarre and unpredictable behavior had left her no other option. Edgar was about to snap, and Shavonne didn't want to be anywhere near him when he finally went off the deep end.

When Edgar's strange behavior had initially escalated to voices inside his head, Shavonne had ignored and rationalized his mental deterioration as a temporary condition. Now, the signs were too troublesome to pass off as mere eccentricities. He hardly ever slept, and when he did, his sleep was plagued by horrible visions and night sweats. During the daylight hours, he sat alone in their depressing, little apartment with the curtains drawn, babbling incoherently to himself in Lakota.

Shavonne didn't know where Edgar went each night, but she found herself anxiously awaiting his nighttime departures. Most nights he left the apartment just after sunset and didn't return until well after sunrise the next day. She assumed he was doing unsavory things to make a little money. She also suspected Edgar was spending more and more time at his uncle's shack on the shore of Coyote Bluff Reservoir, because he was convinced the spirits were more willing to speak to him at the place of Buddy Red Bird's death.

An hour ago, she had injected the last of the heroin Edgar had given her on Monday night. She had saved just enough to stave off the side effects of withdrawal but not enough to incapacitate her. After she had finished, Shavonne threw the syringe in the kitchen garbage can. She would no longer need her little, black kit if everything went according to plan. The first step in her plan was to check herself into the Mountain View Women's Shelter four blocks over on Eleventh Street. Once she was free of Edgar and safe at the women's shelter, she would call Mr. Jelaco and tell him where to find his daughter. She had even written his home phone number on a scrap of paper that was safely tucked away in her purse. After her call, Mr. Jelaco would have plenty of time to rescue his little girl before Edgar returned from his nightly prowl.

Shavonne had toyed with the idea of taking the child with her, but she wasn't strong enough, at least not yet. Besides, there was no logical explanation for how she had come to possess the little girl. If she took the child with her, there was a good chance she would end up in prison for kidnapping and murder. The beautiful, little girl was fast asleep on top of the soiled bedspread when Shavonne went to tell her good-bye. She watched her sleep for a few moments and then removed a small blanket from the foot of the bed and carefully covered her tiny body. She had developed a bond with the little girl over the course of the past three weeks and couldn't bear the thought of Edgar harming her. Shavonne gently smoothed the child's long, brown hair and kissed her lightly on the forehead. The little girl stirred momentarily and then was still again.

"Don't worry, sweetheart. Your daddy will be coming for you soon," Shavonne whispered to the child.

Shavonne returned to the living room with tears in her eyes and gathered up the black garbage bag that contained the sum total of her personal belongings. As she hoisted the plastic bag over her shoulder, she was saddened by the realization that she was a fifty-year-old woman whose worldly possessions were too few to fill a garbage bag. Shavonne was tired of living each day just to survive, and this time, she was serious about making it through rehab. When she reached the front door of the apartment, Shavonne paused briefly to glance back at the bedroom where the child lay sleeping, and then she quickly opened the battered wood door and vanished into the night.

CHAPTER 39

Wednesday night, October 25

Edgar had been waiting for ten minutes in the shadows of the old Lakeland National Bank building, which had been converted into a discount furniture store after the local bank had relocated. The furniture store had long since closed for the evening, and Edgar was about the only living thing stirring in Lakeland's downtown business district. The person he was waiting for was scheduled to arrive any minute now. The agreed-upon plan was for Edgar to climb into the lawyer's car when he stopped at the Jefferson Avenue stop sign. The two would conduct their business while the lawyer drove through the deserted downtown streets. As soon as their business was concluded, he would return Edgar to the original pickup spot, and their partnership would come to an end.

At eleven o'clock sharp, a Cadillac pulled up to the designated stop sign. It was the lawyer's car, right on time. Edgar silently moved from the shadows and made his way toward the passenger door of the waiting car. When he heard the click of the automatic lock, Edgar quickly opened the door and eased into the heated leather seat.

"Have you been waiting long?" the lawyer asked in an unnatural attempt at small talk.

"Not long," Edgar answered flatly.

The lawyer turned right onto Main Street and drove slowly past the decaying buildings. Felix Mendelssohn's "War March of the Priests" was playing softly on the Cadillac's radio. Edgar had frequently listened to classical music before the voices in his head had overpowered the soothing effects of the music.

"Do you like Mendelssohn?" Edgar asked the lawyer.

"What?"

"Felix Mendelssohn is a classical composer," Edgar explained, sorry he had brought up the subject.

The lawyer looked confused. "Classical music all sounds the same to me."

Edgar's business associate appeared nervous and distracted as they drove south on Main Street. When he reached the industrial district on the outskirts of town, he turned right onto Bannock Boulevard.

"Your money's above the visor," he informed Edgar.

Edgar retrieved the letter-sized envelope and casually peeked inside. The envelope contained a thick stack of fifty- and one-hundred-dollar bills. He didn't count the money, but it appeared as if the envelope contained the entire $5,000 contract price.

"This concludes our business," Edgar said with finality.

The lawyer was anxious to be rid of Edgar, but there was one piece of business he needed the crazy Indian to take care of before they permanently terminated their partnership.

"I need your help tying up a loose end."

"I can't take the job," Edgar replied without hesitation. "I'll be leaving Lakeland first thing tomorrow morning."

"It's a simple job that won't take long."

"The nature of the job is inconsequential."

"I need you to kill Detective Gates."

"I'm not a hired killer," Edgar replied indignantly. "I take my orders from the spirits who have passed before me."

"Do your spiritual advisors care about your freedom?" the lawyer mockingly asked. "Detective Gates can connect me to

Cole Panache, Jefferson Hughes, and Janis Jones, which means he's a direct threat to you as well."

"I'm done working for you," Edgar emphatically replied.

"The job pays ten thousand dollars," he coaxed. "With that kind of money, you could put some real distance between you and Lakeland."

Edgar had to fight off an overpowering urge to kill the manipulative lawyer on the spot. When he finally regained control of his inner rage, he calmly replied, "That's not possible."

The lawyer was clearly angered by Edgar's outright defiance but maintained his composure. "It's a simple job for a man with your abilities."

The voices in Edgar's head were making it difficult for him to concentrate on the lawyer's deceitful words, and to make matters worse, his business associate had taken on the form of a large black snake with gleaming eyes and a forked tongue. Edgar knew the spirits were allowing him to see the true essence of the man.

Edgar struggled to push the voices from his head and said, "I made a mistake while I was stealing the file."

"What kind of mistake?" his employer barked.

"I took off a glove while I was inside the house," Edgar explained.

The lawyer's facial muscles tightened, and he asked through clinched teeth, "Did you leave fingerprints inside the home?"

Edgar shrugged indifferently and said, "I'm not sure, but if my fingerprints turn up at the crime scene, it won't take the police long to connect me to the murder." Edgar then paused for a second and added, "Perhaps that's what the spirits have intended all along."

The lawyer now had two problems on his hands, a detective who knew too much and a babbling, insane Indian. His only traceable contact with Edgar Ellenwood had occurred almost thirty years before, and it would take some serious digging to uncover his involvement in the plea agreement. Detective Gates was another matter altogether.

"Your screwup complicates things for me," the lawyer agreed. "It sounds like a change of scenery is in order."

Edgar nodded his head in agreement and said, "I need to deal with a personal matter before I leave Lakeland. The spirits have been talking to me, but I can't understand their words."

"I hope the spirits realize that you're on a tight schedule."

"After I visit the place where their counsel and guidance is clear, you'll never see me again."

"Take care of your business and vanish," the lawyer replied dismissively. "I hear Indians are good at becoming one with nature."

"I will vanish into nothingness when the time is right," Edgar said with a cold stare.

"Did you get rid of the little girl?" he asked, abruptly changing the subject.

"Yes, it's done," Edgar lied.

The unlikely pair concluded their business as the Cadillac pulled up to the Jefferson Avenue stop sign. Edgar stuffed the envelope in his pants' pocket and placed his hand on the door handle.

"One more thing," the lawyer added. "Don't ever seek me out again."

Edgar gave him a piercing stare and then exited the car without responding. The lawyer breathed a deep sigh of relief when the huge Indian disappeared into the night. He was thankful that his twenty-eight-year relationship with Edgar Ellenwood had finally come to an end. He removed a can of air freshener from the glove box and sprayed the passenger seat. The large man's physical appearance and body odor were quite disgusting, and all that inane chatter about the spirits was more than a little unsettling. The lawyer took one last look at the shadows where Edgar had vanished before he shifted his Cadillac into drive and turned toward home.

CHAPTER 40

Wednesday night, October 25

The Mountain View Women's Shelter was a privately funded rehabilitation facility for women whose lives had been derailed by serious drug addictions. A pleasant young woman named Paige had cheerfully checked a very nervous Shavonne into the shelter. Paige had been candid about the personal demons in her own life after Shavonne had recounted her thirty-year battle with drug addiction. In theory, residents of the shelter would be transitioned from the safety of the facility to productive lives in society once they had acquired the skills needed to cope with their addictions. Shavonne knew that rehabilitation for someone like her was a long shot, but she was determined.

Paige had thoroughly explained the shelter rules to Shavonne during the check-in procedure and made it abundantly clear that there were no exceptions to the rules. Because she was a drug addict, she would not be permitted to leave the facility for the first four weeks of her treatment program. During that same period of time, she would not be allowed visitors or phone calls, and she would be required to attend at least two counseling sessions each day. If Shavonne was unable or unwilling to follow the rules, she would be asked to leave the shelter, and another woman would take her place.

Paige had carefully searched Shavonne's personal belongings for drugs and other contraband before escorting her to her new bedroom. Shavonne's sleeping quarters were clean and decorated in bright colors. The room's colorful décor reminded her of a child's bedroom, but perhaps that was appropriate, given the fact that Shavonne was hoping for a rebirth of sorts. Although new residents were not allowed to make or receive phone calls, after some persuasive pleading, Paige had reluctantly agreed to bring Shavonne a portable phone after she was squared away. Once Paige left her alone, Shavonne removed her personal belongings from the plastic garbage bag and carefully placed them in the top drawer of the dresser she was assigned. It was an enormous change for Shavonne, yet she felt strangely at home in her new room.

It didn't take Shavonne long to unpack, and she was already sitting on the bed, worrying about the child, when Paige returned carrying a portable phone and a yellow nightgown. Paige placed the nightgown at the foot of Shavonne's bed and said, "A clean nightgown might make you a little more comfortable on your first night in a strange place."

"Thank you," Shavonne replied before meekly asking, "Is it okay if I make my phone call now?"

Paige tentatively handed her the telephone and with a furrowed brow said, "I'm allowing you to make this call because you haven't officially started the program, but after this one call, you won't be allowed to contact people on the outside."

"There's no one I need to talk to after this call," Shavonne sadly replied.

"I'll give you some privacy while you make your call," Paige said in a softer tone before she left the room.

Shavonne removed the crumpled scrap of paper from her purse and nervously dialed Mr. Jelaco's home telephone number. The phone rang three times before a man's voice came on the line and said, "You've reached Nick Jelaco's voice mail. If it's important, leave a message."

Shavonne's heart began to race the instant she heard the first beep. What if Mr. Jelaco did not pick up her call before Edgar returned to the apartment? After the last beep, Shavonne blurted out, "Hello, Mr. Jelaco, my name is Shavonne Nolan. I'm so very, very sorry for what I've done. I should have called sooner, and I'll never forgive myself if he hurts her. I know where you can find your daughter. Please call me as soon as possible. Hurry…you don't have much time. Oh no…I don't know the phone number here. I'm at the Mountain View Women's Shelter on…Eleventh Street. Please hurry."

Shavonne hurried from her bedroom and tracked down Paige at the front desk. Paige looked up from the admittance papers she was filling out and smiled at Shavonne. "Did you make your call?" she asked.

"I'm expecting a phone call from a man named Nick Jelaco," Shavonne said in a rush. "It's urgent that I speak to him the instant he calls."

Paige tilted her head to the side and frowned disapprovingly at Shavonne. "You know the rules. You're not allowed to entertain visitors or receive telephone calls for the next four weeks," Paige explained as if she were talking to a child.

"This is a matter of life and death," Shavonne pleaded. "I won't even think about bending the rules again if you let me take this one call."

Paige gave Shavonne a patronizing smile and said, "Why don't you get a little rest? Everything always seems a little brighter after a good night's sleep."

"What about my call?" Shavonne demanded in a more frantic tone.

"If your Mr. Jelaco calls, I'll let you speak to him," Paige lied.

Shavonne breathed a deep sigh of relief. "Thank you, Paige."

Paige felt guilty about lying to Shavonne, but she wasn't about to jeopardize the new resident's treatment by allowing her to violate the rules on her first day at the shelter. Shavonne needed to be isolated from the outside world and that included Mr. Jelaco.

CHAPTER 41

Wednesday night, October 25

Phil Gates didn't spend much time in his small, sparsely furnished apartment, and when he did, he felt like a stranger in his own home. His wife had divorced him fifteen years ago, and since that time Gates's living quarters had been nothing more than a place where he could sleep, shower, eat, and drink. When his wife and kids had first moved out, he had hoped the pain and loneliness was temporary. Over time he had discovered that it was not. The loneliness had actually become more acute with each passing year. Gates secretly feared that he would end up a lonely old man who died in his home with no one to discover his decaying body until weeks later. Gates was tired of being alone and miserable; perhaps he would reach out to his estranged children and ex-wife when the Jelaco case was closed.

Detective Gates found a half-empty can of cat food behind a six-pack in the refrigerator and absentmindedly dumped its contents into a small bowl. His cat, Tiger, brushed against his leg before attacking the food. Gates felt a twinge of guilt when he realized that he had not fed the cat for a couple of days.

"No wonder my family wants nothing to do with me—I can't even take care of a cat," Gates mumbled to himself.

In 1984, Phillip Gates had been an upstart police officer who could barely pay the rent, yet life had been good. He had built a solid and loving relationship with his wife and two children and worked at a job he truly enjoyed. Unfortunately, all of that changed in 1985 when young Officer Gates did what was expected of him and not what was right. Since that lapse of judgment nearly twenty-five years ago, his career had been the only part of his life that hadn't fallen into shambles. He had successfully closed case after case and gained the respect and admiration of his colleagues, but the accolades meant nothing to him. He knew the real truth: he was a fraud and a phony, no better than the criminals he pursued.

After Cole Panache's trial and conviction, Gates had become moody and withdrawn. At first, he had tried to convince himself that participating in the frame-up was just part of the job, but the guilt had continued to gnaw at him. Gates's wife, Sherry, had hung on as long as she could, but after several months of trying to make their marriage work, she had asked for a trial separation. During the separation, their relationship had gone from bad to unbearable, so Sherry had filed for divorce in the spring of 1987. Gates hadn't contested the divorce and had agreed to her demands without putting up a fight. The detective had tried to settle into the role of weekend father for his two children following the divorce, but the weekly visits had soon turned into monthly visits, and by 1989, he had been lucky to see his kids once or twice a year. It wasn't his ex-wife's fault; she had pleaded with him to make time for his children. When his kids had become involved with friends and school activities, his contact with them had ceased altogether. It had now been several years since he had spoken to his son, Ryan, or daughter, Stacey.

Gates pulled out a frozen dinner and a Miller Genuine Draft. He couldn't remember the last time he had eaten something that wasn't either frozen or purchased from a fast-food restaurant. He shoved the processed dinner into the microwave and set the timer for five minutes without reading the instructions. While the seconds slowly ticked off the microwave, Gates twisted the cap off the cold beer and casually dropped it on the counter beside a dozen others just like it. He took a long swig of beer and walked into the living room to turn on the TV. The detective didn't watch much television, but he needed something to take his mind off the Jelaco investigation. Gates quickly cycled through the channels until he recognized one of his favorites, the classic Western *Shane*. He could relate to the flawed gunfighter who was trying to find salvation by protecting homesteaders from a ruthless cattle baron. Perhaps, it was because the same thoughts of redemption were floating around in the back of his mind.

When the microwave timer beeped, Gates tossed the remote control on the sofa, which had been doubling as his bed for the past few months, and returned to the kitchen. The exhausted detective retrieved the frozen dinner and wearily plopped down on the sofa. Gates knew he needed some form of nourishment, but after a couple of bites, he gave up on the tasteless frozen dinner and took another long swig from his beer. It also didn't take him long to realize that the old Western wasn't going to provide a distraction from his dark thoughts. He tried to focus on the movie's storyline, but every few seconds, his focus would return to the missing little girl.

Phillip Gates had been living under the weight of his unbearable secret for so long that he could scarcely remember the man he had been before the Panache investigation. After an objective evaluation of the way the Jeloco homicide was playing out, he was convinced that his past misdeeds were on a collision course with the investigation he was currently working. Gates could feel it in his bones; he would soon be forced to make another life-altering decision, and he honestly didn't know if he had the courage to make the right choice this time.

Gates finished the last of his beer in one long drink, pulled off his boots, and lay down on the lumpy sofa. His instincts were telling him the investigation was coming to a head, but he needed to get a little sleep before he went back to work. Gates closed his eyes and tried to clear his mind long enough to drift off to sleep, but his thoughts kept returning to the Jelaco case. Finding Edgar Ellenwood's fingerprints at the crime scene and his connection to Walter Burton had theoretically confirmed the detective's suspicions about the intersection of his past and present. He was certain that Edgar Ellenwood was responsible for Julie Jelaco's murder, and he was pretty sure Walter Burton was the man pushing Ellenwood's buttons. Gates believed Walter's motivation was about as simple and straightforward as motives got; he wanted to cover up his involvement in the Panache case.

Apparently, Janis Jones had stumbled onto the truth about Jefferson Hughes's perjured testimony and the incriminating evidence planted by Clyde Parks—the evidence that had ultimately led to Cole's murder conviction and Janis's own death. He still had no idea how Ms. Jones had come to possess the information that had been buried for more than twenty years, but if she could figure it out, so could someone else. For some unknown reason, Walter believed the Janis Jones case file contained evidence that could incriminate him, which meant the file probably contained evidence that would eventually lead back to Gates as well. In a perfect world, Walter Burton would pay dearly for his crimes, but Gates knew it would be nearly impossible to balance the scales of justice unless he was willing to sacrifice himself in the process.

The troubled detective tossed and turned on the old sofa for an hour or so as images of Darby Jelaco and Cole Panache bounced around inside his head. He may have dosed off once or twice, but by midnight, he had accepted the fact that an uninterrupted night's sleep was out of the question. With his frustration nearing its boiling point, Gates sat up and angrily pulled on his cowboy boots. Even though he was headed back to the police station, Gates still made a quick detour through the kitchen to pick up another beer. One way or the other, the Jelaco investigation was going to end. When it did, he would sleep.

CHAPTER 42

Thursday morning, October 26

Nick backed the sputtering Mustang out of William Forsythe's garage at three fifteen on a frigid Thursday morning. He still didn't have a clear picture of his next move, yet he sensed it was time to go on the offensive. Prior to their second trip north, he had been somewhat optimistic about the prospect of acquiring critical information from Jefferson Hughes. Instead, he had only found another corpse at the end of a promising evidence trail.

A light snow had dusted the Wood River Valley while Simone slept on William's big leather couch. Nick had tried to get a little sleep as well, but he had been unable to block out the chilling images that kept invading his thoughts. His daughter was running out of time; he could feel it in his gut. Another misstep might be fatal for his little girl. Nick was convinced Walter possessed information that would lead him to Darby, and he was trying to figure out how to extract the information from his former employer when a loud beep from his cell phone caused him to jump. It wasn't the less intrusive humming the phone made when he had an incoming call. This distinctive beep alerted him when he had an unopened voice mail.

"Is there something wrong with the car?" Simone asked as she nervously glanced at the dashboard.

Nick shook his head and said, "Someone left a message on my cell phone."

"Why didn't you take the call?"

"The battery was going dead, so I plugged the phone in the cigarette lighter while you were asleep," Nick explained and then mumbled to himself, "I wasn't expecting any calls after midnight."

A troubled look spread across Simone's face. "Who called?" she asked, clearly worried.

Nick frowned while he scrutinized the unfamiliar number displayed on the caller ID and then haltingly answered, "I don't recognize the number, and I've only given my cell number to a handful of people."

Nick quickly entered his four-digit security code. An automated female voice informed him that he had one new message and then told him to press the number one if he wanted to listen to the message. Nick wasn't sure if he wanted to hear the content of the message, but he pressed one just the same. He listened to the strange message in its entirety, while Simone stared at him with pleading eyes. When the message ended, he immediately punched the number one and listened to the entire message for a second time. After he had listened to the woman's disjointed message twice, he punched the number two and saved the message.

"What's wrong?"

"We need to find a phone book," Nick replied as he replayed the message in his head.

"Nick, you're scaring me."

Nick gave Simone a look meant to reassure her and said, "It's probably nothing, but it was a very strange message from a lady named Shavonne Nolan."

"Strange?" Simone repeated.

"Ms. Nolan claims to know the whereabouts of my daughter," Nick answered in a flat tone that belied the racing of his heart.

Simone wrinkled her eyebrows and gently cautioned, "What if she's some kind of crackpot?"

"Ms. Nolan is probably a bona fide nutcase," Nick agreed. "But I'm running out of time, and I can't afford to ignore a potential lead."

"Of course not, but don't get your hopes up until you talk to her," Simone countered.

"There was something about the tenor of her voice that seemed genuine," Nick mused aloud. Nick had been wondering how Shavonne Nolan had come to possess his cell number and when the simple truth finally hit him, he blurted out, "She actually called my home."

"Who called your home?"

"Calls to my home phone were forwarded to my cell after I moved out, and my home number is listed in the phone book," Nick explained. "The woman who left the message probably called my home phone."

"Is that important?"

Nick shrugged and said, "I don't know, but I was afraid Walter might be involved when it appeared as if Ms. Nolan had my cell number."

It took Nick less than five minutes to cover the six-mile stretch of two-lane highway that led into Ketchum. Just inside the city limits, he spotted a twenty-four-hour convenience store with a payphone and swerved into the parking lot. He left the car running while he raced to the tattered phone book. Nick's frustration began to mount when a quick survey of the yellow pages came up empty, but he did find the shelter's number listed in the white pages. The directory was chained to the pay phone, so he ripped the needed page from the book and returned to the Mustang. His hands were clumsy and trembling as he punched the ten digit long-distance number into his cell phone.

"Is anybody there?" Simone asked impatiently.

After the fifth ring, Nick shook his head and sarcastically replied, "What kind of shelter doesn't take calls in the middle of the night?"

"What do we do now?"

"Drive to Lakeland as fast as humanly possible," Nick answered, but before he could snap the cell phone shut, a woman's voice said, "Mountain View Shelter for Women, Paige speaking."

Given the nature of the facility, Nick knew that he needed to sound composed and in complete control. He exhaled slowly and calmly said, "My name is Nick Jelaco, and it's critical that I speak with a woman staying at the shelter."

After a brief silence, Paige replied, "I'm sorry, Mr. Jelaco. Phone calls are a violation of the shelter's rules."

Nick was afraid Paige might hang up before he could convince her to call Shavonne Nolan to the telephone, so he cut right to the crux of the matter. "Listen closely, Paige. Your next move will determine if a child lives or dies."

"I'm sure your call is very important, but I don't have the authority to put your call through," Paige responded in a bored voice that made Nick believe she was accustomed to dealing with men who stretched the truth.

"Is a woman named Shavonne Nolan staying at the shelter?" Nick asked in a more pressing tone.

There was another noticeable silence before Paige said, "We protect the identity of our residents."

Nick heard a trace of indecision in Paige's voice, so pushed the issue, "It's imperative that I speak to Shavonne Nolan immediately."

"I can't help you, Mr. Jelaco," Paige responded with less conviction.

"Please! Do the right thing, Paige."

"I'll lose my job if I ignore the shelter's rules."

"Forget the rules," Nick barked. "This is a matter of life and death."

"You'll need to present your request to the shelter manager,

Judy Hernandez," Paige snapped, obviously put off by Nick's tone. "She starts her work day at about eight o'clock."

Nick had decided to give the receptionist all the pertinent facts, but before he could explain the details of his wife's murder and three-year-old daughter's abduction, Paige hung up the telephone. He quickly dialed the shelter's number a second time, but this time, Paige did not answer the incoming call. Nick glanced at the digital clock on the dashboard and mentally noted that traffic would be nonexistent at three thirty in the morning. Barring bad weather or car problems, he could be knocking on the shelter's front door by five o'clock. Nick shifted the Mustang into drive and roared away from the convenience store.

"Maybe we should call the police," Simone suggested as they sped through Ketchum.

"I can't trust the police," Nick replied in a curt tone that indicated he wasn't willing to discuss the topic.

"What if Shavonne Nolan isn't staying at the women's shelter?"

"She's definitely there."

"How can you be sure?"

"I could hear it in the night attendant's voice," Nick answered with confidence. "She could have avoided the entire confrontation by subtly implying that Ms. Nolan wasn't a resident, but she didn't offer any kind of denial."

"It's hard to pick up subtle inferences over the phone," Simone cautioned.

"Her inferences weren't all that subtle, and for a split second, I thought she might let me talk to Shavonne," Nick countered.

"I pray you're right, Nick."

"That makes two of us."

CHAPTER 43

Thursday morning, October 26

The old Mustang skidded to a stop in front of the Mountain View Shelter for Women at 4:52 a.m. Nick had briefly considered dropping Simone off at her apartment, or checking her into a motel, but time and safety concerns had caused him to reject both options.

The instant the car stopped moving, Nick sprang out of the driver's seat and barked, "Wait for me here."

True to form, Simone ignored his order and followed him down the sidewalk. When Nick realized that Simone was right on his heels, he growled, "This isn't a game; wait in the car."

"Think about it, Nick—it's a women's shelter," Simone offered as an explanation for her defiance.

"I'm not taking up residency," Nick snapped.

Simone ignored the sarcasm and said, "A strange man storming a female rehab center before sunrise might be a little overwhelming for a bunch of traumatized women."

Nick didn't have the patience or energy to argue with her, and when he thought about it, he realized she had a valid point. If his first conversation with Paige was any indication, there was a good chance Simone would be more persuasive with the receptionist than an overwrought man. Nick rolled his eyes and waved at her to join him. With Simone by his side, Nick ran to the front door of the shelter and rang the doorbell several times in rapid succession. When there was no immediate answer, he checked the door. It was locked, so he rang the doorbell again. Nick was about to start pounding on the door when Paige's voice came over the intercom speaker beside the door.

"If you don't go away, I'll call the police."

Nick pushed the talk button on the intercom and in a voice choked with emotion, responded, "Please hear me out—my daughter's life is at stake. My name is Nick Jelaco, and my daughter's been kidnapped. Shavonne Nolan called me last night and told me to contact her at this location. According to her, she knows where I can find my little girl."

Nick removed his finger from the black button and waited for Paige's reply. After several seconds of agonizing silence, he assumed she had gone to call the police. Nick took a step back preparing to kick in the front door when Paige's voice finally broke the silence. "I thought your name sounded familiar," Paige said in a more sympathetic voice. "I've been following your family's story in the local paper."

"Then help me," Nick pleaded.

"Give me a minute—I need to check on something," Paige hastily replied before the intercom went silent.

"What do you think she's doing?" Simone whispered.

"She's either verifying my story with Shavonne Nolan, or she's calling the police."

"Which way are you betting?"

"At this point, I'd say it's a toss-up."

Nick and Simone shuffled around on the front porch for an agonizing three or four minutes. Nick was half expecting to hear police sirens as the seconds ticked away. Instead, Paige's voice crackled through the intercom's speaker.

"I'm going to open the door, Mr. Jelaco. Shavonne is anxious to speak with you."

Nick exhaled in relief. "Thank you."

After the distinct click of two deadbolts, the shelter door swung open. There were two women standing just inside the door, and Nick immediately identified the older one as Shavonne Nolan. She bore no resemblance to the mental image he had formed in his mind, but he knew it was her as soon as their eyes met. She was dressed in a yellow nightgown and was timidly hiding behind the younger woman. Nick would have guessed Shavonne's age at around fifty-five, but it had definitely been a hard fifty-five years. Stringy bleached-blonde hair hung to her shoulders, and her skin had an unhealthy grayish hue to it. She was of average height but probably weighed less than ninety pounds.

Nick took a step toward her and said, "Hello, Ms. Nolan. I'm Nick Jelaco." When Shavonne didn't respond to his greeting, he calmly said, "Do you know where I can find my daughter?"

Shavonne inched a little closer to Paige and weakly said, "I'm so sorry—I should have called you sooner."

Nick gave the frail woman an understanding smile and said, "We can't change the past. It's my daughter's future I'm worried about."

Shavonne stared at the floor and meekly replied, "Your daughter was in an apartment on Seventh Street a couple of hours ago. A man named Edgar Ellenwood took her from your house."

"Is Edgar with her right now?"

Shavonne shrugged her stooped shoulders and said, "She was alone when I left the apartment."

Nick wanted to ask what kind of person left a three-year-old unattended in the middle of the night but instead asked, "What's the apartment's address?"

"Two hundred thirty-seven Seventh Street."

"How about the name of the complex and the apartment number?" Nick urged.

"The place is called the Cherry Wood Apartments, and she's in apartment sixty-six," Shavonne answered without hesitation. "The little darling's been sleeping through the night, so I figured it would be okay to leave her alone for a couple of hours."

Nick ignored an urge to point out the idiocy of her logic and merely asked, "Can you describe the apartment's layout?"

Shavonne seemed confused by the question at first, but before he could restate it in simpler terms, her eyes widened, and she said, "It's a small apartment with only four rooms. There's a living area, a small kitchenette, one bedroom, and a bathroom."

"Where was Darby when you left the apartment?" Nick asked.

"She was sleeping in the bedroom."

"Where's the bedroom located in relationship to the front door of the apartment?"

Shavonne's face contorted as if she was trying to solve a complicated physics problem, before she said, "The front door opens directly into the living room. There's a hallway on the far wall of the living room. The bedroom is the only door on the right side of that hallway."

"Thanks, Ms. Nolan," Nick said and turned to rush back to the Mustang.

"Wait a minute, Mr. Jelaco," Shavonne blurted out. "I think Edgar killed your wife."

Nick nodded at Shavonne, but didn't bother to tell her that he had already arrived at the same conclusion. His first priority was to rescue his daughter, yet he would not hesitate to kill the man who had murdered his wife if an opportunity presented itself.

"When will Edgar return to the apartment?"

"Most mornings he doesn't show up until well after sunrise. You need to be very careful, Mr. Jelaco. He's not right in the head," Shavonne added.

"Does he carry a weapon?" Nick asked.

"He keeps an old shotgun in the trunk of his car."

"What kind of car does he drive?"

"An old Lincoln Town Car that barely runs," Shavonne answered.

"What color?"

"White."

Nick was about to leave for the second time when he realized Simone intended to come with him. He held up his hand and forcefully said, "You're waiting right here." When Simone started to protest, he firmly said, "Don't argue with me. My mind is made up."

Simone must have realized he was dead serious because all she said was, "Bring your daughter home safely."

CHAPTER 44

Thursday morning, October 26

Nick was not surprised to discover that the Cherry Wood Apartments on Seventh Street were both filthy and run-down. The once stylish apartments looked as though they had slowly evolved into transient housing for Lakeland's drug addicts and petty criminals. Nick felt sick to his stomach when he thought about his little girl being held hostage in one of the squalid apartments by the psychopath who had killed her mother. Nick pushed the unpleasant thought from his mind and retrieved the .40 caliber Glock from beneath the driver's seat. He had intentionally parked fifty yards up the street and tried to appear nonchalant as he walked toward the apartment complex. In an attempt to avoid unwanted attention, he had tucked the handgun into the waistband of his pants and covered it with his jacket. Nick was trying to appear relaxed and unconcerned as he approached the apartments, but his heart was beating like a bass drum. Even though he had been in life-and-death situations during his stint in the military, it had not been his daughter's life that had been at stake.

The dilapidated apartment complex was constructed of faded red brick that local gang bangers had nearly covered with spray painted graffiti. Nick assumed the tenants of the

Cherry Wood Apartments placed the aesthetic appearance of their housing well down on their list of priorities, while cheap rent and a landlord who minded his own business was near the top. Darby's home for the past three weeks was a ground-floor apartment on the southwest side of the ramshackle complex. Under ideal circumstances, Nick would have covertly observed the apartment prior to making a forced entry. Unfortunately, concern for his daughter's safety didn't afford him that luxury.

Nick tried to appear uninterested in the activity going on inside apartment 66 on his initial walk past, and, as expected, the living room curtains were drawn. He hoped anyone watching his movements would assume he was visiting one of the tenants who lived further down the sidewalk. Approximately ten feet past the front door of apartment 66, he abruptly stepped off the sidewalk and flattened himself against the brick wall. After quickly scanning the area, he cautiously inched his way along the wall until he was right beside the only entryway into Edgar's apartment. Outside the door he listened for sounds of movement or chatter from inside. After several seconds of silence, he carefully removed the Glock from the waistband of his pants with his right hand as he slowly turned the doorknob with his left hand.

Much to his surprise, the door handle turned without resistance. *It's now or never,* Nick thought as he exhaled slowly in an attempt to clear his head. When his nerves were steady, he rushed through the door with his weapon in the ready position. Inside the dingy apartment, Nick quickly scanned the small living room through the sites of his .40 caliber Glock. It didn't take him long to determine that Edgar Ellenwood was not in the living room or adjacent kitchenette, and his instincts were screaming that he had arrived too late. Nick pushed the thoughts of failure from his mind and rushed to the bedroom at the rear of the apartment. The door to the bedroom had been left ajar, and he quickly realized the room was unoccupied as well. Even though the bedroom was empty, something on the double bed caught his attention. The bedding had not been turned down, but a single blanket lay crumpled on top of the stained and faded bedspread. Nick immediately knew his daughter had been sleeping beneath that blanket just a short time ago.

The profound disappointment that overwhelmed him after running headlong into another dead end was almost paralyzing. There was no doubt in Nick's mind that Edgar had taken Darby and vanished again, yet he searched the entire bedroom just the same.

The bedroom contained nothing of interest aside from the crumpled blanket, so Nick shifted his search to the small bathroom directly across the hall. It was there that a seemingly innocent discovery forced him to stifle an anguished cry. Wadded up on the floor beside the moldy and corroded bathtub, he found a small pair of light blue pajamas decorated with little pink teacups and purple teapots. Nick immediately recognized the tiny pajamas as Darby's favorites. She always insisted on wearing those exact pajamas whenever they weren't in the laundry. Now, he knew what his daughter had been wearing the night she was abducted, but he had no idea how she was currently dressed or where Edgar had taken her. When a host of very unpleasant mental images began to flood his thoughts, he forced the distasteful pictures from his mind and focused on the present.

Edgar Ellenwood had apparently returned to the apartment sooner than Shavonne had expected, discovered her absence, and fled with Darby. Nick was now wasting precious time at the abandoned Cherry Wood apartment. It appeared as if a second question-and-answer session with Shavonne Nolan was in order. With a little bit of luck, perhaps she could shed some light on where the madman had taken his little girl.

CHAPTER 45

Thursday morning, October 26

Edgar had intended to return to his uncle's shack on Coyote Bluff Reservoir after his rendezvous with the lawyer. He desperately needed to seek enlightenment from the spirits, but the voices in his head had become so overpowering that he was forced to alter his original plan. In fact, the voices were now louder and angrier than ever before. Edgar wondered if the little girl and her mother were the cause of the spirits' displeasure. The voices used to come and go, but now they were constantly inside his head and becoming more agitated with each passing day. Perhaps it would quiet the spirits if he killed the little girl so she could reunite with her mother.

Edgar immediately sensed that something was amiss when he arrived at the Seventh Street apartment. He found the child asleep in the bedroom, but Shavonne was not in the apartment. It was unusual for Shavonne to venture out alone, and her absence troubled him. Edgar had planned to load the little girl and their belongings into the car while he waited for her to return. His plan changed when he opened the closet door and discovered that Shavonne's clothing and personal items were gone as well. He didn't know what it all meant, but the voices in his head were telling him to leave Lakeland without her. Somehow, the evil spirits had used their trickery to turn Shavonne against him. Her disappearance made one thing clear: it was time to kill the little girl and make a run for the one place he would find peace.

Edgar removed his tattered woolen poncho and an ancient .45 caliber revolver from the hall closet. The old revolver had sentimental value because it had belonged to his uncle Buddy Red Bird. Edgar had discovered the old handgun while rummaging through Buddy's cabin shortly after his death. He pulled the decorative hand-woven poncho over his head and tucked the revolver into his belt. Edgar then placed both hands over his ears and pushed down hard in a futile attempt to quiet the voices in his head. It was no use; the angry voices would not be quieted. After a couple of minutes, he gave up and refocused his attention on the task at hand, the small child who was sleeping in the back bedroom.

The child was curled up in a tiny ball and sleeping peacefully in the center of the bed when Edgar entered the bedroom. She was breathing deeply and completely unaware of the large man's presence. Edgar had no desire to kill the child. Still, he would do what had to be done. He moved silently to the edge of the bed and stared at the child. After watching her sleep for a couple of minutes, he gently placed one of his enormous hands around her slender neck. The little girl's eyes opened with a start, and her tiny body tensed noticeably at his touch, but she didn't cry out. A sliver of moonlight that flickered through the lone bedroom window cast a surreal glow on the child's beautiful face. Edgar recognized the look of fear and confusion in her eyes.

Edgar tightly shut his own eyes. He could not bear to see the little girl's anguished face as the life drifted from her body. Free of her paralyzing stare, Edgar slowly began to tighten his grip on her delicate throat. The little girl's face vanished from his sight, but her mother's face had taken her place in his mind's eye. The voices were still inside his head, but they were less angry.

The girl's mother looked at him with the same pleading blue eyes that had haunted him since the night of her death, and in a melodic voice, she said, "Don't kill my baby—it's not her time."

Edgar loosened his grip on the child's neck and slowly opened his eyes. Now, he was more confused and unsettled than before. Deep in his soul, Edgar believed that killing the woman had been a terrible mistake. He had hoped that reuniting the child with her mother would pacify the spirits, but perhaps he had been wrong. Edgar scooped up the small child and gently pressed her against his massive chest. He would take the little girl with him to Coyote Bluff and wait for guidance from the spirits. If it was the child's time to die, another few hours wouldn't matter.

CHAPTER 46

Thursday morning, October 26

Nick raced back to the women's shelter in a state of absolute panic. Darby had obviously been held captive at the disgusting little apartment on Seventh Street, and if Shavonne's timetable was accurate, he had missed her by no more than an hour or two. At least he knew for certain the identity of his daughter's kidnapper and that she was still alive. Now, he needed to find out where the psychopath had taken his little girl. Nick stashed the .40 caliber Glock under the driver's seat and sprinted toward the shelter's front door. A feeling of déjà vu hit him as he sprinted up the concrete sidewalk for the second time. Simone must have been watching through the window because she met him at the front door with Paige at her side.

"Where's Darby?" Simone frantically asked.

"She wasn't there," Nick panted, out of breath. "I did find a pair of her pajamas, which corroborates Shavonne's story."

"How does that help?" Simone demanded, unable to contain her disappointment.

Nick turned to Paige. "I need to talk to Shavonne. She might know where Edgar has taken my daughter."

Paige didn't hesitate or ask questions this time. She immediately disappeared into the hallway. Nick nervously paced back and forth in the reception area while he waited for them to return. Simone sat down on one of the two sofas and buried her face in her hands. When the two women entered the room a few minutes later, Nick was shocked by Shavonne's appearance. She was trembling noticeably, and her face was drenched in perspiration. Given the rehabilitative mission of the facility, Nick assumed Shavonne's deteriorating physical condition was the result of heroin withdrawal.

Nick struggled to keep his anger in check when he addressed Shavonne. "The apartment was empty," he informed her through clinched teeth. "Where would Edgar take my daughter?"

Shavonne began to shake her head and cry softly. "I never should have left her alone in the apartment."

"Where would he take her?" Nick repeated.

"I was so scared and confused—I didn't know what to do," Shavonne mumbled to no one in particular.

Nick walked over to Shavonne, firmly grabbed her by the shoulders, and looked her square in the eye. "You need to pull yourself together," he commanded in a resolute voice. "I can't find my little girl without your help."

"I really don't know," Shavonne whimpered. "He used to talk about moving to the Oregon coast or returning to his tribe in South Dakota, but lately he just rambles on and on about the Indian spirits."

"Give me something," Nick urged.

Shavonne shrugged and said, "He spends a lot of time at the reservoir. It's where his uncle died."

"I need an exact location," Nick demanded.

"I really don't know specifics," Shavonne responded apologetically. "I do know his uncle died at his place on the shores of Coyote Bluff Reservoir."

Nick suddenly recalled bits and pieces of Jason Davidson's story. "Edgar's an Indian?" he asked. He'd been in such a rush during his first conversation with Shavonne that he had forgotten to get a detailed description of Edgar Ellenwood.

"That's right," Shavonne agreed, seemingly pleased that she could give a definite answer. "He's a full-blooded Sioux Indian."

Nick already knew the answer, but he asked the question anyway. "Can you describe Edgar's physical appearance?"

"Edgar is abnormally large. He must be at least six-foot-nine, and he weighs more than 350 pounds. He wears his black hair long, well past his shoulders." An involuntary shudder ran through Shavonne's body. "His face is scarred quite badly. He was stricken with a bad case of chicken pox as a child and then got sliced up pretty bad in a knife fight." Then in a small voice she added, "People are cruel to him because of his appearance."

There was no longer any doubt in Nick's mind that Edgar Ellenwood was the same man who had abducted and terrorized Jason Davidson all those years ago. He was also convinced that Walter Burton was pulling Edgar's strings from somewhere in the shadows. If Walter had given the order to steal Janis Jones's case file, he was also undoubtedly behind the bribery and perjured testimony that had led to Cole Panache's murder conviction.

J ason Davidson had been held captive in a rundown shack near the reservoir, and according to Shavonne, Edgar spent a great deal of time at his uncle's shack that was located on the reservoir. Nick was not a gambling man by nature, yet he was about to bet everything that Edgar had taken his daughter to an old shack on Coyote Bluff Reservoir.

"I need directions to Edgar's shack," Nick said to Shavonne.

Shavonne appeared completely befuddled by the simple request. "I've only been there a couple of times, Mr. Jelaco, and I was stoned out of my mind on both occasions," she stammered.

Nick wanted to shake a coherent answer out of her but realized aggression would do more harm than good. "Please try to remember," Nick pleaded. "Any little detail could make the difference between me finding my daughter and …" He trailed off.

Shavonne scrunched up her ashen face. "We had to walk quite a distance to get to the cabin," she said hopefully.

"Why did you walk?" Nick pushed.

"The road didn't go all the way to the cabin."

"Can you describe the landscape on your walk to the cabin?"

"Actually, Edgar always carried me because the terrain was pretty rough for a person in my condition."

"Did he carry you through trees?" Nick urged.

Shavonne closed her eyes, and after a brief silence said, "I remember pine trees and lots of big rocks."

Jason Davidson believed he had been held captive on the northern side of the reservoir, and Nick now agreed with his deduction. Most of the reservoir was surrounded by upscale houses, but the northern shore was still underdeveloped because of its rugged topography. The hilly, rocky terrain made it too costly for real estate speculators to access the area.

"Were there any houses or cabins near his uncle's place?" Nick continued.

"Not that I can remember," Shavonne answered without much confidence.

"Was there anything special or unique about the cabin?"

Shavonne stood there with a blank look on her face for several seconds. Finally, after a maddening silence, she said, "The old cabin was made out of wood planks, and every single window was boarded over. There was a small porch out front with a couple of broken steps leading up to it."

"That's good, Shavonne, real good," Nick said encouragingly. "How close is the cabin to the water's edge?"

"I don't know exactly, but I think it's fairly close."

"Why do you think it is close to the water?" Nick immediately encouraged her.

A look of complete certainty appeared on Shavonne's face. "The old shack was built two or three feet above ground level just in case the water level got too high," she explained. "I remember because the cabin looked like it was sitting on top of stilts."

"Do you know his uncle's name?"

"It was a funny-sounding Indian name. Something like 'Running Bird' or 'Red Bird,'" Shavonne answered with a frustrated shake of her head.

Nick gently placed his hand on the woman's boney shoulder. "Thanks, Shavonne. What you did took real courage."

"Please find your little girl before something bad happens," Shavonne pleaded. "My life has been a long string of regrets, but I couldn't live with myself if Edgar harms that beautiful child."

"Don't worry. I'll find her," Nick said with resolve.

CHAPTER 47

Thursday afternoon, October 26

The perception of how quickly time passes is a strange phenomenon. When Nick was forced to kill a couple of hours in an airport lobby or sit through a boring business meeting, time seemed to stand still. Now, when each tick of the clock could mean the difference between life and death, the hours seemed to fly by. It was a quarter past noon by the time Nick was completely packed and speeding toward the north shore of Coyote Bluff Reservoir. After some deliberation, Nick had decided a land approach would be too risky and more time-consuming than a water assault on Edgar's shack.

Once the attack logistics of the mission were worked out, Nick stopped by his house to retrieve his scuba gear and .45 caliber Smith and Wesson. By all accounts, Edgar was an extremely large and powerful man, which called for the additional stopping power provided by the Smith and Wesson. His plan was to scan the north shore from a boat, identify Edgar's shack, and then put his scuba diving skills into action. If everything went according to plan, he could approach the shack undetected from beneath the water.

Nick wasn't about to subject Simone to any unnecessary risks this close to the finish line, so he dropped her off at a Comfort

Inn and gave instructions to check in under an assumed name. When he had first told her about his decision to hunt Edgar alone, she had vehemently insisted that their partnership remain intact until their ordeal was resolved. During a short but heated argument, Nick had finally convinced her that working alone provided him with the best chance for a successful mission. He then gave her explicit instructions not to leave the motel or make any phone calls unless he failed to make contact by midnight. In that event, she was supposed to contact Detective David Sato of the Lakeland P.D.

After several maddening yet unavoidable delays, Nick was finally headed toward Coyote Bluff Reservoir without detailed information as to the exact location of Edgar's shack. He had briefly considered searching the Monroe County archives for the physical address of the land formerly occupied by Edgar's uncle. However, numerous unknowns caused him to abandon that course of action. Edgar's uncle may not have been the legal owner of the property, and if he had owned the land, there was a good chance the transfer deed had not been filed in the County's records. Besides, Shavonne did not seem overly confident about the uncle's legal name. After discarding the unacceptable options, Nick was basically left with a half-baked plan to locate and assault the shack from the water.

A former coworker, an associate lawyer named Craig Barlow, docked his small fishing boat on the west end of the reservoir. Even though they weren't the best of friends, they had fished together on a couple of occasions, and he remembered the no-frills fishing boat could be fired up without an ignition key. It was Nick's intent to borrow the boat for the rest of the afternoon and then return it to the dock before anyone noticed it was missing. As he raced toward Coyote Bluff Reservoir, Nick realized that his daughter's life was riding on a bunch of *what-ifs*. Unfortunately, time was running out, and *what-ifs* were his only shot.

CHAPTER 48

Thursday afternoon, October 26

A mere handful of cars were scattered around the Rocky Point parking lot, which was exactly what Nick expected to find on a weekday afternoon in late October. After parking beside an old Ford pickup, he made a preliminary trip to the boat docks. The twelve-foot aluminum boat was moored in its usual place, so he returned to the car and quickly donned his black neoprene wetsuit. He then unloaded the remainder of his gear and stowed it in the fishing boat. After determining that the gas tank was almost full, Nick tried to fire up the boat's sluggish motor. At first, the engine wouldn't turn over, but after several tugs on the manual starter, it reluctantly roared to life. When the motor was idling smoothly, Nick untied the mooring line and slowly chugged away from the dock.

Even though the weather had been perfect all morning, climate patterns in the high desert of southern Idaho were unpredictable and an afternoon storm appeared to be blowing in. The wind had picked up substantially, and the sky had darkened noticeably since Nick's arrival at the reservoir. He tried to look at the bright side of things; maybe an overcast sky would provide some additional cover when he began his advance on Edgar's shack.

Nick's tentative plan was to position the boat approximately three hundred yards off the northern shoreline while he cruised the length of the reservoir from west to east. With a little luck, the boarded-up shack would be situated near the northwestern end of the reservoir. He was fairly confident he would be able to identify the shack with the aid of high-powered field glasses and the descriptions provided by Shavonne and Jason Davidson. Once he located the shack, Nick would anchor the small fishing boat, don the rest of his scuba gear, and then begin the underwater rescue attempt of his daughter. He had not yet worked out the most critical element of his hastily concocted plan: how he would access the inside of the shack. The most viable options were to enter through the elevated floor or a drop-down entry through the ceiling. Ultimately, the physical layout of the structure would dictate the manner of his entry.

Jason Davidson had mentioned a trapdoor positioned in the floor of the wooden shack. If it actually existed, the trapdoor would be the best access point. Assuming it was unlocked. The other, more risky, alternative was to enter through the ceiling. If the shack had an attic, he could access the roof from the tree line and surprise Edgar from above. A ceiling assault was certainly not his first choice. It would force him to expose himself while he accessed the rooftop, and it would create more noise than a breach from the ground up.

Nick had just begun his search of the north shore when the freak storm hit full force. High winds created three-foot white caps that rocked the small boat and made progress across the reservoir nearly impossible. The cold easterly winds also brought a driving horizontal rain that dropped the temperature fifteen degrees in a matter of minutes. The severe weather would make it more difficult for persons on the shore to detect the boat, but it would also make it harder for Nick to scan the shoreline. It now appeared as if Mother Nature had made a nearly impossible rescue mission that much more difficult.

CHAPTER 49

Thursday afternoon, October 26

The storm made west to east navigation of the reservoir much slower than Nick originally anticipated. The small fishing boat had been bucking driving headwinds for the better part of two hours, and Nick had only covered about four miles of the shoreline. He had passed a dozen or more rundown houses and cabins but nothing that even remotely resembled the vague description of Edgar's shack. He was beginning to question the logic of basing his entire plan on the twenty-year-old memories of a traumatized lawyer and the hazy recollections of a junkie when a dilapidated cabin suddenly appeared on the shoreline.

Nick grabbed the Steiner field glasses off the bench beside him and wiped the lenses with the palm of his right hand. The bitter cold and a rush of nervous energy caused his hands to tremble as he raised the field glasses to his eyes. A tingle went down his spine when he fixed the binoculars on the beat-up structure approximately three hundred yards away. Given the severe weather conditions, he couldn't be positive, but the wind-swept shack seemed to match Shavonne's description of Edgar's place. Visibility was poor and getting worse. Nick tried to curb his enthusiasm until he had a better view of the structure. He guided the fishing boat past the shack, looped a little closer to the shore and began motoring in a westerly direction. He tried to appear nonchalant as he scanned the shoreline with his field glasses, paying special attention to the dingy hovel's doors and windows.

The rickety old shack was small. No doors and only two small windows were positioned on the southern wall of the shack, the wall that directly faced the water. Both windows were boarded over with ten-inch wooden planks. Nick didn't know how difficult it would be to pry the planks loose, but two planks would need to be removed before he could squeeze through one of the windows. Edgar would surely detect his attempted trespass before he made it inside. As the small boat chugged past the structure for a second time, he also noted that the two windows located on the east side of the shack presented the same roadblock to a quick and easy breach. Lastly, there was nothing about the cabin's design that made him believe it had been constructed with an attic, which meant a ceiling entry was out of the question.

Shavonne did accurately remember the most important characteristics of the cabin's design. The old cabin was situated approximately thirty feet from the existing shoreline, and the entire structure had been elevated several feet above ground level. Nick's best chance for an undetected breach would undoubtedly be from the ground up. Once beneath the floor, he could monitor Edgar's movements inside the shack and adjust his plan accordingly. If any portion of the floor was decaying, he might be able to crash through the distressed floorboards, surprising Edgar before he could react. It was unlikely, but there was still an outside chance that the trapdoor described by Jason would be unlocked. Perhaps he'd get a clear shot at Edgar through the wooden floor, and actual entry wouldn't be necessary. Nick realized his success was contingent on far too many *ifs*, but his options were limited at this point. He'd play the hand he was dealt and pray for the best.

Nick maneuvered the twelve-foot motorboat past Edgar's shack for the second time, this time from east to west. The howling tail wind made westerly movement almost effortless.

When he was a good distance past the cabin, Nick guided the aluminum boat around a jog in the shoreline and dropped the thirty-pound anchor. About twenty feet down, the anchor came to rest on the rocky floor of the reservoir, and the boat jerked to an abrupt stop. Gale force winds battered the small aluminum boat and pulled the nylon rope taut, but the anchor held the lightweight craft in place.

With the fishing boat pitching violently from side to side, Nick fastened the dive belt around his waist and checked his waterproof pouch one last time. His cell phone, the .45-caliber semiautomatic, and one back-up eleven-round magazine were secure and dry. A Blue Tang dive knife with a five-inch double-edged blade and an underwater flashlight were attached to the belt as well. Nick wasn't expecting any hand-to-hand fighting. Still, he wanted a back-up weapon handy just in case. Next he slipped into the dive harness that had only one oxygen tank attached for this dive. The single tank would allow him to remain under water for approximately thirty minutes, more than enough time for his one-way trip to Edgar's shack. After securing the harness, Nick pulled a neoprene hood over his head, slipped off his tennis shoes, and donned a pair of fins.

Finally, Nick checked the dive tank's regulator to make sure the flow of oxygen was unimpeded. Everything seemed to be in perfect working order, so he pulled on the dive mask, inserted the regulator into his mouth, and stepped off the boat into the cold murky water of Coyote Bluff Reservoir. Even though the neoprene wetsuit provided some measure of protection, the frigid water momentarily shocked his system. Nick had endured harsher conditions during basic training, but three years of law school and six years of sitting behind a desk had definitely made him soft. It took his body several seconds to adjust to the near freezing water. The instant his faculties were restored, Nick began to flutter kick the fins.

Visibility in the murky water was poor, limited to a foot or two, but the illuminated dial of the compass strapped to his wrist told him that he was moving in the right direction. After swimming east for approximately five minutes, Nick briefly surfaced to check his location. He was still about 250 yards off shore, but now, Edgar's shack was due north of his current position. With his current location verified, Nick dropped below the water's surface for a second time and propelled himself in a northerly direction.

Nick knew he was approaching the north shore when the rocky floor of the reservoir suddenly appeared directly below him. A few seconds later, the water became too shallow for swimming, so he kicked off his fins and quickly crawled from the reservoir on his hands and knees. Then, without pausing to catch his breath, Nick leopard crawled across the open expanse of beach between the reservoir and cabin. When the shack was close enough to touch, he abandoned the leopard crawl and barrel rolled beneath the cover of its elevated floor. If his deductions were on target, his daughter was now somewhere directly above him.

CHAPTER 50

Thursday afternoon, October 26

Nick immediately slipped out of the dive harness and retrieved the .45 caliber Smith and Wesson from the waterproof pouch around his waist. He had already chambered a round prior to stowing the weapon, so with one click of the safety the semiautomatic would be ready to fire. Nick took a deep breath and exhaled slowly in an attempt to steady his nerves before he started moving toward the center of the cabin's floor. It didn't take him long to pinpoint Edgar's position inside the cabin. The large man was pacing back and forth on the rickety floor near the northwest corner of the structure. Once Edgar's whereabouts were pinpointed, Nick rolled onto his back and used the soles of his feet to silently propel himself face up across the damp, musty ground. Small gaps between the floorboards, and an occasional knothole, allowed him brief glimpses inside the shack. As he neared Edgar's location, Nick realized the large man was fervently chanting in a strange language.

After positioning himself directly beneath Edgar, Nick briefly contemplated unloading his Smith and Wesson through the rotting maple floor. The idea was quickly discarded as too risky, because Darby's location inside the rickety structure was still unknown. Nick was about to go in search of a suitable point of entry when Edgar's chanting suddenly ceased and he abruptly stopped pacing midstride. At first, Nick feared the large man had detected his presence beneath the floorboards, but then he heard the faint sound of Darby's voice.

Nick's heart was thumping like a bass drum as he struggled to regain some measure of control over his emotions. The tiny voice was scarcely louder than a whisper, but it had undoubtedly belonged to his daughter. It was sheer agony to be so close to his little girl and not be able to reach out and touch her. With some effort, Nick managed to pull his stare away from the direction of Darby's voice while he quickly scanned the floor for a suitable entry point. He finally spotted the trapdoor Jason had described and had just started to move toward it when Darby's voice froze him for a second time.

"I want my daddy," she whimpered softly.

"Do not cry, child," Edgar urged. "You will be with your loved ones very soon."

Darby continued to cry softly, so the large man tried a different approach. "I'll sing you an Indian song I learned as a child. It's a song my people sing before we pass into the spirit world. The song lets our ancestors know we have begun our journey to the other side."

Edgar slowly shuffled to the center of the room and sat down heavily with Darby in his arms. Once seated, he began to sing in a sorrowful voice that sounded more like an anguished moan than a song. Even though the language was foreign to Nick, the song's melody clearly conveyed its haunting message. All of a sudden, it hit him; Edgar was getting ready to kill Darby.

In a state of panic, Nick crawled on all fours toward the trapdoor. He was moving further away from Edgar, but the Indian's pitiful singing was getting louder and more distressed with each passing second. Edgar's death song was building toward its crescendo, and it was up to Nick to stop him before the song reached its deadly climax. Edgar was still singing when Nick reached the trapdoor. Without pausing, he pushed hard on the wooden door with the palms of both hands. The trapdoor didn't budge. Nick immediately rolled onto his back and kicked the heavy wood door with all the force he could muster. The trapdoor creaked but didn't open. Nick was loading up to give it a second jolt when Edgar's disturbed chanting abruptly ceased. Nick was so close, but he was out of time.

Nick pulled both knees against his chest and screamed at the top of his lungs as he thrust both feet upward. The trapdoor finally gave way with a resounding crash. Nick scrambled into the musty old shack without hesitating, but he was too late. Just as he pulled himself through the trapdoor a second, much louder, blast reverberated off the walls of Edgar's death shack. Nick knew the blood chilling sound all too well. It was the unmistakable report of a handgun. Edgar Ellenwood had killed his little girl.

CHAPTER 51

Thursday afternoon, October 26

The full weight of Nick's body crashed hard onto the dusty wooden floor of the old shack. Edgar had murdered his wife and now his daughter. Nick wanted the pain to end. He wanted to join his wife and daughter, but first Edgar would suffer a slow and painful death. Nick readied his semiautomatic and waited for the sound of Edgar's heavy footsteps to signal the large man's approach, but the cabin remained deadly quiet.

"If Ellenwood won't come to me, I'll hunt the animal down," he mumbled under his breath. Nick had only just struggled to his feet when the faint sound of a child crying drifted from the other room. At first, he thought his mind was playing tricks on him. He listened. The child's crying was definitely real. Nick didn't know how it was possible, but Darby was still alive. Adrenaline was pumping through his body as he lowered his Smith and Wesson and raced forward.

Nick found his little girl sitting cross-legged on the dirty floor beside Edgar Ellenwood's lifeless body. She was whimpering softly and staring at nothing in particular. Aside from being afraid, she seemed fine. The same could not be said for the enormous Indian. He was laying faceup on the wooden floor with an old Colt .45 revolver clutched in his right hand, a peaceful expression on his face, and an expanding pool of blood surrounded his massive head. He would never know why, but for some inexplicable reason, Edgar had decided to spare his daughter's life. Perhaps the troubled man had followed the commandments of the voices inside his head.

The instant their eyes locked, his little girl leapt to her feet and rushed toward him with her arms outstretched. Nick scooped up his daughter and pulled her tight against his body in one motion.

She immediately wrapped her tiny arms around his neck and said, "I've been waiting for you, Daddy. Mommy told me you were coming to get me."

Nick fought to hold back his tears. "Daddy's here now, baby, and I won't let you go," he promised.

"Where were you?" Darby asked with the unknowing innocence of a three-year-old.

"Looking for you," Nick answered, his voice choked with emotion. "Sorry it took me so long to find you."

"That's okay, Daddy," Darby reassured him. "When I was really scared, Mommy would sit with me and hold my hand."

It was up to Nick to tell his daughter that her mother was gone, but he didn't know how to go about it. Tears ran down his cheeks while he searched for the words to make his three-year-old little girl understand.

"Mommy went to heaven," he finally whispered. "She's watching over us all the time, but we won't be able to see her anymore."

Darby pulled her beautiful little face away from his chest and looked up at her father with wide, quizzical eyes. "I know, Daddy. Mommy already told me."

A chill ran throughout Nick's entire body. "What did Mommy tell you?" he asked, choking back a sob.

"Mommy said she could only stay a little bit longer," Darby answered softly. "She told me you were coming to get me today and then she would have to go away forever. I don't want Mommy to go away."

Nick choked back another sob and said, "Me either, baby."

It would always be a mystery to him if Darby had been dreaming about her mother or if Julie had found some extraordinary way to communicate with their little girl. Nick believed Julie had been guiding him, but he lacked the faith and innocence possessed by his daughter. It was the kind of untarnished faith that would have allowed him to completely accept the seemingly unexplainable.

Nick clutched Darby to his chest and said, "It's time to go home."

He was careful to shield his daughter's view of Edgar's body as they walked past the enormous man. When they were safe in another room, he dialed the Comfort Inn on his cell and asked for Tracey Ryan's room. Simone answered on the first ring. "Nick?"

"Yes, it's me," Nick answered, but that's as far as he got.

"What happened? Did you find Darby? Is she all right?"

Nick kissed Darby lightly on the cheek before answering, "I'm holding my daughter as we speak."

"Thank God," Simone said with a deep sigh of relief. "I can't believe this ordeal is finally over."

It wasn't over yet, not by a long shot, but Nick wasn't going to let that minor detail ruin the way he felt right now. Walter Burton needed to be brought to justice for a litany of transgressions that had spanned two decades, and Cole Panache was still rotting away in prison for a crime he didn't commit. Nick needed to remedy those past wrongs, but it wouldn't be tonight.

"Listen carefully, Simone," Nick said. "Take a cab to your apartment and pick up your car. Don't call anyone or stop along the way."

"I'll leave the instant we hang up," Simone agreed. "Where do you want to meet?"

"There's an old restaurant called Harry's Diner on the old Monroe County Highway—"

"I know the place," Simone cut in.

"I should be there in about thirty minutes," Nick estimated, after a quick glance at his watch to mark the time.

"I'll hurry, but it could take me a bit longer."

"Simone."

"Yeah, Nick…"

"Don't let your guard down," he cautioned. "The man who murdered Jefferson Hughes is still out there somewhere."

"Don't worry about me. I've been looking out for bad guys ever since I was a little girl," Simone answered before she hung up the phone.

Nick then turned his full attention to Darby. "Are you ready to go home, baby?"

"Yeah, Daddy, I need to take care of Buddy," Darby said with a concerned frown. "He's missed me an awful lot."

Darby hardly ever let her stuffed animal Buddy, a shaggy brown dog, out of her sight when she was at home. In fact, most nights she drifted off to sleep with the tattered little dog tucked under her arm.

"We'll stop by the house and pick up Buddy, first thing," Nick promised.

Darby smiled and said, "Thanks, Daddy. Buddy gets lonely when I'm gone."

CHAPTER 52

Thursday night, October 26

The afternoon storm that had blown through while Nick was crawling beneath the cabin had left a clean, fresh smell in its wake. If his calculations were correct, the old Monroe County Highway and Harry's Diner were about a mile due north of their current location. Nick should have been exhausted, but suddenly he had enough energy to walk ten miles with Darby in his arms. He carefully navigated the wobbly steps leading from the front porch and gingerly stepped into the knee-high grass in front of Edgar's cabin. Unfortunately, the rain-soaked front yard was as far as he got.

"Don't take another step, Jelaco," a man's voice shouted from the cover of the tree line.

"You're a long way from home," Nick called out, angry he'd let his guard down.

"Get your hands above your head," the familiar voice commanded. When Nick ignored the order, the man screamed, "Do it now!"

"I can't," Nick defiantly shot back. "I'm holding my daughter."

"Do it, Nick," he yelled with a bit more urgency. "I'm not playing games."

Darby began to cry softly after Nick reluctantly placed her on the damp ground directly behind him. He then felt her tiny arms wrap around his leg as he slowly raised his hands above his head.

"Remove the semiautomatic from your belt with your left hand," the man ordered. "And don't try any of that fancy Delta Force stuff they taught you."

"Don't be concerned about me," Nick calmly replied. "It's your itchy trigger finger that has me worried."

"Remove it slowly with your thumb and index finger."

Nick slowly pulled the .45 caliber semiautomatic from his belt and held it nonthreateningly at his side.

"You're doing real good. Now toss it to the ground."

Nick dropped the handgun onto the ground and flatly asked, "What now?"

Detective Gates slowly emerged from the shadow of the tree line. "We need to clear the air between us."

Nick nodded toward Darby and mouthed, "Not here. Not now."

Detective Gates had his .38 caliber revolver pointed directly at Nick's chest. Nick wondered if the same handgun had been used to kill Jefferson Hughes. "We've got one complicated mess here," Gates said with an annoyed frown. "And I'm not sure how to clean it up."

"The case is closed as far as I'm concerned," Nick replied emphatically. "Ellenwood is dead, and my daughter is back where she belongs."

"I wish things could be that simple, but they're not," Gates continued. "Your wife is still dead, and Cole Panache is still rotting away in prison, paying for a murder he didn't commit."

"Ellenwood murdered Julie, and now, he's dead," Nick said matter-of-factly.

"What about Cole Panache?"

"That's not my fight," Nick lied.

"The real bad guy is still out there somewhere," Gates shouted.

Detective Gates couldn't afford to let him walk away. Nick had uncovered enough evidence to put the cop in prison for the rest of his life, and they both knew it. "Cole Panache's situation doesn't involve me or my daughter."

Gates furrowed his brow. "You don't seem like the type of guy who walks away from unfinished business."

"Whatever's left is police business," Nick answered unconvincingly.

Gates inched a little closer to Nick and his daughter. "You know too much to walk away without a second thought."

"Try me."

"It's time I put right a mistake I made twenty years ago."

"How can you make things right?" Nick demanded. "By killing me and my daughter the same way you killed Jefferson Hughes?" It may have been the tone of Nick's voice, or maybe she had understood the content of his words. Either way, something had frightened his little girl, and she suddenly clutched his leg again.

Nick's accusation and his daughter's reaction seemed to catch Detective Gates off guard. "Jefferson Hughes is dead?" he asked, genuinely surprised.

Nick changed the tone of his voice in an attempt to lessen his daughter's fear. "I found Jefferson's body yesterday morning, and he certainly didn't die of natural causes. The old man had two .38 caliber slugs in his chest," Nick said, staring at the detective's revolver for emphasis.

Gates shook his head from side to side, seemingly confused. "Jefferson moved away years ago," he muttered. "Where did you find the old man's body?"

"On the kitchen floor of his cabin—right where you left him," Nick snapped. When Gates didn't respond, Nick added, "He was shot in the chest at point black range, presumably by someone he knew."

"It sure wasn't me," Gates angrily replied with a quick glance at Nick's daughter. "I've done some bad things, but cold-blooded murder isn't anywhere on the list."

"You paid the old man fifty thousand dollars to commit perjury," Nick said in disgust.

Detective Gates took Nick's accusation in stride. "Let's get the facts straight before we move on," Gates countered. "I didn't pay Jefferson anything to lie about Cole Panache. I was the bag man for someone else."

"And that somehow exonerates you?" Nick asked.

"There's no absolution for what I've done. But if I go to hell, I'm not going there alone."

"Who wanted Cole Panache in prison bad enough to put up that kind of money?" Nick asked.

Gates shrugged. "My partner, Clyde Parks, gave me the cash."

"Who gave Clyde the cash, Detective?"

Detective Gates lowered his weapon. "Come on, Nick, you're a smart guy."

"Walter Burton..." Nick answered slowly.

Detective Gates nodded his head and said, "And someone needs to take him down."

"He isn't the only bad guy."

"That piece of garbage has ruined a lot of lives," Gates said, his hatred obvious. "I'm not an innocent bystander, but I'm willing to pay for my mistake."

"How do we take Walter down?" Nick asked. "He's insulated."

"You're the lawyer. What kind of evidence will it take to convince a prosecutor?"

"All the witnesses are dead," Nick said, thinking aloud. "There's nothing that directly connects him to Julie's murder or Jefferson Hughes."

"I can testify that Walter had a questionable working relationship with Clyde Parks, and Clyde personally gave me the cash to bribe Jefferson Hughes."

"That's weak circumstantial evidence at best, but I suppose it's a start."

"As a co-conspirator, we'll need tangible proof to corroborate my accusation," Gates said with a knowing nod of his head. If we don't dig up something else, it will be my word against Walter's, and he's slippery."

Nick thought about the man who had been his boss for the past six years. "Walter won't talk unless he truly believes he's in the clear. He's not the brightest guy in the world, but he knows how to cover his tracks."

"Okay, Nick. You were smart enough to track down Edgar Ellenwood. Now figure out a way to nail the snake you work for," Gates urged.

"Correction, Detective. The slippery reptile I *used* to work for. Remember, Walter fired me last week."

"Correction noted. Got any brilliant ideas?" Gates asked.

Walter certainly had more than his fair share of character flaws that made Nick believe they could find one to use against him. "Walter's the most egotistical man I've ever known," Nick tentatively began. "He overestimates his own abilities, and underestimates the abilities of his adversaries. His unbridled arrogance is definitely a weak spot."

Detective Gates looked at Nick like he might be on to something. "I'm listening," he said. "What do you have in mind?"

"I'm not sure, Detective, but Walter loves the sound of his own voice," Nick continued. "If he thinks he's in the clear, he might feel a need to blow his own horn,"

Gates was obviously skeptical about Nick's idea. "Given our history, Walter Burton will see me coming a mile away, and I can't turn this over to another detective."

"Let me have a crack at him," Nick suggested.

"That's out of the question," Gates replied without hesitation. "Instead, maybe I should throw him in jail and see how a few hours in county lock-up impacts his state of mind."

Nick shook his head and forcefully replied, "That's a bad idea, Detective. Walter loves to run his mouth, but the guy's watched enough episodes of *Law and Order* to know when it's time to keep his trap shut."

"All right then, you tell me," Gates said. "How do we get Walter to spill his guts?"

"Walter will be more at ease if we play the game on his turf," Nick proposed. "I could catch him off guard when he shows up for work tomorrow morning by questioning him about Cole Panache and Jefferson Hughes."

"Have you ever interrogated a criminal suspect?" Gates asked.

"Not exactly, but I can read people and situations. If our little chat takes a bad turn, I'll walk away," Nick promised.

Gates holstered the .38 caliber revolver that had been dangling at his side for quite some time. "Pick up your daughter and your semiautomatic. I'll think about your harebrained scheme while we walk."

"Can we stop by Harry's Diner on the old county highway?" Nick asked.

Detective Gates widened his eyes and looked incredulously at Nick. "You gotta be kidding, Jelaco. You're hungry?"

Nick shook his head and sheepishly said, "I told Simone Panache to meet me there in about fifteen minutes."

"Why not?" Gates replied dryly. "Given your detective work, I'm sure I'm a big hit with the Panache family."

CHAPTER 53

Thursday night, October 26

It had taken some fast talking and a little begging on Nick's part, but Detective Gates had finally acquiesced. It would be Nick who confronted Walter Burton about his involvement in Julie's murder. The lawyer and the detective then agreed to meet at the Lakeland Police Station the following morning to finalize the specifics of their plan. Even though the gruff detective had made his share of mistakes, Nick trusted his new partner. Simone had driven Nick and Darby to the Rocky Point Boat Landing after Gates's departure from Harry's Diner. Nick's thoughts momentarily flashed to Craig Barlow's fishing boat when he saw the other boats moored at the docks. He made a mental note to phone Craig when his business with Walter was concluded.

Simone had hugged Darby as if she'd known her for years and then tried to gracefully excuse herself at the boat landing. According to her, Nick needed some time alone with his daughter. Nick appreciated her sensitivity and agreed with her assessment but asked her to stay. He needed someone he trusted to watch Darby during his meeting with Walter, and his daughter seemed comfortable with Simone.

CHAPTER 54

Friday morning, October 27

The critical elements of their hastily concocted sting operation included a one-way radio transmitter, a miniature microphone, and a receiver capable of recording any incriminating statements Walter Burton happened to make. Gates had taped the radio transmitter to the middle of Nick's back, and a small microphone had been secured to his chest. Nick's job was to get Walter talking about Edgar Ellenwood, Jefferson Hughes, Brooke Schaffer, or anything else that might indicate his involvement in Julie's murder. Detective Gates's 4-Runner was parked a couple hundred yards down the block, and it was his job to record the entire conversation. Nick hoped the outdated receiver would pick up the subtleties of his conversation with Walter. The outdated equipment made it fairly obvious that state-of-the-art surveillance gear was not high on the Lakeland Police Department's list of budgetary priorities.

Nick understood the success of their set-up was contingent on two variables. First, it was essential that Walter was the first person to arrive at the law office, and second, Nick had to get the egomaniac talking before he called the cops. If he failed to get Walter on tape, his former boss had an excellent chance of beating the justice system yet again. The thought of Walter walking away unscathed made Nick sick to his stomach. He vowed that would not happen under any circumstance.

A car finally pulled into the law firm's parking lot at six fifteen. If it was Walter Burton, their plan would move forward. If another lawyer wanted to get an early start on his billable hours, Nick would be forced to improvise, because they had not developed a contingency plan. Nick didn't have to wait long. Moments later, Walter came strolling through the door of his office. When he discovered his former employee waiting in his office, Walter's anger was evident. "How did you get in here?" he demanded.

"How I broke into your office is unimportant. Why I'm here is a much more interesting question," Nick answered with an arrogance intended to provoke Walter's ire.

Walter began to move toward his telephone. "You're trespassing, Jelaco."

"It's in your best interest to hear me out," Nick smugly replied.

"I have a better idea," Walter snapped. "I'll have the police toss you in jail."

"Go ahead, call the cops," Nick replied indifferently. "Maybe they'll throw us in adjoining cells."

Walter hesitated near the telephone before he took a seat behind his desk. "What could you possibly say that would interest me?"

"How about two names for starters: Cole Panache and Jefferson Hughes?" Nick answered.

"One is a convicted murderer, and the other is the eyewitness who testified against him. All that stuff is a matter of public record," Walter responded, trying to appear disinterested.

"I'm well aware of the public record," Nick countered. "I've seen the Panache case file. Quite frankly, I didn't find the case file nearly as enlightening as my conversations with Jefferson Hughes and Detective Gates."

The constipated look on Walter's face spoke volumes. "The absurd ramblings of two social misfits don't concern me," Walter scoffed.

Nick stared unblinkingly at Walter for several seconds before he continued. "According to Jefferson Hughes, he was paid $50,000 to lie on the witness stand, and Phil Gates delivered the blood money," Nick said in disgust.

Walter shrugged his shoulders and said in a voice intended to convey indifference, "If that's the case, Jefferson Hughes and Detective Gates have a problem, not me."

"My story gets better. Detective Gates claims that you were the one who ordered the payoff and it was your $50,000 he delivered to Jefferson," Nick stated as if it was an indisputable fact and not pure speculation.

Nick could tell by the pained expression on Walter's face that he was trying to figure out his next move.

Finally after a lengthy silence, he stammered, "If that's the case, it will be my word against the word of Detective Gates."

"Not quite, Walter. It'll be your word against mine, because I killed Detective Gates last night," Nick lied. "He wanted to die with a clear conscience, so he told me everything."

A big smile spread across Walter's face. "Then you've got squat, Jelaco."

"I know the truth, and the truth isn't squat," Nick growled through clenched teeth.

"Correction, you know Detective Gates's twisted version of the truth."

"I believe the detective's dying declaration, and I won't quit until you've taken Cole Panache's place in prison," Nick continued, trying to push the button that would get Walter talking.

"Go ahead, Nick, bring it on," Walter replied with an unconcerned shrug. "You killed Detective Gates, not me."

"You killed Gates twenty years ago when you pulled him into your web of lies and deception," Nick shouted.

"I suppose your paranoid delusions are understandable given your recent personal tragedy," Walter said, faking sympathy. "The mental stress must be too much for you to handle."

"I didn't kill Jefferson Hughes."

"Jefferson Hughes is dead?" Walter replied in mock sadness. "What a shame."

Walter was beginning to enjoy their game of cat and mouse. Nick sensed that Walter's cocky arrogance would be his downfall if he could just hit the right nerve. "The rest of Cole Panache's life is worth something."

"That's certainly debatable."

"You're not God," Nick yelled. "It's not up to you to decide the fate of mankind."

"Cole Panache is white trash," Walter growled, outwardly losing his composure for the first time.

"You sacrificed his future to satisfy your insatiable hunger for power and public recognition."

"His bleak future was predetermined at the time of his unfortunate birth. A life of crime and substance abuse was all that bottom-feeder had ahead of him. I probably did him a favor by locking him up."

"You ruined a man's life!" Nick shouted.

Walter shook his head at Nick, clearly disappointed his former employee didn't understand the obvious justification for his actions. "I traded his life for mine. It was a fair trade given the circumstances. I've done a lot of good for the people of Lakeland over the past twenty years."

When the underlying meaning of Walter's words hit Nick, everything suddenly made sense. "You framed Cole Panache because you killed Brooke Schafer," Nick said in amazement.

Walter grinned at Nick. "Let's assume for argument's sake that you've guessed correctly. It's not by happenstance that I'm a rich and powerful man. When I see an opportunity, I seize it."

"Cole Panache is an innocent man," Nick shot back. "Doesn't that bother you on some level?"

"It's completely irrelevant who gets hurt along the way. The weak and subservient never acquire power, wealth, or status. They're nothing more than disposable resources for people like me."

"You're a complete psychopath."

"Really, Nick, lowering yourself to name calling," Walter said, pretending to be offended. "Life is a game without any clear-cut rules, and I'm a natural born winner. You, on the other hand, will always be a loser. You lack the intelligence and intestinal fortitude to do what it takes to fight your way to the top."

"You're probably right, Walter, but at least I can look at myself in the mirror."

"You're pathetic, Jelaco," Walter hissed at him.

"You murdered an eighteen-year-old girl, framed an innocent man, and you have the nerve to call *me* pathetic?" Nick responded with contempt.

Walter shrugged his shoulders and said, "You're entitled to your opinion."

"Cole Panache claims that Brooke used sex to manipulate men in positions of power," Nick said, thinking aloud. "Is that why you killed her? Was she threatening to expose your sexual relationship?"

"I did what had to be done and nothing more," Walter replied indifferently. "Brooke Schaffer no longer understood the dynamics of our relationship, and her ignorance was unacceptable to me."

"You murdered Brooke to teach her a lesson?" Nick asked incredulously.

"Her death was an accident, but that's completely beside the point," Walter explained.

"What is the point?" Nick demanded.

"To set the record straight, my relationship with Brooke was never about the sex. It was about *my* power and control over every aspect of her life."

"Was she beholding to you because of a sweetheart plea bargain?" Nick asked.

Walter nodded and said, "I dismissed a felony drug charge, but it wasn't in exchange for sex. I dismissed the case to gain control over her. The sex was just another way to prove my dominance over her."

"In other words, you used your office to victimize the people you were elected to represent."

"Don't all politicians?" Walter asked, seemingly oblivious to the fact he'd done something wrong.

"You're completely insane," Nick said in disbelief.

Walter leaned back in his chair and began to speak as if he was an expert witness sharing his vast knowledge with an unsophisticated jury. "The little whore tried to blackmail me, imagine that." Walter then paused for a second and chuckled softly to himself.

"Did I miss something funny?"

"I must admit, I misjudged Ms. Schaffer," he scoffed. "It never occurred to me that trailer-park trash like Brooke would have the audacity to stand up to me. When she picked up the phone and threatened to take her story to the media, it infuriated me. Naturally, I tried to stop her, but she fought back. During the struggle, she fell and hit her head on the side of my desk."

"Brooke Schaffer was murdered in the prosecutor's office?" Nick asked, hoping the old microphone was picking up their conversation.

"Somewhat ironic, isn't it?" Walter replied. "Clyde Parks and your good buddy Detective Gates stuffed her body in the trunk of their squad car, and when the coast was clear, they dumped her body in her apartment."

"Why frame Cole Panache?" Nick asked. "You could have covered up your involvement in her murder without ruining another man's life."

Believing all his co-conspirators dead, Walter couldn't resist the temptation to brag about his brilliance. "The unsolved case would have been a thorn in my side until Brooke's killer was brought to justice. Besides, the good people of Lakeland demanded and deserved a conviction," Walter added like a conscientious public servant.

"So you sent an innocent man to prison for the rest of his life?"

"Quite frankly, I initially feared my life of privilege was over. Yet true to form, I turned my biggest mistake into a glorious victory," Walter answered with an infuriating grin. "Once I came up with the plan, the rest was easy. Cole and Brooke had quite the checkered past. It was child's play to portray him as the jealous ex-boyfriend with a violent streak. Officer Parks planted Brooke's jewelry and bloody scarf in Cole's car, and the rest is prosecutorial history."

"How does Edgar Ellenwood fit into the mix?"

"He doesn't," Walter answered with a confused expression on his face. "Still, I'm surprised to hear you've had the pleasure of making his acquaintance. I wasn't aware Edgar had returned to Lakeland."

"Oh yeah, Mr. Ellenwood was in Lakeland, but we never actually met," Nick corrected him. "He committed suicide before I had a chance to question him about my wife's murder."

"You believe Edgar Ellenwood killed your wife?" Walter asked. "Well, I can't say that I'm shocked. The big Indian was never right in the head."

Walter's acting was getting better, or he was truly surprised to hear about Edgar's involvement in the crimes.

"As long as we're clearing the air, why don't you shed some light on your relationship with Edgar Ellenwood?"

Walter shrugged indifferently and said, "There's really not much to it. Mr. Ellenwood killed a local boy back when I was the Monroe County prosecutor. Edgar was a mixed-up kid. I decided that prosecuting the young man would have been contrary to the interests of justice."

"You let him walk away from a murder charge?"

"Edgar was the victim of a sad and troubled childhood. Rehabilitation seemed like the most humane course of action," Walter explained.

Nick rolled his eyes before he asked, "Did you order the break-in at my house?"

Walter became indignant at the very suggestion. "What a ludicrous accusation," he bellowed. "I had absolutely nothing to do with the tragic events that befell your family."

"When was the last time you spoke with Edgar Ellenwood?" Nick prodded.

"I haven't seen or spoken to Edgar in years," Walter said without hesitation. "He used to stop by the office every once in a while, but that was quite some time ago. Erma and Jackson went out of their way to befriend young Edgar, but I personally avoided him like the plague."

Walter had admitted to killing Brooke Schaffer and framing Cole Panache, but he had yet to utter a word about Nick's wife. If he was behind the break-in, Walter was an accessory to murder and kidnapping. Nick wanted him to pay for Julie's murder, so he pushed just a little harder.

"You ordered Edgar to steal Janis Jones's case file."

"You've lost your mind," Walter shot back. "I wouldn't ask Edgar Ellenwood to fetch me a cup of coffee. He was an unpleasant man, and his mere presence made me uncomfortable."

"Your denial has a hollow ring to it," Nick countered.

"Your opinion is meaningless. Now if you'd be kind enough to leave, maybe I could get some work done," Walter said with a dismissive gesture toward the door.

Even though he was done talking, Walter had said plenty. If the receiver in Gates's 4-Runner was working properly, he had talked himself into a nice long prison sentence. Nick stood and leaned over his former boss' desk.

"You're going down this time, Walter; and there's nobody around to clean up your mess."

"If you take your wild accusations public, I'll sue you for everything your worth," Walter threatened and then added with a laugh, "Which I'm sure isn't a lot."

"You're going to prison," Nick growled through clenched teeth.

"You've got unsubstantiated allegations and a couple of dead bodies. If you're smart, you'll keep your mouth shut," Walter advised.

"Jefferson Hughes told me that he was paid $50,000 to lie on the witness stand. According to Detective Gates's dying declaration, you were the source of the payout."

"Both statements are hearsay—not admissible in a court of law," Walter smugly replied.

Nick shook his head at Walter in disbelief. "I can't believe you actually passed the bar exam. Both statements are admissible hearsay under the statement against penal interest exception."

The insults directed at his intellect were more than Walter could tolerate. "You're playing games with the wrong guy, Jelaco," he screamed. "No one talks down to Walter Burton."

Watching Walter unravel before his eyes was even more gratifying than he had imagined. "I almost forgot to mention my best witness," Nick goaded.

Walter was so angry his entire body was shaking. "Who's this mystery witness?"

"You're the witness, Walter."

Walter appeared confused by Nick's statement and then hesitantly said, "Ever hear of the Fifth Amendment? Citizens of this great country have a constitutional right to remain silent. No judge or jury will hear a single word of the story I just told you."

Walter was doing his best to appear unconcerned about his ill-advised diatribe, but the potential ramifications of his colossal blunder were starting to sink in.

"You don't need to repeat your story for a jury, Walter," Nick taunted. "The taped version will more than suffice."

Walter frantically looked around his office. "What do you mean, 'taped version'?" he demanded.

As if on cue, Detective Gates casually strolled into Walter's office. The pained expression on Walter's face was priceless. He looked like a man who had just seen a ghost.

Gates grinned at Nick as he held up a micro-cassette. "I got it all, Nick. Old Walter came through loud and clear."

"Is it enough to put him away?" Nick asked.

"More than enough," Gates said with an incredulous shake of his head. "I couldn't believe it. The idiot just kept on talking."

"I thought you were dead," Walter stammered.

Detective Gates winked at Walter and said, "Truth be told, I haven't felt this good in years."

Walter just stood there speechless. Detective Gates snapped him out of his trance when he informed the ex-prosecutor he was under arrest.

"You've got to be joking. Under arrest for what?" Walter demanded.

"We can start with the murder of Brooke Schaffer, obstruction of justice, evidence tampering, and public corruption,"

Gates said while he handcuffed Walter and informed him of his Miranda rights.

Walter was red-faced as he tried to plead his case to the unsympathetic detective. Gates didn't say a word as he led Walter Burton from his office in handcuffs. A few of Walter's early-arriving coworkers looked on in stunned silence as the firm's senior partner was escorted from the building.

As they crossed the parking lot, Walter blurted out, "This is an illegal arrest, Gates, a clear case of entrapment and an unlawful search. Without a search warrant, you don't have a prayer of getting that tape admitted in court."

Nick didn't have the inclination or energy to tell Walter that he was wrong on both counts. That job belonged to the unlucky lawyer he would hire to represent him.

"I'll give you a call after he's booked and resting comfortably in the Monroe County Jail," Gates said as shoved Walter into the backseat of his 4-Runner.

"Thanks, Detective," Nick said with genuine gratitude. "If I hurry, I'll be home before my daughter wakes up."

CHAPTER 55

Friday night, October 27

Nick and Darby were having an early dinner at one of Lakeland's finest fast-food restaurants when his cell phone rang. He would have ignored the incoming call, but he recognized the displayed number as Detective Gates's cell.

Nick flipped open the phone and said, "Good evening, Detective."

"Hey, Nick, I wanted to provide you with an update on your ex-employer's new living arrangements."

"I trust he's adjusting nicely," Nick wisecracked.

"He was dressed in a stylish orange jumpsuit with 'Monroe County Inmate' stenciled across his back the last time I saw him."

The thought of Walter behind bars brought a smile to Nick's face. "Has Walter accepted the bleakness of his legal situation?"

"Not really." Gates laughed. "He was threatening to sue anybody within earshot the last time I saw him."

"That's vintage Walter," Nick scoffed. "Blaming everybody else to the bitter end."

"On a more serious note, the Monroe County Prosecutor heard the tape, and he's absolutely dying to prosecute Walter,"

Gates remarked. "Evidently, there's no love lost between the two of them."

"So he was impressed with the tape?" Nick asked.

"Very impressed, but you know lawyers—he wouldn't commit to anything concrete."

"Walter's taped statement incriminates you as well," Nick reminded him. "What steps have you taken to protect yourself?"

"Covering up my transgressions is not one of my priorities right now," Gates answered flatly.

Nick liked the detective and believed him to be an honorable man. "Don't be a martyr, Detective. Throwing yourself on the sword won't turn back the clock. You did the right thing in the end, and that should count for something."

"Maybe, Nick . . . I don't know," Gates hesitantly replied. "It does feel good to have the monkey off my back."

"The prosecutor will need your testimony to make his case against Walter," Nick suggested, implying that Gates should hold out until he had a deal in place.

"I thought about resigning from the police force and then offering to testify in exchange for no prison time," Gates countered. "If the prosecutor turns me down, I'll still cooperate and take my lumps."

"I'd represent you, Phil, if I didn't have a conflict of interest," Nick added, wishing he could do something more for the detective.

"You're one of the few lawyers I would trust to represent me," Gates answered truthfully. "Take care of your daughter, Nick. I'll let you know if anything significant happens with Walter's case."

"Thanks, Phil. I'm a phone call away if you need anything."

"Count on it," Gates said, before he hung up the phone.

CHAPTER 56

Saturday morning, October 28

Nick was frozen in time, staring at one of his favorite pictures of Julie when the harsh ring of the bedroom telephone jolted him back to the present. Nick and Darby had returned to the house at 434 River Crest Drive to throw a few things into a suitcase before they hit the road together. Nick had decided that a few days away from Lakeland were in order. However, the details of their impromptu trip still needed to be worked out. Nick briefly debated whether or not he should answer the incoming call before he reluctantly walked to the nightstand and picked up the cordless handset.

"Did you hear about Walter Burton?" Gates asked, obviously worked up about something.

Nick wasn't expecting an update quite so soon.

"What's going on?" Nick asked, not sure if the detective was the bearer of good or bad news.

"You won't believe it, Nick," Gates said in a rush. "He killed himself last night."

"What? That's impossible," Nick said in disbelief. "He's in jail."

"Actually, he made bail," Gates explained. "Judge Montgomery set his bail at one million dollars, and Walter's good buddy, Jackson St. James, put up the money."

"Jackson St. James posted Walter's million-dollar bail?" Nick asked in surprise.

"You know how it works," Gates replied. "Jackson paid some sleazy bail bondsman a hundred grand. Then the bondsman actually covered Walter's million dollar bail."

"Walter committed suicide?" Nick mumbled in disbelief. "Was his wife at home?"

"Evidently, it took her about five minutes to jump ship. As soon as her husband was arrested, she packed up and went to stay with her sister in Salt Lake City."

"Who found Walter's body?"

"Jackson St. James discovered it when he dropped by Walter's house earlier today," Gates said without the least bit of sympathy.

It was hard for Nick to comprehend the full impact of Detective Gates's shocking news. He had mentally prepared himself for a long drawn-out trial or plea bargain, followed by a symbolic slap on the wrist. Now suddenly, it was over.

"How did he do it?" Nick asked.

"I don't have all the details, but according to Detective Sato, Walter stuck a .38 caliber revolver against the side of his head and pulled the trigger early this morning. I guess the public humiliation was too much for him," Gates theorized aloud.

"Perhaps ..."

"You have to give him credit," Gates continued. "He saved the taxpayers the cost of a murder trial."

"All that self-serving rhetoric about doing whatever it takes to come out on top, and the coward blows his brains out," Nick said in disgust. "What a bunch of crap."

"Let it go, Nick. Walter is dead."

"How does his suicide affect your legal situation?" Nick asked.

"I don't know yet. I'm hearing rumblings that the attorney general may release Cole Panache from prison with as little fanfare as possible."

"Less publicity would be good for you."

"Yeah, I suppose …" Gates reluctantly agreed.

"As strange as it sounds, I'm sorry he's dead."

"Why? The world's a better place without Walter Burton in it."

"I wanted him to live a long and very unhappy life in prison," Nick explained. "I'm sure an ex-prosecutor would have been a big hit in the state pen."

"I'm glad his fate isn't in the hands of our screwed-up justice system," Gates shot back.

"You're probably right. Thanks for the news, Phil."

The line was quiet for several seconds while Detective Gates searched for something meaningful to say. Following the awkward silence, he said, "No problem, Nick. Take care of yourself."

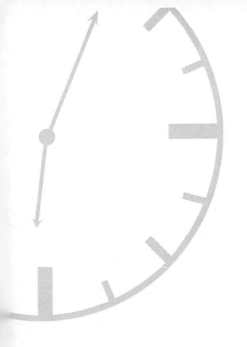

CHAPTER 57

Saturday morning, October 28

After living in a waking nightmare for the past twenty-three days, Nick didn't think he could be shocked by anything. Yet he was truly stunned by Walter's suicide. Not in his wildest dreams did he envision the self-absorbed egomaniac taking his own life. Walter Burton was the kind of man who would deny wrongdoing until the bitter end—no matter how many people he hurt along the way. In a way, suicide admitted defeat, and that seemed out of character for Walter.

Nick tried to refocus his attention on the simple task of packing a suitcase, but he had been standing in front of the open closet for five minutes, and his suitcase was still lying on the floor, empty. Something small had been gnawing at his subconscious since Detective Gates's phone call. He couldn't put his finger on it. Still, his intuition was telling him that an important piece of the puzzle was missing. Walter had admitted his culpability in Brooke Schaffer's death. Yet, when questioned about the break-in that led to Julie's death, he had appeared genuinely confused by Nick's accusation. *Why?* Nick wondered. *Was Walter playing mind games with him? If Walter didn't order Edgar Ellenwood to steal the Janis Jones case file, who did?*

Nick glanced at his daughter sitting cross-legged on the floor near the foot of his bed. She was quietly playing with one of her dolls she called Sophie. All of Darby's dolls looked alike to him, but to his daughter, each had its own unique personality. The capacity of a child's mind to block out the real world was a truly amazing gift. Nick hoped that ability would help his little girl cope with the loss of her mother. Unfortunately, he didn't have the same ability to compartmentalize the present while blocking out the past. Instead of looking forward to an adventure with Darby, Nick was dreaming up conspiracy theories about Walter's suicide.

"This is nuts," Nick muttered to himself. "I'm not going to waste another second on Walter Burton."

Nick had finally managed to push Walter Burton's suicide from his thoughts long enough to pack a couple of suitcases. The process had taught him that packing a week's worth of outfits for his three-year-old daughter was more difficult than he had imagined. He was about to toss the suitcases into the trunk when the truth hit him like a slap to the face. Jackson St. James had ordered Edgar to steal Janis Jones's case file, not Walter Burton. The answer had been sitting in a cardboard box in the trunk of his car since the day he was fired from Burton, St. James, & Summers. When Jackson had handed him the cardboard box, he had specifically mentioned Nick's house key. Nick didn't know how he'd missed it before, but sure enough, perched on top of his family pictures and coffee mug was a legal-sized envelope labeled "house key." And there was no doubt about it, the elegant script on the envelope belonged to Jackson St. James.

How was Jackson able to specifically identify the key that opened our front door? Nick asked himself. Detective Gates had theorized that Julie had inadvertently left the door unlocked the night she was murdered or the alternative, that her killer had possessed a key. Julie would have checked and then double-checked the door before retiring for the evening. Suddenly, the answer was right there in front of him. Jackson could identify Nick's house key because he had provided Edgar Ellenwood with a copy of the same key. Jackson St. James had given Edgar Ellenwood his marching orders, not Walter Burton.

Nick had been blindly searching for answers since his wife's murder. Now the pieces fit together perfectly, and his intuition was telling him that he had it right this time. Walter didn't commit suicide; Jackson had killed him. Walter didn't kill Jefferson Hughes; Jackson had been the triggerman. As far as he knew, Walter didn't even own a gun. Jackson, on the other hand, was always boasting about his prowess with a handgun and had flaunted his collection of weapons whenever an opportunity presented itself.

After twenty-four hours of relative peace, Nick realized his three-week nightmare wasn't over quite yet. There was one piece of unfinished business. Nick buckled Darby into her car seat and phoned Simone on the drive to her apartment. Although uneasy with Nick's plan to confront Jackson alone, Simone reluctantly agreed to babysit Darby.

Simone was waiting at the door when they arrived at her apartment. She guided Darby into her apartment and gently said, "I'll be there in a second, sweetheart, but first I need to talk to your daddy."

"What is it?" Nick asked in an abrupt tone meant to squelch a potential debate.

"You should let the police deal with Jackson St. James," Simone answered with a troubled look on her expressive face. "If your theory's correct, he's killed at least two people and probably more."

Simone was right, but Jackson was too smart to make a mistake if he sensed any kind of danger.

"He'll be on guard if the cops get anywhere near him," he told Simone. "Jackson's been committing crimes for twenty-five years, and no one had a clue. A man like that knows how to keep his mouth shut."

"Then how are you planning to make him talk?" she asked.

Nick smiled, and in a futile attempt to lighten the mood, he joked, "I thought I'd play it by ear. It's worked for me so far."

"Seriously, Nick, he's dangerous. Don't take him lightly," she pleaded.

"Don't worry, Simone. I know exactly what Jackson's capable of. Tell Darby I won't be long," Nick said and then quickly walked away.

CHAPTER 58

Saturday morning, October 28

Nick phoned his old law firm on the drive across town to make sure Jackson wasn't working on the Saturday morning of Walter's death. He wasn't expecting an answer, yet Erma Sliger picked up after the third ring.

"Good morning, St. James and Summers Law Offices," she answered in a subdued voice.

Nick noticed her omission. Erma had previously answered the telephone by saying, "Burton Law Offices."

"Hello, Erma. It's Nick Jelaco," he greeted her in a tone intended to convey an appropriate amount of grief.

"Hi, Nick, it's good to hear your voice," Erma sadly replied.

"I just heard the news about Walter," Nick fibbed. "How are you holding up?"

Erma sighed deeply and said, "As well as can be expected. Walter's been my boss for more years than I care to admit. He wasn't always an easy man to work for, but I'll miss him just the same."

Nick couldn't bring himself to say anything good about Walter, so instead he asked, "Did Jackson come into the office this morning?"

"No, he was at home when I spoke to him earlier. I truly believe Walter's death has hit him a bit harder than the rest of us. They've been the best of friends and work associates for the past thirty years."

"Maybe I'll drop by his house to pay my respects."

"That would mean a lot to Jackson. He always liked you, Nick."

Nick was certain that he was the last person Jackson wanted to see, but he didn't mention that to Erma. "You have my cell number, Erma. Let me know if you need anything."

"Thanks, Nick. I will. Maybe you'll come back to work for the firm after the dust settles," Erma said hopefully

Nick didn't have the heart to tell Erma that the law firm where she had worked for the past twenty years had probably seen its last days. "I'm not sure what my future holds," Nick replied truthfully. "Right now I just want to be a good father to my little girl."

"You do that, and take care of yourself as well," Erma said.

"I will," Nick promised.

CHAPTER 59

Saturday morning, October 28

Jackson St. James resided in one of Lakeland's more upscale neighborhoods. An ornate security gate kept unwanted nighttime visitors from entering the neighborhood without a security code, but the gate remained open to the public throughout the day. Jackson and his wife had hosted a couple of Christmas parties during Nick's short tenure at Burton, St. James, & Summers, so he was somewhat familiar with the location of his home.

Even though his previous visits had taken place at night, Nick immediately recognized the house when he saw Jackson's white Cadillac parked in the driveway beside a brand-new convertible Mercedes-Benz Roadster. For some reason, it occurred to Nick that the total purchase price of the two vehicles was more than the cost of his house. Nick parked his beat-up Mustang on the street in front of Jackson's house and retrieved the .40 caliber Glock from beneath the driver's seat. It was warm outside, and Nick didn't need a jacket, but his loose-fitting windbreaker provided an inconspicuous place for him to hide the semiautomatic.

Nick struggled to keep his emotions in check as he approached the house and rang the doorbell. If he wanted to catch Jackson with his guard down, it was essential that he maintain his outward composure. Nick heard some muffled shouting inside the house before Jackson's wife answered the door. She appeared stunned at first but quickly put on her hostess face and greeted him with a disingenuous hug. Living with Jackson couldn't be easy, and Nick liked Phyllis St. James despite her exaggerated and phony personality.

After returning her embrace, Nick said, "I heard about Walter and wanted to offer my support."

"That's sweet of you to worry about Jackson after all you've been through," Phyllis replied with a forced smile.

"Jackson has always been good to me," Nick lied.

It was usually difficult to end a conversation with Phyllis, but on this occasion, she seemed uncharacteristically nervous and anxious to cut their chat short. As soon as the pleasantries were over, she glanced longingly in the direction of her car and said, "I was so sorry to hear about Julie's death. If there's anything I can do, please don't hesitate to call."

"Thanks, Phyllis, but I'm through the worst of it," Nick lied again.

"I'm off to brunch with the girls, but Jackson could use a friendly face. Walter's death has come as quite a shock."

"Don't let me keep you."

"Jackson's in his office, Nick. Go ahead and let yourself in," Phyllis said before she quickly headed for her car.

Nick found Jackson St. James slumped behind his big oak desk with a bottle of scotch and an empty glass in front of him. When he saw Nick approaching, Jackson waved him into his office and motioned toward a leather chair directly in front of the desk. Nick didn't know what a cold-blooded killer was supposed to look like, but there was nothing remarkable or sinister about Jackson St. James' physical appearance. He was a short man, no taller than five foot six. Nick often wondered if the countless hours he spent in the gym lifting weights and jogging were the result of an unspoken little man's complex. An associate lawyer had once commented that Jackson reminded him of a muscle-bound pit bull, and the description was fairly accurate. The top of his head was completely bald, so Jackson shaved his entire scalp each morning. The resulting five o'clock shadow created a graying horseshoe on his round head. Jackson always wore thick glasses with tortoise shell frames, perhaps in an attempt to create an intellectual persona. To make room for his bulging neck, he left the top button of his shirt unbuttoned and his tie loosened when he wasn't in court.

As soon as Nick was seated across from him, Jackson asked, "How have you been, Nick?" But before Nick had a chance to respond, Jackson immediately moved on to a different topic. "It was certainly good news to hear about your daughter's rescue. The local news is making you out to be a big hero and rightfully so."

Nick was trying to keep his temper in check, but it wasn't easy. "Darby wasn't harmed physically, but it's too early to fully understand the emotional impact of her ordeal."

"I suppose that's true," Jackson responded in a tone that implied he couldn't care less about Darby's mental health. "Enough with the small talk, what can I do for you, Nick?"

"A couple of things have been bugging me—" Nick began cautiously.

"If you want your old job back, I'm sure we can work something out," Jackson interrupted. "The firm's dynamics have changed with Walter permanently out of the picture."

"I'm not here to inquire about a job," Nick replied flatly. "I want to set the record straight between us."

"I respect that, Nick. Right to the point, no beating around the bush," Jackson said as he enthusiastically clapped his hands together. "Why don't you tell me what's on your mind?"

Nick was now sitting across the desk from Jackson St. James, still unsure of his next move. Jackson seemed to appreciate the forthright approach, so Nick decided to start strong. "You arranged the burglary at my house, which makes you responsible for my wife's murder," he stated as if it was a fact and not speculation.

Jackson shook his head patronizingly from side to side in a halfhearted attempt to deny the accusation. "There's no denying you've been through a lot, Nick. However, if you think about the situation logically, you'll realize the bad guys have all been brought to justice," Jackson calmly responded.

"Not *all* the bad guys," Nick corrected him.

"Go home, get some sleep, and move on with your life," Jackson urged in a condescending tone of voice.

"I'd like nothing better," Nick angrily replied. "Unfortunately, there is still one loose end that needs to be tied up before I can move on."

"Which loose end is that?" Jackson asked indifferently.

"You're the loose end," Nick shot back. "Your partner in crime, Edgar Ellenwood, provided the details of your unholy alliance before he embarked on his one-way journey to the spirit world."

Jackson appeared unfazed by Nick's reference to Edgar's pre-death confessions. "Are you trying to imply that Edgar Ellenwood implicated me in some way?" he asked incredulously.

Nick slowly nodded. "He did more than just implicate you, Jackson. Edgar told me flat out that you personally arranged Janis Jones's murder and ordered the burglary at my house."

"Why didn't you come forward with this outlandish accusation sooner?" Jackson scoffed. "Your timing seems a bit suspect given the fact that Edgar's been dead for two days."

"It's really quite simple; I originally jumped to the wrong conclusion," Nick countered. "At the time of Edgar's near death confession, I wrongly assumed that he was talking about Walter Burton. It wasn't until yesterday when I read his journal that I realized you were the one manipulating Edgar," Nick lied.

Jackson leaned back in his chair, stretched his muscled arms above his head, and then heavily dropped both hands into his lap. "That's complete nonsense, Nick. Why would a respected professional, like myself, get involved in such unsavory matters?"

"I know what you did, Jackson. I just don't know why," Nick replied.

"Edgar Ellenwood was a paranoid schizophrenic with a borderline personality disorder. The man was completely delusional and antisocial," Jackson replied dismissively. "Check out his medical history—it's all well documented."

"Edgar seemed lucid enough to me," Nick said matter-of-factly. "His journal contains names, dates, and the specific dollar amounts he received from his business dealings with you." Nick had always sensed Jackson resented living his professional life in Walter's shadow, so he hit Jackson with a low blow. "To be honest with you, at first, I didn't believe what Edgar had written in his journal. I always saw you as Walter's *yes man*, a guy afraid to take a piss unless Walter gave him permission."

A flash of anger momentarily caused Jackson's face to redden, but he quickly regained his composure. By the time Jackson spoke, he was actually calm and smiling.

"To be completely honest with you, Nick, Walter was a complete moron. Without my guts, vision, and superior intellect leading the way, he was nothing," Jackson boasted. "But I bet a smart guy like you already knew that."

Nick sensed that Jackson wanted to sing his own praises. It was written all over his face. He just needed the right nudge to get him started.

"You're pathetic, Jackson. Now that Walter's dead, you want to take credit for his accomplishments in the legal profession."

"Your version of reality couldn't be further from the truth," Jackson indignantly replied.

Nick shook his head thoughtfully before he continued. "Walter made all the tough decisions when he was the Monroe County prosecutor. He had the brains and balls necessary to get things done. From what I hear, the legal community considered you to be nothing more than his incompetent sidekick."

"You're entitled to your opinion," Jackson snapped.

"I'm familiar with Walter's climb to the top of the legal profession. He litigated all the important cases, while you carried his briefcase and shined his shoes." Nick suddenly stood as if he was about to leave and then dismissively said, "I had it all wrong. Walter manipulated and used you just as he used Edgar, Brooke, and Jefferson Hughes. I apologize for wasting your time, Jackson."

The mere suggestion that he'd been Walter's unsuspecting dupe caused Jackson's anger to reach its boiling point. He jumped up. Unfortunately, there was another development Nick wasn't expecting. Jackson had a .38-caliber revolver clutched in his right hand. Nick had been so focused on pushing his former employer over the edge that he had foolishly let his guard down.

Jackson aimed his gun at Nick and growled, "I'm not a complete idiot, Nick. Why don't you hand over your weapon so can we finish our little chat?"

When Nick didn't immediately react, Jackson screamed, "Do it now."

Nick slowly pulled the Glock from his jacket pocket and placed it on Jackson's desk.

Jackson kept the revolver trained on Nick's chest and said, "Put both your hands on top of your head, then slowly step away from the desk."

Nick followed Jackson's instructions without putting up a protest. He certainly wasn't going down without a fight, but he wasn't about to commit suicide either. With a little luck, he'd get an opportunity to turn the tables on Jackson without resorting to a mad rush. After he stepped away from the desk, Jackson picked up the .40 caliber Glock. "Your semiautomatic will be Exhibit 1 in my self-defense claim."

"You're planning to kill me just like the others?" Nick asked.

"You haven't left me an option," Jackson answered, implying the whole situation was somehow Nick's fault.

Nick needed more time, which meant he had to keep Jackson talking just a little longer. "For my own peace of mind, did you kill Janis Jones and order Edgar to steal her case file from my house?"

Jackson smirked like a mischievous child. "That's right, Nick. Walter had absolutely nothing to do with Janis Jones's murder or your wife's unfortunate death."

"Why was it necessary to steal her file?" Nick demanded. "That file didn't contain one shred of evidence that incriminated you or anyone else."

"Sit down, Nick, but keep both hands on top of your head. If you make any abrupt movements, I'll put a bullet between your eyes, and I won't think twice about it," Jackson said almost as calmly as he gave dictation to his secretary.

There were two leather chairs positioned directly in front of Jackson's desk. Nick did as he was told and sat down in the chair to his left. Once he was seated, Jackson leaned forward and asked, "Do you remember that Monday morning when you brought up Janis Jones's drug-possession case?"

Nick nodded.

"I immediately realized that Walter and I had a big problem on our hands. You see, I already knew Janis Jones was Jefferson Hughes's niece. In fact, I had memorized Jefferson's entire family tree," Jackson boasted.

"According to Jefferson, it was a fairly small tree," Nick sarcastically replied.

Jackson ignored the snide comment and continued his self-serving explanation. "When you casually informed the group that Ms. Jones had information about an old, high-profile murder case, I instantly surmised that her uncle had broken his twenty-year silence. I mentioned my concerns to Walter, but the pompous jerk called me paranoid and laughed in my face. His ego was so out of control, he felt invincible. Obviously, he wasn't," Jackson said with a wry smile.

Nick shook his head incredulously. "Janis Jones was dead, her case was closed, and there was nothing in the file that implicated you or Walter in any way. Your crimes would have gone undetected for another twenty years if you had just left well enough alone."

"Hindsight is twenty-twenty. Unfortunately, the decision-making process wasn't that simple—it never is. After some deliberation, I decided to have a chat with Ms. Jones and took Edgar along to keep me company." Jackson stopped talking, and a strange smile appeared on his face. After the brief pause, Jackson continued. "Anyway, Edgar and I visited Janis in her motel room on the night of her unfortunate death."

"You mean the night you murdered her," Nick cut in.

Jackson gave Nick a disappointed look and said, "Now, you're trying to be difficult. If my story is boring you, we can dispense with the clearing of the air and get on with your demise."

Nick raised his eyebrows and pretended to zip his mouth shut.

Jackson nodded his approval, clearly enjoying his position of control. "I had to find out what that worthless junkie told you about the Panache case. Poor Ms. Jones nearly wet her pants when she got a look at Edgar, so I promised he wouldn't harm her if she was completely honest about the specifics of her meeting with you. Evidently, Ms. Jones did not take my assurances at face value, because she lied through her rotting teeth. She claimed she had written a detailed statement regarding her uncle's perjured testimony and had included the name of the man who had paid him to lie. She also told me that she had left you a sealed envelope with explicit instructions to open the envelope in the event of her untimely death."

"And you found her story credible?"

Jackson grinned and shrugged his broad shoulders. "Honestly, Nick, I didn't know what to believe. The months following her death were excruciating for me. I kept waiting for you to reveal the contents of her last testament, but no disclosure was forthcoming. I searched the files in your office and the closed files archived in the basement. No matter how hard I tried, I could not track down that file. To be perfectly honest with you, the uncertainty was causing me to lose sleep at night."

"I'm really sorry that file caused you so much grief."

Jackson ignored the sarcasm this time and went right on justifying his actions. "After searching every square inch of your office and the basement, it occurred to me that you had taken the file home and had forgotten all about the sealed envelope. I had no choice but to retrieve the file when a legitimate opportunity presented itself."

"After two months, why didn't you just assume that Janis had fabricated the story to protect herself?" Nick asked.

"I never assume anything," Jackson replied indignantly. "There was always the chance someone might go through the contents of that file and discover Janis's letter. The Peterson trial in Las Vegas provided an opportunity to break into your home and acquire the file before it caused me any serious problems."

"That decision worked out well for everyone involved," Nick growled through clinched teeth.

"Now I know there was no letter, so all those months of lost sleep and endless worrying were for nothing." Jackson said as if he was the one who had been victimized.

Even with Jackson's handgun pointed at his head, Nick still had to fight the almost uncontrollable urge to climb over the desk and break the man's neck.

When Nick regained his composure, he said, "In other words, my wife was murdered because you were losing sleep."

"I suppose that's one way to look at it," Jackson halfheartedly agreed.

"Did you personally kill Janis Jones?"

Jackson thought about the question for a few seconds. "Technically, I suppose I did. Even though Edgar held her down, I was the one who injected the lethal dose of potassium. With degenerates like Janis Jones, the county doesn't spend a great deal of time or money trying to determine the actual cause of death. I suspected the medical examiner would rule her death an accidental overdose without an autopsy, and I was right."

"You're completely twisted, you enjoyed murdering her."

"I took no pleasure from the killing," Jackson countered without conviction. "After I injected Ms. Jones, she went into convulsions, vomited, and it took several minutes for her to die. The entire episode was quite disturbing, but unavoidable given the circumstances."

Jackson's indifference to human suffering was maddening, but Nick realized that the longer Jackson talked, the longer he stayed alive.

"Did you help Walter cover up Brooke Schaffer's murder?"

Jackson grinned and said, "I did more than cover up Brooke's murder—I'm the one who actually killed her."

Jackson was obviously capable of anything. Still, his last admission caught Nick off guard. "Walter claimed he accidentally killed Brooke during a violent struggle," Nick replied in confusion.

"Walter was a complete moron, plain and simple," Jackson scoffed. "Brooke Schaffer was playing him for a fool, and that pathetic excuse for a man was too weak to put an end to it."

"But Walter looked me straight in the eye and told me that he killed her," Nick repeated a bit louder.

"Perception is not always reality," Jackson philosophically explained. "When she threatened to go public with their affair, Walter tried to stop her. During the struggle, she fell and struck her head on a coffee table. I'm no doctor, but I do believe prompt medical attention would have saved her life."

"So you and Walter just stood there while a young woman bled to death?" Nick asked.

Jackson leaned forward in his chair and paused for dramatic effect. "Walter wanted to call an ambulance. He was running around his office, wailing like a frightened child. I told him to go home so I could take care of the situation. Brooke started to regain consciousness shortly after Walter's departure, which would have complicated things for both of us. If you evaluate the situation objectively, you'll realize that I really didn't have another option. I removed a throw pillow from Walter's couch and suffocated her."

"Let me get this straight. You convinced your best friend and business partner that he was responsible for a murder you committed?" Nick asked in disbelief.

"Why not?" Jackson demanded. "Walter was like putty in my hands after that fateful day. I never had to fight for my fair share of the pie, and Walter went out of his way to make sure I was happy."

"Whose idea was it to kidnap and terrorize Jason Davidson?"

Jackson nodded his head approvingly and with sincere admiration said, "Very impressive, Mr. Jelaco. You've been extremely diligent and surprisingly resourceful in your investigation."

"Thanks, Jackson, that really means a lot coming from a guy like you," Nick replied.

"Again, I must take full credit for the Strickland verdict," Jackson boasted. "Walter was so clueless. The idiot actually believed his skill as a lawyer had something to do with the outcome of the case."

"Walter didn't commit suicide, did he?"

Jackson rolled his eyes as if Nick had asked a question that was beneath the intellectual level of their conversation. "It takes guts and a sense of duty to end one's own life. I don't want to speak ill of the dead, but Walter had neither."

"Don't preach to me about duty," Nick snapped. "You murdered Walter to protect your dirty secrets."

Jackson solemnly shook his head from side to side and did his best to appear saddened by what he was about to say. "I prefer to view Walter's death as a mercy killing. He would have been absolutely miserable in prison."

"What kind of person shoots his best friend in the head?"

"A dang good friend," Jackson barked indignantly. "Walter didn't suffer one iota."

"Oh, I see now…you killed Walter for his own good."

"The poor guy was distraught, really falling apart at the seams," Jackson said, seemingly convinced he had taken the most humane course of action.

"I'm sure Walter would thank you if he were alive today," Nick deadpanned.

Jackson glared at Nick with obvious contempt. "Joke all you want, funny man, but Walter was in agony. He was sobbing uncontrollably and wailing nonstop about his ruined life. I couldn't bear to see him suffer. It was pitiful."

"So you put a bullet in the side of his head?"

"I reached out to Walter like I was about to console my old friend, and when he returned my embrace, I pressed the muzzle against his head and pulled the trigger," Jackson said matter-of-factly.

"I didn't realize you had a compassionate side," Nick said, his disgust apparent.

"It was a clean and humane kill," Jackson shot back. "Walter never knew what hit him. He was actually in the process of thanking me when the bullet ended his life."

Nick sensed that Jackson was tiring of their conversation. If he wanted to postpone the inevitable, he needed to create some doubt in Jackson's mind. "If you kill me, Edgar's journals will be made public."

Jackson locked eyes with Nick for a second before he hesitantly replied, "I don't think so, Nick. You're trying to buy yourself a little time."

"How can you be sure?"

"I don't know how you pieced it all together, but I'm willing to gamble there aren't any journals."

"The cops will have plenty of questions."

"And I'll have an answer for every single one of them," Jackson said with a chuckle. "Your stupidity has provided me the perfect defense. You barged into my home distraught, irrational, and armed with a semiautomatic. The stress of your wife's death and the lingering horror of your daughter's ordeal had apparently forced you over the edge."

"The old reliable self-defense claim, huh?"

Jackson held up his hands and pretended to be confused. "For some inexplicable reason, you blamed me for the loss of your job and your wife's death. I tried to reason with you, but in the end, you didn't leave me an alternative."

"You'll never pull it off. Too many people know the truth," Nick countered in a last-ditch effort to buy himself a few more seconds.

"No one knows a thing, Nick. What you have are a collection of unsubstantiated conclusions, but you can't prove a single one," Jackson accurately concluded. "You'll be killed with your own weapon. Then after you're dead, I'll fire a second shot while you're holding the gun. Ballistics tests and gunpowder residue will corroborate my version of the facts."

Nick could tell Jackson was about done talking by the abrupt change in his demeanor. The time had come to tie up the final loose end. "It sounds as if you've covered all your bases."

"I didn't scratch my way to the top of the heap by leaving my destiny in the hands of chance," Jackson boasted and then his face brightened. "Oh, I almost forgot to mention my plans for your daughter."

In his haste to confront Jackson, Nick had failed to consider how his death would impact his young daughter. "If you harm my little girl, I'll kill you. I swear to God, I'll kill you."

Jackson smiled, nodded in the general direction of the handgun aimed at Nick's head, and then calmly said, "You're in no position to threaten me."

"Please, Jackson, leave my daughter out of this," Nick pleaded.

"I'm not a monster," Jackson assured him. "My plans don't include harming your little girl. In fact, I'll do everything within my power to make sure your father-in-law gets full custody of his granddaughter. I've heard the two of you are real close."

"There's no way William Forsythe will raise my daughter," Nick screamed at Jackson.

"We'll see about that," Jackson replied as he glanced at his watch. "Stand up, Nick. We need to get this unpleasantness wrapped up before my wife returns from her luncheon."

Nick slowly stood and said, "That's the problem with psychopaths—you think you're smarter than everyone else. I figured out who was behind the curtain, which means someone else will do the same."

"I'll deal with that unlikely development if and when it occurs," Jackson said as he cautiously stepped from behind the desk. "Don't worry, I'm an expert marksman, and I'll do my best to hit a vital organ."

The man responsible for his wife's death was now standing directly in front of him with a crazed looked in his eyes and the .40 caliber Glock pointed at his head. Nick would undoubtedly suffer injuries in his blind rush for the semiautomatic. Still, he knew it was now or never.

CHAPTER 60

Saturday afternoon, October 28

Nick would never know if it was dumb luck or if some kind of divine intervention saved his life, but the telephone rang just as he made his move. The unexpected ring distracted Jackson just long enough for Nick to drop to the ground and sweep kick the stocky man's legs out from beneath him. Jackson managed to squeeze off a wild shot, but it was too late—Nick was no longer standing in the Glock's line of fire. A second errant shot grazed Nick's temple and embedded in the ceiling before the entire weight of Jackson's body crashed hard onto the tile floor. Before he could shake off the effects of the fall, Nick grabbed his right arm and pried the semiautomatic from his grip.

Without hesitating, Nick jammed the muzzle of the Glock into the side of Jackson's head and in a calm voice said, "Your old friend Walter is waiting for you—in hell."

Jackson closed his eyes and curled up in the fetal position. "Please don't kill me, Nick. I don't deserve to die," he whimpered softly.

"I can't think of a single person who deserves to die more than you," Nick growled in disgust.

"Please, Nick, do the right thing," Jackson begged. "If you let me live, I'll pay you a million dollars."

"A million dollars? A million dollars won't bring my wife back!" Nick screamed. "Money can't fix everything, you psychotic freak."

Jackson began to wail in agony when he realized that he was about to die. Nick was going to splatter his brains all over his imported tile floor, and money wouldn't buy him a reprieve. Just as he began to apply pressure to the Glock's trigger, a voice behind him shouted, "Drop your weapon, Nick."

Nick relaxed his trigger finger but kept the Glock's muzzle pressed against the side of Jackson's head as he slowly turned. Detective Sato was standing in the hallway with his service weapon aimed at Nick.

When their eyes met, Sato said, "Gates thought you might need some backup. Now drop your weapon," he continued in a composed yet firm voice.

"I can't do that, Detective," Nick countered, his voice thick with emotion. "This heartless excuse for a man killed Walter Burton, Janis Jones, and Jefferson Hughes. And the way I see it, he murdered my wife."

"I know all about it. Gates brought me up to speed," Sato responded calmly.

"Then you know that death is too good for this worthless piece of garbage."

"Don't throw your life away," Sato pleaded. "He's not worth it."

"My life is already over," Nick shouted back.

"Your wife is dead, Nick, but your daughter is still alive. Think about your little girl before you pull that trigger," Sato urged.

Nick's eyes filled with tears as his mind flashed to the brown-eyed, little girl who was waiting for her daddy to return. "My wife deserves justice, and we both know people with money can beat the system," Nick said with less anger in his voice.

"You have my word," Sato countered. "Jackson St. James will spend the rest of his life in prison."

Nick leaned toward his ex-boss and whispered, "You better pray you end up in prison for the rest of your life, because if you don't, I'll hunt you down, and you will die an ugly and painful death."

"Put down the gun," Sato said. "I won't ask again."

Detective Sato had it right. His daughter was alive and she needed her father. Killing Jackson wasn't going to bring Julie back. Nick slowly pulled the Glock away from Jackson's head and then after a sudden change of heart, he backhanded Jackson with the butt of the semiautomatic. The blow sent Jackson's head crashing into the tile floor. Instead of shutting him up, it seemed to restore his brash cockiness. Blood was dripping from his mouth and nose, but he was grinning like a madman. In fact, Jackson actually smirked and then laughed when their eyes met. There was obviously something on his mind, but Nick had heard enough. Before he could utter a single word, another thump with the semiautomatic silenced him.

Jackson was still trying to shake off the effects of the second wallop to his head when Detective Sato shoved his bloody face into the tile floor and violently yanked his right arm behind his back. Once Jackson was immobilized, Sato removed a pair of handcuffs from his belt and forcefully slapped the metal cuff around Jackson's right wrist. Sato then repeated the procedure with Jackson's left arm and roughly jerked him to his feet.

"Nick, I'll need your semiautomatic," Sato said, extending his hand.

Nick handed over his .40 caliber Glock without a protest and then nodded toward Jackson. "I'd have a ballistics expert check his weapon against the slugs someone left in Jefferson Hughes's chest."

Sato nodded and said, "He's probably just crazy enough to hang onto the murder weapon."

"Arrogance and insanity are certainly two of his more notable personality traits," Nick agreed.

"Backup is on the way," Sato continued. "Once Jackson's out of here, I'll bag his revolver and call in an evidence technician to process the crime scene."

"I suppose you'll need a statement from me."

Sato glanced at his watch. "First, I need to tie up a few loose ends around here, and you should have a doctor to take a look at that wound. Why don't you meet me at the station in a couple of hours?"

Nick gingerly touched the bleeding gash above his left ear. "It's nothing."

Sato shrugged. "It's your head."

"Detective Sato."

"Yeah, Nick."

"I'm glad you showed up when you did."

Sato smiled. "Me too."

CHAPTER 61

Monday morning, October 30

Julie's Honda Accord was packed and gassed up for Nick and Darby's trip south. Arizona was their first destination, but after that they had no definite plans. Nick wanted to reintroduce Darby to her grandmother, and he needed to reconnect with his mother as well. So Darby would not be subjected to another night in the house where her mother had been murdered, Nick had arranged for their things to be moved into a rental house. The old Mustang had finally given up the ghost with a loud and smoky bang as Nick drove home from Jackson's house. Perhaps it was a symbolic end to the most bittersweet chapter of his life.

Even though it felt a little strange to drive Julie's car, Nick was slowly learning how to embrace his memories of her. Simone had phoned earlier in the day to say good-bye and wish them a safe trip. Nick and Simone would be forever linked by their brief, but life-changing time together. At this point, it was impossible to know what his future held. Still, his intuition was telling him that Simone would play at least a small part in his life. Detective Sato's timely appearance at Jackson St. James's house was no coincidence. Simone had grown increasingly anxious after his abrupt departure from her apartment. Finally, after battling her fears for a short time, she had decided to phone Detective Gates. The detective was afraid his prior indiscretion might cloud the issue, so he had asked Detective Sato to check in on Nick.

Nick had promised to check in with Simone when they returned from their trip, and she had promised to keep him updated on the progress of Cole's release. Nick didn't have any female friends, so their friendship was definitely uncharted territory.

Nick and Darby had just returned to the car after a brief stop at a convenience store on the outskirts of Lakeland when Nick's cell phone rang. He instantly recognized the incoming phone number as Detective Gates's cell phone.

"Good morning, Detective," Nick said as he answered the phone.

"It is a good morning," Gates agreed in an uncharacteristically upbeat tone. "Are you on the road yet?"

"We're about three miles south of Lakeland," Nick answered. "What's up?"

"The Monroe County prosecutor charged Jackson St. James with three counts of first-degree murder this morning, and more charges are on the way. Jackson's not talking, but the courthouse rumor mill is buzzing, because your ex-employer has already retained the services of Benjamin Sinclair."

Nick whistled and said, "Benjamin Sinclair—he's high profile. It sounds like Jackson is gearing up for a trial."

"That was my read of the situation."

"Did the judge set a date for the preliminary hearing?"

"Not yet, but I'm guessing it will take place sometime before Christmas," Gates suggested.

Nick groaned. "I'm sure I'll be the prosecution's star witness."

"You're probably right, but don't let that ruin your vacation. Just enjoy the time with your daughter," Gates said, sounding more like a friend than a cop.

"Are you giving me fatherly advice?" Nick asked with a chuckle. "Speaking of daughters, did you call yours?"

"I'm having lunch with both my kids tomorrow. And to be perfectly honest, I'm nervous as a cat on a hot tin roof," Gates admitted.

"It may take some time, but things will work out if your kids know you're serious."

"I hope so," Gates replied and then added, "I've wasted so much time living in the past that the future scares me."

"The past is the past. Don't let it screw up the future," Nick said, as much to himself as the detective.

"There are still some unanswered questions in regard to my past."

"Is the prosecutor threatening charges?"

"Nothing is etched in stone, but at this point, he seems focused on Jackson," Gates answered.

"The statute of limitations for an accessory-after-the-fact charge has already expired. Besides, the State needs you to make its case against Jackson."

Gates seemed to be searching for something meaningful to say, but after a short pause, he simply said, "Enjoy your trip, Nick."

"Thanks, Phil. I'll see you in a couple of weeks."

Nick and Darby were just north of Twin Falls when Nick's cell phone rang for the second time. The area code of the incoming call was from out of state, but Nick didn't recognize the number. After a moment of deliberation, he reluctantly answered the call.

"Hey, big brother," the familiar voice of his brother greeted him.

"Luke. Where have you been?" Nick asked, skipping the pleasantries.

"I'm sorry, Nick," his brother apologized. "I just heard the news about Julie and Darby. I should have been there for you."

"You just heard the news," Nick repeated in disbelief. "Where were you? The moon?"

"It wasn't the moon, but it was pretty close."

"What's that supposed to mean?"

"Believe it or not, I've been on a fishing boat off the coast of Alaska."

"I didn't even know you had left Lakeland."

Nick was afraid the call had been lost when the line went silent for several seconds.

Finally Luke said, "I needed a change of scenery. My life has been headed in the wrong direction for a while. Putting some distance between me and my friends in Lakeland seemed like a good idea."

"When are you coming home?" Nick asked.

"My boat's putting out to sea first thing in the morning," Luke explained. "But if you need me, I'll be on the first plane to Lakeland."

"Stay put," Nick answered back. "Darby and I are on our way to visit Mom in Arizona. We'll be gone for a couple of weeks."

"If that's the case, I'll see you in a month or so."

"Luke..."

"Yeah?"

"I love you, little brother."

"I love you too."

"Call me when you get back to Lakeland."

"You'll be the first person I call," Luke promised before hanging up.

Less than an hour into their journey, Darby was sleeping peacefully as Nick drove through the bleak desert landscape of northern Nevada. His daughter was wearing the heart-shaped locket he had placed around her neck at the start of their journey. Darby had stared at the locket wide eyed as he explained that it was a gift from her mother. Nick remembered how he had clasped the same gold locket around Julie's neck while celebrating their first wedding anniversary. Vivid memories of that special night caused his thoughts to wander to happier times. A simple inscription on the back of the locket read "I will always love you." Julie always read the words aloud before adorning the dainty necklace. After Darby was born, her blue eyes would sparkle when she talked about passing the locket on to their daughter. A smile actually appeared on Nick's face when he thought about Julie's giving nature and zest for life. The smile quickly disappeared when the harsh ring of his cell phone returned him to the present. Unfortunately, this time he recognized the incoming phone number. Nick didn't feel like speaking with the caller, but he answered after the third ring anyway.

"Hello?" Nick barked, making no attempt to hide his disdain for the person on the other end of the call.

William Forsythe's unmistakable voice immediately growled, "I suppose you think you've beaten me."

"This isn't about you and me," Nick snapped. "My wife is dead, and my daughter is trying to adjust to a life without her mother."

Nick could hear the hatred in William's voice. "Don't you dare believe this is over, because it's not," he hissed. "My daughter was crazy to marry a man like you, and you're not fit to raise my granddaughter. I plan to seek full custody of Darby. In fact, the wheels are already in motion."

"I'm not in the mood for your inane babble," Nick shot back. "Darby is with me, and that's not going to change."

"You're certainly not man enough to stand in my way," William snarled.

"Just know one thing," Nick calmly replied. "If you try to take Darby away from me, I'll stop you by whatever means necessary."

Nick snapped his cell phone shut just as William had started to respond, cutting his ex-father-in-law off in midsentence. Nick then turned to gaze at his sleeping daughter. Her beauty, innocence, and vulnerability caused a tear to roll down his cheek. Julie's father was gearing up for a fight, and he didn't like to lose. Nick wasn't dumb enough to take his threats lightly, but William Forsythe and his bullying tactics could wait. After everything he'd been through, Nick wasn't willing to sacrifice today for a tomorrow that might never come. Life was too fragile to waste a single second of the time he was given, and Nick needed only to look into the backseat to realize just how fragile.